THE
ARTFUL
EGG

BY THE SAME AUTHOR

The Blood of an Englishman

The Caterpillar Cop

The Gooseberry Fool

Rogue Eagle

Snake

The Steam Pig

The Sunday Hangman

NONFICTION

Spike Island

Cop World

THE ARTFUL EGG

JAMES McCLURE

PANTHEON BOOKS · NEW YORK

All rights reserved under International and Pan-American Copyright Conventions. Published in the United States by Pantheon Books, a division of Random House Inc., New York.

Hardcover edition originally published in Great Britain by Macmillan London Limited, London, in 1984, and in the United States by Pantheon Books, a division of Random House, Inc., New York, in 1985.

Library of Congress Cataloging in Publication Data
McClure, James 1939–
The artful egg.
I. Title.
PR9369.3.M394A87   1985   823   84-25359
ISBN 0-394-53472-7
ISBN 0-394-72126-8 (pbk.)
Manufactured in the United States of America
9 8 7 6 5 4 3 2

for Wendy Robinson

1

A HEN is an egg's way of making another egg.

This was the thought uppermost in the mind of Ramjut Pillay, Asiatic Postman 2nd Class, at the start of the horrific Tuesday morning that altered the course of his life. He tried to have an uppermost thought every morning, for fear of being lulled into intellectual stagnation by the sort of reading his work required of him:

> *Mrs W M Truscott*
> *4 Jan Smuts Close,*
> *Morningside,*
> *Trekkersburg,*
> *Natal,*
> *South Africa*

Not that most envelopes, being mailed locally, had anything like as much on them, making this example – an air letter from Cincinnati – the workaday equivalent of *War and Peace*.

Not that there was ever any real need to read further than the first couple of lines anyway, because nothing reached his sorting-frame that hadn't already been set aside for Morningside, but he prided himself on being conscientious.

Ramjut Pillay slipped Mrs Truscott's air letter through the slot in her front door, sidestepped her dachshund with nimble disdain, and continued on his way. There was nothing today for the Van der Plank family at number 6, and only a few bills and a holiday postcard for the Trenchards at number 8.

He no longer perused postcards; the sheer inanity of their scribbled messages was more than his rather remarkable mind could bear.

'So let us ponder more profoundly and afresh', he murmured, as he opened the gate to 8 Jan Smuts Close, 'the devilish cunning shown by the aforesaid egg, and its

7

consequent effect upon the wretched fowl in question . . .'

Ramjut Pillay invariably used the plural form when addressing himself, being exceedingly conscious of the fact that there was a lot more to him than met the eye – which, admittedly, wasn't much.

Bespectacled, standing five-two-and-a-quarter, slightly bow-legged and as spare as a sparrow's drumstick, he 'reliably informed' his pen pals the world over that he was 'wholly Gandhi-esque' in appearance 'save for a head of truly healthy hair'. What he didn't tell his pen pals was that people frequently looked right through him, just as though he wasn't there, and that, as a child, his mother had kept losing him on buses, in shops, and at the Hindu temple down Harber Road.

Once, when he was about twelve years old, his father and mother, after a frantic search of the bottom end of town, had found him seated in the midst of the temple elders, under a sacred fig-tree. 'Ramjut,' his mother had cried out, 'don't you know how worried your father and I have been? Just what are you up to, child, with these wise old men?' To which he had replied: 'Eating figs.'

The front door to 8 Jan Smuts Close opened before he could slip the mail through its letter-slot.

'I wondered if—' began blowsy Mrs Trenchard, her green eyes darting to the mail in his right hand.

He knew what she was after. All last week it'd been the same, the constant hope against hope that her son had written to her from army camp. 'You keep hearing these stories', she had explained to him, 'that they're no sooner given their boots than they're sent to fight in the bush in Namibia.' Indeed, her motherly anguish would once again have been pitiful to behold, were Ramjut Pillay paying the slightest attention to it.

Instead, he was slyly stealing a look at seventeen-year-old Suzie Trenchard – he'd delivered her recent birthday cards in their unsealed envelopes – who was languidly descending the staircase, engrossed in a glossy magazine. The white girl's legs were bare all the way up to the frilly-edged panties she wore beneath a shortie nightie. What legs! Broad thighs,

8

smooth knees, calves with a truly heavenly curve to them. The full breasts were also quite exquisite, a pair of bobbing sweet melons which jutted the sheer fabric and gave it a delicate shake each step she took. Several split-seconds passed before he could reluctantly collect himself.

'You were wondering, madam?' said Ramjut Pillay, fanning the mail like a conjuror and suggesting she picked the postcard.

'Blast,' said Mrs Trenchard, hardly glancing at it. 'Is that the best you can do?'

'The picture is most pretty and informative,' Ramjut Pillay pointed out.

'Don't be cheeky!' snapped Mrs Trenchard. 'What I want to know is, haven't you anything else for me?'

There was really no need for her to be so rude, so he indulged a simple pleasure by handing over the bills one by one. Then, with a final forbidden glance at Suzie Trenchard, whose delectable bottom was giving a ripe jiggle as she disappeared down the passage towards the kitchen, he turned and went on his way.

'Suzie!' he heard Mrs Trenchard shouting out, a moment before the front door was slammed shut. 'Suzie, will you come downstairs this minute for your breakfast? And see you're decent, do you hear? Don't forget the servants.'

Two letters, an electricity bill and a small packet of colour prints went sliding through on to the hall carpet of 10 Jan Smuts Close.

'A hen is an egg's way of making . . .'

But his uppermost thought had changed.

It was always so when Ramjut Pillay felt a stirring in his loins. A condition, moreover, that tended to elevate his thoughts still further, reminding him of his deep affinity with the Mahatma.

'Brahmacharya...' he whispered reverently, not noticing that he'd given 12 Jan Smuts Close the mail for numbers 14 and 16 as well, so great was his preoccupation at this moment with Higher Things.

The brahmacharya experiments, as any devotee of Mohandas Karamchand Gandhi knew full well, had entailed the

Mahatma lying all night with naked young girls beside him, testing his will to abstain. Gandhi's will had reportedly never failed him, and neither would Ramjut Pillay's, he felt sure, given the opportunity to undergo a similar ordeal.

'There's the rubbing,' he muttered to himself, hurrying on up the close. 'The damnable rubbing . . .'

The rub being quite simply that, try as he might, Ramjut Pillay had yet to find a young girl in Trekkersburg who was willing to lie naked beside him all night. Once, he had come very close to emulating the Mahatma, that was beyond dispute – although her father still did not see it that way, and he had to make a two-block detour whenever he chanced to be in that part of town. And once, having decided that tender years might not be an absolute requirement of a brahmacharya experiment, he had attempted a night with Sophia, a middle-aged Tamil lady well known for her accommodating disposition. That had worked very well for the first hour; and then, growing restless, Sophia had given a deep sigh before suddenly heaving herself on to him.

'I say,' called out old Major MacTaggart from the porch of 14 Jan Smuts Close, 'dash it all, I was expecting a copy of the club minutes this morning. You weren't just going to trot by, were you?'

'M-Major?'

'Big brown envelope.'

Ramjut Pillay seemed to remember a big brown envelope in his Jan Smuts Close bundle, but a quick check revealed that his memory, usually so perfect in every way, must have played a trick on him. 'So sorry, Major,' he said, 'no can do today.'

'Humph,' Major MacTaggart snorted unpleasantly. 'I've my doubts about you as a post wallah, Pillay, *serious* doubts. Well, don't just stand there looking holier-than-thou, you bandy old rascal – you're late enough as it is.'

Seething with indignation, yet no better placed to protest than when Sophia had clapped a hand over his mouth before having her vigorous way with him, Ramjut Pillay continued on up Jan Smuts Close.

By jingo, how the world took advantage of an avowed pacifist.

'A ruddy hen', he said crossly, 'is an egg's—'

No good. He simply couldn't be expected to concentrate, certainly not under these circumstances. *Post wallah?* What a damnable impudence! What a way to speak to a highly educated man, qualified ten times over in any number of things. Why, the principal of the Easiway Correspondence College, the world-famous Dr Gideon de Bruin, was forever congratulating him on the variety of diplomas he continued to be awarded, ranging from Automotive Engineering (Theory Only) to Elementary Philosophy, Newspaper Cartooning and Conversational Afrikaans.

'That's a pretty stamp,' remarked Miss Simson at 20 Jan Smuts Close, as she signed for a registered letter. 'On that cream envelope, half-sticking out of your bag.'

Ramjut Pillay glanced down. Great heavens, he'd quite forgotten he had this to look forward to. 'Yes, the new UK issue, madam,' he said, 'and the first time I am ever seeing one.'

'So, are you going to ask them if you can have it?' said Miss Simson, smiling as she handed back his ballpoint pen. 'To add to your collection?'

'Most assuredly,' Ramjut Pillay replied, nodding.

But it wasn't until he had actually reached the top end of Jan Smuts Close that his mood changed properly, allowing him to appreciate again what a beautiful morning it was, and to anticipate to the full becoming the proud owner of such a fine example of British stamp design.

'Now, let us see...' he said, pausing to take out the cream envelope and to rummage about for the rest of the mail for Woodhollow.

There was always quite a bit of it, the bulk coming from overseas and being addressed to Naomi Stride. Yes, just 'Naomi Stride', with no 'Mrs' or 'Miss' in front, which was because, she had explained to him, it was her 'professional name', whatever that meant. Then, to complicate matters, she also received post for Mrs Naomi Kennedy, for Mrs N G

Kennedy, and for Mrs W J Kennedy, although nothing ever arrived for a Mr Kennedy.

To the cream envelope Ramjut Pillay added six other personal letters, four business letters and a circular, then started up the long drive. Woodhollow, or 30 Jan Smuts Close as it really should have been known, wasn't strictly speaking part of the cul-de-sac of modest middle-class bungalows at all, but stood well back, behind a screen of Scots firs up at the top end, facing away over a wooded valley. It always took a minute or two, in fact, before someone approaching on foot actually saw the house, so dense was the surrounding vegetation.

'Ah, such beauty,' sighed Ramjut Pillay, and inhaled again the heavy scent of the flowering shrubs on either side of him.

He pictured the lady coming to the door, his asking for the stamp most politely, and her agreeing as always, giving that throaty little laugh. Perhaps she would want to ask him more about preparing curries, which she did from time to time, and he would have a glass of chilled orange juice brought out to him by the servant.

Just then, there was a stirring in his loins, making him wonder why on earth the problem of the brahmacharya experiments should return to bother him at such a time. Then, without warning, a truly shocking insight provided the answer to that, tempting him to think the unthinkable.

He gave in.

There would be no servant to answer the door when he knocked. The hall would ring empty. Then he would hear the slap of her sandals, and the door would swing inwards, revealing her in her voluptuous glory. Her face would soften sweetly when she saw who was standing there, then a flush would rise to her throat. 'Come in,' she would whisper hoarsely, 'I have great need of you.' And there would be no mistaking what she meant by those words. In another minute, his postbag cast aside, he would enter—

'Ho, what balderingdash is this?' Ramjut Pillay scoffed out aloud. 'Have we taken leave of our senses, post wallah?'

Not entirely, another side to him insisted. The lady in question had already shown herself to be unusually sympathetic to his race. What other house on his round always smelled of incense? What other lady wore toe-thong sandals on her feet, and dressed in long, loose-fitting garments so clearly inspired by the sari? What other lady asked him intelligent questions about the God Kali, about yoga and yoghurt, and knew words such as 'Sanskrit'?

'None,' admitted Ramjut Pillay.

Well, said this other side of him, at last we're getting somewhere. And is it not true that she has several times listened with fascination to your accounts of the Mahatma Gandhi, confessing herself to be in awe of his great spirituality? Has she not herself said that she would dearly love to be able to follow in his footsteps, too? Then, is this not her great opportunity? If properly cajoled, I am sure she would be willing to join a true disciple such as yourself in a brahmacharya experiment, and to—

'Bosh!' said Ramjut Pillay. 'Bosh, bosh, bosh! Immorality Act!'

That old thing, sighed another side to him. What has that to do with it? Without hanky-panky, there can be no contravention of the Act, surely? OK, OK, so you are of different races, but all you're asking her to do is to lie naked beside you, while you—

'Enough!' declared Ramjut Pillay. 'This is mad talk, and I will hear no more of it! I have forgotten it already. There, now, it's all gone...'

Even so, there was still such a stirring in his loins that, for want of a loincloth, he had to move his postbag round to cover his upper thighs before reaching up for the doorbell.

Nobody answered his ring.

The house remained silent.

He rang again, two short rings and then a long one.

Nothing.

How uncanny, that all should be just as he'd imagined it, only a minute or so ago. And were those approaching sandals he heard? Glancing round first, he then bent low and peered through the letter-slot. The hall was empty.

Well, perhaps the servants were taking their breakfast break, and she was out in the garden somewhere. He was

13

about to slip the letters through the slot anyway, when his hand rebelled, not wanting to release the cream envelope until he had been promised the stamp on it. Perhaps he could just take a quick look round, and hope to spot her with her gardening things or beside the swimming-pool.

Bump, bump, bump, moving a little awkwardly because of the postbag, Ramjut Pillay set off to circle the house anti-clockwise.

The swimming-pool lay without so much as a ripple on its surface. The garden looked quite empty. There was no sign of life anywhere. Then something that flashed caught his eye.

Needing new lenses in his wire-framed spectacles, Ramjut Pillay had to cross the patio beside the swimming-pool before he could make out what was reflecting the sun's rays in this unusual manner: it was an electric fan with shiny metal blades, purring away just inside a room that opened out through huge sliding glass doors. Edging a little closer, he took a quick peep into the room, which was proably what he'd seen described somewhere as a sun-lounge. There was certainly enough sun in it, bouncing in off the pool outside, so no wonder someone had the fan on.

'Oh, heavens!' gasped Ramjut Pillay.

That someone was none other than the lady of the house, who lay stretched out on the black-leather sofa directly in line with where he was standing. She must certainly have seen him peering in, for he had been able to see *her* well enough, and would now doubtless expect some very good excuse for his intrusion. All the more so because she was virtually naked, save for a glittering bluey-green bikini.

'Er, madam?' Ramjut Pillay said hoarsely, stepping over to where the sliding doors stood ajar, but keeping his eyes humbly averted. 'Good morning, madam, so sorry for the disturbance – many, many apologies, madam.'

There was what he took to be a stunned silence, so he went on hastily: 'All in the line of duty, you see, madam. When I feel the weight of this cream letter in my hand, I say to myself: "Pillay, you are the bearer of some very important tidings – see there is no delay in the conveyance." And so, when I am ringing at your bell and there was no immediate

14

answer, I . . .' He had just taken another peep at her, and now realised her eyes were closed. 'Asleep?' he whispered, hardly believing his good fortune.

Why, he need only sneak away as quickly as possible, and nobody would ever know he'd been there.

Then he hesitated for a fateful fraction of a second.

Long enough anyway to want a closer look at those splendidly rounded white limbs, at those womanly breasts, at the gently domed belly, and in that same blink of an eye another side to him took possession. This frightened Ramjut Pillay – in fact, it scared the wits out of him – but it also somehow excited him, and excited him enormously, if the situation behind his postbag was anything to go by.

At first, he acted with cold calculation. He cleared his throat loudly, and when this failed to produce a reaction he gave a rap on the glass door. He did not rap a second time, however, having satisfied himself she was not merely dozing. And then he took his boots off, leaving them outside on the patio before setting off on tiptoe across the wooden floor of the sun-lounge.

This was when a feverish, dizzying feeling overcame him. He would never have believed such a perfect pallor of exposed skin possible, not in a million trillion years, and wanted desperately to caress it, to feel its cool sheen soothe his brown fingertips like magnolia blossom. Nothing could stop him now, and if she awoke suddenly, too bad – he'd just have to do something drastic.

There was a low buzzing in the room. He ignored it.

He marvelled instead at the glittering bluey-green bikini, shimmering as though stitched over by thousands of iridescent sequins, and moved closer, his weak eyes greedy for strong detail. The bikini had some red in it, too, he noted. The blurry face was as he remembered it – rosebud lips and long sweeping eyelashes. The breasts seemed heavier than he had suspected, the mound between her thighs far more pronounced than he could have dreamed. All of a sudden, he hated that bikini and wished it away, wanting to see beneath it.

He got his wish.

No sooner had his advancing shadow fallen across the female body lying languorously before him, than the bluey-green glitter disintegrated into a buzzing swirl of angry flies, rose up and disappeared over his shoulder.

2

TUESDAY morning had started well for Lieutenant Tromp Kramer of the Trekkersburg Murder and Robbery Squad. At 5 a.m. exactly – the Widow Fourie's body clock came complete with its own alarm – he'd been woken by her blowing gently in his left ear. 'Trompie,' she had said, 'it's any moment now, hey?' He'd lit a Lucky Strike, wanting to stay awake long enough to mark the moment. 'Is it over yet?' she'd whispered a few minutes later. Her timing was perfect, because even as she said this he had seen in his mind's eye a trapdoor, five hundred miles away, fall with a crash and the hangman's rope snap straight, before beginning its slow twirl.

And Tuesday morning had progressed from there. When he'd been woken again, it had been by the Widow Fourie making secret love to him, which he had pretended not to know about; and then, when he'd woken for the third and final time, it had been to find his favourite breakfast waiting on the locker beside her bed. Two jam doughnuts and a bottle of ginger beer.

Burping quietly – he found the burps that went with this breakfast one of its more attractive and lasting features – he had then taken himself out on to the veranda, there to scratch at the pelt on his chest in remarkably contented fashion.

A note, sticky-taped to a veranda-post, had read: 'Me and the kids have gone out for the day to Myra's and I've told Johannes to take the day off also so you can have peace and quiet for a change. XXX'

Quite what he had done with the time between then and

now, which had to be somewhere around eleven o'clock, he wasn't at all certain, except that he'd enjoyed himself. There had been the long, deep bath, which had lasted until the water had lost its heat, and then the change into fresh clothes, his first in over a week. After that, he had wandered round the old farmhouse, visited the pumpkin patch, and had eventually settled down in a crude hammock that her children had rigged between two peach-trees.

He lit another Lucky Strike, noticing that the match flame was almost invisible in the brilliance of the blazing sun. There would be a storm later on, there always was when the weather turned as hot as this, but for the moment it was as near to a perfect day as anyone with nothing to do, and absolutely no intention of doing anything, could wish.

A butcher bird came to sit on a branch above him. It had a fledgling in its beak, still struggling feebly. After a while, the fledgling hung limp, but the butcher bird remained where it was.

Kramer looked down and away. The coarse lawn was burned almost the colour of the tinder-dry veld beyond the barbed-wire fence surrounding the property; and far off, murky-grey at this distance, Trekkersburg lay in its wide bowl, brimmed by rocky outcrops. Nothing was distinct; the scraps of bright colour, the metallic glints, the little white shapes were like ants' eggs, bits of beetle, gaudy scraps of butterfly wing and other insect debris caught at the centre of a cocooning spider web. Poke it with a twig, and God knows what might come crawling out.

The butcher bird had its head cocked, watching him.

He twisted round in the hammock, facing downwards through its wide mesh, finding a hole through which his blunt nose fitted comfortably. Below him, in the fine red dust, were two conical depressions made by a couple of ant lions. The ant lions were buried out of sight at the bottom of each depression, waiting for an unwary ant to come slithering down the treacherous walls of the pits they'd dug. A tiny moth, dizzy in the daylight, rang the changes by becoming a victim, and he turned away as the ant lion closed its pincers.

The butcher bird had gone.

17

He tried to doze. He left the hammock and went indoors, where he strapped on his shoulder holster. A minute later, having made sure all was secured and locked, he climbed into his Chevrolet, started it up, and drove off.

'Naomi Stride?' said Colonel Hans Muller, pausing to blow hard into his pipe-stem. 'Damn, the bloody thing's properly blocked this time. I best send out for some cleaners.'

'Ja, Naomi Stride,' repeated Lieutenant Jacob Jones. 'Do you know who that is, Colonel, sir?'

'Is her dad that Jewish tailor on the corner opposite the prison?'

Jones, an Afrikaner to the core, despite such a ridiculous name, gave one of his tight little smiles and said: 'Let me give you a clue, sir . . . Books.'

'Just a minute,' growled Colonel Muller, setting his pipe aside and glowering up from his desk. 'This is the CID, hey? The Criminal Investigation Department! I haven't got time to bugger around with bloody clues!'

'Sorry, Colonel, I just—'

'So spit it out, man! Let me hear what is so important that it's OK for you to come running in here, just banging open the door like that, making me break off the match I'm using to—'

'She's dead, Colonel – murdered.'

As accustomed as he was to receiving reports of sudden death, Colonel Muller needed a moment or two to adjust to this information. He spent the time wondering why Lieutenant Jacob Jones had such a pale, bloodless complexion, and why Mrs Muller had confided to him, during the last police ball at the city hall, that the detective's brooding eyes and sensuous lips gave her the creeps.

'Oh ja? Where?'

'Here in Morningside. There's just been a report from a Uniform van. It seems they got a tip-off from some neighbours, went round to the house and there she was. She'd been stabbed.'

'I see,' said Colonel Muller, choosing the sharpest of his two dozen 2B pencils, and making a note of the name on a

18

pad. 'Naomi Stride. . . But what has this got to do with books?'

'She wrote them – you know, a world-famous novelist! Hell, when this gets out, you're going to have the press here from every —'

'Oh, no,' said Colonel Muller very firmly. 'Not unless I give the word. And, anyway, she can't be as famous as you say, because I always look in the bookshop window down the road, and I don't have any memory of—'

'Well, you wouldn't, Colonel, sir. Her books are all banned.'

The pencil point snapped. 'Banned?' echoed Colonel Muller, staring at the name on his pad. 'God in Heaven, now I do smell trouble. Remember how it was when that stupid bloody political detainee – What's-his-name – hanged himself in the cells here?'

'Ja, and the overseas press tried to prove we'd done it to put a stop to his—'

'Please! I need no reminders, hey?'

'But, Colonel, sir, it was you who—'

'Quiet, Jones. We must nip all such talk in the bud.'

Colonel Muller glanced at his blocked pipe, pointed to the packet of cigarettes in the pocket of Jones's safari jacket and snapped his fingers. Having accepted a light as well, he then rose from behind his desk and began to pace the strip of worn carpet by his window, never taking the cigarette from his lips.

'Lieutenant Kramer,' he said. 'Where is he?'

Again Jones gave another of his tight little smiles, making this one look even more like he was sucking something sweet through a straw. 'I thought you'd want to know that, sir, so I put my head in his office on my way up. Just his boy was there, playing at doing a report.'

'What did Zondi have to say?'

'Oh, the usual cock-and-bull story you can't follow, so I thought that you'd like me to take charge, Colonel, sir, seeing as Kramer's decided to take the day off to go round his popsies and give them all a—'

'Ah, talk of the devil,' interrupted Colonel Muller, turning from his reflection in the window to wink at the big man standing behind Jones on a less worn part of the carpet.

Ten minutes later, Kramer was ready to leave for Morningside. All he needed now were the keys to his police car. There was a jingling from the steel fire-escape leading from the CID building into the vehicle-yard, and down it came a trim, jaunty Zulu in a snazzy suit and snap-brim hat, making those steps ring like a tap-dancer. Reaching the asphalt, he did a soft-shoe shuffle, spun round on his heel, then switched to a casual saunter, both hands deep in his pockets.

'So the world is good today, Bantu Detective Sergeant Michael Zondi?' grunted Kramer.

'Boss, the world is beautiful!' replied Zondi, taking out the jingling car-keys again, and getting in behind the wheel. 'Have you looked to see what day it is? I had forgotten, and then I saw the calendar on my way out of the office. Today, early this morning, far away in Pretoria, a certain Fritz—'

'Christ, kaffir, you're not going morbid on me, hey?'

'What is the derivation of this difficult word "morbid", master?'

'*Drive*,' ordered Kramer.

And they were both laughing as the big Ford bucked out of the vehicle-yard, slewed round and dived into a gap in the passing traffic. After this, Zondi made his own gaps, ran two red lights and generally had a good time, until they reached the dual carriageway out to the suburbs, where there was too much room to make his kind of driving interesting. So he eased back and took the Lucky Strike that Kramer had lit for him.

'Ja, I also noticed it was execution day,' murmured Kramer. 'I'm still not sure you should have stopped me that time. I tell you, his throat felt good in my hands.'

Zondi shrugged. 'The same throat that was squeezed shut this morning in Pretoria. Your reach is long, boss.'

'And so is yours. Was your evidence that really nailed him.'

'Hau, a pair of *dangerous* men . . .'

'Too true, old son.'

And again they both laughed.

The police mortuary van went rocketing past them with the considerable bulk of Sergeant Van Rensburg crouched over its wheel, his tongue curling up into his moustache in intense concentration.

'Do you know of this woman who has died?' asked Zondi.

'Ach, just that she's a banned writer or something,' replied Kramer. 'The Colonel's having pups that it'll cause a big fuss.'

'Then he wants results right this minute?'

'Something like that . . .'

They left the dual carriageway and plunged down a slip-road into Morningside. Every house was different, every house a testament to the taste and pocket of its original owner; some were big, some were small, some exotic, some very plain, but they did have two things in common: a bonding of lush tropical vegetation and an air of earnest middle-class pretension. This made it a terrible place to work in uniform, because if you were called to a man-and-wife fight the violence would be all verbal, and they'd be saying intellectual things about each other in English that the average constable had a hard time understanding. 'Ach, lady,' Kramer could remember a colleague remarking with a sigh, 'if it's just your husband has anal fixations, why don't you get him one of those blow-up rubber rings he can sit down on?'

Zondi's memory, developed as a pupil at a mission school which never had enough textbooks to go round, came into its own on an occasion like this. Show him anything, even a map of the more complicated parts of Trekkersburg, and it was imprinted for good, allowing him immediate and easy reference. Without taking a single wrong turning, he found his way to Jan Smuts Close and accelerated towards the top end of it.

'Hey, slow down,' said Kramer. 'There's some woman with an old man who's shaking a golf club at us.'

Zondi was already slowing down. He stopped outside 20 Jan Smuts Close, and Kramer lowered his window.

'Excuse me, but are you the police?' asked the woman. 'Only Major—'

'Ja, lady – and who are you?'

'Er, Miss Simson, actually. I live on my own here at number 20.'

He had already guessed as much. Miss Simson's petticoat dropped beneath the hemline of her skirt, which was something that anyone on an even vaguely intimate basis with her would surely have pointed out before breakfast. He put her age at around thirty-eight, and noted her very small chin. He lamented the fact that she stooped a little, spoiling the effect of two very fine, rather girlish breasts, and wondered if she bought her sanitary towels by mail order.

'Major Hamish MacTaggart, Cameron Highlanders Retired,' gruffly announced the stumpy, grey-haired warrior standing beside her with his golf club at slope arms. 'Neighbours. Bloody poor show.'

Kramer liked these old lunatics, who really should have been dead and buried long ago, but persisted in staining their corners of the globe Empire Red with shakier and shakier pourings from the port-bottle. 'What's a bloody poor show, Major?' he asked.

'Dammit, man, you can see the state this young woman's in, having that infernal idiot left on her doorstep! Good God, when she first came battering at my door I thought we'd another uprising on our hands, and her—'

'No, honestly, Major, I'm really quite all right now,' said Miss Simson, 'although it was very sweet of you to rush to my rescue.' Then she turned to Kramer and said: 'I'm afraid it's the poor Indian postman, you see. He just came tearing down here, dived on to my veranda, and began the most dreadful howling. I couldn't get a word of sense out of him until the Major—'

'An accident of some sort, I gathered – blood and that sort of thing,' Major MacTaggart explained. 'Got him calmed down long enough to sound that out, then gave the local police station a ring. Any idea what's happened to the poor woman?'

Kramer exchanged glances with Zondi, before replying, 'We're not sure yet. But let me see if I've got this straight: the postman was the one who raised the alarm?'

'Correct.'

'And what precisely had he seen?'

'No idea. The man's a gibbering—'

'He's obviously very upset,' said Miss Simson, 'and we do think something ought to be *done* about him, if you know what I mean. All the other police we've seen have just shot past.'

Kramer shook his head, wearied by the juvenile excesses of the uniformed branch, which had grown far worse since the introduction of television in the mid-seventies. 'And you say this witness's still over there on your veranda?'

'Yes, sitting huddled up in the corner.'

'Doing what?'

'Well, mumbling away to himself, actually.'

'Gibbering,' said Major MacTaggart.

'OK, fine. I'll leave my sergeant here,' said Kramer, and moved over to take the wheel as Zondi slipped out of the driver's seat. 'Just get a brief statement, and then meet me up at the—'

'I trust,' cut in Major MacTaggart, 'you are going to arrange for him to be carted off as quickly as possible? I can't see how what he's saying is going to be of the slightest—'

'That's for my sergeant to decide, hey?' said Kramer, putting the Ford into gear and releasing the handbrake.

'Humph,' snorted Major MacTaggart, giving Zondi a sharp glance. 'Then I take it this chappie has an uncommonly lively interest in eggs.'

'Eggs?'

'Hen's eggs,' explained Miss Simson. 'Poor Mr Pillay appears quite obsessed with them.'

Two patrol vans, a police Land-Rover and the District Surgeon's Mercedes Benz were parked haphazardly on the circle of gravel outside the Spanish-style house at the end of the long drive. There were palms to go with the curved red tiles of the low roof, and bougainvillaea to hint, like festoons of crumpled pink tissue-paper, at fiesta time. For the pretty senorita, seeking something bright to wear in her hair, there were hibiscus and azalea blooms, and for the dead grasp of the woman within there were some arum lilies.

Kramer kneed shut his car door and went up the steps of the uncovered veranda. The front door was wide open, so he carried on through into the large hallway, hesitated a moment, then continued across it and down a wide corridor. A curious feature of this corridor was that its gaily coloured rugs weren't spread over the polished black floor-tiles, but had been placed on the walls, of all impracticable places.

Two young constables were standing outside the last door on the right. They glanced round, saw who was approaching and stiffened to attention, hiding their cigarettes in cupped hands.

'Relax,' said Kramer. 'It isn't your arse I've come to kick. Who's in charge here?'

'What's this?' demanded a high-pitched voice, and an orang-utan in a warrant officer's uniform and a ginger crewcut stepped into the doorway behind them.

'Oh Christ,' said Kramer, 'I might have known . . . How goes it, Jaap?'

And Jaap du Preez grinned good-naturedly up at him, exposing more gum than tooth in a mouth as wide as a saucepan. 'It goes fantastic, sir. Everything's under control. So why am I going to have my backside kicked?'

'Ach, I've changed my mind,' said Kramer. 'I don't want to cause brain damage.'

'Sir?'

So Kramer used short words and simple sentences to get across to Jaap du Preez the seriousness of a key witness being left unattended down at Miss Simson's place, and Jaap du Preez promised to kick the two constables for failing to mention the postman to him; and the constables protested, saying that the message they'd received from Control had made no mention of any postman, just that the householder at Woodhollow was in trouble.

'Then, let that be a lesson to you,' said Jaap du Preez, cheerfully booting them all the same. 'And now, Lieutenant, if you'll just follow me, sir.'

They went through the doorway, crossed a room with its walls covered in bookshelves, and then into an adjoining room that had a huge sliding window on one side. The first things Kramer noticed were a postbag lying in the middle of the floor and, just outside the partly open window, a pair of black boots.

'Why are you barefoot?' Zondi asked Ramjut Pillay, yet again.

But the postman still wasn't responding to even the simplest questions. Lost in a world of his own, he kept muttering on about eggs.

'What happened to you up at that house?' Zondi persisted. 'What did you see there?'

'A ghost by the look of it,' whispered Miss Simson, awed by the postman's blank stare, greatly magnified behind smudgy wire-rimmed glasses.

'Time the brute was brought to his senses,' grumbled Major Hamish MacTaggart, practising a swing with his golf club. 'Give him a good clip round the ear, Sergeant – can work wonders with his sort. I remember a dhobi wallah having the damned cheek to try a spot of dumb insolence on me once, some hardly trivial matter of betel stains on a dress kilt, and I—'

'Oh, no, please don't resort to violence!' begged Miss Simson, catching a hand to her throat. 'I simply won't allow it!'

And yet her eyes flashed, Zondi noted.

'You could at least try prodding him,' suggested Major MacTaggart, holding out his golf club. 'Mind you, you're dealing with a frightful idiot there, even in the best of circumstances. God knows how he got the job – beggars the imagination.'

Ramjut Pillay turned to the old man and glared indignantly. Then his hand went to his tunic pocket, extracted a worn and bulky wallet, and from it he took a sheet of folded paper that he slapped down hard on the veranda floor.

Opening it out, Zondi read:

Dear Student,

It is with regret that I note you have once again failed to obtain a desired position despite having attained a Distinction in the relevant Diploma. Do not be downhearted! DO NOT LISTEN *to those who, as you report in your latest communication, say that your diploma isn't worth the paper it's written on. (You'd soon realise what rubbish that was if you could see my printing bill, believe me!) Persevere, my friend, persevere, always remembering that the road to Rome was not built in a day. And, while I'm on the subject, I wonder if you have seen that, owing to the acute manpower shortage, non-white persons of Asiatic extraction are now permitted to obtain gainful employment as Postal Operatives? I would not hesitate to recommend a person of your talents and aptitudes for such a Position, and will gladly furnish you with a Reference to that effect should one be required (when writing, enclose return postage).*

Yours sincerely,

PRINCIPAL, EASIWAY CORRESPONDENCE COLLEGE
Dr Gideon de Bruin, DD (Alabama), BA Hons. (Univ. of SA), AFRPS

P.S. Attached you will be pleased to find the latest Supplementary List of Courses, now on offer at 20% off to all Honour Roll Students such as yourself. I am confident that Tax Law (Part I) and/or Coastal Navigation are well within your grasp, by the way.

Zondi folded up the letter again and then motioned politely to Major MacTaggart, indicating he would value a private word with him, if this were at all possible.

They moved down to the far end of the veranda.

'Sir, I would like to do as you suggest,' said Zondi in a very respectful whisper. 'What this bloody coolie needs is a good slapping – maybe some fist.'

'Thought it'd have to come to that. Well, just you carry on, Sergeant! Not really any need to ask, not when a fella's doin' his duty.'

'But . . . er, well, the young madam, sir . . .'

'Ah,' said Major MacTaggart. 'Tricky'.

'Unless, sir, it would be possible for you to take the young madam inside the house – maybe to the back veranda? For a few minutes only?'

'Ah,' said Major MacTaggart. 'A nod's as good as a wink, what?'

Uncertain of quite what this meant, Zondi was relieved to see Miss Simson being coaxed away, with several backward glances, a minute or so later, leaving him free to interrogate the postman as he saw fit.

'Well, well,' he said, handing Ramjut Pillay back the letter, 'who was that old fool calling an idiot? Anyone can see from that you are indeed a very educated man – and it isn't often we detectives get a chance to speak with such a scholar, so this is for me a great privilege.'

'It is?' said Ramjut Pillay, sitting up and polishing his glasses.

The body lay quite naturally, thought Kramer. So often the limbs had an ugly twist to them, an arm bent at an impossible angle, or a leg turned in underneath, but here it suggested simple repose, relaxation.

'I think she was probably lying just like this when it happened,' remarked Dr Christiaan Strydom, the diminutive District Surgeon, scratching at the back of his shock of grey hair. 'But why she was nude at the time, don't ask me.'

'Ach, I don't think I have to,' said Kramer. 'There's her clothes over there, and right here, by the couch, is her wet swimming-costume. I reckon she had just taken the cozzie off, and felt like a bit of a lie-down. Y'know, a couple of minutes to get her breath back after twenty lengths – then *choonk*.' And he made a downward stabbing motion.

'H'm,' said Strydom, probing deeper into her side and altering the angle of his penlight torch. 'Ja, that would fit the

27

facts as we see them, only what was she doing swimming at about one in the morning? You saw what her temperature was – she can't have died any earlier.'

'She was a writer, hey? Maybe she liked to work late, only she decided on a swim to freshen her up again. I see she left a page in the typewriter next door, so she could have been going back to it.'

'And what if a servant had seen her?'

'You don't expect servants in the house at one in the morning, do you? Besides, no servants seem to have been on the property, although Uniform is still checking.'

'You're very full of guesses today, Tromp,' grunted Strydom, taking up his magnifying glass. 'Try to guess what she was stabbed with.'

But Kramer remained where he was for the moment, several feet away towards the sliding window. This was the last chance he'd have of seeing Naomi Stride looking reasonably human, and he wanted to build up a picture of her, something personal he could hold in his memory when everything else about her was coming to him secondhand.

She was basically what the buxom Widow Fourie would describe as petite, being five-one at the most and as light, in all probability, as the average well-filled golfbag. The Widow Fourie often resorted to this comparison with golfbags, which was consistent with the irrational, poorly disguised envy that such women aroused in her. As for the shape of Naomi Stride's body, it wasn't at all bad for someone middle-aged, once proper allowance had been made for the fact that the belly had begun to distend with death a little, it being a day well up into the nineties. Perhaps the thighs were slightly plumper than they might have been, yet the cushioning effect this gave to the area around her dark triangle was undoubtedly attractive; and, as for her breasts, they were surprisingly youthful, suggesting that if she'd had children she had certainly fed them with bottles. It was a pity that blood, pouring from the hole in her upper left side, had streamed down over the nipples, congealing into an unconscious attempt at posthumous modesty. Even so, a little of the textured areola on either side was still visible, defining a neat circumference the size of a cent, and reinforcing that youthful illusion. Her heart-shaped face had a touch of innocence in it, too, but was wholly without laughter-lines, rather surprisingly. Such a mouth, small and perfectly formed for planting light, fondly amused kisses, should have had a bracketing of fine wrinkles, and the intense blue eyes had no crow's feet at their corners to confirm that she'd often seen the funny side of things, this despite the high forehead.

Then too much detail began to impose itself. The fly trapped in the sticky blood on the lower breast, another glutted in her pubic hair, where there had been seepage, and most unpleasant of all, for no particular reason, the nail missing from the smallest toe on her left foot - a recent injury that'd been healing. So Kramer half-closed his eyes, and looked at the body again, this time intent only on forming a general impression.

What he saw this time made him smile, as the pallor of her skin, her jet-black hair and red lipstick combined to create a *risqué* image of Walt Disney's Snow White, with obviously one of the Seven Dwarfs in attendance.

'What's so funny?' demanded Strydom.

'Nothing, Doc! But I must be right in saying this lady was in the habit of using her swimming-pool at night. See how pale she is? Where's her tan, if she was used to going out there in the daytime?'

'Oh ja, that's a great help – any of her friends could probably tell you that,' said Strydom. 'What I still want to know is how this stabbing was done.'

Kramer took the magnifying glass from him and bent low over the wound.

'Ja, I can see what you mean . . . The hole's a funny shape, isn't it? Why a stabbing? How can you tell this wasn't a big bullet?'

'From the way the skin's been turned and pushed in. Besides, there's no burn marks of any kind. Whatever went in there can't have been hot.'

'Uh-huh, that sounds logical.'

'I'll just have to get her back to the mortuary and cut down through here, try to work it out that way.'

'When will this be?'

'Well, as soon as Fingerprints has arrived and taken pictures, I suppose. To hurry things up, I'm having her own doctor to come round and identify her.'

'Can we fix a time, so I can be there?'

'Say two'clock, then, Tromp,' said Strydom, glancing at his watch. 'Which reminds me, where has that bloody fool Van Rensburg got to with the mortuary van? I don't suppose you passed him on the way out here, did you?'

'Not exactly,' said Kramer.

3

THEN the usual party atmosphere began to establish itself, as more and more police vehicles came up the drive, spilling out men who joked nervously and laughed a lot. Many arrived by invitation, ready to perform the tasks that made them specialists at a murder scene. Most of the others were gatecrashers, uniformed patrol officers from neighbouring beat areas whose curiosity had been aroused by the flurry of radio calls. The new arrivals mingled on the patio, stealing glances through the sliding window at their hostess for the afternoon, now wearing a pink sheet from the airing cupboard.

When Dr Strydom left, giving a curt nod to Jaap du Preez, two Fingerprint officers were admitted. One immediately set about doing conjuring tricks with dusting powder and sable brushes, producing latent prints from nowhere, while his partner flicked back the sheet and started taking pictures, bobbing around his subject with all the deference of a Society photographer.

The murmurings on the patio became a cocktail titter, several rather bitchy things were said about middle-aged spread, and then they all looked behind them, distracted by a loud diversion. This was provided by a police dog which, entering into the spirit of things, had decided to go skinny-dipping in the swimming-pool, inadvertently dragging its master, who'd been on tiptoe, off balance and into the water with it. This earned the pair of them, both dog-paddling furiously, a ragged cheer, and an athletic uniformed sergeant leaped up on to the springboard to bawl directions, almost falling in himself. More cheering, and when everyone turned around again the sheet had been replaced and Sergeant Van Rensburg, looking like some form of extremely pompous and obese butler, was to be seen carrying in his mortuary tray.

At this point, Kramer, who never had much time for parties, did what he generally did at them, and took himself off into a quiet room, closing the door behind him.

The room he chose for this was the one that had the typewriter in it and books filling the shelves on every wall, all the way up to the beamed ceiling. Seating himself in the large swivel chair at the desk, he lit a Lucky Strike, tucked the spent match into his breast pocket, and leaned back, delaying the moment when he would look to see what Naomi Stride's last words had been. He had a feeling they'd come as something of a disappointment.

Not that Kramer had any high literary expectations of the woman, still less had he ever read anything of hers before, having no interest in the much thumbed collection of banned works which the Vice Squad kept in its office. It was just that if working Murder and Robbery had taught him anything, then it was the dreary fact that most people died when they were least prepared for it, and very rarely with any style. The most he could hope for was that she'd just typed: 'And then . . .'

He turned his attention instead to the room and its furnishings. They were curiously unsettling, and reminded him of something. He allowed his mind to go blank, while concentrating on the burning tip of his cigarette. Then he had it: Boy Joshua's wheelbarrow.

Boy Joshua was one of the best-known figures in Kwela Village, the vast black township of identical two-roomed, concrete-block houses where Zondi had once lived with his family. Each and every day, Boy Joshua could be seen trundling that cloth-covered wheelbarrow about, carrying in it, as the victim of a tropical disease that enlarges testes to monstrous proportions, his balls. People marvelled at their size, and even those well used to the sight seldom failed to accord Boy Joshua a certain veneration, which he found very pleasing – as did his three wives. Once a white doctor, working at the township's tuberculosis clinic, had sent for Boy Joshua and promised to rid him of his remarkable condition almost overnight, as there happened to be a very simple cure for it. Boy Joshua, according to bystanders, had left that clinic very quickly indeed, pushing his wheelbarrow all the way to the top of the hill without once stopping, which was in itself a feat that won him further notoriety. One had only to glance at the barrow to gauge the considerable weight of it, even when the contrivance stood empty. Boy Joshua had been decorating it for years, twisting coathangers and other short lengths of wire to form a high arch across the front, and then attaching to this arch every interesting trifle that caught his eye. Among the more readily identifiable were old spark-plugs, keys, gear-wheels, used ballpoint pens, pieces of mirror, broken combs, wheel-nuts, chrome-plated petrol-caps, light-bulbs, copper tubing off-cuts, soft-drink cans, throwaway cigarette-lighters, piston rings and colourful circuit-boards.

Kramer had thought he'd never see its like again, but here in this room, in what Naomi Stride had presumably called her study, was evidence of much the same thing. Without getting up, he could count three large bowls filled with beach pebbles, and in the copper vase on the mantelpiece was a handful of old feathers. Egg-shaped stones and pieces of wood lay dotted about everywhere, there were quite a few shiny white bones, oddments of driftwood, a baboon's skull, yellowing greetings cards, three stuffed finches under a glass dome, small picture frames crammed with too many snapshots, old-fashioned green bottles in different shapes, bulrushes in one corner, and dozens of tortoises made of everything from porcelain to dough, occupying the front edge of the bookshelves. More greetings cards, postcards, letters and even a telegram or two protruded from between the books themselves, and into what space remained she had squeezed further collections of rubbish, such as strangely shaped corks, pencil stubs, toy cars, a military badge, some blue marbles and, for reasons only Boy Joshua could possibly understand, little stacks of used typewriter ribbons.

Suppressing a mild shudder, Kramer got up and walked over to the red filing cabinet beside another, smaller desk where the telephone stood. He pulled open the top drawer, taking care not to smudge any potential fingerprints, and was surprised to find everything neatly filed away in blue folders, each of which was clearly labelled. He wasn't sure why he'd looked in there, although a start had to be made somewhere on the tedious business of filling himself in on the dead woman's background, and letters, even business ones, could be useful in this respect. But the sight of so much paper to wade through, and so many lines to read between, weakened his resolution, and he began to push the drawer shut again. If only, of course, he could simply ask the dead woman a few simple questions about herself, how much easier life would be.

Then he gave a slight smile and took out a folder he'd just noticed, earmarked INTERVIEWS. Inside it were a score of cuttings, at least three of which promised to reveal the *real* Naomi Stride, prizewinning authoress, housewife and mother.

'That, too,' he murmured, pleased with his discovery, and returned with it to the swivel chair.

But, before settling down to the first of the articles, he leaned forward to take a look at the sheet of paper left in the typewriter. What he saw was:

p/237

a fine membrane, paler than the moon,
  "II, ii!"

Puzzled, he glanced round for the preceding page, and found it in a wire basket under a glass paperweight. A quick scan revealed that it was a sexy scene between two youngsters

33

in the dunes near Durban, both of whom seemed unusually alive to the odours of each other's body.

'Yes. And you?'
'Yes.'
'Abelard.'
He nodded.
'I don't know the words for this,' she said. 'Not your words.'
'There are no words,' he said, reaching out for her.
She smiled gently, hearing nothing trite in that, knowing he knew no clichés. 'Like wood smoke,' she said, as his chest brushed her lightly, raising her nipples. 'A deep, dark gorgeous smell . . .'
'Like wild mint,' he said. 'Sharp in the nostrils. No, slowly. We must be slow, maybe this is the only time.'

And then followed the descriptive passage that carried over on to the last page ending abruptly with "II, ii!", a totally enigmatic statement, even when taking into account the bewilderingly cryptic dialogue that had come before it.

Kramer shrugged and opened the folder of recent interviews. They were also in English, but far better written, being quite clear in their meaning; and one from the *Washington Post*, which really did try to get to the facts about Naomi Stride, became his favourite. He read it again and again.

At two o'clock Ramjut Pillay was suspended from duty, pending a full Post Office enquiry into how he had come to abandon a postbag, not to mention a pair of Post Office boots, in a reckless and unthinking manner, thereby putting at risk the safety of the Republic's mail.

This came as a bitter blow to him, all the more so because he now believed every word of the story he'd told the remarkably understanding black detective sergeant who had interviewed him after his ordeal – a story which he was still trying to repeat to Mr Jarman, his supervisor, whose powers of concentration were obviously so poor that they'd certainly

34

never gain *him* a diploma in anything worthwhile.

'But I am telling you, Mistering Jarman,' Ramjut Pillay patiently persisted, 'and I am telling you truly, the spirit was present with the remainders of this poor lady, and the spirit said unto me, "I have great need of—!" '

'Pillay,' said Mr Jarman, pointing to his door. 'Out.'

'A moment more, Mistering Jarman, suh! There is much you are not fully comprehending of a religious and cultural nature! One example, if you will permit, concerns the wearing of leather articles upon the feet when in the close proximity of—'

'Out . . .' hissed Mr Jarman, becoming quite threatening.

Sergeant Van Rensburg's own frame of mind could hardly have been much worse when two o'clock came, and the only people in his mortuary were all dead.

'Ja, you can bloody laugh,' he said savagely to a travelling salesman who was baring his teeth in a rigored grin on the first slab along. 'You're not trying to run an efficient department, are you? Christ, you couldn't even drive a motor car in a straight line, or you wouldn't be here, would you?'

Clanking and rattling his trolley over the duckboards, Van Rensburg returned to the refrigerator room, yanked the big double doors open, and grabbed hold of the end of a tray near the foot of the right-hand stack. The tray, a sort of metal stretcher designed to hold a corpse during transportation or storage, wouldn't budge. He heaved at it, and realised a split-second too late the thing was empty, before it suddenly shot out and caught him on the shin.

'You bastard!' bellowed Van Rensburg, hopping about on one leg. 'You think you can play games with me, hey? Don't worry, I know that you're in there, and when I—'

'Taken up Scottish dancing, Van Rensburg?'

The sudden voice badly unnerved him, making him spin round with a loud expletive. 'Oh my God,' he added in frantic haste. 'That wasn't meant for you, Colonel!'

'Just as well, my friend; these are new trousers I have on today.'

'And aren't they terrific?' smarmed Van Rensburg, missing

35

the point as usual. 'Just look at those creases!'

'Who', asked Colonel Muller, 'were you talking to when I came in? Is Doc Strydom here? I didn't see his Mercedes parked outside, and so I assumed—'

'Ach, no, that was just a dead coon, Colonel – the burglar CID shot last night in the supermarket. Only I was catching a bit of a panic on account of the Doc not being here yet; and Lieutenant Kramer hasn't pitched up, either; and, with one thing and another, matters are getting a bit out of hand.'

Colonel Muller pondered this reply, tapping his swagger-stick against his front teeth. 'Sergeant Van Rensburg,' he said at last, 'I hope you haven't been drinking this lunchtime.'

Kramer looked up as the study door opened and Zondi poked his head into the room. 'Hey, Mickey, how did it go, man? That postman had all the answers?'

'No chance,' said Zondi, coming in and closing the door behind him. 'The man is a happy fool.'

'Didn't you get anything out of him?'

'Some nonsense about hens and eggs to cover up how he had tried to take a look at a white woman with no clothes on. Correct, boss? She was naked?'

Kramer nodded. 'Nothing else?'

'I went seeking information from servants who know the people working at this house – they have all gone home for six weeks' holiday.'

'*Holiday?*' echoed Kramer, astounded. 'What were they, white?'

Zondi laughed at the very idea. 'No, two Zulus, husband and wife – house boy and cook; there was also a Xhosa, garden boy. It seems that it was the custom of this madam when she was going to be away on a long journey.'

'But who'd look after the place?'

'She hires special guards with big dogs.'

'But—'

'All I can tell you, boss,' said Zondi, shrugging, 'is that the servants left here on Sunday, and that was when the madam was supposed to leave, too.'

'Ja, to go to some prize giving in England. All the details are

36

there in that pile of bits and pieces from newspapers.'

Zondi took up one of the cuttings. 'Maybe', he suggested, 'the son can tell us what is going on.'

'I've been trying to contact him,' said Kramer, nodding at the telephone. 'Seems he's away today on a business trip, but the girl in his office is still ringing different places. Hey, there could be a quicker way of finding out . . .' He crossed over to the red filing cabinet.

'What is the son's work?' asked Zondi.

'African curios,' replied Kramer. 'So you'll have to watch your back, hey? I bet he could get a good price for you.'

'H'm,' said Zondi, preoccupied by the newspaper cutting.

There was a knock at the door.

'Who is it?' demanded Kramer, extracting a folder marked HOUSEHOLD.

'It's Jaap, Lieutenant. Can I see you a moment?'

Zondi palmed the cutting and moved several paces away from Kramer.

'Ja, come in,' said Kramer.

Jaap du Preez entered breezily. 'Sorry to disturb, Lieutenant,' he said, 'but I should have knocked off quarter of an hour ago, and I was wondering how many blokes you need up here from the next shift – you know, to help you.'

'The next shift? Jesus, is it after two o'clock already?'

'Two-sixteen, to be exact.'

'Then, I'm late, bugger it,' said Kramer, throwing the folder into the swivel chair. 'How many do I need? Let's say just three Bantu constables to secure the property, and tell the van sergeant to keep an eye on them.'

'Fine, sir. Also, Fingerprints was wondering when they should do this room?'

'When I'm finished with it.'

'Whatever you say, Lieutenant,' said Jaap du Preez, moving back to the door before adding: 'This is going to be quite a case, hey?'

'Not if I can help it,' said Kramer.

Then, when Jaap du Preez had gone, he gave Zondi a pile of reading to do, explained he was overdue at the post-mortem, and took a short cut through the window.

Zondi plumped down in the swivel chair and tried a few revolutions, three clockwise, three round the other way. He'd never had the chance of sitting in such a chair before, and could see its attractions. Then he tipped back his hat, reached for the clippings and shuffled through them, searching for a picture of the deceased woman.

There were several single-column head-and-shoulder shots among the newspaper stories, all a bit smudgy and probably very dated, for she looked about twenty in them. Then he found what he wanted: a full page from the glossy magazine *Fair Lady*, which showed Naomi Stride seated exactly where he was seated, her fingertips resting on the keyboard of her electric typewriter.

Zondi wondered if she were beautiful. He was never too sure when it came to white women. He had seen some on film posters that puzzled him deeply: jaws like a man, cheeks flat and hard, the shoulders straight, the hips too narrow to bear a child worth having. This woman, however, was at least plainly feminine and there was a neatness about her features that was pleasing, even though the large eyes seemed too open and vulnerable, like windows without any glass in them.

Keeping the picture in front of him, he arranged the clippings in chronological order and read them through once. Then he lit a cigarette, leaned back in the chair, and sorted through all that he'd learned, paring it down to the bare bones of a life so abruptly ended.

– Naomi Stride had been born Naomi Esther Cohen forty-seven years ago, the only child of Emmanuel and Esther Cohen, proprietors of a small jewellery store in Johannesburg.

– She had won a scholarship to the University of the Witwatersrand at seventeen, and at the early age of twenty-two had been awarded her doctorate in English Literature. 'A brilliant student,' her professor had said.

– That same year, she had failed to take up a post as lecturer at the University of Natal, having in the meantime met and married William James 'Big Bill' Kennedy, an eminent heart surgeon.

– While pregnant, she had begun a short story that grew into *The Last Magnolia*, her world-famous first novel that critics said 'penetrated to the very heart of the tragedy of apartheid'. It'd won five prestigious awards in Europe and America. Success after success had followed with each new novel; all of which had been banned in the Republic.

– When she was forty-two, her husband had died of a heart attack, leaving her a very rich woman. She had spoken of leaving South Africa and of taking up residence in London, to be at 'the hub of the literary world', but had moved instead to Trekkersburg, where her son was at university.

– Naomi Stride had not written a word for several years after her husband's death, but had confined herself to encouraging creative talent in others – young writers, poets, painters and sculptors of all races. Then, roughly two years ago, she had begun *Ebbing Hill*, the novel that had just been shortlisted for the Booker Prize, and she had agreed to be there at the presentation ceremony in London this week.

– The various descriptions given of Naomi Stride tended to repeat the same set of adjectives: unequalled, modest, masterly, sensitive, articulate, passionate, tender, acute, outraged, apolitical.

Apolitical? The last of these words was lost on Zondi, so he decided to remedy this by leaving the swivel chair and going over to the bookshelves to find a dictionary. But on the way there he became sidetracked by all the things she had collected to have around her.

He liked the feathers in the brass vase over the fireplace, and enjoyed the feel of the egg-shaped rocks. The dozens of tortoises amused him, too, especially the one made in dough, which was growing mildew, and he saw how interesting the different green bottles were, and the same applied to the assortment of oddly shaped corks. He remembered what it was like to be a child, pockets bulging with salvaged trifles, and as he moved from one to the other, touching and admiring, he let his imagination roam.

Yes, thought Zondi, a writer of books would probably have need of a child's mind, that same capacity for wonder and for making up stories based on little or nothing.

Sometimes, being a detective was a bit like that, too.

'What requisition sheet?' snapped Dr Strydom, lifting out Naomi Stride's brain.

'Ach, the one I handed you last Wednesday, of course,' said Sergeant Van Rensburg, picking bone dust from the teeth of the saw he used to take the tops off heads. 'I'm getting really short of some of the stuff on it – you know, stitching thread, DH-136, sample-bottles, all sorts. Can't you just sign it, Doc?'

'I've already signed it!'

'You couldn't have, because—'

'Do you two never stop arguing?' said Colonel Muller, looking up with a frown from the midday paper.

'Sorry, Colonel,' said Van Rensburg, 'it's just that a bloke tries to run an efficient—'

'*Efficient?*' said Strydom. 'Since when was this mortuary —?'

'God in Heaven, surely—' began Colonel Muller, and then stopped, having noticed that Kramer had joined them. 'Anything to report from the scene, Tromp?'

'No, nothing Doc can't have told you already, sir,' said Kramer. 'Except that we know now she had a son, and I'm trying to find him to explain why his ma didn't go to England on Sunday as planned. I'll also want to get from him how many people would've known she'd be alone in the house without any servants.'

'Last night, you mean?'

'Uh-huh.'

Kramer looked Naomi Stride over and recognised only the legs and feet. The face was hidden by a glistening flap of scalp pulled down to expose the cranium, and the body had been opened up from pubic arch to chin, so that the breasts faced the other way now, hanging down by her sides.

'Brain's weight is average,' declared Strydom, taking it off his scale and cutting it into thick slices. 'No unusual characteristics – so who says the lady was a genius?'

'This paper does,' said Colonel Muller. 'Mind you, they waited until she was dead first.'

'It's in there already?'

'Ja, just the Stop Press. I wonder who the bastard was who tipped them off?'

'What progress on the murder weapon?' asked Kramer.

Strydom looked up with a wink. 'I've been saving that till you got here, hey?'

'Something special, is it?'

'Unusual, certainly. I won't be a sec.' Strydom left the brain on the draining-board of the sink for Van Rensburg to replace later, and crossed over to the slab, picking up a pair of long forceps from his instrument-tray. 'Take a peep in that chest cavity.'

'Hell, she bled a lot,' remarked Kramer, stooping low. 'Must be half a bucketful in there.'

'Actually, we've gone metric now,' Van Rensburg pointed out. 'So really—'

'Here', said Strydom, using the forceps to follow the path of a weapon through the tops of the lungs, 'is the culprit. That silvery thing stuck in the anterior scapula – ach, shoulder blade – with just the end showing. No knife could have travelled so deep.'

Kramer leaned closer. 'What is it, then? Tip of an arrow head?'

'No, but you're warm, I think,' said Strydom, applying his forceps to the object, and beginning to draw it out. 'Something a bit old-fashioned . . .' Then he held it up to the light and said, with a grunt of self-satisfaction: 'As I thought, the broken end of a rapier.'

'Come again?' queried Van Rensburg, his perpetual frown deepening.

'I said "rapier", man – which is English for one of those thin swords they used to use for sword fights.'

'Ah,' said Van Rensburg. 'It was the "rape" part that fooled me.'

But Colonel Muller didn't share his look of sudden enlightenment. 'A *sword?*' he said, lowering a corner of the newspaper. 'That's a bloody funny thing to go round sticking into people – especially lady writers.'

'Not if you don't like blood on your clothes,' said Kramer.

Zondi turned another page of *Ebbing Hill*, astonished by how well Naomi Stride was able to describe the conditions in a municipal hostel for Bantu males. He couldn't imagine a white woman ever being allowed in such a place, let alone permitted to observe day-to-day life in one, and anyway, even if she had, the occupants of those bleak eight-man rooms would certainly not have behaved normally. Yet here were four instantly recognisable characters, doing the sort of things they would ordinarily do, squabbling, sharing a small orange, pining for their wives and their children, hoping that this year they'd be able to return to see them again. Two pages further on, the story switched to the distant families, and to the difficult lives led by the wives trying to bring up youngsters on their own – youngsters whose bellies were never full, just as their hearts always had an emptiness in them. Again, he could see and hear these people, almost as though he were a lizard in the grass roof above their heads.

Then he became restless. Supposing that he was feeling slightly guilty about the time he'd squandered on reading banned literature, Zondi returned the book to its place on one of the shelves in the study, resisted an impulse to see what was in the typewriter, and lit another Lucky. His glance fell on the folder marked HOUSEHOLD.

Why had the Lieutenant taken it from the filing cabinet? Something to do with finding out about the dead woman's delayed departure. . .

Zondi opened the file. It was filled with bills and business letters. Leafing through the latter, he came on one from Cyclops Security, confirming the arrangements made to safeguard Woodhollow while Naomi Stride was away for a period of six weeks, beginning the previous Sunday evening.

He noted the security company's telephone number, moved across to the smaller desk and used a pencil to dial, although he very much doubted that the killer had been the sort to leave fingerprints anywhere.

'Oh ja, Cyclops Security?' he said in Afrikaans and the most guttural of accents. 'Police here, lady, with a couple of questions, hey?'

'Anything at all we can do to help, sir,' she replied.

Driving back to Morningside with the car windows down, trying to get the stink of the mortuary out of his nostrils, Kramer took a small bet with himself: somewhere in Naomi Stride's house would be a room that had old guns and spears and Zulu shields and other such items on its walls – houses like hers often went in for things like that, just as they favoured a big brass gong outside the dining-room and he'd already spotted one of those. Discovering where the murder weapon had come from would be no problem.

But who could have used it on her was another matter. The simplest answer – and the one most likely to prove correct – lay in the idea of an intruder having stumbled across her. Most whites, even of her class, tended to be early risers, and could be expected to have been in bed long before midnight. The intruder had probably imagined he had the whole ground floor to himself, and then, hearing noises from the sun-lounge, had taken down a sword from a wall display and had gone to explore. Or had he already armed himself with the sword as a precaution? Ja, that did seem more likely. Burglars, as a breed, tended to be very nervous people.

An Indian urchin darted into the traffic at an intersection, taking advantage of the red light to sell copies of the afternoon paper to waiting drivers. Reminded of Colonel Muller, hiding behind his first edition back in the mortuary, Kramer had to smile. Marriage had certainly softened the old bastard up and no mistake, even allowing for the fact his new bride would be about the same age as the late Naomi Stride.

The light changed to green, giving the driver in the car ahead an excuse to accelerate off with the afternoon paper without paying for it.

Perhaps, thought Kramer, the intruder theory was a trifle simplistic: a crime is discovered, and automatically the assumption is that a criminal must have committed it. Yet the world was filled with evil bastards, with scum who wouldn't think twice about cheating a ragged kid out of his profit on fifty papers – or, if it seemed worth it to them, somebody out of their three score years and ten – while maintaining every outward appearance of the model citizen. On top of which, murder was a rather unusual type of crime in that, the chances were, the victims generally knew their killers, and it always paid to take a close look at those closest to them at the start of any investigation.

The bunched traffic reached the dual carriageway and spread out. He moved over into the fast lane.

Motive, that came next. The woman had been rich, she'd been famous. Greed could have provided one reason for wanting her dead, jealousy another. Perhaps patriotism had had something to do with it, if she'd been writing about South Africa in a subversive manner – but he wasn't sure yet whether her books had been banned for that or for being too sexy. And then of course, on a more basic level, motivations like hatred had to be considered, because being rich and famous didn't exempt a person from the passions which made so many of the humblest citizens kill each other. The best idea was simply to start collecting information and to allow it to produce its own patterns; this sort of theorising without proper facts wouldn't get him anywhere.

The turn-off to Morningside was coming up, so he slapped down the sun-visor on his passenger side, bringing into view a notice clipped to it that read POLISIE–POLICE, held his hand on the horn, and forced the car travelling in front of him to draw over sharply to the kerb. As he got out and walked back, the startled driver emerged, tugging a driver's licence from an inside pocket.

'Look, I don't know what this is about,' he said, smiling and politely deferential. 'I've only driven two blocks and I know I didn't do anything wrong. I didn't jump the lights, I wasn't speeding.'

Kramer looked at him blankly. What a mother's joy the man was: a winsome, open face; clean teeth and fingernails; a freshly laundered pale-green safari suit and beneath it, without a doubt, an impeccably clean pair of underpants which would uphold the family's honour in the event of an accident.

'Ach, I'm sorry,' the man apologised, switching smoothly

44

from English into Afrikaans, 'it's just I'm forced to speak the bloody language most of the day because of my job – software, you know. The name's Hennie Vorster, sir. Here, you can see it on my licence, and it's clean.'

Kramer took the licence, then glanced over the car.

'A beauty, isn't it?' the man went on. 'I'm afraid, if this is one of those spot checks, you're not going to find a thing to give me a ticket for – I only took delivery on Monday. Oh, thanks very much.'

And he reached for the licence which Kramer had just held out to him, giving a sharp little cry as the handcuff snapped over his wrist.

'Jesus Christ!' he gasped, in English. 'You can't be arresting me! Whatever for?'

'Theft of one newspaper,' said Kramer. 'But don't worry,' he added, attaching the other handcuff to the man's steering-wheel. 'I'll leave a little note for the next patrol van coming by, explaining all about it.'

4

ZONDI had three things to tell Kramer when he arrived back at Woodhollow and went into Naomi Stride's study. The first concerned what he had learned from Cyclops Security.

'They said, boss, Mrs Stride rang up last Friday to inform them she had changed her plans and would be leaving for London tomorrow, Wednesday, and they were not to worry about guarding this place until then. They were not very clear why she was leaving later, but it had something to do with her being at a point in her latest book where she did not want to stop until the chapter was finished.'

'Uh-huh, and what else?'

'The son's secretary has phoned. He is on his way here, should be arriving any time now.'

'Does he know his old lady has—?'

'No, just that the police want to contact him.'

'Fine. What was the third thing?'

Zondi did a three-quarter turn in the swivel chair and pointed to the sheet of paper in the typewriter. 'I have been looking at that last line, boss.'

'Oh ja? Something about "two, comma, two" – didn't make any bloody sense to me, unless it's just that two and two make four. But, then, the whole book seems to be so bloody strange that—'

'Boss, I don't think this Naomi Stride missus wrote that. Take another look.'

Kramer took another look, leaning low to view the paper at an angle to the light coming in through the window. 'The pressure used on the keys is the same as with the lines before it – which is only logical, since this is an electric typewriter. What's there to tell apart?'

'Here,' said Zondi, taking down at random a novel from the bookshelves. 'Have you ever noticed that in books, when they show the words people speak, they don't always use double inverted commas for quotation marks, they just use one?' And he held out a page for Kramer to inspect. 'Ordinary people, though, use the double quotation mark, because that's what they learn at school . . .'

'Wait a minute,' said Kramer, taking up some sheets of manuscript from the wire tray. 'Ja, but Naomi Stride actually typed the same way as the printers, with one mark.'

'And suddenly there are double quotation marks around that last line...' murmured Zondi. 'I don't think that someone who typed so much would break a habit just once in more than two hundred pages.'

'You've looked?'

Zondi nodded. 'I can't find any other place she has used double marks.'

Kramer walked over to the window and stared out of it for a while. Then he turned and nodded. 'You're right, Mickey,' he said. 'It can't have been her, and so it had to be – well, bugger it, the murderer? Leaving us some kind of message? Having a little joke?'

'It seems so, boss.'

'But "two, comma, two" means nothing to you, either?'

'No idea, boss,' replied Zondi, shrugging.

Ramjut Pillay was exhausted by the time he reached Gladstoneville, a sprawling shanty town set aside for Asiatics on the north-western edge of Trekkersburg. Normally, he had permission to use his Post Office heavy-duty bicycle for getting to and from work, but now that he was under suspension this privilege had been withdrawn from him. Barefoot, too, because his boots had been retained for forensic examination by the police, and because he was in no position to requisition another pair, his progress had been slow and painful, especially over the last three kilometres, a dirt road down from the asphalt highway skirting Gladstoneville. The heat hadn't helped, either, seeming to become more intense each weary step he took.

'Ten thousands five hundred and ninety-one, ten thousands five hundred and ninety-two,' he murmured, reaching the corner of Apricot Street, 'ten thousands five hundred and – ah, jolly good! – ninety-three.'

He was home.

'Ramjut?' his mother croaked from her wicker chair on the slanting porch. 'Where have you been, you shameful son of respectable parents? Your poor aged father is out looking for you, begging news of a fully grown-up boy who should have returned from his work many hours ago. What have you to say to your—?'

'Mother, would you like to know how many pacings it is from the Post Office to—?'

'Pah!' she said, dismissing him with that familiar wave of her fly-whisk.

Which, for once, pleased Ramjut Pillay immensely, because all the way back to Gladstoneville he had been turning over in his mind the most exciting thought he'd entertained in years, not excluding several associated with brahmacharya experiments.

And so, indifferent to his limp, he went through the house and out to the corrugated lean-to in which he lived at the back. It was like stepping into an oven, save for the fact that few ovens held such a pungent odour of warm horsehair mattress, and for several seconds he was tempted to leave the door ajar. But, no, that would be wholly unprofessional, so he closed it firmly and did up its seven bolts and two chain locks. Then, feeling a little faint, he edged his way between his divan and the bookshelves he had constructed out of orange-crates, and drew aside the faded curtain in the far corner. Behind it, hanging from a sagging length of string, was his entire wardrobe: shirts, trousers and a couple of jackets, motor mechanic's overalls, a chemist's white coat, an advocate's black gown, a loincloth, a Scout uniform, a grey plastic raincoat, a tracksuit, nineteen ties in various designs, and a pillowcase containing hats, caps, helmets and a gas-mask. From a termite-proof tin box hidden beneath all this he selected a diploma and pinned it to the edge of one of the orange-crates. He stepped back to admire it, collided with his divan and had to sit down suddenly.

Ramjut Pillay, said the diploma, in beautifully curly writing, *Has Passed With Distinction All The Exacting Requirements Of This Course & Is Henceforth Qualified To Practise As A Private Investigator.*

Theo Kennedy, only child of the late Naomi Stride, arrived at Woodhollow in a Land-Rover painted black and white in wavy stripes to resemble zebra hide.

'"Afro Arts",' murmured Zondi, reading aloud the signwriting on the cab doors. '"Wholesale and Export".'

'You'd best bugger off and find yourself a good place to listen from outside the window,' suggested Kramer.

'On my way, boss!'

Kramer walked out on to the front veranda at much the same moment as young Kennedy started up the steps. He looked angry, very pale.

'I've just heard on the radio,' he said, 'that my mother's been murdered. What the hell are they talking about? That can't be true!'

'I'm sorry, Mr Kennedy, but for once they've got their facts right.'

'Rubbish! Next of kin would have to be informed first, and

48

nobody's—'

'We've been trying to get hold of you, sir. We rang your place of work just as soon as we knew where to contact—'

'But—'

'As for the press and radio, there'll be an enquiry into who told them, and—'

'I don't give a shit about that! My only—'

'Hey, come inside,' said Kramer, motioning him into the house. 'You tell me where your ma kept the brandy, and I'll get you one – hell, I'll even have some, too.'

Kennedy half-smiled, let his shoulders drop, and led the way, walking like a man who finds the floor a long, long distance beneath him. They went into a large living-room furnished in a mixture of skinny wooden drinks-tables and plump easy chairs covered in a floral pattern. Kramer directed him to sit in one of the chairs, and crossed over to the mahogany cabinet to the right of a huge fireplace. The cabinet was well stocked, containing no less than four different brandies. Choosing the Oude Meester, Kramer poured two double tots, handed Kennedy his glass and sat down on the arm of the sofa.

Nothing was said for a while. They just sipped their brandy and found something to stare at. Kennedy stared at a brass poker, propped beside the grate. Kramer stared at a round, bulging kind of mirror, which gave him an interesting view of the dead woman's son. Shortened by the mirror's distortions, which took about twelve inches off his six-foot-two, Kennedy looked a lot like her in a way, having the same dark hair, neat build and high forehead.

'I can't believe this is happening, that it's true . . .'

'It's true,' said Kramer.

Kennedy looked up at him.

Unlike the mother, there were laughter-lines on the son's deeply tanned face – not that he was using any of them right now.

'How?' he asked brusquely, forcing the word out.

'A stabbing,' said Kramer. 'Just the once. She died instantly.'

'Jesus . . .'

49

'In the early hours of this morning. She had been in for a swim and was changing back out of her costume. It was on the floor and her clothes were—'

'You mean she was – not dressed?'

Kramer nodded. 'But there'd been no sexual interference, if that's what you're thinking. More brandy?'

Kennedy didn't seem to notice the glass being lifted from his grasp. He was staring at the poker again, nibbling gently on his lower lip. Turning from him, Kramer went back over to the drinks cabinet, hiding a frown. He was puzzled by his own behaviour, by the way he'd not attempted to see whether Kennedy had known how many times his mother had been stabbed, when she'd been stabbed, what her state of dress – or undress – had been. It was often amazing, the way even the cleverest killers could let something slip right at the start, before their nerves had steadied and they'd grown accustomed to being questioned Yet Kramer had played no games with him, had simply given the main facts to him straight, just as though it'd never crossed his mind that Kennedy, being the deceased's closest relative, should be treated as a major suspect.

Carefully, he poured another double tot, still frowning.

A major suspect? Christ, he hadn't regarded the man as a suspect at all, not from the first moment of setting eyes on him. He had liked the bloke; it was as simple as that – an intuitive response based on God knows what. On top of which, Kennedy's reactions had since struck him as entirely genuine, reinforcing the same feeling – but of course this nonsense now had to stop.

'Look, sir,' he said, turning with the refilled glass, 'it is necessary for me to ask some questions.'

Kennedy did not appear to hear him. He went on staring at the brass poker, his teeth clamped hard on his lower lip and a trickle of blood running down his chin.

'God in Heaven,' muttered Colonel Muller, glancing at the proffered press card, 'how did you get here so fast?'

'I lucked out, I guess, sir. Flew down from our Johannesburg bureau on another assignment and—'

'But why should *Time* magazine want to poke their noses into this as well? Why not stick to writing about clocks and watches, for Pete's sake? They're much nicer things than murders – and more useful, too.'

'Pardon me, sir, it seems we have a communications failure. *Time* is a major news—'

'No communications failure,' interrupted Colonel Muller, handing the card back. 'I think I've communicated things quite clearly, young man: the answer is no – *no* exclusive interviews, *no* further information for the present.'

Then he went into his office and closed the door firmly.

Lieutenant Jones was waiting for him. 'I've got something highly significant to show you, Colonel,' he said smugly, hugging a docket to his chest. 'I hope you have no objection to me exercising a bit of initiative?'

'Huh!' grunted Colonel Muller, seating himself at his desk and reaching for his pipe-cleaners. 'What've you got there? Plane tickets to send all these bloody reporters to bloody Timbuktu, I hope. I want them banned from the building.'

'I'll see to that in a sec, Colonel. But first, if it's OK, I'll explain how I've already made a breakthrough. Do you remember there was a story in the local paper not long ago, to the effect that Naomi Stride had agreed to settle out of court in a libel case? You know, when that person accused her of—'

'No,' said Colonel Muller.

'Well, anyway,' Jones hastened on, 'I remembered there was some sort of statement made by her lawyer, and so I looked up the paper to see what his name was. When I'd got that, I went round to his offices, had a few words with the right person, and here, in this docket, is a photocopy of the deceased's last will and testament. It will amaze you.'

'No, never,' said Colonel Muller.

But it did. The woman had been worth a million rand or more, made up partly of what her husband had left her, and partly of her own earnings as a best-selling writer.

'Which isn't counting', Jones pointed out, 'the royalty

money her books will go on making, especially now there'll be such good publicity. And do you see where it nearly all goes to?'

'To the son . . .'

'That's right, Colonel. I bet he's happy, hey? The spoiled young bugger won't need to put in another day's work for the rest of his life.'

Zondi glanced upwards. Another fat drop of rain fell, splashing on his cheek. He cursed softly under his breath, and then began to edge his way out of the hydrangea shrubs in which he'd been hiding, right below an open window to the living-room. A storm had been inevitable that afternoon after the heat earlier on, but it could have held off for half an hour or so; Theo Kennedy had only just started talking, and all he'd done so far was to declare himself as a white adult male, aged twenty-four, living at an address on the far side of town.

Momentarily at a loss to know what to do next, Zondi sprinted round to the rear of the house and found shelter in the sun-lounge. He wasn't the only one with this idea. A young Bantu constable from the local police station, brought in to guard the property against invasions by the press and other sensation-seekers, was standing just inside the sliding windows, wiping the rain from his face with a khaki handkerchief almost a metre square.

'Hau, Sergeant!' the constable exclaimed guiltily, surprised by his sudden appearance. 'My intention was not to—'

'Your intention', said Zondi, 'was to stay here under cover as long as possible – correct? It's what any sensible man would do.'

The constable chuckled. 'My name', he said, 'is Hopeful Dumela.'

'Dumela? Did your father work CID five – six years ago?'

'It is a common name, Sergeant, but, yes, that was my father. He always spoke of you with great respect.'

'I do not remember that he owed me money . . .'

Dumela grinned from ear to ear.

Outside, the rain became heavier, sweeping at almost

forty-five degrees across the lawns and making the surface of the swimming-pool dance. Lightning flashed, but the thunder was faint and distant.

'Would the Sergeant like a drink of tea?' offered Hopeful Dumela.

'You know where to find the kitchen?'

'I have found it many times before,' replied Dumela, displaying a certain dry humour of his own. 'This is my beat.'

Excellent, thought Zondi. There was nothing quite like a thick stew of cook's gossip for information, and the spicier it was, the better.

Kramer waited, black ballpoint poised above his notebook.

'Yes, I know why my mother put off going to London on Sunday,' said Theo Kennedy. 'She'd been fighting this writer's-block thing – couldn't get a word down for days – and then she suddenly could. Well, she didn't want to stop again until she absolutely had to, so she—'

'And when did you speak with her last?'

'On . . . on Saturday. She came over to where I live and told me she'd postponed her flight. Yes, it must've been Saturday, because I had the Land-Rover in bits and couldn't hear the phone from outside. She'd rung me originally, you see, and not getting an answer she thought she'd drop me a note. Then she saw me fixing the shocks, and . . . well.'

'It was a good visit?'

'Sorry? Not sure what you mean.'

'You parted on good terms, Mr Kennedy?'

'As good as we ever do.'

'Were any family problems discussed?'

'No.'

Kramer raised an eyebrow fractionally. 'You said that fast,' he remarked.

'No quicker than I could have said "yes", Lieutenant.'

The note that Kramer made in his notebook was *Shampoo*. Then he asked: 'Did anything your mother say – or hint at – suggest to you that she had reason to fear for her life?'

53

'No, nothing at all. She was in a very good mood, as her writing was going so well.'

Kramer wrote down: *Toothpaste*.

'In fact,' Kennedy added, 'I can't remember her ever suggesting she felt in any danger.'

Blades.

'Never ever, sir?' queried Kramer.

Kennedy shrugged. 'Once or twice, after she'd got some really disgusting hate mail – people threatening her with acid, that sort of thing.'

Coffee.

'Oh, really? Was there a recent one, sir?'

'Not that she told me about.'

'I don't suppose she kept any of them?'

'Hell, no! Had them destroyed immediately.'

Sardines.

'Did any of this hate mail seem to be coming from one person, sir?'

Kennedy shrugged. 'I'd not heard of that happening.'

'And so', said Kramer, jotting down *Sugar*, 'we can't say your ma was afraid of anyone, but she did have enemies . . .'

'Lots. She'd become a celebrity, a public figure of a kind.'

'Uh-huh.' *Rent*. 'Go on, sir.'

'Automatically, that starts upsetting people. First, there are the straightforward cranks, and then come the buggers who don't like what you do to be called a celebrity. You know, some don't like your actual writing, with others it's the sex scenes – or, as happens more often, it's what is called the "subversive slant".'

'There was lots of politics in the stories your ma made up?'

'Obliquely, yes. Her settings were always South Africa.'

'And she was anti-Government?'

'Anti-suffering.'

'Uh-huh. Now, what about plain jealousy? Greed? Things like that?'

'Sorry . . .?'

'Your ma was famous, right?'

Kennedy smiled wryly. '*Rich* and famous.'

New chequebook, wrote Kramer.

． ． ．

Hopeful Dumela made a fine pot of tea, and he knew how to
sweeten it properly with condensed milk, scorning the
sugar-bowl. Zondi took his mug over to the window. There
had been a pause in the storm, but now the thunder and
lightning were back, crashing down much closer.

'So tell me,' he said. 'Why do you say this murder is no
surprise to you?'

'Hau, many strange things have already happened in this
place.'

'Such as?'

Dumela scratched vigorously at the side of his head. 'There
was once a naked Coloured woman here, and the people sat
around her and made pictures of her on big sheets of paper.'

'What people?'

'Friends of the missus. Would you believe it if the cook
told you that some of these people were black men, just the
same as you or me?'

'Hau!'

'Oh, yes,' went on Dumela, suitably encouraged. 'There
have been parties, too, all races – many bad men.'

'How could the cook tell that?'

'Because she saw them laughing behind the back of her
missus, sometimes it was only their eyes. These men would
come to the house carrying a piece of polished wood one day,
maybe a stone with holes in it the next day, and they would ask
much money for them.The cook swears to me she would pay it.'

Zondi glanced away, distracted by lightning striking close
by. 'What has the cook told you of the son?'

'A good man, always polite when asking for anything. But
him and his mother – it was always fight-fight-fight-fight,
the cook says.'

'What is the reason for their quarrelling?'

'Mainly, it is money. The mother says her son thinks of
money too much.'

'He has wanted her to give him some also?'

Dumela shrugged. 'That I do not know, Sergeant. But let me
tell you another of the strange things that has happened here.'

． ． ．

The storm clenched the house in its fist, darkening rooms, rattling windows, shaking it to its foundations. There was a brilliant flash and then a tremendous bang; a piece of chimney-pot clattered down the tiles. Leaping to his feet, Theo Kennedy took a step, paused and looked foolish.

'Christ,' he muttered, 'my nerves must be all shot to hell.'

'Come,' said Kramer, rising from the sofa's arm.

This seemed an excellent moment to test the suspect's reactions to the scene of the crime. He led the way through the gloom of the long corridor with mats on its walls and into the study.

Kennedy's attention went immediately to the sheet of paper in the typewriter. 'What a strange line...' he remarked, touching a fingertip to "*II, ii!*"

'Any idea what it means?' murmured Kramer, watching him closely.

Kennedy shook his head, and then turned towards the door through into the sun-lounge. 'If she was changing at the time, that's where it must have happened,' he said. 'Is it all right for me to take a look?'

Which neatly defused the small bombshell Kramer had been about to drop by taking him through there. 'Ach, there's not much to see, sir,' he said.

'I'd still like to,' Kennedy insisted quietly.

Kramer let him go through alone. Bugger it, the man was genuine – he felt sure of this. Nobody could fake the pain in those eyes, the anguish in the way Kennedy was struggling to act casually, passing on nothing of what he was feeling. So what if – as Kennedy had himself revealed a few minutes ago – his mother's death left him a rand millionaire? Plainly, to judge by the off-the-peg casuals he wore, and the inexpensive watch on his wrist, Theo Kennedy wasn't someone who cared a great deal about money – most definitely not enough to kill for, and least of all his own mother. On top of which, if he'd been in need of money, surely he could just have asked her for it?

'She had that sun-lounge built on to the house specially,' said Kennedy, returning to the study. 'Called it her second-favourite room.'

'What was her most favourite?'

56

'This one, the study. It has – well, a lot of her in it.'

'Oh ja? Can you tell me if anything's been disturbed?'

'No, I can't, not really,' replied Kennedy. 'It's been ages since I last had a proper look around in here.'

'Why's that?'

'Er, strained relationship – that sort of thing. Look, do you mind if . . .?'

Kramer caught his arm to steady him. 'Hey, you've gone a bad colour,' he said. 'Best you go through somewhere else and have a lie-down.'

'No, I've got to get out of here.'

'That's what I was suggesting, so if you'll —'

'*Right* out, if you've no objection,' said Kennedy, so pale now he looked on the point of collapse. 'I don't think I can take this house another minute.'

For a moment, Kramer stood undecided, uncertain whether he ought to make the most of this moment, while Kennedy was at his weakest, or to act as his instincts dictated. 'I'll run you home,' he said.

'Thanks, but there's no need. I can drive myself quite—'

'Bullshit, man! You can't even bloody stand properly!'

The trouble was, decided Ramjut Pillay, it was very difficult to feel like a private investigator, dressed up in your plastic raincoat, when just about everybody else on the streets of central Trekkersburg was wearing a raincoat. The worst of the storm had passed, but now a steady downpour had set in.

Still, he did have something few other people had – a gold badge (*Issued Free with Every Diploma*) pinned to the underside of his jacket lapel – and that at least set him apart from the common herd. Turning his collar up even higher, he moved like a shadow along the inside of the pavement, pondering where to begin probing into the foul murder of Naomi Stride.

'Ats-zoo!' sneezed Ramjut Pillay. 'Gods blessing me and dammit!'

A head cold was the last thing he needed, right at the start of his first major case. Muttering about the changeable weather in Trekkersburg, he put his hand through the slit in the right-hand side of his raincoat and into his trouser pocket, groping for a handkerchief. He felt instead a wad of crumpled envelopes, and realised with a sickening lurch that not only had he forgotten to change out of his Post Office trousers, but he'd also somehow absconded with some of the mail.

The seriousness of his situation weighed so heavily on him that he was forced to find a place to sit down, and went into the public lavatory reserved for males of his race behind the city hall. There, bolted into the last cubicle in the line of four, he gingerly withdrew the mail from his pocket and looked to see what names and addresses were on it.

He should have guessed: every item had been destined for Woodhollow – and there was the new English stamp he had coveted.

'Oh, dearie me,' sighed Ramjut Pillay, now with a faint recollection of stuffing the envelopes into his pocket as he fled from the house in wild panic. 'We are in a considerable pickling, are we not?'

And he shuddered as he pictured what would happen if he took these items of mail round to his superior at the Post Office. From the outset, Mr Jarman had made it very clear that the worst, *the very worst* crime any postman could commit – no matter what his excuse – was pocketing mail instead of leaving it at the given address. Instant dismissal would be automatic, with instant arrest on a criminal charge of tampering to follow, Mr Jarman had warned.

'Ah!' exclaimed Ramjut Pillay, having a sudden bright idea. 'There is no difficulty here. I am delivering these tomorrow, just as if—'

But how could he, now he was under suspension? A prickle of icy sweat broke out on Ramjut Pillay's brow. He was trapped, forced into a corner from which there could be no escape. Unless . . .

He counted the envelopes – six were missing, if he remembered correctly. Six letters and a circular he must have dropped in the room where he'd discovered the deceased lady. Good, then those would account for why he had called at the house, and the rest he could destroy, claiming he'd never seen them. None was registered, none had been recorded in any way.

And he was about to begin tearing them up into very tiny pieces, for flushing down the contrivance upon which he sat, when he had another sudden bright idea. What if a vital clue to the murder lay in one of the letters he held in his hand? Shouldn't he first take a look before destroying possible evidence? After all, he had been trying to think of a good place to begin his investigation . . .

You're right, said another side to Ramjut Pillay, filling him with that same cool detachment as before. Go on, take a look – I dare you.

But he hesitated, intimidated by the sound of someone coming in to use the cubicle next to him. The someone, however, soon proved to be beset by severe flatulence problems, and made such a noise, what with his loud sighings and the rest of it, that it seemed impossible he'd overhear a few envelopes being carefully opened. With trembling fingers, Ramjut Pillay set to work, and moments later he was unfolding the first of the letters, turning it the right way up.

What he saw written on that sheet of blue notepaper made his eyebrows leap in horrified amazement. 'Phee-*eeeew*!' exclaimed Ramjut Pillay.

'No need to be so rudely personal,' grumbled the someone next door.

5

WITH Theo Kennedy at his side, and Zondi following behind in the zebra-painted Land-Rover, Kramer drove across town to Azalea Mansions.

'Have you got a girlfriend?' he asked Kennedy.

'Not any more. Why?'

'You're going back to an empty flat, man – that's why.'

'I'll be all right.'

'Or maybe there's some bloke you could go and stay with. The press and television won't take all that long to find out where you live, and then—'

'The hell with them!'

'Then, at least take your phone off the hook, hey?' said Kramer, switching off his windscreen wipers.

Azalea Mansions was made up of five two-storey blocks of flats set at odd angles on an uneven slope of untidy brown lawn. Over the road, where Charlton Heights housed the better-off in an imposing high-rise, the lawn was green, weeded and watered. The sign outside it said, *Keep off the Grass – No Ball Games*, while the chipped enamel notice, askew at the foot of Azalea Mansions' potholed drive, warned: KIDDIES AT PLAY – DRIVE CAREFULLY.

Not that there were any about, as the rain had only just stopped, and Kramer hardly slackened speed on his way up through the puddles.

'My flat's over there,' said Kennedy, 'but this is far enough, so just—'

'Hold on, my sergeant has to know where to park your jalopy, hey? Which number is it?'

'That one, Number 3.'

Kramer took him almost to his front door, and moments later Zondi drew up beside them.

'Well, Mr Kennedy, I'm not sure you're doing the right—'

'No, I'll be fine, but thanks anyway,' he said, opening his car door and getting out. 'It's just I need—'

'T'eo, why aren't you in zebby car?' demanded a little girl, running up to him. She was immaculately dressed, fair, dimpled, and looked like something straight off a chocolate-box. 'Why's there a boy in zebby car? Did you let him?'

Kennedy forced a smile. 'It's all right, Amanda – and how are you today?'

'Been to the shops and to the slide!'

'That must've been nice,' said Kennedy, adding in an aside to Kramer: 'Er, this is a young lady who comes out and watches me when I'm working on my "zebby car", as she calls it. The zebra stripes fascinate kids.'

'Ja, I bet.'

'T'eo, why are your eyes red?' asked Amanda, frowning.

'Look, maybe—' began Kramer.

'Amanda! What are you doing out in the wet?'

'But, Mummy, you said—'

'*Amanda* – and you're making a pest of yourself again!'

'No, she's not,' said Kennedy, 'really she's not.'

Kramer watched the approach of the child's mother. She was a slim woman of about twenty-six in slacks and a jumper and a red headscarf patterned with horseshoes. Her manner was shy, over-anxious.

'I'm sorry,' she said. 'I've so much to do, and no sooner do I turn my—'

'Please, Mummy,' broke in Amanda, '*please* can I sit in T'eo's zebby car? He says I can't unless my mummy says so.'

Perhaps that made it one 'mummy' too many for Kennedy, his having so recently joined the ranks of the motherless. He mumbled an apology, pulled his latchkey out of his pocket, and made for his front door.

'Goodness,' said Amanda's mother, looking at Kramer. 'Is there something the matter?'

He nodded. 'Mickey,' he said, 'scoot after Mr Kennedy and give him his car-keys – tell him we'll be in touch.' And then Kramer murmured very softly, trying not to let the child hear: 'The "something" is that his mother was murdered last night.'

'His *mother* . . .?'

'Ja, and so he's naturally a bit—'

'Oh God, how dreadful! Are you the police, then?'

'CID. We've just brought him back from the scene. Tell me, how well do you know Mr Kennedy, Mrs. . . er?'

'Stilgoe, Vicki Stilgoe. I'm afraid I've hardly ever exchanged more than the odd word with him. It's been Amanda, you see, and of course Bruce, but as far as—'

'Bruce?'

'My brother. He and Mr Kennedy both tinker with their engines out here at the weekend, and—'

'Does Bruce know him well enough to drop in tonight, maybe take him a few cans of beer? I'm a bit worried about—'

'Him being left on his own? Oh, I agree! Don't worry, we'll – well, Bruce will know what to do. He should be home any minute.'

'Excellent,' said Kramer, noticing that Amanda had become all ears.

'But if only I'd *known*. There was me, carrying on as if—'

'A bloke in his position', said Kramer, 'needs normal things happening around him more than anything, I promise you, Mrs Stilgoe. Can I have your phone number?'

'Pardon?' she said, as though startled by sudden propositioning.

Kramer smiled. 'Ach, no, it's just that I've advised him to take his phone off the hook – I suppose you know his ma was a famous writer?'

'Oh, yes, everyone in the flats knows that.'

'Then the press and television will get here all the sooner, and I'd like some way of being able to contact him after the siege begins. I'm not asking you to go to too much trouble?'

'Don't be silly! Our number's 444893.'

It wasn't until a few minutes later, while Zondi was driving him back to CID headquarters, that Kramer began to question the purity of his inspiration regarding Trekkersburg 444893. There had been something about Vicki Stilgoe that had excited him in an oblique, tantalising way and, on reflection, he was sure he'd sensed a reciprocal excitement, hidden behind that timorous exterior.

'That will be two rand fifteen cents,' said the bored brunette behind the cash register. 'You don't want a bag for them, do you?'

Ramjut Pillay did want a bag for his purchases, being somewhat sensitive about their nature, but obligingly shook his head as he paid over the money. He could always find himself a suitable container in the litter-bin down the street.

'Your change,' she said, placing it on the counter for him to pick up, avoiding any chance of their fingers touching.

And yet, mused Ramjut Pillay, as he returned to the street, had she the slightest idea of what was pinned under his jacket lapel, then it would have been a very different story. One

62

touch of his hand, and she'd probably not have washed for a week. Poor common shopgirl, he went on to think kindly, how drab and dull your life must be, when compared with the glamorous, excitement-filled world of the private detective. Which somehow led him on to wonder exactly how often the average common shopgirl *did* wash in a week, and he finally came to a conclusion which, while charitable enough, still had a deeply depressing effect on him.

So much so that he walked right by the first litter-bin in the street, his eyes downcast, and he might have missed the second one had it not been directly in his path.

'Ouchy ow...' said Ramjut Pillay, rubbing at his barked shin.

Then he picked out a crumpled shopping-bag, used a screw of newspaper to wipe the melted ice-cream off it, and carefully stowed away the labels, lemon, pen nibs, notebook and twelve plastic sandwich-bags he'd just bought, before catching the bus back to Gladstoneville.

At six o'clock that evening, Colonel Muller was waiting where he said he'd be, seated in the far corner of the officers' mess on the first floor of divisional headquarters. He was smoking a new briar pipe, and had two large Scotches on the table before him.

'What will you have, Tromp?' he asked, waving a hand at the bar. 'Just tell young Vermaak your pleasure, and I'll pay for it later.'

Kramer brought back a lager.

'I'm in here because I can't take the telephone any longer,' explained Colonel Muller. '*Time* magazine is already on our backs – it'll be *Newsweek* and *Der Spiegel* next! On top of which, Pretoria is on the line in my office every five minutes, with the Brigadier wanting results yesterday. Have you got anything I can tell him?'

'To get stuffed, sir?'

Colonel Muller smiled briefly before raising a finger to his lips and using a sideways movement of his eyes to draw Kramer's attention to the huddle of Security Branch officers sitting two tables away to their left.

'Or alternatively —'

'Er, cheers,' said Colonel Muller, swallowing half a large Scotch.

Kramer raised his glass.

'But seriously now, Tromp, what have you got to tell me? You've interviewed the son, I hear. What's he like?'

Kramer glanced round the mess to see if there was anyone there who bore some resemblance to Theo Kennedy. It was like trying to pick out a cocker spaniel in a kennel of guard dogs.

'Ach, six-two, age twenty-four. Medium build.'

'No, but what *sort* of bloke, I mean. All artistic, like his ma was?'

'Ordinary, Colonel – nothing flash. A good bloke, that's all. Naturally, he is totally bombed out of his tree by what's happened. I took him back to his place and fixed up for some neighbours to keep an eye on him.'

'Oh ja?' said Colonel Muller, sipping at his Scotch. 'And where was he last night?'

Kramer had drunk half his lager. 'He'd had this phone message from some bloke who said he had some business to offer him. The arrangement was they'd meet in the cocktail room at the Florida Hotel in Durban at nine, but the bloke never turned up. Kennedy waited around until ten-thirty, then drove back to Trekkersburg, had a shower and a couple of drinks and went to bed.'

'Alone?'

'Ja, alone. He hasn't got a girlfriend at the moment.'

'You've not accepted that as an alibi?'

'I don't see he needs one, sir. Kennedy doesn't rate as a suspect.'

'Oh, no? One of the lawyers connected with the will has let slip to Jones that mother and son "had their differences concerning money", which suggests an important line of enquiry – at least, to me it does.'

'What will?'

'Naomi Stride's, of course – in which she leaves him the best part of a million rand, with more to come from her book sales.'

Kramer shrugged. 'Typical Jones thinking,' he said. 'In a flash, he comes up with the obvious: the lady was killed for her money. Never mind the fact she wasn't just any rich woman, but a famous writer; never mind that her son obviously doesn't give a damn about money, or that she's killed by a sword, of all things. Let's not complicate the issue.'

'Agreed,' said Colonel Muller, handing him a smudgy carbon copy of a list of names and addresses. 'She was killed for her money. Here's a list of other beneficiaries, all except one of them local.'

'Huh! The fourth one down is for only a piddling thousand rand!'

'But look at the name beside it – Kwakona Mtunsi. How many coons do you know that have ever even dreamed of so much money coming their way?'

'Oh, I think they all dream,' said Kramer.

'The point remains', went on Colonel Muller, showing some irritation in the way he knocked the dottle from his new pipe, 'that everything is relative. What a white wouldn't think was worth killing for, a black could easily—'

'There are two assumptions being made here,' interrupted Kramer. 'The first is that all the beneficiaries were aware of being included in her will.'

'She could have told them, Tromp. Have you any way of proving she didn't?'

Kramer shrugged and shook his head.

'So what is the second assumption?' asked Colonel Muller, opening his tobacco-pouch.

'The one that's already been made, that she was killed for her money, sir. It could have been for all sorts of other reasons.'

'But have you any evidence of a different motive so far?'

'No, sir,' Kramer had to concede, 'apart from a sword being a bloody funny weapon in this day and age. But neither have I had a chance to make the usual checks on who she's been seeing lately, whether the neighbours had noticed anything suspicious, the likelihood of—'

'Fine, then this list at least gives us somewhere to begin,

and the Brigadier is pleased with it. He suggests that you take the first five names, and Jones does the second five, with me co-ordinating in the middle.'

'But, Colonel—'

'I know, Lieutenant, I know . . . You're not a man who likes teamwork. Usually, I'm willing to go along with that; only in these circumstances, with the pressure we're getting put on us, I can't oblige right now. And, on second thoughts, can I have your list back a minute?'

Kramer handed it over to him, and watched him make an alteration with a ballpoint.

Zondi said nothing. Just drove.

Down long tunnels of violet jacaranda blossom, avenues of palm-trees, and over the bridge into the oldest part of town, where the Victorian houses had faded tin roofs, fancy cast-iron railings surrounding their balconies and dim verandas, high hedges with narrow gates opening on to mossy paths of red tile. Little-old-lady territory, where carefully darned pastel petticoats hung on the washing-lines each Monday, and the cats sat combing best cream from their whiskers. But here and there, like vivid fungi beginning to sprout from a mouldering log, colourful blinds shaded freshly painted window-frames, and shiny new cars, vivid as toadstools, stood in clumps, signifying the gradual return of new life to the neighbourhood.

Still without saying anything, Zondi drew up in front of a narrow two-storey house, blazing with light from every window.

'Christ,' grunted Kramer, 'what's it supposed to be? A warning to shipping?'

The silhouette of a stocky figure appeared at an upper window and gazed down on them. It vanished for a moment, the light in that room went out, and then the figure returned again, to stand motionless.

'Now he thinks we can't see him,' murmured Zondi. 'I am beginning to wonder about his politics.'

'Ja, he's acting like an old hand at the game,' agreed Kramer. 'Like he's had cop cars outside his house before. . .'

66

'Let him stew for a minute, boss?'

'Could be useful – why not?'

Zondi lit two Luckies and passed one across. 'And so', he said, 'why the dark face, boss? What happened when you met the Colonel?'

Kramer told him.

'Hau, hau, hau . . . Lieutenant Jones? And that lazy baboon, Gagonk Mbopa? They take half the list?'

'Uh-huh. Including Theo Kennedy, although he was mine originally.'

With a low whistle, Zondi settled back in his seat. 'They get the Number One Suspect! You know, Hopeful Dumela's information about the money fights Boss Kennedy had with is mother, plus—'

'Ach, not you, too!' protested Kramer, flinging open his door.

'Boss?'

But Kramer was out of the car the next second and striding up the path to the house of the second person named on the beneficiaries list.

'Can I help you?' asked the stocky figure, now appearing against the dazzling hallway light.

'You'd bloody better,' growled Kramer. 'Anton Leonard Carswell?'

'That's right, but just who do you—?'

'Lieutenant Kramer, Murder and Robbery.'

Carswell swallowed hard. 'Er, then, perhaps we ought to go inside,' he said. 'This must be about poor Naomi. . .'

God, the house stank. Turpentine, paint, over-ripe fruit. The excessive wattage in the light fittings didn't contribute much, either, for they showed quite plainly that the floorboards were totally bare, the whitewashed walls un-evenly plastered, and that the colours used in the huge pictures stuck up everywhere were childishly garish.

Carswell stumped hurriedly down the hallway corridor. He went through the second door on the left, and came to a stop on the far side of a pine dinner-table, turning to face Kramer.

'My wife Pamela,' he said, a pleased note of warning in his

voice, as though now he had all the protection he needed.

Kramer winked at the woman seated at the head of the table. 'Hello, Pamela,' he said. 'Tromp Kramer, CID, hey?'

'Mrs Carswell, *if* you don't mind,' she said icily. 'Do you want to sit down?'

Kramer took the chair opposite to her and waited to see how long it would be before Carswell seated himself, too. They were an odd pair and no mistake. The man was about thirty-two and wore baggy white shorts, red sandals, and a T-shirt the same colour as his baby-blue eyes. He was almost hairless, except for a few reddish wisps growing across the pate of his very round head, and his limbs had dimples at the elbows and knees, accentuating his chubby smoothness. By way of contrast, the woman had a very full head of hair, drawn back tightly into a braided knot the size and colour of a large pastry. It was the nearest she came to indulging in frivolous femininity. The long serious face bore no make-up, the capable hands had their fingernails cut straight across, the swell of her breasts was lost in a loose-fitting garment that fell to her ankles, which were pink and pressed tightly together. It would undoubtedly take a great deal more than missionary zeal, decided Kramer, to get this lady into any sort of position.

Zondi glanced up from the paperback edition of *The Last Magnolia* which he had let slip into his pocket as he was leaving Naomi Stride's study. There was a car approaching with only its sidelights burning. He switched off the small torch he had been reading by, tipped the rearview mirror so that he could use it as a periscope, and lay down across the front seat of the Ford, hidden from sight.

He heard the car slowing right down and then stopping Carefully, he manoeuvred himself until he could read its licence plate in the angled mirror, ready to make a note of the number. Then he began to smile. The number of the vehicle was all too familiar to him.

So Jones and Mbopa had decided on a detour to check up on the Lieutenant's progress, although it was impossible to guess what they hoped to deduce by peering into the house

68

from the street. They acted strangely at the best of times, however, and anybody trying to establish rational reasons for their behaviour was probably expecting too much of them.

'Where's that bugger Zondi?' came Jones's nasal whine.

The gravelly response by Mbopa was impossible to make out.

'Just see he doesn't,' said Jones, 'or you'll be back in uniform double-bloody-quick, my fat friend.'

The car began moving again, and for an instant Zondi glimpsed its two occupants in the mirror above him. They were both looking straight in his direction, but evidently – and predictably – had seen nothing.

Anton Carswell sat down suddenly in an awed slump. 'I can't believe it,' he said. 'Naomi has left us *how much* . . .?'

'Forty thousand rand,' said Kramer, 'give or take a few hundred. Are you implying you weren't aware until now of being a beneficiary?'

'Aware? I didn't even know she thought of us as special friends of hers!'

'Obviously the bequest must be in recognition of your work,' said Pamela Carswell, taking the news quite calmly. 'Yes, that makes perfect sense to me.' And to Kramer she said: 'Anton has been hung in New York, you know.'

'Really, hey?' said Kramer, resisting the temptation to say he knew quite a few who'd been hung in Pretoria.

'In fact, if he hadn't to spend so much of his time teaching, my husband would've long since—'

'To hell with that now, Pamela! Forty grand means we can—'

'I want', cut in Kramer, 'to go back to something you came out with a couple of seconds ago: this business of not being "special friends" of the deceased. What exactly was your relationship?'

'Um, artist and patron would cover it, I suppose.'

'Patroness,' said Pamela Carswell. 'Naomi came across Anton's work not long after moving here, to Trekkersburg, and made a point of acquiring several of his pictures for her private collection.'

'I see, so it was all just buying and selling between you,' said Kramer.

She coloured slightly. 'No, not entirely.'

'Far from it!' said Anton Carswell. 'We were often invited to parties at Woodhollow, weren't we, Pamela?'

'Well, I wouldn't say we'd—'

'Quite intimate ones, too,' he added.

'Ah,' said Kramer, consulting a blank page in his notebook. 'That's what I thought. I have some dates here.'

A beautiful moment. The couple exchanged uneasy glances and each sat up a little straighter, as though bracing themselves. But Kramer said nothing more; he simply waited.

'All right,' said Anton Carswell, 'I'll admit that, on one level, Naomi and I were unusually close.'

So it was 'I' now all of a sudden, instead of 'we', which indicated he was taking care to keep his wife out of this. But, no, it couldn't be sex, thought Kramer, and opted for: 'Politics, Mr Carswell?'

'Anton, you needn't have said any—'

But Carswell ignored her. 'Politics, human rights, call it what you like, Lieutenant. Naomi Stride and I shared certain beliefs, and through our work we both attempted to convey the same message, if you like. Every nation, as someone once said, must look to its artists to act as the watchdogs of its soul and its future!'

'Which I also believe,' Pamela Carswell said quietly.

Kramer turned and stared at the canvas filling half the wall behind him. It looked as if the paint had been smeared on by hand, the way a toddler has fun with its mashed pumpkin while its mother is answering the front door to the electricity-meter reader. There was plenty of yellow, and plenty of orange, with dribbles of gory red here and there, coinciding roughly with skinny black shapes that almost had arms and legs but didn't.

'Well?' demanded Anton Carswell, lifting a dimpled chin in proud defiance.

'I'm sorry, but I don't think you stand a hope of getting it

70

banned,' said Kramer. 'Only, you probably realise that, don't you?'

'You bastard!' hissed Pamela Carswell.

With great care, Ramjut Pillay sealed each piece of correspondence addressed to Naomi Stride in its own plastic sandwich-bag, and labelled them *Exhibit One* to *Exhibit Five*. Then he adjusted the wick of the paraffin-lamp on the orange-crate locker beside his divan in the lean-to, cleaned his glasses, and began his forensic examination in earnest.

The bill from the suppliers of swimming-pool filtration equipment seemed to be quite genuine, if such huge figures could be believed, and he set it aside after only a few minutes.

He spent far longer on the letter in a cream envelope sent from a place called Bumstead in England, suspecting something decidedly fishy about such an address. In the end, however, he had no choice but to discount it as a fan letter of sorts. Although the signatory had been 'appalled at the way the book sided with the terrorists', he had gone on to say that the esteemed authoress of *Winter Sun* had 'caught the Rhodesian landscape magnificently', just as he remembered it.

Exhibit Three was a moving letter from the father of a boy with an incurable disease asking, on his behalf, for her to autograph the five pieces of white card enclosed.

After which *Exhibit Four*, a request from some magazine or other for a photograph it could use with an article on South African novelists by Professor Andre P. Brink, seemed very dry stuff indeed, and took no more than a minute or so to authenticate.

Ramjut Pillay made another adjustment to the lamp wick, and then steeled himself for *Exhibit Five*, the sheet of cheap blue stationery that had earlier so horrified him, but which he now felt able to study with the necessary professional detachment.

'Bad speller,' he noted, tut-tutting. 'Deduction: person of low intellect, minimal educations. . .'

Right you Filthey JUW bitCH. You haVe haD all tHe

WARNingS you Are goING to Get. I suPPose You tHInk yOu can Put ME in a BooK and MaKe a Mock of Me and GeT aWAy wiTH it. you Know I can'T sue you beCoz tHe booK is Banned here (anD so It shOULd be!!!!) but Peopele still gett coPies and so I hAVe had enouGh and nOw yoU Are reALLy goINg to Pay For It. ReMEMber Richelieu, Act II, Scene ii – "The PEn iS mighTier than THE swORD"? Ha ha ha. We'll soon see AboUt tHAT – jUsT you WAit!!!!!

Zondi's torch batteries were almost flat when Kramer returned to the car and found him engrossed in a dimly lit page of *The Last Magnolia*.

'No wonder they say it's a mistake to teach you buggers to read,' he said, getting in on the passenger's side. 'You'll all end up bloody blind at this rate.'

Zondi smiled and pocketed the book again. 'The Lieutenant sounds as though he has also learned something,' he said, turning the ignition key. 'What was this Boss Carswell like?'

'Ach, you saw for yourself, Mickey! One word to him out on the porch and he goes running inside to Mummy – the sort of arty-farty character you imagine puts a rubber teat on his wine-bottle. Go back over the bridge and I'll have decided by then where we go next.'

The Ford churned up the verge, bit into the asphalt of the street and took off. 'So that's why all the lights in his house are on? He is afraid of the dark, too?'

'Could be – although when I made some remark about it he came back with a whole lot of crap about "an artist must have light all around him" or something. Anyway, that's beside the point.'

'Except this artist does not sound like a murder suspect.'

'No chance, but I'll give you the main points of the interview later. The important thing, old son, is that Anton Leonard Carswell was able to explain all this nonsense about the "fights over money" that Theo Kennedy had with his mother.'

'Uh-huh?' said Zondi, reaching over to re-adjust the rearview mirror.

'It was the son's job,' said Kramer. 'His way of making a living. His mother kept wanting him to give it up, claimed he was "corrupting the Zulu culture" – accused him of exploitation. She said it disgusted her that a son of hers should be part of a "cheap and shoddy" operation, et cetera, where only money—'

'Exploitation, how?'

'Ja, I asked that. Apparently the son got into the curio business after some birdwatching trip he took in a jeep to a really remote area, up near the border. He came across this village where there was a man who had made some really good heads out of clay – you know, heads of different people – and the bugger was willing to sell them at fifty cents apiece or around that. Kennedy saw straight away that the same heads could be fetching twenty – thirty times that back in Durban, and that's how his business began. He offered this bloke five rand a head, cash in hand, and said he'd be back in a month to pick up more of them to—'

'*Five rand?*' queried Zondi, giving a low whistle. 'The son must be a good man. Many would have said, "OK, fifty cents," and—'

'Ja, I didn't follow where the exploitation came in, either, when you take into account transport and all the other overheads. On top of which, you know how bare-bummed poor those buggers are, out in the sticks.'

'Too true. Five rand by itself would be much, much money. The man made more heads?'

'He's still making them, apparently, and he's got half the village helping him, finding the right clay, looking after the ovens he bakes them in. Mind you, he's not the only one supplying Kennedy these days. There's woodcarvers, women doing beadwork, people using cowhide for Zulu shields – ach, all sorts.'

Zondi took the lit Lucky Strike being offered him. 'But . . .'

'I know, you want to know what the mother thought was so wrong about this? Shall I tell you what Carswell said when I asked him the same thing? He said all the heads the first bloke made, for instance, were still the same six heads

Kennedy bought the first time.'

'And so?'

'I'm buggered if I can see the crime in that, either,' said Kramer, winding down his window.

'What was the connection between this Boss Carswell and—'

'The Stride woman? Basically, she paid big money for his paintings after he'd given her all the right sort of chat, I'd say.'

'His pictures are no good?'

Kramer shrugged. 'Christ, how can you tell, Mickey? They all looked the bloody same to me, except some were different sizes.'

6

COLONEL MULLER was halfway across the vehicle-yard at eight the following morning when Jones drove in off the street and stopped beside him. 'I've already seen two of the suspects on my list, sir,' he said, getting out. 'And my boy ran a double-check by interrogating their servants. Cast-iron alibis for both lots, I'm afraid.'

'How can you be so sure?' asked the Colonel, not pausing, but forcing Jones to fall in step with him. 'And, anyway, it's me that's doing the co-ordinating, taking the final decisions in these matters.'

Jones flipped open an immaculately kept and detailed notebook. 'Roger Michael Slater, white adult male, fifty-five years of age, poetry-writer and bookshop-owner by occupation. At approximately seven-fifteen last night, a lady friend came up to his flat to show him some etchings.'

'Oh ja? That's a new twist.'

'Pardon, Colonel? Have I missed something I should've—?'

'Just get on with it, man.'

'This lady friend – namely Shareena Gordon, thirty-eight

74

years of age – then had an evening meal with the aforesaid Roger Slater, prepared by Moses Tetwe, house boy, who resides in Kwela Village. Tetwe was asked to serve coffee at approximately ten-twenty, by which time he had fallen asleep in the kitchen. Slater reports that the lady had by now "had a few drinks" and was in a "boisterous mood". She knocked over the first pot of coffee and another one had to be ordered. When Tetwe arrived in the lounge with this second pot, he informed his employer that he could not return to Kwela Village as curfew was at ten-thirty and he was not in possession of a late pass. Slater offered to drive him home personally, and to make the right excuses if stopped by a patrol van, but Tetwe said that as his boss had just knocked the second coffee-pot over perhaps he was not really in the mood for driving. Slater agreed with him, and told him to make himself comfortable for the night on the kitchen floor, using any bedding he liked to take from the basket beside the washing machine. He then wished Tetwe "happy dreams" and said not to bother with more coffee, as he had just remembered he had some cognac somewhere. According to Slater, "I thought cognac might help Shareena to calm down", and at approximately midnight she was calm enough to be left to sleep on the couch in the lounge while he retired to his bed. Tetwe reports that he himself did not fall asleep again until approximately four-twenty by the kitchen clock, owing to the lady visitor frequently saying prayers out aloud such as, "O God, that's beautiful – Jesus, I love you!" – which he, as a self-confessed pagan, grew very tired of. Personally, Colonel, I think—'

'Ja, ja, so do I, Jones. But surely the point is, this Tetwe can vouch for the fact Slater was on the premises all night?'

'Exactly, Colonel. As to Slater's connection with the deceased—'

'Who was the other suspect you interviewed, hey?' said Colonel Muller, making a show of consulting his wristwatch at the foot of the fire-escape.

'Miss Yvonne Frobisher, white adult female—'

'Can't I just have the main drift for now?'

'Er, certainly, Colonel,' replied Jones, his mouth going

sulky. 'The aforesaid, a librarian by trade, claims to have had an early night after listening to some concert on the radio, and the maidservant, resident on the premises, who helps her with her wheelchair, corroborates the above statement.'

'Excellent, Jones!' said Colonel Muller, clapping him on the shoulder. 'Now, I really must—'

'Any news from Kramer, sir?'

'Aha,' said Colonel Muller mysteriously.

Two reporters and a television crew were hanging about outside Theo Kennedy's flat at Azalea Mansions, eating what smelled like bacon sandwiches. Kramer walked right past them.

'Bugger it!' he said under his breath, not having expected the press to be out and about so early.

Then a familiar figure came running up to him. 'Mummy says you must come,' she said, reaching for his hand. 'Come with Amanda.'

'Oh ja? But what does Daddy say?'

'Daddy's not there – Daddy's in Heaven, silly! Come *on*, or I'll pull you!'

He let her tug him all the way to the door of Number 7. The reporters, he noticed, gave him no more than a glance, having no interest in the commonplace. A moment later he was inside the flat, which also smelled of bacon, and the front door had been closed behind him.

'I hope you didn't mind that,' said Vicki Stilgoe, smiling shyly and showing that she, too, had a dimple or two. 'But I guessed you probably wanted to see Theo, and we've got him in here with us.'

'*T'eo's in the bath*,' Amanda confided. 'Washing.'

'Really?' said Kramer.

'He'll be out in a moment, though,' said Vicki Stilgoe. 'Can I offer you a cup of coffee in the meantime? Come through to the kitchen.'

Kramer followed her down the short passage, wishing he could see whether she had more dimples where her neat little bottom joined the small of her back. But she was fully dressed, in pressed blue jeans and a crisp cotton blouse, and he had to content himself with admiring her earlobes.

'With milk, or without?' she asked, lifting a coffee-pot.

'With, please.'

She laughed. 'At least someone took it quietly last night,' she said. 'Bruce and Theo have been drinking theirs black and *very*, very strong, I'm afraid.'

'Ja, I packed in early, about seven-thirty – this artist bloke got right up my nose – and decided it'd be better making a fresh start this morning. But what happened here?'

'Bruce went over to Theo's, who didn't want to know him at first, and then, so I gather, one thing led to another. I heard them coming in about two, and noises while they tried to find more booze for themselves; and, the next thing I knew, I had two corpses on my hands in the living-room. God knows how Bruce pulled himself together enough to leave for work – I'd hate to be one of his factory boys this morning!'

'The lady's a widow,' Kramer was telling himself. 'Is that why she gives me this feeling? Christ, I must have some sort of thing about widows! Is it they're touched with death in some way, and this appeals to me because death is my business – my life even?' He had never thought of himself as a pervert before, and stood mildly shocked by the very suggestion.

Joseph 'Gagonk' Mbopa was looking at the single rose which grew in the courtyard of the CID building. A black prisoner on loan as a cleaner from Trekkersburg jail, distinctive in his red jerkin, khaki shorts and leather sandals, squatted nearby, brushing cigarette ends into a small dustpan, and giving him anxious sideward glances. Mbopa was not a man generally reputed to have an interest in horticulture, let alone a gentle, whimsical side to his nature.

Very nearly as broad as he was tall, perpetually scowling and given to deep booms of displeasure, the detective sergeant had been given the name 'Gagonk' early on in his police career, and it had suited him so perfectly nobody had ever thought to change it. Not even the purists, who did, however, point out that strictly speaking it should have been 'Igogog(o)', the Zulu word for the ubiquitous four-gallon paraffin-can, much in use for fetching water, which has thin, almost square sides that make a 'gog-gog' or 'gagonk-ish' sort of sound when being carried empty.

The rose trembled in the pink palm of Mbopa's cupping hand, its stem between his fat fingers. He thrust his broad flat nose up close and sniffed, grimacing appreciatively. Yet his sharp, red-rimmed eyes never left the main entrance, and Zondi, who had chosen to come in through the rear entrance for a change, noticed this.

The prisoner could have spoiled what happened next, but wisely averted his gaze and moved crablike until his back was turned on Zondi's advancing figure. The soft dust of the courtyard absorbed footsteps without a sound. The Walther PPK automatic left its shoulder holster as silently. Moving swiftly, holding a hand against his left trouser leg to keep his loose change from giving a telltale clink, Zondi closed the gap and then poked his gun muzzle into the small of Mbopa's broad back.

'Hey-bar-bor!' exclaimed Mbopa, wildly startled, leaping into the air and spinning round with clenched fist raised.

'Good morning, Gagonk,' said Zondi, grinning and putting his gun away.

'Bastard son of a bastard!' snarled Mbopa, the fist still high. 'Pox-ridden whore's whelp conceived on a dung—'

'Don't do anything stupid, the Colonel's watching,' Zondi said out of one corner of his mouth.

Mbopa glanced up at the balcony behind him and saw this was true. He brought his clenched fist down and laughed heartily as though he and Zondi were just indulging in a little friendly horseplay.

'It's OK, he's gone now,' said Zondi. 'But tell me – why were you waiting here to see me as I came in?'

Mbopa cast another wary look behind him.

'The Colonel's gone – like I told you. Don't you trust your comrades, Gagonk?'

'I wasn't waiting to see you!'

'Rubbish,' said Zondi. 'You were hoping to have a little chat. Hoping to find out how far me and the Lieutenant had got with our investigations last night.'

'Huh, what you and Spokes—'

'The big question being, where was I myself when you drove past the Carswell house last night?'

'We never came anywhere near the—'

'I'll tell you,' said Zondi, beckoning him closer. 'I was attending to one of our big clues: the last magnolia . . .'

'That what?' asked Mbopa.

'*Magnolia* – you know, man, it's English for a kind of big flower. I thought, from the way you were sniffing away, flowers must be a special subject of yours.'

'Zondi, you—' Mbopa began threateningly.

'Just a minute, Gagonk,' said Colonel Muller, striding towards him from the foot of the stairwell. 'What have you done to that rose, hey?'

Zondi gave a polite nod and discreetly withdrew, followed by the prisoner who had probably learned, after a spell in Trekkersburg jail, that Afrikaans spoken in a certain silky tone boded little good.

'I asked you', Zondi heard Colonel Muller say behind him, 'what the hell you'd done to that rose I look at every morning?'

'But, Colonel,' protested Mbopa, 'I hardly touched—'

'Open that fist, you heathen monstrosity. Open that fist! There, now tell me what that is. . .'

Whistling, Zondi started up the stairs, taking them two at a time.

'Ramjut?' came his mother's querulous voice from outside the door to the lean-to. 'Ramjut, are you there? And, if you are there, why are you there? This is not a Sunday, not a day of rest, Ramjut. Ramjut, can you hear me. . .?'

'Go away, Mother,' he said rudely. 'Go away and dropping dead.'

'What, boy? What did you say to me?'

'Please go away, Mother,' he sighed.

Then turned back to what he had been doing the whole night long, caught up in a fever of excitement mixed with uncertainty. He read, for the umpteenth time, the threatening letter on cheap blue stationery that described Naomi Stride as a 'Filthey JUW bitCH' and, again for the umpteenth time, he wondered whether it hadn't in fact been written by her killer.

Everything seemed to point to this being so. Each word of the letter was charged with murderous hatred, and there, quite plainly, was a promise that she would be made 'to pay for it' through what the writer would do to her. And yet...

'Ramjut!' came his mother's voice again, quavering pathetically. 'I'm an old woman, the sun is already hot, I cannot stand here many minutes longer, pleading for a word from you. What is the matter? What is going through your mind?'

'A postmark!' snapped Ramjut Pillay.

Monday's postmark, to be exact, and this was where his half-formed theory foundered. Naomi Stride had been murdered on Monday night, before the letter could reach her. What sense was there in that? Obviously she had been intended to read the thing and to feel shame for what she had done. Just as obviously, the writer had wanted to gloat over the mounting terror she would feel while she waited for him to strike. Why jump the gun, and let her off so much terrible punishment, when there was such hatred in your heart?

'Ah!' said Ramjut Pillay, with sudden inspiration. 'Because, we must remind our dear selves, the aforesaid lady victim might take such colossal frights she will run away, or tell the police of her problems, thereby making it difficult to be executing such a devilish scheme!'

But, no, something wasn't quite right about that notion, either, as logical and rational as it seemed.

'Ah!' said Ramjut Pillay.

Logic and rationality were not to be expected from the sort of madman who had written the letter. To have done so at all, risking the letter being traced back to him by the CID, showed he was not one for astute reasoning but a bloody foolish fellow.

Which did not necessarily make him a killer, though.

'Oh dear, oh dear, if only I am knowing of some proper link,' sighed Ramjut Pillay.

Kramer sipped his tea and tried not to think about Vicki Stilgoe. He concentrated instead on the fact that Theo

Kennedy had seemed much calmer when he'd come sidling into the kitchen, a terrible hangover notwithstanding. It was obviously doing him good to have Amanda around, because her chirpy remarks made the poor bugger keep smiling. On top of which, Vicki was the perfect—

'Right, Mickey!' he said to Zondi, who was fitting a new lead to the electric kettle. 'Enough of this pissing about, let's have your ideas on where we should start today. With Carswell out of the way, that leaves four others on our list to see. Jesus Christ, this is a stupid bloody way of going about things.'

Zondi nodded. 'The money in each case is now small,' he agreed. 'And was it only to people here in Trekkersburg that Mrs Stride left these presents in her will?'

'Ach, I don't know, man – and I care even less. What I want are practical suggestions.'

'Then, to do this quicker, we split up, boss.'

'You crafty bugger,' grunted Kramer, picking up the list. 'That means you get just the one – this Kwakona Mtunsi bloke – while I get the other three.'

'Are you not three times the man I am, O Great White Father?'

'*Six times* the man, kaffir,' Kramer replied. 'Because, the way I feel right now, I'm likely to go out and bite each one of these bastards in half.'

Gagonk Mbopa was becoming heartily sick of questioning domestic servants. His idea of an interrogation was something a good deal more lively, less inhibited, and best carried out after dark, well away from squeamish people with sensitive hearing. His favourite place had long been a children's play-park, hidden in a remote grove of wattle-trees on the edge of one of the city's more prosperous white suburbs, but then some over-imaginative housewife had noticed bloodstains under one end of the seesaw, and he had reluctantly decided to change venues for a while. Time and place weren't the only things, neither was improvised equipment; a real man like Gagonk Mbopa needed another real man to get his teeth into, not this assortment of overfed,

81

hysterical women, or the obsequious, head-bobbing creatures who passed for males among them.

'And, like I say, while I do that,' Jones was whining on, 'you get round the back and sort out the farm boys and everything, OK?'

'Ermph,' said Mbopa, and then, as a grudging after-thought, 'sir.'

They carried on up the steep dirt road, watching out for a sign to direct them to a farm called, for some very strange reason, Cold Comfort. Twice, Jones hit huge potholes that could have been easily avoided, and Mbopa gave an involuntary grimace to hear the police vehicle labouring in quite the wrong gear.

'So what gives you the right to make faces?' Jones demanded. 'The first and only time I allowed you to drive me anywhere, you nearly ruined the bloody gearbox and the clutch, and we spent half the time trying to get back on the road. Honest to God, a drunken bloody gorilla, with a bucket over its head, couldn't have done any worse than you – do you know that? I've never seen such an example of dangerous, completely crazy kaffir-driving in all my life!'

'Hau, I am ashamed,' said Mbopa, who could genuinely handle any car with consummate skill, but preferred, for reasons associated with his ego, to make Jones act at what he called 'my little pink chauffeur'.

Yawning, Kramer reached for the door-knocker and clattered it impatiently, hardly pausing before he clattered it again. He wasn't too sure he had scribbled down the correct address, because this place seemed a lot more like an old warehouse than someone's home.

Then the small door within the big door opened very slightly, and a bleary but bewitching green eye took a look at him. 'Go away,' a sleepy voice said in English.

'Here,' said Kramer, pushing his warrant card through the crack. 'It tells you who I am, lady. The rest comes when you let me inside.'

'And if I don't?'

'I'll stand here and sob my heart out.'

She laughed. 'How grotesque! No, I don't think I could stand that . . .' And there was the sound of a chain lock being unhitched. 'Count to ten and then let yourself in,' she said. 'You got me out of bed to answer this, and I'm not really in a state to be seen receiving visitors.'

Kramer began to take an interest in the morning.

He counted to ten, pushed the door open and stepped into a vast room that had been partially divided into two levels. The ground level had a polished wooden floor, a circle of enormous cushions almost dead-centre and, over in the far corner, an L-shaped kitchen area, equipped with the biggest spice-rack he had ever seen. Also on a grand scale was the huge wall-mirror that rose a good six feet from the skirting and had a curious banister or handrail running across it.

'I'm up here,' said the sleepy voice.

Having closed the door behind him, Kramer crossed over to a spiral staircase made of cast iron and painted fire-engine red, hesitated for only a moment, and then started up it. The lady, he reflected, would have to be quite a little mover to have covered the same distance so silently and in only ten seconds.

The first thing he saw on the second level was the cross-section of a thick white carpet. This was followed by the foot of a very wide, low bed, and then by two large built-in wardrobes on either side of it, each painted black. It was not until he actually left the spiral staircase that he finally got to take a proper look at what went with that one green eye.

Another green eye, thank God – just as bewitching.

A nose, too, and a mouth.

A face straight from a make-up ad, high-cheeked, finely modelled, impeccable in its detail, framed by a tumble of long hair the Coca-Cola brown of a Cape mountain stream.

It wasn't often Kramer felt poetic.

'Theresa Mary Muldoon?' he said.

'Usually just "Tess",' she said. 'But fine, if you prefer to be so formal.'

'Always,' said Kramer, sitting down on the foot of her bed.

'*I* see,' she said. 'And?'

'I'm here because I'm enquiring into the death of a friend of yours, the writer Naomi Stride.'

'God, I can't bear to think about it!'

'You were close?'

'I adored her. She was. . .'

Kramer raised an eyebrow.

'*Good*,' said Tess Muldoon. 'Would you rub my foot?'

He thought about it, then turned back a corner of the patchwork quilt. The foot wriggled its long toes in greeting.

'M'm, gorgeous. . .' she said, closing her eyes and letting herself relax totally. 'What big strong hands you have – how did they get like that?'

'Ach, pulling the wings off flies,' said Kramer.

Zondi blinked, not entirely sure he was seeing right. But there, against the skyline, was undeniably a gigantic dragon-lizard, akin to those whose bones were on display at the Trekkersburg Museum, held together by iron rods and wire. It stood on four great pillars of legs, its long body arched, its slender neck and almost identical tail dipping down to the ground.

Then the rough track took a sudden twist and some mimosa-trees got in the way. A dilapidated noticeboard announced: *Tebeli Mission School*. It took another hundred yards of cautious driving before the dragon became visible again, very much closer, and revealed itself to be more mythical than reptilian, for it had two rows of mammary glands under its belly. There were also children climbing all over it.

'Mad!' said Zondi, chuckling as he stopped the car.

From each pair of teats hung the ropes of a swing, and the tail of the creature was actually a slide, reached by climbing the rough steps fashioned in its neck. Never in all his life had he seen such a marvellous contraption, not even at a school for whites.

'Greetings, my brother,' said a Zulu of his own age, appearing at his car window. 'May I be of service to you?'

'Greetings. Yes, you can tell me who made this thing.'

84

'Kwakona Mtunsi, with much help from the children.'

'Are you Mtunsi?' asked Zondi, alerted by the modesty of the reply.

'Yes, my brother, I am he.'

Zondi got out of his car. Mtunsi was tall and thin, as loosely connected at the joints as a Railway Street drunk. He wore workman's blue dungarees, kept his long thumbs hooked behind the shoulder straps, and on his head was a wide grass hat, frayed around its brim. His feet were bare, just like the feet of the children in his charge. Zondi had never seen a teacher before who didn't try to keep up appearances in a patched jacket and pants, shiny tie, sagging socks and lace-up shoes with many cracks in them.

'What is your job here at the school?' he asked.

'I am the principal,' Mtunsi replied, adding with a slow smile, 'and the only member of staff.' He held out his hand.

'Detective Sergeant Mickey Zondi, Trekkersburg CID.'

Mtunsi nodded, widening that smile. 'I understood you were from the police. Usually, when any visitor comes to Tebeli, the children run to greet the car, and to beg a ride.'

'Only they saw the radio aerial on the back?' said Zondi, smiling, too, and completing a Zulu handshake.

'Something like that, Sergeant – I'd not noticed it myself. But how is it you knew my name. . .?'

'The writer woman, Naomi Stride.'

'Mrs Stride?'

'You must know her.'

'Of course,' said Mtunsi without hesitation, yet showing some puzzlement. 'She was here last Friday.'

'Doing what?'

'Sitting.'

Zondi cocked his head to one side, puzzled himself now.

'Come,' said Mtunsi, 'permit me to show you. . .'

And he loped off towards a round mud hut set a little apart from the rest of the school's rudimentary buildings. Chickens squawked from Zondi's path as he followed him, and a small child, hugging a broken slate, suddenly leaped up from a hollow in the long yellow grass and made its escape, too. The hut had an unusually large doorway, no door, and the far wall had an oversize window-space in it.

Mtunsi motioned Zondi to pass through the doorway ahead of him. To his left was a long trestle table, covered in crudely made pots; to his right were two forty-gallon oil-drums, filled almost to the brim with plastic bags of dark brown clay. There wasn't much else in the room. Just a wooden crate with an old cushion on it, and several feet away, where the daylight was strongest, stood a very tall and strangely narrow stool on top of which rested a large lump wrapped in wet sacking.

Mtunsi took the end of this sacking and started to unwind it. Gradually a dark brown head was revealed, so strikingly lifelike that, for a moment, it seemed about to utter a few choice Zulu words in protest over the rather undignified way it was being handled.

'Hau, but I know that face...' began Zondi, tantalised by an elusive quality that mocked his photographic memory.

'Of course, I must still put the curls of her hair on,' remarked Mtunsi, 'once I've finished the—'

Zondi laughed softly. He'd just realised his mistake, and that, in effect, this was the *negative* in dark clay of the portrait he'd seen of novelist Naomi Stride in the magazine.

'So cold, like this,' murmured Mtunsi, touching his long fingers to her cheek.

'Yes, cold...' said Zondi. 'My brother, I think I have some bad news to tell you.'

Kramer came back up the spiral staircase with a cup of black coffee in each hand. Real coffee, not the instant stuff, and it smelled pretty horrible.

'What a sweetie you are,' said Tess Muldoon, sitting up eagerly in her bed and exposing the top half of her bare self with not so much as a blink. 'Oops, you nearly got that on your trousers.'

He sat down where he had been massaging her foot, and handed over her coffee. She had firm, fairly flat breasts with nipples like pink icing.

'Oh, naturally I thought about it when I first heard,' she said, taking a sip. 'Went utterly to pieces. I had to get Gareth

86

over in the end, told him to bring a bottle of something large, and we held a sort of wake last night. Apparently, or so Gareth insists, I kept wanting to telephone the police and tell them I knew who'd done it. But as Naomi'd—'

'Not so fast, Tess, hey? What gave you the idea you—?'

'A feeling, mainly. Have I told you I spent the weekend before last at Woodhollow?'

'No, but go on.'

'Well, *part* of the weekend, anyway. Naomi had asked me to dinner on the Friday evening – an awful flop, poor darling – and she begged me to stay behind when the others were leaving. We thought those borrrrriiing Carswells would never go, but finally the two of us had the place to ourselves, and we sat beside the swimming-pool and gossiped for absolutely ages. In fact it got so late that I flopped out on the couch in the sun-lounge, while Naomi was fetching more ice from the kitchen, and that's where I woke up on Saturday morning, covered with a rug she'd found for me. She really was a—'

'Was it something you'd gossiped about that gave you this "feeeling"?'

'No, no, I'm still coming to that. I woke late, right? My God, the time! So I decided to sneak through Naomi's study and – well, that wasn't very clever, was it? The post had just arrived, and she was going through it at her desk. I caught her gazing at a letter on cheap blue paper, the kind with lines ruled, and it was a second or two before she realised I'd barged in. "What's the matter?" I asked – it just popped out. "Oh, just another crank letter," she said, as if it didn't bother her one bit. But I could see she was badly shaken by something.'

'You got to see this letter?' asked Kramer, setting his coffee aside.

Tess Muldoon shook her head. 'Naomi slipped it quickly into the middle drawer of her desk and locked it in there,' she said. 'But, as she did so, I glimpsed something.'

'Let me guess – another blue envelope already in the desk?'

'*Two* others, my love.'

'Same size?'

'They looked identical.'

'How were they addressed?'

'Oh, it was all too fast for that. As I said, a glimpse and she shut the drawer again.'

'But . . .' Kramer rose and went over to examine a Japanese fan on the wall. 'OK, then tell me what happened next. How long did she stay looking "badly shaken", as you call it?'

'About three seconds – which you'd know, if you'd ever met Naomi. She hated to dump her problems on anyone else, said that sort of thing was so unfair. Next moment, she was chattering away, coming out with the most marvellously bitchy remarks about Erica Jong you've ever heard, and—'

'This Erica woman,' interrupted Kramer, 'could she in fact be connected in some way with the blue letters? Was Naomi giving vent in a roundabout way?'

With a giggle, Tess Muldoon shook her head. 'Erica Jong's an American novelist,' she explained. 'And the stamps on those envelopes were definitely not foreign ones.'

'Uh-huh, that narrows things down a bit. Was the handwriting on them big or small?'

'No idea. I thought I'd said—'

'Go on with what else Naomi Stride chattered about,' prompted Kramer, turning from the Japanese fan and digging into his jacket pocket for his Lucky Strikes.

'You're not going to smoke, are you? Because I was rather hoping. . .'

'Oh ja?'

'That you'd give another bit of me a rub,' said Tess Muldoon, flinging the quilt completely aside and rolling, over stark naked. 'It's my gluteus maximus. I did something silly with it on Monday, and it's been an absolute bastard ever since.'

GROWING desperate in his attempts to come to some conclusion about the anonymous threat sent to Naomi Stride, Ramjut Pillay tried pacing his room. Unfortunately, it was not of a size conducive to undisturbed thought, as he had to keep stepping on and off the corner of his divan, and after ten minutes of this he was in a muck sweat and no closer to solving the paradox of the postmark.

'By golly,' he said to himself, flopping down for a rest, 'a case, we think, for Sir Sherlock Holmes!'

This reminded him that somewhere, buried in among all sorts of useful little items he had picked up, he had a magnifying glass and a pipe with a big bend in it. The pipe was easily found, still tasting of the terrible trading-store tobacco he had briefly experimented with, and after only about another five minutes or so the magnifying glass came to hand.

Seated on his divan, puffing at the empty pipe and studying the hairs on the back of his left index finger, his spirits soon improved. He wondered what else he might look at, and picked up the plastic bag containing the cheap blue envelope in which the dreaded *Exhibit Five* had been mailed.

'Euripides!' cried out Ramjut Pillay, whose brush with Ancient Civilisations (Parts I and 2) had taught him that the Greeks had a word for it. 'How could we be so blind, dammit?'

For there, too faint for his spectacles, but distinct enough under a magnifying glass, he could see four tiny numerals printed on the right-hand side of the postmark.

0730.

All was explained in a twinkling.

The only time letter-boxes were cleared on a Saturday was at 11 a.m. Anything posted at the weekend after that 'cut-off' was not processed until 0730 hours on Monday morning, making it too late for delivery until Tuesday. The trouble was, however, many members of the public had the idea that noon was the deadline – as indeed, not too long ago, it had been – and kept posting things well after 11 a.m. in the expectation that they would be included in Monday's local delivery. Obviously, the anonymous writer of terrible threats had made this same all-too-common mistake, and his apparently contradictory behaviour was a mystery no longer. He'd simply *wrongly supposed* that Naomi Stride would read his letter before he murdered her.

Then Ramjut Pillay, instead of continuing to feel elated by the brilliance of his deduction, suddenly shuddered. 'Oh, dear, dearie, dear,' he lamented, as he reeled under a full realisation of what all this signified.

Not only had he proved fairly conclusively that the letter *was* without doubt the work of Naomi Stride's killer, but he'd also confirmed the fact that he was in illegal possession of vital evidence that the police would willingly give his right arm for.

Cold Comfort was now making much more sense as a name than it had done on Gagonk Mbopa's way up to the farm. He was finding it very cold comfort indeed to be confronted by so many real men, and yet, because of the circumstances, to be frustrated by the namby-pamby way in which his interrogations had to be conducted.

'Well, what have you got for me so far?' asked Jones, coming out of the farmhouse and taking him to one side.

'So far nothing, sir,' replied Mbopa, very nearly allowing the hint of an apology to creep into his voice. 'These farm boys are not as other farm boys that I have ever come across.'

'Ja, they certainly seem a cheeky lot,' agreed Jones, coldly surveying the group of confident-looking, well-fed and decently clothed black men gathered outside the cowshed. 'Mind you, this is a bloody weird set-up and no mistake. The suspect here has just been trying to explain it to me.'

Everyone *tried* to explain things to Lieutenant Jacob Jones, reflected Mbopa, and some tried so hard they very nearly succeeded. Maybe this time it would be worth saying, 'Ermph, sir?'

'This place', confided Jones, dropping his voice, 'is what the farmer – I mean, suspect – calls a workers' "korropativ", which must be a Russian word by the sound of it, although he denies this with a big laugh. What it means, apparently, is that the boys you see here do not get the usual bag of maize meal, some meat and a few rand for wages. Ach no, what they get instead – and I'm not bulling you – is a share in the farm's profits.'

Mbopa gave a surprised and disbelieving hoot.

'Show more respect, you black monkey!' snapped Jones, glancing uneasily at the group outside the cowshed.

'Sir, do not misunderstand me. It is not sir's statement that causes amusement. I am laughing at what fools these boys are.'

'In what way?'

'Thinking they get a true share of the profits, sir. How do they know the farmer doesn't just pretend a much smaller number is the profit?'

'He claims he holds meetings with them where they talk about the farm's finances, and every month a different boy gets a chance to look after the accounts.'

'Hau, hau, hau...' said Mbopa, shooting his own glance at the men he had assembled. 'Is sir going to give Security Branch a tip-off about this place?'

Jones turned to go back into the farmhouse. 'Too right, man. You can never tell where something like this could lead to – if it hasn't done so already.'

A happy smile came to Mbopa's lips. He noticed that it had an immediate effect on the farmworkers which he didn't altogether understand. But he knew enough to keep the smile going, and saw the general nervousness increase as he returned to his interrogating.

At nine-forty Warrant Officer Jaap du Preez turned up at Colonel Muller's office, bringing with him the results of routine enquiries made in and around Jan Smuts Close.

'Nothing, Colonel,' he said.

'*Nothing?*'

Du Preez ran a hand over his ginger crewcut and grimaced, reminding Colonel Muller of some remark of Kramer's about an orang-utan. 'Absolutely not a thing, sir,' he confirmed, 'although, God knows, we've tried hard enough. Nobody in Jan Smuts Close has any memory of a vehicle travelling up or down the road at or about one o'clock on the night in question. Nobody around there has any idea of who may have felt sufficiently strongly about Naomi Stride to want to murder her. The neighbours aren't the sort of folk she associated with.'

'But Jan Smuts Close can't have much late-night traffic, man! Surely somebody must've—'

'Not a soul, Colonel. Not even Mr Parry Evans, who says he's an insomniac. Mind you, he also added he was in a bedroom at the back of his place, listening to music on some headphones.'

'Terrific,' sighed Colonel Muller, slumping back in his chair. 'What about the search of the house – y'know, Woodhollow? Has that been completed?'

'Nothing, sir. Or, at least, nothing that looks suspicious in itself.'

'You've been through all her correspondence?'

'The three detective constables you sent out are still working on it, sir,' said Du Preez, standing there and scratching his right knee without having to reach for it. 'There's not been anything "sinister", as you might say, for the last year anyway.'

'No sign of the murder weapon, either?'

'None, Colonel. The grounds are now being searched for the second time.'

Colonel Muller grunted and started to dig about in his new briar pipe. 'You've sent someone to fetch the deceased's servants back?'

'Hopeful Dumela, sir – he volunteered.'

'Dumela? Oh ja, a good man, his pa. How's Hopeful turning out?'

'For a coon, first class, sir.'

'And when do you expect—?'

'His instructions are to be back by nightfall, sir.'

'Then we have that to look forward to,' Colonel Muller remarked gloomily. 'Not that I can see what they're going to contribute. Don't ask me why, Jaap, but I've got a feeling we're really up against it this time.'

．　．　．

'Give us a ride!' begged the children of Tebeli Mission School, tugging at Zondi's coat tails. 'Just a short ride, Mr Big Town Detective, down to the mimosa-trees and back.'

'You've made an impression,' said Kwakona Mtunsi, the great sadness leaving his face momentarily.

'Huh, I have you to blame for that!' grumbled Zondi, winking his offside eye. 'Many thanks for inviting me to drink tea with you.'

The sadness came back. 'When you catch this man, tell me.'

'If it was a man,' agreed Zondi, with a nod.

Again, Mtunsi smiled, very slightly. 'There speaks the policeman I could never be,' he said. 'Surely no woman—'

'But you said earlier you couldn't imagine *anyone* taking such a life, my brother.'

'Verily, those were my words,' admitted Mtunsi.

'Then have you since had thoughts which suggest to you some male person who might've—?'

Mtunsi shook his head. 'I have no knowledge of Mrs Stride, apart from her coming here to Tebeli to encourage me in my sculpture and to bring the children small gifts. She never spoke of her own life, although once—' And he paused. 'Yes, that is correct: once she told me I must never have any dealings with her son. I had forgotten.'

'Did she say why?'

'No, and I thought it impolite to ask. I could see from her face muscles that there was much conflict within her.'

'When was this?'

'Long ago – maybe last year.'

'What has her face told you recently?'

Mtunsi used a thumbnail to scrape dried clay from a brass button on his dungarees while he did some thinking. 'About a month ago – she came here each Friday – Mrs Stride was so unhappy inside that I made some excuse not to begin work on her portrait. Hers was the tired head of an old woman, sunk down on its neck.'

'And since then?'

'The chin has been up, although once I saw a strange fear take the brightness from her eyes. That was two Fridays ago, when the nose was giving me—'

'What happened to cause this fear?'

'Nothing here at the school, I am sure of it. A memory, maybe; some idea that forced its way into her mind. Little Ntombifikile had come into the hut to show Mrs Stride a letter she had written in class, and just as Mrs Stride took it in her hand to praise the child, that's when the look came.'

Zondi took out his car-keys. 'Could it have been – something contained in the wording?' he asked. 'Can you remember what the letter was about?'

'I remember it was full of bad spelling and capital letters in the wrong places! Oh, a very short note to Ntombifikile's father, who lives in a factory hostel in some very far-away place. Ntombifikile asked him by which year he hoped to have saved enough money to come home again for ten days.'

'Ah,' said Zondi, remembering Naomi Stride's description of a Bantu men's hostel. 'Can you be sure what you saw in those eyes wasn't fear, but understanding and sorrow?'

'I am sure it was fear,' said Mtunsi, 'although you are right; I cannot swear to it.'

'Give us a ride, please give us a ride!' chorused the children.

'Perhaps soon your teacher will have his own vehicle in which to take you to the mimosa trees and back,' said Zondi, opening his car door. 'You heard what I told you about the thousand rand, Mtunsi?'

'I heard, my brother. But what we really need is a tank so we can catch rainwater for drinking.'

Tess Muldoon sprang out of bed and reached for her turquoise silk kimono. 'I hate to say this,' she said, 'but much as I'd like to lie here all day, having my back rubbed and gossiping about poor Naomi, *some of us* have work to do! My first private pupil is at twelve-thirty, and she's only got her lunch-hour.'

Kramer nodded, preoccupied by seeing her upright and moving so lightly. 'Christ, lady, you're beautiful.'

'I know,' she said.

He laughed. Ballet dancers were not as other women, or so his first encounter with one seemed to suggest. They had this

94

down-to-earth, very professional detachment from themselves which was, in a land of preening females, so refreshing.

'And, anyway, I doubt if there's anything more I can tell you.'

'True,' he agreed. 'Ja, I'd also best get going. I've still two other people to see by eleven.'

'C'est la vie, my love. Although. . .'

'What?'

'I will be free again later.'

'Oh ja?'

'After nine this evening?'

'But I thought we'd run out of things to talk about?'

'Oh, I do hope so,' she said, smiling wickedly.

Kramer smiled back. 'Well, maybe until later, hey, Theresa Mary Muldoon?' And he made his farewell bow very formal.

Lieutenant Jones's driving came close to being passable on tar roads that ran reasonably straight and level. Almost effortlessly, he and Gagonk Mbopa were heading back into Trekkersburg, intent on checking out at least one more suspect before reporting at eleven o'clock to Colonel Muller.

'I wonder if Kramer has come up with anything this morning,' mused Jones.

Mbopa shrugged.

'Hey, who asked you to butt in? Can't you tell when I'm talking to myself?'

The *Welcome to Trekkersburg* sign came and went.

Daydreaming, Mbopa spent a few pneumatic moments with an old friend, Zsazsa Lady Gatumi, and then found himself in Leonard Street, where the witchdoctors had their shops, buying a very potent aphrodisiac. Just two drops of which he'd sneak into Jones's coffee at eleven tomorrow, and when the hullabaloo had died down, and the ambulances had evacuated the CID typists' pool, then Colonel Muller would come across and say, 'Bantu Detective Sergeant Joseph Mbopa, expect news of promotion within the week. If you hadn't been on hand, to restrain a very sick man, God in Heaven, what else might have happened!' And Mbopa would give a small, self-effacing laugh.

'What was that?' snapped Jones.

Mbopa looked round at him, all innocence.

'You're giggling away to yourself again,' Jones complained. 'Honestly, there are times when I seriously wonder what I've done to deserve a Bantu like you! But, that aside for the moment, did you see any magnolias at the farm? I'm buggered if I did.'

'White flowers? Uh-uh, Lieutenant.'

'You don't think that little bastard Zondi isn't just trying to have us on by letting slip "the last magnolia" is a clue?'

'The Lieutenant may be right, but he plays a sly game, that one.'

'Ja, and "magnolia" definitely rings a bell somewhere . . .' conceded Jones, nibbling his lower lip [nsively. 'Mbopa, put your thinking-cap on, hey? We mustn't let ourselves be beaten by those two.'

On that, if on nothing else, the pair of them were agreed.

The suspect next on Kramer's list made his life easy.

'Dead,' said the hard-faced woman who opened the door of the boarding-house which had been given as the address of Richard Pomeroy, short-story writer and civil servant. The place smelled of boiled turnip.

'Oh ja? Dead for how long, lady?'

'Sunday.'

'He died in what manner?'

'Choked.'

'How? On what? Or did somebody—?'

'Vomit.'

'Ah, so he—'

'Alcoholic.'

'And where exactly did this death take place?'

'Here.'

'In his room?'

'Lavatory.'

'And I suppose the local police have all the rest of the details?'

'Yes.'

'Then I must love you and leave you,' sighed Kramer. 'But tell me first, do you always reply to every question you're asked with only one word?'

'No,' she said.

With time on his hands before having to be back at the CID building to exchange information with the Lieutenant, Zondi decided to drop in on Bantu Constable Hopeful Dumela at Woodhollow. It was just possible that the youngster had remembered other things he'd heard from the cook about goings-on in the big house.

But when Zondi reached the top of Jan Smuts Close he remembered with a click of his tongue that Dumela had been part of the two-to-ten shift the day before, making this a wasted journey. He stopped the car and began backing it into a driveway.

'Coooo-eee!' called out Miss Simson, waving at him from her veranda over the way. 'Aren't you the African detective who was here yesterday?'

So Zondi completed his turn, parked on her side of the close, and got out to see what she wanted. Miss Simson had pinked her cheeks and was wearing a dress that had frills at the neck and cuffs. Having a murder on her doorstep was obviously making her feel life was worth living.

'Any news?' she asked, as Zondi came to stand at the foot of the veranda steps.

'Sorry, madam?'

'You know, have you people caught anybody yet?'

'No, madam, not yet. This will be a very difficult case.'

'I know. Isn't it *shocking* to think anybody would – what was it they did to her exactly?'

'I'm sorry, madam, I am not party to such information.'

'Oh, no, I don't suppose you would be,' she said, looking cross. 'I really can't understand why there aren't more details in the papers.'

'That is sometimes best, madam.'

'But to think of her son – that poor, poor boy! What can he be going through?'

'It must be hard for him, madam.'

Miss Simson paused, as though awaiting a much more satisfactory reply, and then said: 'He isn't – er, *with* you people, is he? He's been allowed home?'

'Yes, allowed home, madam.'

'I *am* relieved! But what about poor Mr Pillay? I noticed we had another postman this morning. He came terribly early, as a matter of fact, so I only caught a glimpse of him and didn't have a chance to—'

'The postman, too, was allowed home, madam,' said Zondi, wishing he could end this silly woman's questioning of him.

'Oh dear, it's so sad in so many ways,' went on Miss Simson, peeling a grape. 'Just minutes before he came running down here, Mr Pillay had been so excited about that letter, poor thing. But as Daddy always said to me—'

'Pardon me interrupting, madam,' said Zondi, 'but what letter is this that you speak of?'

'The one with the new English stamp on, of course.'

'The new English stamp?'

'Mr Pillay collects stamps,' said Miss Simson. 'Hasn't he told you? I thought detectives always found out everything there was to know about people. Anyway, we'd both admired the stamp, right here where you're standing, and I'd encouraged him to ask the people if he could have it.' Then she gave a little shudder and added: 'Oh, I say! Do you think it could have been one for Mrs Stride? Perhaps you'll see the one I mean if you take a quick look through your exhibits or whatever you call them.'

But Zondi rather doubted that. He had a mental picture of the letters found delivered to Woodhollow the day before, and an envelope with a new (or even an old) English stamp hadn't been among them.

Then, at ten-thirty, Colonel Muller had another caller, Captain Tiens Marais, the new head of Fingerprints. He was a quiet man with a taste for loud clothing who always wore gloves. White cotton gloves which, he would explain, hid the horrible results of an allergy he had to certain chemicals used in his darkrooms. This morning he also had on an emerald-green shirt with yellow polka dots, red slacks, a wide green belt and yellow shoes. Some people called him 'Tickey' behind his back, in memory of a famous circus clown.

'I've got a few bits and pieces for you, Colonel,' he said, drawing up a chair to the desk. 'Nothing too special.'

'The Naomi Stride case? Excellent!'

'First, what my scene-of-crime officers have come up with. Two samples of vegetable matter.'

'Dagga?' said Colonel Muller, most surprised. 'At her age? Granted, she was an arty type, and they tend to go in for that kind of thing, but—'

'No, not dagga, marijuana, hashish or any of the other names you care to use. Something much stranger. . .'

'Then, what is it?' asked Colonel Muller, examining the small plastic packet he'd been handed.

'Rosemary.'

'Hey?'

'It's an English herb, used in cooking.'

'I see,' said Colonel Muller, who didn't like being made to play guessing games. 'I'm glad your highly trained officers had the sense to give her kitchen a good going over.'

'Ach, no, that's not where they found it. This came from the floor of the sun-room where she was murdered. What is more, when they did check her kitchen, she hadn't got any in stock.'

Colonel Muller sat up a little straighter. 'You mean it'd been dropped or something?'

'Weirder than that, Colonel. Looked like it'd been sprinkled.'

'Oh ja?'

'And now the other sample,' said Tiens Marais, handing over another small plastic bag. 'These are petals found inside her swimming-costume. They looked like they'd been sprinkled there, too.'

'Man, I know what this flower is – pansies?'

'Correct, Colonel. But what you probably don't know is that pansies don't grow in the garden at Woodhollow. We've checked.'

This seemed a good moment to pause and light a pipe.

Colonel Muller used three matches, tamped his tobacco thoughtfully, and sat back. 'Well, bugger me,' he said eventually.

Tiens Marais scratched his red nose – a mysterious affliction for a complete teetotaller – and shrugged. 'The best we can come up with', he said, 'is that the murder was, er, ritualistic in some fashion. The use of the sword, plus the rosemary and the pansies, having a hidden symbolic meaning.'

'I can see that,' Colonel Muller concurred. 'Rosemary's a girl's name, right? And pansies are – dammit, they're pansies! Everyone knows the art world is "cockablock" with homosexuals.'

'"Chockablock",' Tiens Marais corrected quietly, his English being slightly better.

'But where do we go from there, Tiens?'

'It's a mystery to me, Colonel. More helpful, perhaps, is what my lab has been able to tell us about the fragment of sword that was discovered. I've had the resident whizzkid, Piet Baksteen, take a look at it.'

'And?'

'He says it's not from a real sword – the tempering is wrong. A real sword wouldn't have broken off in the same way. He suggests it's home-made, probably a sword produced and sold for decorative purposes, something like that.'

'Ah! That narrows things down a bit!'

'The lab has already checked with the Firearms Squad, in case they've had a report of a similar sword stolen, but nothing doing. Piet suggests we now divulge publicly what type of weapon was used, and see if anyone comes forward, saying they've had one stolen off them.'

'H'm,' said Colonel Muller. 'I'm not too happy about that. We were withholding the type of weapon to cut down on the crank letters, keep the headlines from being too lurid, and because that way – well, it was a bit of a trump card up our sleeve.'

Tiens Marais waggled his eyebrows, which were unnaturally bushy and stuck out a mile. 'You don't think you should now reconsider that decision, sir?'

There was a long silence. 'Only perhaps,' said Colonel Muller.

'The time being wasted!' Kramer muttered to himself, as he reached the last address on his list of suspects. 'Fine! Why should I worry?'

Number 18 Ladysmith Terrace was one of the really old bungalows in a twisting road by the Town Stream. Red brick, corrugated iron roof, fancy woodwork in the twin gables, and behind it red-brick stables with a bright-yellow door. This door was ajar, and through it drifted a pretty blue smoke, smelling of hot lead. Kramer used his car-keys to rap twice, loudly.

'Sweet Jesus! Who's that?'

'Sorry if I gave you a fright, hey? Lieutenant Kramer, Murder and Robbery. You're Mr Gareth Telford?'

'Come in, come in, for Christ's sake! I can't be expected to drop everything just because. . .'

So Kramer stepped through the doorway, expecting a glamour-boy comforter of ballerinas, and saw a squat figure bent over a stained-glass window that lay in pieces on a huge, paper-covered table.

'Holy Mary, Mother of God,' said Telford, using both hands to steady the soldering-iron he was using, 'don't ever do that again – promise me. I've put six months into this little lot, and you nearly made me balls the bloody thing.'

'Sorry,' said Kramer, who'd never spoken to a white hunchback before.

'I suppose this is about Stride?' Telford went on, still without looking up from his task of joining together the lead strips between segments of coloured glass superimposed on a pencilled pattern. 'You'll be going round all the bloody beneficiaries.'

'Oh ja?'

'Stands to reason. Almighty God, look what I've done now! Could you stand further out of my light? No, I didn't kill her – haven't had the time.'

'You knew her well?'

101

'Patronising bitch.'

'You sound like a man with a chip on his shoulder.'

'It's a hump, or hadn't you noticed?'

'I'd noticed,' said Kramer, stubbing out his Lucky Strike. 'Tell me, how long can you last in the desert on just one drink of water?'

Telford barked a laugh and glanced in his direction, showing for an instant a broad, flat face as expressionless as a welder's mask. His eyes were a bright iridescent blue, like the reflections of the flame of an acetylene torch adjusted to sear through thick metal. 'All right,' he said, 'what is it you want?'

'How do you know there was money bequeathed to you?'

'She told Tess Muldoon, and Tess told me last night.'

'When you had the bottle of wine together?'

'Yes, I was bitching about what the bloody thing had cost me, and Tess said I could deduct it from my thousand,' replied Telford, showing no surprise at what Kramer already knew, which made a nice change in an interview. 'Jesus wept! Why leave me anything? I never done anything except insult the woman!'

Kramer pondered the heated way the man spoke, and toyed with a fragment of rose-tinted glass, holding it in front of his eye so that Telford turned a much more attractive colour. 'You were once in love with her?' he asked.

Again the man laughed and glanced across, but this time he wasn't showing any amusement. 'It's as obvious as that, is it?' he said. 'I suppose I was, for all of two months.'

'And then?'

'I couldn't take it any more, that indiscriminate *pity* she lavished on everything. I began to think she was bogus, on a glorified guilt trip.'

'Sorry? You've lost me. . .'

'I took her one weekend', said Telford, putting his soldering-iron aside, 'on what was supposed to have been a camping trip into the bush. She empathised all bloody day with the wretched rustics we came across and then, when it was time to pitch our tent, she absolutely refused to sleep on the ground. I had to drive inland about fifty kilometres to find a hotel for her.'

'And so?'

'God Almighty! Isn't it obvious enough? No wonder she felt so sorry for blacks! Don't they sleep on the floors of their huts?'

'Some, but sleeping on the floor can be a cultural thing,' objected Kramer.

'My point exactly,' cut in Telford. 'Stupid cow wasn't really interested – only in how *she* would feel under the same conditions.'

Kramer nodded. 'So when did you last see Mrs Stride?' he asked.

'When we got back from that trip a day early – oh, about four weeks ago.'

'But while you were still in cahoots, so to speak, with the deceased, did she ever mention having trouble with hate mail?'

'Poison-pen stuff, you mean?'

'Ja, anything along those lines.'

'No, can't help you there,' said Telford, stepping back to review his work. 'Although, from what I gathered, her son had some bother with something like that not long ago. I don't know the details, just that it caused quite an upset.'

'In what way?'

Telford shrugged, his gaze still fixed on the stained glass before him. 'These things are always such bastards to judge until you can get a proper light behind them.'

'Ach, I don't know,' demurred Kramer. 'Holy Mary looks OK to me, and the same goes for God Almighty and Sweet Jesus.'

8

FEET UP, hat tipped back, Zondi had made himself comfortable in his corner of the office and was waiting for the electric kettle to come to the boil, when he'd brew himself a pot of tea. It was just after eleven.

There came the sound of heavy breathing outside on the landing overlooking the CID courtyard. One day, unless he did something about his weight, those stairs were going to be the death of Gagonk Mbopa – or possibly Zsazsa Lady Gatumi's strenuous demands would see him off in much the same way. A happier death, which would enrage a lot of people.

'Zondi,' said Mbopa, appearing in the doorway and blocking almost all the direct sunlight entering the room, 'you have to pay half – it is only right.'

'Half of what?'

'The new rose-bush I must buy the Colonel. Hau, I have just made enquiries about the price of such things, and they are very, very expensive.'

'Huh! It wasn't me who pulled the rose off the—'

'But it was still your fault!' growled Mbopa. 'If you hadn't—'

'Tea?' asked Zondi, swinging his feet down off the table that served as his desk. 'Come in and sit down, Joseph. Let us discuss this matter in the manner of reasonable men.'

Mbopa hesitated, eyeing him sharply as though suspecting a trap in this somewhere. Then he grunted and moved into the room.

'Have my seat,' invited Zondi.

Suspicion mounting, Mbopa shook his head and stood instead beside the filing cabinet, where he produced a small horn. He uncorked it, took two great pinches of black snuff between thumb and forefinger, and pushed them a considerable distance up each nostril.

'You remind me of my father,' remarked Zondi, switching off the kettle and reaching for the teapot. 'He was always taking snuff. Kept his snuff-horn in his earlobe, with a big wooden plug in his other lobe to balance it.'

'Is that so?' said Mbopa, plainly even more disconcerted by this pleasantry.

'What a morning,' sighed Zondi. 'Did you have the same trouble that we had? You go round all these addresses, hoping the suspects will be at home, and how many answer the door?'

Mbopa gave a snort. 'So that's what this is all about?' he said. 'You're trying to trick me into telling you how well our investigations have been going! Like you falsely accused me of doing this very same—'

'That's rubbish,' said Zondi, a shade too quickly.

'Interesting...' murmured Mbopa, enjoying this. 'I know I'm right, and so what does that tell me? It tells me that things have not been going so good for you and Spokes.'

'More rubbish!' scoffed Zondi. 'And will you look? There are still tea-leaves in the pot from last time – I must first go and wash them out.'

Mbopa didn't spare the teapot a glance; he seemed too busy suppressing some silent laughter. 'Yes, you do that,' he said, taking out a crackly handkerchief to wipe the tears away.

So Zondi went downstairs, round the back of the CID building to the Bantu Males' lavatory, and marked time there with the perfectly clean teapot under one arm. A good five minutes went by before his return to the office, where he found Mbopa on his way out.

'But what about the tea? What about this business of me paying half of—?'

'Not now,' said Mbopa airily, 'there is no great urgency. It's more important that I go and make a check with Records about a suspect we interviewed this morning – I had nearly forgotten all about it.'

'Huh! You just don't think you could win the argument, that's all!'

'Later,' said Mbopa, hurrying off.

Zondi watched him go, then turned and entered the office with a broad smile. A smile which grew into a grin when he looked for a book he'd hidden in rather an obvious place. To his immense satisfaction, the book had vanished.

'Ja, ja, ja,' said Colonel Muller, cutting short Jones's second reading from his immaculately kept notebook, 'it may be the gospel truth, but spare me all the verbatims. The farmer could tell you nothing, and now what does the interview with this composer suspect boil down to? He wasn't in town on Monday night?'

'That's true,' admitted Jones. 'Like I said, he was returning from Johannesburg by train, only—'

'Is that a fact which can be verified?'

'I suppose so, Colonel. Well, he was in charge of forty kids from the school he teaches at, the senior orchestra. My interest was more in his—'

'Forty alibi witnesses are enough for any man,' declared Colonel Muller very firmly.

'But Colonel—'

'Tromp,' said Colonel Muller, turning to the corner of his desk where Kramer sat, 'let's hear what you have been up to this morning. I'm relying on you to keep to the bare facts as usual, hey?'

Kramer tightened the knot in his tie. 'First off,' he said, 'I went to see this beautiful little popsie. In ten seconds, I'm up in her bedroom, two minutes later I'm massaging her foot, next she's showing me her boobs and asking me to fondle her bum. So I—'

'God in Heaven,' sighed Colonel Muller, slumping back, 'and you call yourself a true-life detective? What *is* this amazing bullshit?'

'The bare facts, Colonel.'

'Kramer! A joke's a joke, all right?'

'Sorry, Colonel. Would you like to hear about a possible lead?'

Colonel Muller nodded. 'Please,' he said wearily. 'I don't think either of you buggers realise the pressure I'm under.'

Life is never simple, thought Ramjut Pillay, as he made for Trekkersburg on a bicycle borrowed from his second cousin's brother-in-law's youngest son. If it were, then all he'd have to do was to go to the police, explain to them that an honest mistake had been made, and hand over the missing mail, including the anonymous threatening letter.

'Ja, we quite understand, Mr Pillay,' they would say. 'Mind you, you did have us running around in the dark for a bit, hey?'

'I only noticed I had them stuffed in my Post Office trouser pocket this very Wednesday morning,' he would reply most earnestly, 'on my way to the dry cleaner's. Better late than never, I suppose!'

'Of course, of course, Mr Pillay! And it isn't we're not grateful. You'll see, once we have made our arrest, using this invaluable clue, we may even come up with a small reward for you. . .'

But he had already gone far beyond the point of being able to do anything like that – far, far beyond. On top of all the Post Office offences he'd committed, he could be charged with tampering with evidence, obstructing the police in the performance of their duty and goodness knows what else. One wrong move now and Ramjut Pillay was done for.

'Oh, woe is we,' he sighed, pedalling along.

Then he took another pull at himself with a stern reminder that he'd not long agreed he could be jumping to too many conclusions. Half of this could be simply his imagination. The anonymous threatening letter had implied that its fiendish writer intended to use a sword on the unfortunate Naomi Stride, a crazy idea if he had ever heard of one. Just say, for example, that she had been shot – what would happen to his theory then? Crashety-crash, it would go! Surely proving that the letter and the murder were not connected, and he'd be able to destroy the evidence of his crime with a clear conscience, knowing it could play no part in bringing a heartless murderer to justice.

And so all he had to do was to establish that Naomi Stride had indeed been killed by a bullet – or anything else, for that matter, so long as it wasn't a sword – and this would put his mind at rest, lifting the terrible burden of guilt from his shoulders.

'Tally ho!' whooped Ramjut Pillay, swooping down the last slope into the city.

Then he wished the borrowed bicycle had better brakes, for it had just occurred to him that he really needed to stop a minute and do some more thinking. Exactly how was he going to discover the manner in which the lady writer had died? He could hardly walk into the police station and demand such information.

'You look pleased with yourself,' remarked Kramer, on his return at one-thirty from the case conference with Colonel Muller. 'Any of that tea left?'

Zondi poured him a cup. 'How did it go, boss?' he asked.

'Jones and Gagonk hadn't come up with a bloody thing, apart from eliminations.'

'That includes the son, Theo Kennedy?'

'No, he's still to be interviewed again, but the priority right now is seeing what can be found out about those blue envelopes.'

'So the Colonel agreed they could give us a lead?'

'Christ, he was delighted to – we've nothing else, hey? Except for all this loony talk about some bloody stuff called "rosemary", pansy flowers and the sword being a fake.'

'Boss?'

So Kramer repeated to him what the Fingerprints captain had told the Colonel, and Zondi nodded and said; 'Very loony, boss. But the sword is surely a good lead, too – why not use it now? And why not go straight to the son? Didn't the stained-glass boss say that Theo Kennedy had been personally involved in some "upset" of a similar nature?'

Kramer drained his cup. 'The Colonel's still trying to play this all very cool. He thinks it'd be smarter to find out more about the alleged letters first, if we can. Jones has sold him a theory that Kennedy could have been sending them to his mother himself, part of a master plan to cover his tracks as the murderer.'

'H'm,' said Zondi.

'I've had an idea,' announced Kramer. 'You know what you were telling me about how Kwakona Mtunsi saw "fear" in Naomi Stride's eyes when she was given that letter to read by the kid at the mission school? He didn't say what colour paper it was on, did he?'

'No, boss.'

'Apart from its contents, did he give any other description

108

of the thing?'

Zondi thought a moment, and then repeated from memory, mimicking Kwakona Mtunsi's slow, gentle voice: 'I remember it was full of bad spelling and capital letters in the wrong places! Oh, a very short note to Ntombifikile's—'

'Hold it,' said Kramer, opening the bottom right-hand drawer of his desk and taking from it a tattered folder.

'But those are our own poison-pens,' said Zondi, surprised.

'Uh-huh, and when you glance at the stuff what strikes you immediately? Especially where attempts have been made to disguise its origin? Look. . .'

With a snap of his fingers, Zondi replied: 'The bad spelling and capitals in wrong places! Now I get the point, Lieutenant – Ntombifikile's note could have reminded Mrs Stride of the letters she had been receiving, and Mtunsi was probably right when he thought she looked afraid.'

Kramer nodded. 'Something like that, old son. Guesswork, admittedly, but it does help to back up the idea that the blue envelopes are mixed up in all this.'

'Then, what is our next stop, boss?'

'Jaap du Preez's told the Colonel that nothing resembling hate mail has been found at Woodhollow, but I'm not satisfied the place has been searched as well as it could be.'

'So we go out there, take another look?' said Zondi, picking up his jacket.

'The Colonel's exact orders,' confirmed Kramer, hooking his own jacket over one shoulder. 'Meanwhile, Jones and Gagonk have been sent to find that Indian postman for a further statement – you never know, if there's been a series of blue letters to the house, he could have noticed something useful about them.'

'That one!' chuckled Zondi, with a shake of his head. 'A hen is an egg's way of making another egg. . .'

'Come again?' asked Kramer.

Jones poked his head into the Bantu detective sergeants' office and snapped: 'Hey, you! Gagonk Mbopa! Get your fat arse out of that chair and come along – hurry! We've got important work to do, man. You're not paid to sit around reading all day!' Then he disappeared again.

'When the jackal is on heat', said Mbopa, rising unhurriedly and pocketing a paperback, 'even the elephant must watch his back. . .'

Which made his grinning colleagues laugh out loud, but he left uncertain of why they had also winked at one another.

'Come on, come on!' nagged Jones, grinding his gears in the vehicle-yard. 'We've got to go round to the main post office.'

Mbopa grunted and climbed into the passenger-seat, where he took out the paperback again and flipped it open at his place.

'Gagonk . . .' said Jones, threateningly, as the car jerked abruptly out on to the street, lurched, and then straightened up for the short journey down to the first traffic lights.

'Lieutenant?'

'Put that bloody book away! How many times must I repeat myself?'

Mbopa kept it in his hands. 'I thought the Lieutenant would be interested to see the name of this book,' he said smugly.

'Oh, you did, did you? Now, let me make one thing quite clear: my only interest, as of this minute, is finding this—'

'A big clue,' cut in Mbopa.

'What's that you say?' asked Jones, looking round as he stopped at the red light.

Holding the paperback up so that its title was impossible to miss, Mbopa said slowly and carefully, trying not to explain too much at once: 'Does the Lieutenant remember the remark made by Zondi, who said "the last magnolia" was a big clue?'

'You mean it's that thing?'

'And can the Lieutenant see who wrote it?'

'Naomi – hey, wait one minute! Where do you get that?'

'I borrowed it, sir.'

'From Zondi and, er . . . They've *lent* it to you? But why would they—?'

'No, but it is true I borrowed it from them, sir, because we can give it back later when we're finished.'

110

Something very close to a smile came to Jones's thin, bloodless lips. 'So they don't know we've got it? But how did you, er, you know. . .?'

'I found it in a very clever hiding-place in their office, sir, and I thought maybe the Lieutenant would like to study it for himself.'

'What's everybody hooting at?'

'The light has turned green, sir.'

'This is a police vehicle – they can bloody wait!'

'Have I done wrong, Lieutenant, in—?'

'No, Gagonk,' said Jones, and he actually laughed then, a sound so strange and unfamiliar that is affected the hair at the back of Mbopa's neck. 'For once, you idle bastard, I'd say you'd done an excellent day's work! Carry on reading. . .'

'Lieutenant?'

'The bloody book, man! Nice and loud, so I can take it in while I'm driving.'

'Where's Hopeful Dumela?' murmured Zondi, as Kramer braked to a halt outside Woodhollow and two unfamiliar black constables came out on to the veranda.

'Ach, I meant to tell you – sorry, Mickey,' said Kramer. 'He volunteered to go and fetch the three servants, and the Colonel says he'll be back by nightfall. Now, what we're expected to do here is—'

Zondi held up a hand. 'Quiet a second, boss! I think I just heard Control calling for you on the radio.'

'Shit, what now?' growled Kramer. 'I suppose Gagonk and Jones have come across some long word they can't understand.'

'Indubitably!'

It helped to share a laugh at a moment when intuition had hollowed the stomach a little. Kramer reached for his radio mike and gave Control his position. There was a slight pause, and then Colonel Muller himself came on the air.

'Lieutenant Kramer, are you receiving me? Over.'

'Loud and clear, Colonel.'

'Drop everything, Tromp, and leave Zondi to deal with Woodhollow. Highest priority. I want you at 146 – I repeat,

111

146 – Acacia Drive. Have you got that?'

'Ja, Colonel – the place is off Brandsma Road?'

'Correct. How soon can I expect you?'

'Say, ten minutes?'

'Sooner, man!'

'Can I ask what the problem is, sir?'

'Just hurry,' said Colonel Muller. 'Over and out.'

Tidying his work locker for the ninth time, Ramjut Pillay reflected on what a boon it was to have been born with a rather remarkable mind. In a flash of pure inspiration, which had come to him just as he'd hurtled down into Trekkersburg through a set of red traffic lights, a brilliant idea had presented itself, making the loud hooting all around him sound like a fanfare of trumpets.

Very simply, he'd remembered that one of his colleagues at the Post Office, Harry Patel, had often boasted of having a brother in the CID – a detective sergeant, no less, who assisted in all the most difficult cases. Just the fellow, in other words, to have the facts of the Naomi Stride case at his fingertips! And, as Harry Patel made a practice of divulging the details of his brother's latest cases at every opportunity, all Ramjut Pillay had to do was to wait in the changing-room at the Post Office for a chance to engage him in idle chatter.

Quite a wait it was turning out to be, but no matter; Harry Patel, who had one of the more distant rounds to do, frequently arrived back after most of his colleagues had already hung up their postbags and gone home. On top of which, it would certainly be more advantageous to encounter him on his own, for that way the conversation could be more easily steered in the desired direction.

'There you are, Ramjut old fellow!' remarked a cheery voice behind him. 'What a coincidence! Only five minutes ago I was being asked the exact whereabouts of our naughty suspended postman.'

Ramjut Pillay turned round. Who should it be but Peerswammy Lal, Asiatic Postman 3rd Class, beaming from ear to ear. The same Peerswammy Lal, let it be remembered, who had last year placed in Ramjut Pillay's postbag a large toad which had done urines over nine items of personal mail and a library postcard.

'There is no rule to say I cannot come in and locker my tidy,' snapped Ramjut Pillay, caught so off guard his speech became garbled.

'My God, you are a card!' applauded Peerswammy Lal, with the heartiest of laughs. 'Always so full of quips and merriment! What, may I ask, is the artful saying you have chosen for today's meditations?'

'Buggering off!' hissed Ramjut Pillay.

Which delighted Lal so much that he clapped him on the back, making his glasses shoot down his nose. For one terrible moment, it was touch and go whether the Mahatma's pacifist teachings were going to be enough to prevent a bloodbath.

'Damn fool! Can't you—?'

'Now, wait one minute, old chum!' warned Lal, a martial-arts enthusiast, moving his weight on to one foot. 'My intentions are entirely pure, I have no wish to engage you in fisticuffs! But, if you are persisting in this fashion, I'll kick you in the ghoolies so damnably fast your navel will hear only the echo.'

Deeply sobered by this thought, Ramjut Pillay let his shoulders drop and said: 'Was it Mistering Jarman who was making enquiries?'

'No, the police.'

'*What?*' gasped Ramjut Pillay.

'As I say, not five minutes ago, I was walking by the boss's office, after overtime working, and I saw two CID fellows talking to him. Or, to be entirely correct in my particulars, *one* CID fellow was talking; the other detective was a black chappie, just listening.'

'S-s-sergeant Zondi?'

Lal shrugged. 'No name was mentioned. All I am hearing is something about the CID thought you would be willing to help them, reference some blue envelopes, and the boss called out and said: "Oi, Peerswammy, you don't know where Ramjut is today, do you?" And I said to him: "I caught one quick glimpse of his flying figure this morning, Mr Jarman, sir, equipped with raincoat and pedal cycle, coming down the topmost end of Club Street. Perhaps he—" '

'No, no, no!' wailed Ramjut Pillay. 'It is impossible you could have done such a thing to me! I am lost! I am finished! Never will I see my old mother again!'

'Ramjut?' said Lal, his smile fading. 'Ramjut, what is the matter? Your *mother*? Why do you despair so greatly you say such mad things?'

'The police will arrest me! Brand me a thief! Cast me in deepest dungeons!'

'My dear chum, you have a misunderstanding. All they seek is some information from you, not to—'

'It is *you* who has the misunderstanding!' cried out Ramjut Pillay. 'O, traitorous dog and betrayer of bosomy brothers!'

And with that he began running.

Zondi was glad to be back in Naomi Stride's study. There were quite a few oddments lying about that he hadn't had time to admire properly before, and one of them was a tortoise made of fired clay, bearing the unmistakable stamp of Kwakona Mtunsi.

Yet it was hard to take full advantage of the moment, what with half his mind still caught up in conjecture concerning Colonel Muller's urgent and mysterious radio call.

There were no blue envelopes in the middle drawer of the desk. Zondi pulled the drawer right out and turned it over. People sometimes tried to hide documents by taping them to the underside, but that hadn't been attempted in this case. He sat back in the swivel chair and allowed his gaze to roam about the room, trusting it to seize upon any other likely hiding-places.

Colonel Muller had sounded badly shaken, too badly shaken for an ordinary run-of-the-mill murder or robbery. Whatever it was he wanted the Lieutenant to help him with would therefore have to be something very *extra*ordinary, something totally outlandish, impossible to imagine.

All the letters and postcards, which Naomi Stride had poked between the books on her study shelves, had been removed, presumably by Warrant Officer Jaap du Preez and his team. But had they troubled to look between the pages of those books themselves? Yes, the big dictionary had changed position, and Zondi had to hunt for the title he remembered having seen previously on either side of it. Obviously the shelves had been emptied and refilled in haphazard order while just such a search could be carried out.

On the other hand, Colonel Muller might have sounded so shaken simply because a crime had been committed that affected him personally. Even a burglary could come as a severe shock to a police officer – all the more so because he had always thought of burglaries as happening just to 'them', to the public, of which he never saw himself a part.

Looking for hiding-places in Naomi Stride's study was ridiculous, thought Zondi. Everything he had learned about the woman indicated that she was fiercely open in all she did and believed. Hiding things would not have been in her nature. The filing cabinet had not been locked, and neither had the middle drawer of the desk, come to that.

But the idea of Colonel Muller being so badly shaken because of some personal involvement was difficult to sustain. So far as he knew, Colonel Muller lived nowhere near Acacia Drive, and neither did he have any relatives residing locally.

There was, Zondi decided, only one conclusion to be drawn: either Naomi Stride had removed the blue envelopes from the drawer herself, presumably to have them destroyed, or else the murderer had taken them at the time of the killing.

But just why this business at 146 Acacia Drive was being given the 'highest priority', over and above the slaying of a world-famous woman novelist, and just why Colonel Muller should have sounded so disturbed, still eluded him.

Or, as the Lieutenant was wont to say, the mind bloody boggled.

The house at 146 Acacia Drive was a bungalow in a street lined by jacaranda trees. Kramer parked his car between Colonel Muller's official vehicle and a patrol van, lit a Lucky, and took a look at the place.

It was neat, it was modest, it seemed to be the sort of dwelling that either newlyweds or a retired couple would choose because, to judge by the depth of the building, it had at most only two bedrooms, one of which would be rather small. The roof was low-pitched corrugated asbestos sheeting, the outer walls were plastered and painted pale yellow, the woodwork trimmings had been done in dark green. There was a garage joined on to the right-hand side of the house, and a short driveway made of crazy paving. It seemed very unlikely that this was the home of anyone of the slightest importance.

Kramer got out and started up the driveway, on which was parked a gleaming red Datsun, expertly fitted out with innumerable extras. The garage door was wide open, showing that it was used also as a workshop, for there were tidy rows of both car and woodwork tools along the back wall, above a solid workbench. On the floor lay several piles of the American magazine *Popular Mechanics*, and beside them stood a large cardboard box. Someone must have been sorting through them when presumably called away.

A uniformed constable of barely seventeen, so pale in the face his pimples looked like cherries on an angel cake, came out of the house. 'Excuse me, but are you Lieutenant Kr-Kramer, please?' he asked, coming to attention and saluting.

'Just seen your first stiff, hey?'

'H-h-hell, no, sir, but this lady's the first white one.'

'Ja, they're often the worst, so I'm told. Well, where is she? Haven't you been sent out to show me the way?'

The youngster nodded and shambled into the house.

'Do you know what all the fuss is about?' Kramer asked him in the spick-and-span hallway, where even the telephone directory had its own ornamental shelf.

'Honest, I can't understand it, sir,' the youngster admitted in a whisper. 'We got a call to come here, because somebody was dead, and it all seemed normal enough to me. But my sergeant, he takes one look, has a word with the son, tells me to keep the husband talking, and he shoots out to the van to get Colonel Muller on the radio.'

116

'Just what exactly—?'

'It's in here, sir,' said the youngster, pausing outside a door and knocking softly on it. 'Colonel, sir? Lieutenant Kramer's arrived.'

'Enter!'

Kramer found himself in a very pleasant bathroom, lined with pale-yellow tiles and smelling of apple. There was a bottle of shampoo with an apple on its label standing on the glass shelf below the washbasin mirror. To the right of it, fixed to the wall, was a chrome-plated device holding three toothbrushes, two of which were for dental plates.

Then Kramer glanced at Colonel Muller and down at his feet.

A dead woman lay there, sprawled on her back, naked, covered over in an orange dressing-gown. A big woman, verging on obese, with legs like bolsters and long grey hair that spread out, tangled, on the cork flooring. She had been wet. Small puddles surrounded her, and water had soaked into the dressing-gown.

The shower dripped.

'My wife...' said the man sitting on the edge of the bath.

He spoke in Afrikaans. He was about seventy, stocky, dressed in khaki shorts, a sports shirt and sandals. His face rang a bell somewhere. It was the puffy bags beneath the eyes, the jut of those thin ears, the feeling that such a jaw had been cast in reinforced concrete. Also, the mildness of the mouth, which made such an odd contrast.

'She slipped in the shower,' said the man, trembling.

Kramer could see wet patches on the man's shirt, and some blood on his collar. He must have rushed in, grabbed his wife, and dragged her out of the shower cubicle. That made sense, only. . .

To be sure here, at 146 Acacia Drive, lay a dead body. But so what? As dead bodies went, this particular body was nothing special at all; everyone knew that mishaps in the home accounted for hundreds of lives every year and, so far as he could see, this body was simply part of those dreary statistics. In fact, it was so ordinary and pathetically humdrum that, when compared with the sort of corpse

117

which usually came his way, the bloody thing was an affront to his intelligence.

He looked questioningly across to Colonel Muller, standing there pinch-lipped and pale.

'She just went into the shower and slipped,' repeated the man. 'The soap must have got under her foot. *It was an accident!*'

Colonel Muller reached out a hand and placed it on his shoulder. 'Now, keep calm, Willem, keep calm,' he said. 'Try not to get too upset, hey? Why not take my advice and come through to the lounge to wait for Doc Strydom?'

Willem? Kramer looked again at the man.

Suddenly the penny dropped. Why, of course, Willem Martinus Zuidmeyer, pensioned off these last ten years or more! And Kramer, caught completely unawares, very nearly gave a laugh.

Before realising with a jolt the extraordinary implications of the situation.

9

'I'VE never yet come across a coolie you could trust,' grumbled Lieutenant Jones, as he and Gagonk Mbopa continued their search of central Trekkersburg for Ramjut Pillay, driving up one street and down the other. 'Ach, just take this description we've been given by that other churra postman for a start! Who, except a raving lunatic, would be going around in a plastic raincoat on a sunny day like this?'

'Ermph,' said Mbopa, turning another page of *The Last Magnolia* and devouring it silently.

'Has that story started to improve yet? Or is that stupid woman still moaning about not having any proper job to do, except having to look pretty for her husband and chase the servants?'

'Ermph.'

'Then carry on keeping it to yourself until you get to an action part. I only like books with plenty of action parts. I wonder what all this business is on the radio, all this fuss about 146 Acacia Drive.'

'Ermph.'

'Christ, fatso, I'm talking to you, hey?'

Mbopa looked up from a fascinating description of two whites engaged in a very vigorous act of adultery. 'Acacia Drive? Is that where this postman lives, sir?'

'Ach, you're impossible!'

'But', said Mbopa, pausing briefly to find a way of redirecting their efforts along more promising channels, 'I thought the Lieutenant must have decided to visit the home of this Pillay. Perhaps he has returned there for his midday meal – perhaps his family can inform the Lieutenant of his present whereabouts.'

'Obviously,' said Jones, altering course. 'Where do you think I'm heading, thick head? But that wasn't what I asked you about.'

'It wasn't, sir?'

'Gagonk, just you get on with that boring bloody book and leave the thinking to me, OK?'

Zondi went through to the kitchen at Woodhollow and then decided he'd had enough tea for the morning. It was simply that, being convinced that the blue envelopes were no longer on the premises, he was now feeling at a loss to know what to do.

He looked at the clock. The Lieutenant had been gone almost half an hour. Was there a possibility that this Acacia Drive call had in fact something to do with the Naomi Stride case? The thought hadn't crossed his mind earlier, yet it made sense of a lot of things. Just say, for example, another writer lived at that address, and had been found with a fatal stab wound and the mysterious line *"II, ii!"* added to the page in his typewriter. A coincidence like that would certainly have put Colonel Muller into an unhappy state of excitement.

Then, again, wasn't that taking the idea of coincidence too far? Did Trekkersburg, which was hardly a major cultural centre, really stretch to more than one proper author? Questions, questions, but no real means of finding out the answers, not while he was stuck at Woodhollow and without a car.

'But wait a minute . . .' Zondi said to himself.

He hastened back to Naomi Stride's study and went straight to a large volume entitled *The Writers' Directory*. He took it down and found an entry for her without any difficulty. So he started flicking through it, reading further entries at random, but failed to come up with any other South African writers. If only he knew the name of the person living at 146 Acacia Drive, he'd be able to test his latest theory very much more quickly.

'Ah!' said Zondi.

Having dialled the Trekkersburg Public Library, and asked for the reference section in his most guttural Afrikaans accent, he then identified himself as a police officer and asked the librarian to check the electoral role.

'Ja, lady, that's 146 Acacia Drive,' he confirmed. 'Many thanks, hey?'

She was back on the line in under two minutes, sounding very self-important and delighted to have her uneventful life enlivened by assisting the police with their enquiries. 'The name of the householder is given as Willem Martinus Zuidmeyer,' she said. 'Are you sure that's all you want to know, sir?'

'Perfect,' said Zondi. 'My, you were quick.'

'Well, being alphabetical, Acacia Drive's very near the start of the roll.'

'Even so, my thanks again, hey?'

'All part of the service! Ring me whenever you like – or pop in, if you're passing.'

'Careful, I might do that,' said Zondi. 'Bye, now!'

Then he sat back in the swivel chair at the desk and spun round three times, saying to himself: 'Willem Martinus Zuidmeyer? *Major* Willem Martinus Zuidmeyer? Hau, it has got to be! But how is he mixed up in this?'

Major Zuidmeyer must have retired from the South African Police at least ten years ago, after spending most of

120

his latter service in the Security Branch up in the Transvaal. And there had been quite a stir when he'd been transferred down to Trekkersburg, following a series of allegations against him which, although never substantiated, had caused sufficient embarrassment for his superiors to want him tucked away in some relative backwater, out of the limelight. Major Zuidmeyer's basic problem had been what he himself had described as 'a lot of bad luck with prisoners'. Two political detainees in his charge had jumped out of the same tenth-storey window in Security Branch headquarters, two more had died after tripping and falling down some stairs at the HQ, and no less than three others had slipped on the soap while taking showers under his supervision, fracturing their skulls and never regaining consciousness.

Could there be a link, perhaps, between such an obvious patriot and the death of a writer whom he'd no doubt have regarded as a dangerous subversive? It was still impossible to guess exactly what the Lieutenant was dealing with over in Acacia Drive, yet Zondi felt certain now that he was getting a lot warmer.

'Ja, my mother and father had been quarrelling,' said Jannie Zuidmeyer. 'They had been having a row that lasted nearly all night, and I heard it start up again before breakfast. I thought, that's *it*, I'm not going to sit around while this drags on and on – and so I took the dog for a long walk. He slipped his lead, ran off, and I spent hours trying to find him again. He's a puppy still, and hasn't been trained properly. Eventually, I decided to leave it to the SPCA to find him, and I came home. My father was kneeling in the garage with his back to me, sorting through his *Popular Mechanics*. I didn't want to talk to him, so I sneaked by and went into the house. I heard the shower going. I felt like a shower myself, after all the running around I'd been doing after the dog, and I hoped my mother wasn't going to use up all the hot water. Our hot-water boiler is not very big, you see – more for two people. So I went to my room at the back, and I kept an ear cocked, waiting for the shower to be turned off, which would be a signal she was nearly finished in the bathroom.

121

But the shower went on and on until I realised something was wrong. I went to the door and knocked. I didn't get an answer. I called out several time to my mother, and still no answer. So I went to get my father. I didn't go into the bathroom myself because I did not think it proper. My mother could have had no clothes on. I tapped on my father's shoulder and he jumped. I saw his face was pale. I said I was sorry I'd given him a fright, but I felt something was wrong in the bathroom and had been trying to keep calm – this was why I hadn't shouted out for him. I asked him to go and see whether my mother was all right. As he stood up, I saw he was trembling. He went quickly into the house and into the bathroom. There is no lock on the bathroom because my mother has always been afraid of becoming faint with the heat when she uses the bath, and has fears of drowning without nobody able to get in and help. She has always liked very hot baths, though, and it isn't often she takes a shower. It's really only when she's upset and not in the mood to lie there reading one of her love stories. She showers when she's wanting to get washed and get going with the day, when she has early-morning shopping to do. I saw my father go into the bathroom. I heard him give a small cry, and the sound of the shower stopped. I heard him saying my mother's name over and over again, and then I heard a grunting noise I could not understand. That's when I went to the door. I saw my father holding my mother under the arms from behind and gently lifting her out of the shower. She was all flopped and looked very heavy. The grunting noise was my father straining to move her backwards onto the floor. He did it slowly, as though not wanting to hurt her, but already I could see she was dead. She was a terrible colour. There was also blood on the top of her head, which was getting smeared on my father's shirt. When he had got her on to the floor, he tucked her dressing-gown over her and put his fingers against her throat to find her pulse. I wanted to tell him to do mouth-to-mouth, hit her on the chest, do anything to bring her alive again. But he just knelt there. I suppose he has seen a lot of dead people as a policeman and knew, in his heart of hearts, none of that would do any good. I felt sick then.

My knees just gave way and I nearly fell over as I came back down the passage. I sat down under the phone shelf. When my father came out of the bathroom a few seconds later, I thought how calm he looked. But when he saw me sitting there his expression changed and I expected him to start crying. He told me that my mother was not with us any more, and that I mustn't look in the bathroom. He reached over me and rang the police. His face went calm again. He told me it was an accident. Mother must have slipped and fallen. A pure accident, he said. Then the police van came and the sergeant saw me first, because my father was sitting in the bathroom to keep my mother company. I said that my mother was dead and my father called it an accident, but it wasn't one. I said it was all his doing. He was a murderer and I could prove it. The sergeant said I was just saying that because of the shock. I asked him if he knew my father, and he said, yes, he did. He remembered him from when he was in the police. I said that he was therefore going to take my father's side, but the fact remained he had killed my mother. The sergeant said I should go and sit in the lounge, and I waited there while he went to the bathroom with another policeman, the young one, and then went out to his van. I waited some more, and this important man in a suit came. The sergeant told him things, out on the lawn, and then the sergeant came to sit with me in here. I have been sitting with him ever since. He says I shouldn't be talking so much, but I can't help it. Sorry.'

The abrupt silence in the room had its own loudness.

Kramer glanced at the sergeant; at Colonel Muller, who completed his shorthand note barely three strokes after the final word of apology; and he looked at the son, who was seated on the floor in front of the television set.

Jannie Zuidmeyer bore no obvious resemblance to either of his parents. Thin and wiry, curly-haired, brown-eyed on the left, blue-eyed on the right, he was all arms and legs, and seemed to rest very lightly on this earth. His face, downy with a mid-teen fuzz, did nothing in itself to declare him much older than that, but made one think of soppy films in which lonely boys had loyal pets with soulful eyes. Young

Zuidmeyer was, in point of fact, all of twenty-one, according to the Colonel, and held a clerical post at the municipal abattoir.

'Tell me, Jannie,' murmured Colonel Muller, 'why did you say to the sergeant that your father was a murderer?'

'Because he is.'

'You'll have to explain that to me.'

'Hadn't he been rowing all night? Wasn't it him that got her so upset that she took a shower this morning and didn't look to see what she was doing? If he hadn't done that, then nothing would have happened. Christ, I hate him! *Hate him!*'

It was hatred that everyone else in the room could feel, striking a chill to the bone. But Kramer, who had been wondering how long the youngster could sit there, describing events so unemotionally, took it as a healthy sign.

Crawling on his hands and knees through the long grass and bedsprings and rusty cans down the slope behind his house on the outskirts of Gladstoneville, Ramjut Pillay experienced a moment when his uppermost thought was to wonder whether, in a former life, he had not perhaps been a *Red* Indian. He was really remarkably good at secretive stalking.

Then panic again took possession of his entire being, and he crawled on with heart thumping and thorns going into the palms of his hands unnoticed. He simply had to reach his room, destroy the evidence of his crime, snatch up his savings, and take to the hills, all before the police could get there. The one good thing that could be said about Peerswammy Lal, may the God Kali persecute him unceasingly, was that he had given those detectives the idea their prey was lurking about town, but of course there was no way of telling when they'd complete their eliminations.

The sound of a car churning up the dirt road to his house made Ramjut Pillay drop flat and close his eyes tightly. But the car carried on by, and when he dared to take a peep at it he saw that it was only Sammy Govender's old Oldsmobile, dragging a broken exhaust-pipe. The same peep sufficed to reassure him that nobody was about to spy on his approach, and so he crawled twice as fast the rest of the way, ending up panting behind his lean-to extension.

Here, he listened very carefully. All was quiet. His father was probably out looking for him somewhere, and no doubt his mother was seated on the front veranda killing flies with her fly-whisk. It wasn't a sight he'd ever imagined would move him, but it was hard to think he might never see it again.

Swallowing the lump in his throat, Ramjut Pillay then sprang into action, nipping nimbly round the corner of the extension and plunging his key into his door-lock. Seconds later, almost choked by the smell of hot horsehair mattress, he stuffed Naomi Stride's letters and their envelopes into his plastic shopping-bag, threw in the knotted sock containing his savings, and snatched up his dog-eared copy of *The Life of Mahatma Gandhi*. Turning, he was outside again in a single jump, locked the door, and then crawled for all he was worth, back up the slope behind his house, exhilarated by his daring.

No sooner had he reached the wattle plantation against the skyline, however, than he realised with a sickening thud that he'd committed two terrible oversights. First, although having decided that fire would be the most effective way of destroying the evidence of his crimes, he had forgotten to pick up a box of matches. Second, and this was possibly even more serious, he'd left behind in his lean-to some secret notes he'd jotted down during the course of the night. Would they not in themselves be totally incriminating?

He had just shuffled round on his knees to begin the descent once again when he was stopped dead in his tracks by the sight of a shiny beige Ford sedan drawing up in front of his house. Two men stepped out. They were too far away to be seen in any detail, but quite plainly one was white, the other black. A whimper escaped him.

Panic-stricken, Ramjut Pillay crawled frantically to the foot of a nearby tree, found a small burrow beneath it, poked the letters and envelopes down into it with a stick, blocked the hole with a stone, found a bigger stone, blocked it with that, looked back once over his shoulder, and fled again.

'Doc Strydom has just arrived, Willem,' Colonel Muller said to Zuidmeyer, who was still sitting in the bathroom, staring at his wife's body. 'I think this is the moment when we must ask you to go through to the lounge. OK?'

Zuidmeyer didn't even look up, and the young constable, who had been ordered into the bathroom to keep an eye on him while the son was being interviewed, tapped a finger on his temple.

'Willem, can you understand what I'm saying?' asked Colonel Muller, motioning Kramer further into the room. 'Would you like Tromp to help me give you a hand in—?'

'No, I can manage,' said Zuidmeyer, getting slowly to his feet. 'Tell Doc I don't want her cut up.'

'But, Willem, you know the procedure when there's a sudden death and—'

'That doesn't concern me. No post-mortem. They're not doing that to my little girl. There are ways round; I have used them myself on other occ—'

'Come, Willem, man. All Doc Strydom wants to do here is a small examination.'

Kramer stood back, allowing Zuidmeyer to pass through the door ahead of him, and then tagged along behind Colonel Muller. They went into the lounge and Zuidmeyer took the big chair by the fireplace, as of habit.

'Where's the boy?' he asked.

'The sergeant's taken Jannie to be treated for shock at the hospital,' said Colonel Muller. 'Don't worry about him; Sergeant Botha is one of the best.'

'He recognised me,' said Zuidmeyer, smiling slightly. 'Knew straight off who I was. There's lots that have forgotten.'

But the English-language newspapers wouldn't have forgotten, thought Kramer, and, given half a chance, would have a field day reminding everyone of Major 'Many a Slip' Zuidmeyer's notorious bad luck in the past. No wonder the Colonel, who hated certain types of human-interest stories more than anything, had the sweats.

126

'Tromp,' said Colonel Muller, bringing out his shorthand-pad, 'would you like to ask our friend here some routine questions, just for the record? Then I can concentrate on—'

'Certainly, Colonel, sir.'

'You see, Willem,' the Colonel explained to Zuidmeyer, getting his ballpoint ready as well, 'what I intend is having Tromp here wrap up this whole unhappy affair as quickly and quietly as possible. That's why I've chosen my best man for the job, a bloke you can trust with your life, I promise you. I know it's only a simple accident investigation but, if I used anybody else, there could be mistakes in the paperwork, procedures not followed correctly, and that's when our problems could start, with the magistrate splitting hairs at the inquest and the press finally getting to hear of it. As you know, they don't as a rule attend inquests, but just take a look at the papers in the Attorney-General's office later on, when I'm sure some slight oversight could be arranged - papers that go astray, that type of thing. Personally, I see no need for any publicity, do you? I can't see how it could serve the public interest.'

Zuidmeyer nodded dully. 'Agreed, Colonel. I have never seen what good it does, and I have had more than my fair share of publicity in my day, so I should know.' Then he looked across at Kramer. 'I put myself entirely in your hands, young man.'

It was a second or two before Kramer responded. The Colonel's little speech had come as a surprise to him, and he wasn't at all sure he liked the role in which he now found himself, although he'd been a fool not to have suspected something of the sort earlier. On top of which, the expression in Zuidmeyer's eyes, now turned in his direction, was so strange that he couldn't think of the right word to describe it. 'Creepy' came close, but wasn't quite right.

'Fine, sir,' said Kramer, taking out his own notebook and a pen. 'All I want you to do is to tell me what happened here this morning.'

'Well, I was out in my garage, sorting through—'

'Sorry, sir, but if you'll go back a bit. I really need the whole picture.'

127

'Tromp—' began Colonel Muller.

But Kramer ignored him. 'I don't want to know what you had for breakfast or anything like that, sir, just a general idea of Mrs Zuidmeyer's state of mind, when she went for her shower, that sort of thing.'

'Of course,' said Zuidmeyer, nodding. 'I'm sorry to sound so like an amateur at this! God knows, I have done investigations like this myself often enough, so I'm fully conversant with what is wanted. Let me see. . .' He sank back in his chair and covered his face with his hands. 'The day began badly – for which I now curse myself.'

Kramer waited and heard a dry sob.

'Curse myself!' repeated Zuidmeyer, his face still covered, then he sat up a little straighter. 'A stupid argument that got so stupid in the end that I just decided to forget breakfast and get out of the house to find some distraction. I haven't any projects on the go at the moment, so I started tidying my magazines. I can't tell you when my wife went into the bathroom. As you can see, I didn't even shave this morning, didn't bother to wash, just went charging out. Usually I shower first, and she uses the bathroom after me. I suppose she could have gone in straight away.'

'Which would have been about what time, sir?' asked Kramer.

'I'd say a quarter to eight, maybe ten to.'

'And so, if it was about eleven o'clock when your son called you to go see what the matter was in the bathroom, your wife could have been lying there for more than three hours?'

Zuidmeyer nodded behind those hands. 'Why? Why didn't I go into the house sooner?'

'Ja, why didn't you, Willem?' coaxed Colonel Muller.

'Because . . . Because – my God, how petty can a man be? – I was still so annoyed with her. I thought she owed me an apology; I was waiting for her to come to me, to say she was sorry. There was that, and also the fact that once I start with my magazines I start reading pieces here and there, and I don't notice how the time flies.'

'Wasn't there a servant who might've—?'

'No servants,' replied Zuidmeyer shortly. 'They are not welcome in my house.'

'Uh-huh. And then what happened, sir? Your son came up to you?'

Zuidmeyer brought his hands down and fixed his eyes on the blank television screen. 'Jannie came and grabbed me, said something was wrong in the bathroom. I told him to stay out of the way as soon as I – as I saw my wife lying there. I turned the water off first, and I felt how cold it was. Because of that, I realised immediately she had been lying there for quite some time. I did not want to look at her. I made some sound when I saw her eyes looking up at me. Then I realised she was still alive. I was sure of it. I went frantic. I got hold of her and tried dragging her out of the shower, to get her on her back to give her the kiss of life. She was slippery and wet and I couldn't get a proper grip. I knew I was being rough, jerking at her and pulling, heaving on her arms as hard as I could – but, Almighty God, she was heavy. It was a struggle, but finally I did it and she came out of the shower with a bump. I'd lost my footing, crouched down like that, and I'd toppled backwards. When I got back on my knees, she was gone. I was too late. I wouldn't accept it. I grabbed her and shook her, I got blood from her head on my chest. I tried mouth-to-mouth. Cardiac massage. I held her to me and cried. Later, before I went to telephone, I covered her with her dressing-gown.' And he went on staring into the television screen, as though doomed through all eternity to watch the same scene repeated again and again.

Kramer turned to Colonel Muller, who had stopped taking shorthand at roughly the point where Zuidmeyer's account had diverged so markedly from that given only a short time ago by his son. The Colonel was even paler now than he had been before.

'Willem,' he said softly, his voice not working properly, 'are you sure that's what occurred here this morning?'

'I'm sure,' replied Zuidmeyer, looking up at them.

'Because, you see, according to—'

'*It was an accident*,' said Zuidmeyer. 'What else could it possibly have been?'

Then Kramer realised what it was about Zuidmeyer's eyes that gave them their strange quality. They were haunted.

'Gagonk, *do* something with this crazy old bitch,' whined Jones. 'I tell you, I can't stand another minute of this.'

So Mbopa picked up the aged mother of Ramjut Pillay, shook her until her fly-whisk fell from her hand and she stopped flailing him with it in the face, then carried her out to the car and put her in the boot.

'Now you can finish what you were saying,' Jones told the father of Ramjut Pillay, who stood smiling nervously before him, one bare big toe hooked over the other. 'When exactly was it your son came back?'

'I have no watch, my master. I am a poor man, my health—'

'OK, OK, just give us a rough idea. Was it long ago? Not so long ago?'

'Not so long ago, my master.'

'And what did he do here? Did he talk to you?'

'No, no, my master! No talk. Ramjut go in his room, come quick-quick out, then run away again on kneecaps.'

'Kneecaps?' echoed Jones. 'Any idea what this silly bugger means, Mbopa?'

'No, sir.'

'Ach, never mind, that can come later. Listen, you, which way did your son go?'

'Up hills and far away, my master.'

'Where?'

'Backside.'

'Hey, you watch what you're—'

'Excuse me, suh,' interrupted Mbopa, who wanted to get back to his book. 'I think what is meant is the hill at the back of this man's house.'

Jones took a look at it, lost interest almost immediately and then asked: 'Why did your son come back here? Have you any idea?'

'I am seated in privy, my master. There are only two nail-holes I am being able to see through. I see only that he takes big bag with him.'

'From his room, you say?'

'Yes, my master.'

'Then we'd better search the place, hey, Gagonk? This is all a bloody mystery to me, but something funny's obviously going on.'

'Room is lock, my master. Ramjut a bad boy, never allow me to keep key.'

'From the look of you, you shifty old bastard, I'm not bloody surprised,' said Jones. 'You'd be straight in and under his mattress for his money-sock, wouldn't you? But never to worry; I've brought my own key with me.'

Thanks very much, thought Mbopa, who was really bored with kicking down doors.

The bathroom at 146 Acacia Drive was a different place with Doc Strydom huffing and puffing about in it, doing tricks with his blue braces. His presence lent a clinical gleam to the yellow tiling, and the body, until now so totally uncommunicative, seemed poised to divulge certain truths, however grudgingly.

'Well, Doc?' asked Colonel Muller. 'There's only me and Tromp present, so I would appreciate it if you just said what comes to mind.'

'H'm,' responded Strydom. 'Difficult.'

'Then, can we start with estimated time of death?'

'*Very* difficult. Shower running, artificial cooling effect . . . Thick layers of fat, well insulated . . . Temperature-loss, h'm, could be misleading.'

'Cause of death?'

'Ah, head injury. Fractured skull?'

'You're the man who's supposed to have the answers, Doc.'

'You can't wait for the p.m?'

'Ja, naturally, but a bit of a conflict of evidence has come up – hard to know who to believe. For my own peace of mind, I'd like—'

'What sort of conflict?' asked Strydom.

'Ah, well, I don't want to prejudice you in any—'

'Tromp,' said Strydom, poking his rectal thermometer at

Kramer, 'can you tell me what your esteemed superior is being so coy about?'

'Let's put it this way, Doc,' he replied. 'We could be interested in any bruises or abrasions, even small ones. Have you come across—?'

Strydom laughed. 'Have I come across bruising? What's the matter with you two? Haven't you taken a look at the lady yet? Are you turning soft?'

'Willem's been in here nearly all the—'

'That's irregular,' remarked Strydom sternly. 'But, in answer to your question, look for yourself.' And he flipped back the orange dressing-gown.

There was bruising on the upper arms, the lower arms, the chest, the shoulders, and on the left jawline. Not deep purple bruising, pale blue in most cases, but bruising all the same.

'Could gentle handling have done that?' asked Colonel Muller.

'Huh, you have to be joking, Hans!'

'More important,' said Kramer, 'did it occur before or after death?'

'Before, almost without a doubt,' said Strydom.

'How long before?' asked Kramer.

'Ah, there you have me. The post-mortem might be able to help us on that one. It could, I suppose, have been hours before.'

'*Hours before?*' repeated Colonel Muller. 'How many hours before?'

'Oh, about two or three.'

'Or about the time something made the lady slip,' said Kramer, watching the Colonel's face. 'The funny thing is, you know, I've just taken another look in this shower cubicle and I can't see any soap.'

10

THE PROBLEM with being on the run, decided Ramjut Pillay, was that unless a poor fellow were in training, then the running itself proved impossible to do after a time. With a stitch in his side, and knees all wobbly, he slowed to a jog, to a fast walk, and finally to a brisk shuffle.

Not long after that, he sat down.

'Mechanise,' said Ramjut Pillay.

So he took out his knotted sock and began to untie it, confident that he should have enough money for a prodigious train-journey. Someone had once told him that Cape Town lay no less than a thousand miles away; exactly what this figure represented in more modern kilometres he wasn't too sure, but it still sounded the right sort of distance to put between himself and his pursuers.

'Thash an inneresting sock,' someone slurred in his ear.

Ramjut Pillay shrank away when he saw who had come to share his bench in the park at the bottom end of Railway Street. Strictly speaking, it was a white man, only his face was the colour of a tomato, and a very rotten tomato at that, with its skin gone all squishy and wrinkly. Some of the red had seeped into the whites of his watery blue eyes, and his teeth, bared in a leering smile, were the yellowy orange of tomato pips. He did not, however, smell anything like a tomato.

'Washa marrer?' asked the man. 'You deaf?'

Lifelong teetotalism, inspired by the Mahatma, had left Ramjut Pillay ill-prepared to withstand the fumes of cheap sherry now being breathed out so close to him, and he suffered an attack of slight dizziness, making the man's deep voice sound terribly far away.

'You wansh me to undo thash knot?' said the man, reaching out a great grimy hand. 'Not take – pardon me – a minute.'

'Many, many thanks,' said Ramjut Pillay. 'But I will untie it later. First I have to—' But as he tried to rise from the bench he felt the weight of a heavy arm draped in friendly fashion around his shoulders.

'Give us the sock!' growled the man.

'That bespectacled gent over there is staring our way,' said another side to Ramjut Pillay.

'Lesh him!'

'But do you know why, sir? It is the bench.'

'Bensh? What bensh?'

'The bench you are presently sitting on, sir. A bench which states clearly on its notice that it is for "Non-Whites Only". Perhaps he is thinking he has never before seen an Indian gent so light-skinned as yourself, sir, and—'

'Wazzat? He thinks I'm a *coolie*? I'm not having thash!' said the man, staggering to his feet. 'Hey, you! Four-eyes! Just who d'you thinksh you're insulting, hey?'

And he lumbered off, gathering terrifying momentum, in the direction of this singularly innocent bystander, leaving Ramjut Pillay to flee in the opposite direction, abandoning his bag but clutching the sock to him very tightly.

Up the steps of the railway station he skipped, through the booking-hall and out on to the platform. Where, behind a porter's trolley piled with suitcases, he finally got the knot undone. 'By jingo!' he chuckled, plunging his hand into the sock. 'How cleverly was a great catastrophe avoided by the one and only ours truly! Cape Town stand by, please, for the privilege of Ramjut Pillay!' But an instant later his ebullience evaporated.

This wasn't a small wad of rand notes he had just taken from his sock. It was a handful of similarly sized scraps of paper.

The telephone rang, making Zondi look first to see what time it was. Four o'clock! He had started to read Naomi Stride's unfinished typescript, supposing that it might well deal with themes which would hint at contemporary problems in her personal life, and had become so completely engrossed he'd not noticed the hours slip by.

'Mickey?'

'The very same, Lieutenant. How are things with Major Willem Martinus Zuidmeyer?'

134

There was a pause. 'Christ, who told you, hey? It's all supposed to be top—'

Zondi laughed. 'The name is all that I know.'

'Ach, now I get it,' said Kramer, laughing, too. 'You've been chatting up some poor unsuspecting female again, hey? Don't worry, I'll tell you the lot later when I get the chance. Meet you back at the office tonight.'

'Boss, the blue letters are not here.'

'Surprise me. OK, pack it in at Woodhollow when you like, and then wait at CID for Hopeful Dumela to pitch up with those servants. The Colonel wants you to be the one who interviews them.'

'And you, Lieutenant?'

'Later, old son, like I said.'

Zondi heard the line go dead as he dropped the receiver back into its cradle. He took another look at his watch, estimated that he had time for two or three more chapters at least, and settled back with the typescript. It was quite a story, this tale of a young black student in love with the daughter of his father's white employer. Switch the sexes of the illicit lovers round, make the employer an intelligent middle-class woman instead of a bearded university professor, and it seemed fairly obvious how Naomi Stride might herself have felt in just such a situation. That a son of hers should be breaking the law would have little to do with it; rather, her preoccupation would be with to what extent he was exploiting the vast social gap that lay between him and his lover, making himself appear the chief's son to her peasant girl.

'Tromp,' said Colonel Muller, sighing as he came out of the lounge at 146 Acacia Drive, 'a private word with you.'

Kramer nodded and stepped out into the garden with him. A dog, he noticed, had visited the property and cocked a leg over one of the stacks of *Popular Mechanics*, which only went to prove the crime prevention campaign had been right about never leaving garage doors open.

'Why the smile?' asked Colonel Muller. 'God in Heaven, I know of nothing to smile about! My mind is in a total state of

135

muddle and confusion. I can't seem to think.'

'But there's a reason for that, Colonel.'

'Oh ja?'

'You can't think because you're stopping yourself from thinking.'

'*Me*, stopping myself?'

'Or at least from thinking along the lines all your experience over the years as a policeman has taught you to do.'

'I don't get it.'

'Then, let me try putting it this way, Colonel,' suggested Kramer, perching on a wing of the red Datsun. 'Say, for argument's sake, this call had been to the house of a certain reverend gentleman with fingers like pork sausages. Do you know the bastard I mean?'

'Hell, I should hope so! The animal who keeps doing indecent things to little kiddies.'

'*Alleged* indecent things,' Kramer corrected him. 'There's been a dozen or more complaints, but have we ever got him to court yet?'

'Ja, but that's because of his position, man. Because it's always been his word against some three-year-old, and he's been careful not to leave any forensic evidence. Only, what this has to do with—'

'Just say,' went on Kramer, 'we got a call to his house right now, and there was a kiddie there who said he'd been putting his hand in her panties. Would you believe her?'

'Why, naturally, man!'

'Because?'

'Because of what we know of him already!'

'So you'd let yourself think that, Colonel? You would let it colour what you—'

'Hey, Tromp,' said Colonel Muller, wagging his pipe-stem. 'I see what you're driving at now, and I don't want any more of that talk. Nothing has ever been proved in connection with the allegations against Willem Zuidmeyer. I have never liked the man, I admit that, but you have to be fair in these matters.'

'Ach, Colonel, you know as well as I do—'

'I know this, Lieutenant Kramer. I know that if what you're hinting is that Zuidmeyer has repeated – what shall we call it, an expedience used in his past? – then that doesn't make sense in the slightest. Why would he do something that'd attract immediate suspicion?'

'Ah, so you're admitting that—'

'I'm admitting nothing. I'm asking you a question.'

'Well,' said Kramer, glancing at the garage, 'could it be because you can't expect an old dog to learn new tricks?'

There was a prolonged silence, which Colonel Muller spent digging carefully about in his new briar with a match, and tamping down the tobacco again. 'I had hoped', he said eventually, 'that you'd be able to help me in forming a nice, clear, unbiased picture of the situation. It's what I need most, Tromp, if I'm to handle matters with the discretion expected of me as the head of CID in Trekkersburg and district.' And he sounded very lonely.

Kramer slid off the Datsun, chastened to see an old friend reduced to being almost human. 'You're right, Colonel,' he said. 'We mustn't prejudge, we must stick to the known facts. Who knows? This could all have been another of God's little jokes. Now, there's a bloke with a bloody sick sense of humour.'

'And the known facts are?' asked Colonel Muller, getting his smile back.

'That father and son repeatedly give contradictory accounts. One says the deceased was alive when roughly manhandled from the shower; the other that she was dead upon removal and there was no manhandling to have caused bruising, which suggests it must have occurred earlier. We now have to turn to the District Surgeon in the hope he can confirm one or other of these two stories, and he has invited us to attend his post-mortem one hour from now. When we know whose story to believe, the father's or the son's, then we will know how this case should be regarded. Either as a simple accident enquiry, or as a full-blown murder investi—'

Colonel Muller shuddered. 'Enough, Tromp! That's all I wanted. Now, let me see; if we go down to the mortuary a little early, do you think Doc Strydom might start sooner than five o'clock?'

'I think,' said Kramer, 'it'll depend more on how the afternoon has treated its resident ghoul, the charming Sergeant Van Rensburg.'

With the smell of hot horsehair mattress thick in his nostrils, Gagonk Mbopa took out his snuff-horn and dosed himself with two large pinches. He also put a little snuff behind his lower lip.

'Now, that,' muttered Jones, poking about between the joists and the corrugated-iron roof of Ramjut Pillay's lean-to bedroom, 'is what I call a truly disgusting habit.'

'Ermph.'

'What did you say?'

'Ermph, Lieutenant.'

'That's better! What do you think he needed this bottle of stuff for?'

Mbopa took the small brown bottle and cautiously unscrewed its top before taking a quick sniff at its contents. 'Lemon juice, Lieutenant.'

'Fresh, is it?'

Mbopa tasted a little and nodded. 'Maybe it is some kind of churra medicine,' he suggested.

'There's also a pen up here he's been stirring it with. God, have you ever seen such an assortment?'

'Never, sir.'

'Then, let's get out in the open again for some air, hey? I need to think about this – it's queer we've still found nothing.'

'The Lieutenant is sure there is something to find? We have searched this place for many—'

'Ja, ja, all afternoon, I know! But I'm sure I'm on to something here; my nose tells me.'

Wiping the sweat from his brow with an already sodden handkerchief, Mbopa stepped out into a mild breeze, wishing it could reach the most uncomfortable part of his anatomy. To this end, he did a couple of deep knee-bends, tugged at his trouser seat and turned his back to leeward.

'Right,' said Jones, taking out a wine gum to suck, 'what

138

we do now is put this place under surveillance, while at the same time we issue out a warrant for this bastard's arrest.'

'Hau!' said Mbopa.

'Just listen, man . . . Who allegedly found the body? Who couldn't explain what his boots were doing outside the sun-lounge? Who stays up all night, doing God knows what in his room? Who borrows a bike and goes rushing into town? Who comes back, not on the bike, and sneaks down here, grabs a big bag and goes sneaking away again, trying not to be seen? *Who?*'

'Er, this Pillay, Lieutenant.'

'And now tell me there's nothing in all that to arouse any normal person's suspicions! You can't, can you?'

'No, Lieutenant,' admitted Mbopa.

'Well, then, what you've got to add to that is all his disguises and—'

'Disguises, sir?'

'You've seen them, man! He's got enough different uniforms and suchlike in there to dress up as almost anything, go out and commit a crime, and who's to know it was only a coolie postman? I bet you that's what he had in the big bag he took away – another costume to disguise himself in.'

'But, Lieutenant—'

'Watch it! How many times must I warn you not to say "but" to me when I'm talking?'

Mbopa fell silent, directing a jet of snuff-brown spit at a locust on a nearby boulder.

'Now, where was I?' said Jones. 'Oh ja, and then there's that detective course he's been taking.'

'That is what I wanted to say, Lieutenant. You speak as though this Pillay is a big, big criminal. Only, why would a—?'

'Ach, don't you ever use your brains? It's obvious he must have taken that course so he'd know what methods would be used against him, giving him a chance to plan accordingly!'

'Hau,' said Mbopa, impressed despite himself, and making up for this by hitting the locust full-on with his second shot. 'So we have found Suspect Number One, sir?'

Jones shrugged and popped another wine gum. 'I wouldn't

go so far as to say that at this stage, Gagonk, but I reckon he'd definitely be worth asking a few questions – out at the playground, maybe?'

'Any time, Lieutenant!' chuckled Mbopa.

'Hey, and you know what else I've just worked out? That he's probably, at this minute, making a run for it in that disguise of his! Didn't you notice he didn't leave a single cent behind? We'd better get on to the bus station and so on straight away, hey? Although there's just one snag. . .'

'Sir?'

'This Pillay's description. We need it quickly to circulate, but neither you nor me has ever seen him. Who can we ask? His pa's obviously half-witted, the Post Office is probably closed by now, and so we'll probably have to end up getting Kra – er, Lieutenant Kramer or his pet monkey to provide the necessary informa—'

'No need, Lieutenant!' said Mbopa, making for the lean-to.

'I've already thought of that,' said Jones. 'You're going to guess his size from those clothes, right? But you can't, hey, because I've already looked and they're all different.'

But Mbopa ignored that remark, and searched at the bottom of a pile of papers for one of the first documents he'd glanced through. 'Ah, here it is, Lieutenant! Just what is wanted!' And he handed over a half-finished letter.

' "Dear Esteemed Pen Pal," ' Jones read out. ' "Allow me to introduce myself. My name is Ramjut Pillay, my age thirty-one years, and I am most Gandhi-esque in appearance, save for a full head of splendidly healthy hair. To help you picture me further, I must modestly reveal that I weigh 81.64 kilos, stand a very fully educated 176 centimetres, and have most excellent eyesight. I work as a postal operative and have the reputation of—" ' Jones broke off, and raised an eyebrow. 'What does this "Gandhi-esque" nonsense mean?'

'Can it be churra talk for Asiatic, sir?'

'Of course!' said Jones. 'Then, we're in business, Gagonk! Everything we need is here, so don't just stand around bloody grinning – let's get to a phone, man!'

Acting like a waiter who has been asked to lay and serve a

table after closing-time, Sergeant Van Rensburg was banging trays about in his mortuary, dropping knives everywhere, making snide remarks about what sort of tip he'd be getting, and pretending that Marie Lousie Zuidmeyer wasn't on the menu.

'Ach, now take a pull at yourself!' remonstrated Strydom. 'You know very well that the deceased was brought here in an ordinary ambulance so as not to tip off the neighbours that there'd been a death.'

'An ordinary ambulance?'

'Ja, the kind with red crosses on. She was on a trolley with a grey blanket over the top.'

'I've had enough of this,' said Kramer, and went through to the refrigerator room, where he took Van Rensburg by the nose and twisted it until his eyes watered and tears streamed down his fat cheeks. 'Fine, then, now you look as though you're putting some feeling into your work, *move*.'

Very shortly after that, Mrs Zuidmeyer's considerable bulk was moved from a trolley on to the channelled stone slab, and Colonel Muller raised a copy of the evening paper in front of him. There was an unusual creaking sound in the room, as Van Rensburg tiptoed about on the wooden duckboards, and Kramer made no attempt to meet Strydom's reproachful looks, which somehow suggested he had interfered with time-honoured tradition. Instead, he concentrated on the dead woman's face, and tried to read a little of her life from it.

Her hands told him more. For a white woman, they were remarkably workworn, and all the more so for a wife in her position, with a good-sized pension coming in. This would naturally have something to do with there being no servant on the premises of course, but he could also see, from the pads on her fingers, that she had done a great deal of heavy sewing, and remembered then that the red Datsun had had new upholstery. The narrow strip of indented skin on her ring finger hinted at a cheap wedding band.

'I've seen fat before, but this is like cutting through a churn of farm butter,' grunted Strydom, his gloved hand disappearing as it parted glistening yellow slopes in search of red tissue.

'Chocolates,' said Kramer.

'What gives you that idea?'

'They go with reading love stories in a hot bath.'

'But wouldn't they melt in the steam?' asked Van Rensburg, and looked even more unhappy when nobody troubled to reply to him.

Mrs Zuidmeyer, on the other hand, was looking quite contented, and for once the phrase 'passed peacefully away' seemed wholly appropriate, notwithstanding her undoubtedly violent departure. Perhaps, mused Kramer, she'd reached the stage when her only concept of peace *was* death, and she'd welcomed it, however it had come to her. Then, again, she might have lived her life as one of those irritating women who always looked peaceful, making one want to drop mice down their fronts, and this expression of supreme superiority had become fixed. Her eyes, he noted, were also one blue and one brown, so he'd been wrong about young Jannie sharing no resemblance. The nose was ordinary enough, but the mouth troubled him; even now it seemed turned in on itself, as though sworn never to impart secrets learned from bad dreams dreamed beside her through many a bad night.

'Jelly beans,' said Strydom, opening the stomach over by the sink.

'Close enough,' said Kramer. 'Any sign of breakfast?'

'None.'

'Uh-huh. And how much of a general picture have you so far?'

'She definitely slipped in that shower cubicle. Extensive bruising to the toes of her right foot, and bleeding under two toenails, consistent with it shooting forward and striking the porcelain surround. Also, massive bruising of the left buttock area, where she landed. Y'know, going down with a helluva bump. When I get inside the head, I'd like to bet we're going to find the base of the skull fractured by upward compression, with maybe secondary fracture-lines extending from it. Overweight people falling hard on their bums are always doing that to themselves.'

Van Rensburg looked round hopefully, in obvious expectation of someone making a callous remark, as would be customary, regarding his own chances of longevity in view of this bleak fact, but again went ignored. With a trembling sigh, he began to saw off the top of Mrs Zuidmeyer's cranium, almost as tenderly as though it were his own.

'All right, for the last time of asking,' said the white constable in the Railway Police office, shaking a broken chair-leg in Ramjut Pillay's ashen face, 'how come you were hiding on Platform One while not in possession of a train ticket, platform ticket, travel warrant, railway employee's pass or other form of necessary authorisation?'

'For the last time of replying sir,' said Ramjut Pillay, 'I was never hiding. I was making a private thing of my grief at having such a ruthless thief for a father.'

'You have a father? Don't make me laugh!'

'I have no wish for humour at this particular moment myself, kind sir, but—'

'Hey, that's enough, coolie!' said the constable, breaking another large piece off the chair-leg by bringing it down hard on the scarred table. 'More than I can stand! There are only two ways you could have got on to that platform without a ticket. *Either* you came in from the street and sneaked through the ticket barrier while old Fannie had his back turned, helping that young lady with her cello, *or* you sneaked off a train here, having travelled to Trekkersburg as a stowaway. Now, tell me, which was it?'

'Er, my throat is very dry, sir – would it be permissible for me to have a little water?'

'Have all the water you like!' shouted the constable, snatching a red fire-bucket off its bracket on the wall and tipping it over him.

'Hey, what are you doing with that, Wessels?' asked a Railway Police sergeant, entering the office at that moment. 'Don't you know I've put fertiliser stuff in there for my ferns?'

'You mean it'll make this loony pregnant, Sarge?'

'Wessels! Atten-shun!'

There was a thunderous stamping of boots behind Ramjut Pillay.

'Right, Constable Wessels,' crooned the sergeant, in a very

unpleasant way, 'that's you finished, once and for all. This isn't the first time I've come across this attitude in you concerning my ferns, and everyone from the stationmaster down, who has one of my ferns hanging *directly* outside his office, seems to be aware of it, too. In fact, old Jannie told me only three minutes ago that he had spied a Peter Stuyvesant filter-tip stubbed out in a fern-basket on Platform Two. What is your brand of cigarette, may I ask?'

'Stuy-Stuyvesant, Sergeant. Only, hundreds of buggers must—'

'Constable, riiiight *turn*! Preee-pare to . . . march! The rest of what I have to impress on you can only be done in complete private, man to man. Understood?'

'Sergeant, I—'

'Quick march, you buffoon! Hup-hi! Hup-hi! Hup-hi. . .'

And at last Ramjut Pillay had a moment alone to himself in which to think. He thought so furiously he found he was straining at his handcuffs and making his wrists hurt. How long had he been manacled to this table? Two hours? Was it three? It was well after five on the big clock behind the charge-office desk.

'By jingo!' he couldn't help blurting out, as a sudden, very sweet realisation hit him. 'SAP are very late in telling Railway Police to beware of Ramjut Pillay, most wanted fugitive! This must mean that they have altogether forgotten! And if they have forgotten, then Railway Police do not have my descriptions. Oh, jolly good.'

But that still left him with the problem of explaining how and why he had been found ticketless on Platform One. Telling the truth would be no excuse, and in no time he'd be appearing in the local magistrate's court for all the world – including the Trekkersburg CID – to see. Telling a lie would simply mean appearing in another magistrate's court somewhere else, on the more serious charge of using public transport without paying for it, and then a WANTED poster would no doubt have been circulated. If only he'd allowed Tomato Face to have his damned sock, how very much simpler life would be!

If only there were another way. . . Just one more

inspiration was all he asked.

'Right, you,' said the Railway Police sergeant, sucking a bruised knuckle as he came back into the charge office, 'I want the truth, the whole truth, and not a word of nonsense. How did you get on that platform?'

'I fall out of the sky, kind sir.'

'Oh ja? What are you? A parachutist or a bloody nutcase?'

'Parachutist,' said Ramjut Pillay.

'I suppose it says that on your papers?'

'I am never reading the papers, sir. Only the prophecies of Allah, who was also a great parachutist.'

'No papers, no money, no bugger all, just one sock full rubbish,' the sergeant muttered to himself, reaching for his telephone directory. 'Are you going to tell us your name now, so I can pass it on to the hospital that'll come to fetch you?'

'Peerswammy Lal,' said Ramjut Pillay.

Hopeful Dumela put his head into the main interrogation room and said: 'Excuse me, Lieutenant sir, but Colonel Muller is coming down the corridor.'

'You'll go far,' murmured Kramer, as he stepped past him through the doorway. 'Hello, Colonel. Any news, sir?'

'Of?'

'Doc Strydom's little games with his microscope.'

'No, not a word yet,' said Colonel Muller, looking very agitated. 'And you? What have Mrs Stride's servants got to say for themselves?'

'A lot, sir – but nothing that's been a big help so far. They say she was a good, kind madam, that she had fights with her son over money, that nobody came as a visitor to the house during the week before they left. The cook remembers her burning some blue envelopes in the Aga stove in the kitchen last Wednesday, but says he didn't see their contents. The most we've got out of them is that nowhere in the house did she keep a sword.'

'What's that noise?'

'The maidservant can't stop crying, sir.'

'Zondi hasn't been—!' Colonel Muller gulped. 'Didn't I tell

you I've got *Time* and all the rest on my bloody doorstep?'

'Ach, nothing like that, Colonel. She says her heart is sore for her white madam.'

'Oh, really? Huh! And is that *it*, the sum total of their statements?'

Kramer nodded. 'Tomorrow,' he said, 'Zondi will take them over to the house to see if they can notice anything missing, et cetera.'

'A long shot, man! But why not tonight?'

'They're in no condition, sir. Dumela's had them on the road all day.'

Colonel Muller shook his head dolefully. 'God in Heaven,' he said, 'unless something happens soon with this Stride case, the press are going to start looking elsewhere for a story – and the last thing I want is them getting hold of the Zuidmeyer business.'

'But I thought Jones was working on a new lead? He sort of dropped a hint to that effect when I crossed paths with him in the courtyard.'

'Didn't he tell you what it was?'

Kramer shook his head. 'I think he wants to keep all the glory to himself, sir. Another of his bullshit theories, I suppose.'

'Actually, he may be on to something. What it boils down to is that Pillay, the postman who found the body, could be involved in some fashion.'

'You're joking, Colonel! Zondi—'

'Zondi can what? Explain where Pillay has vanished to and all the rest of it?'

'The rest of what, Colonel?'

'Tromp,' said Colonel Muller, glancing at his watch, 'it's not really your worry, hey? I'm the one who's doing the co-ordination, and for now you're supposed to be concentrating on the Zuidmeyers, OK? That is *top* priority. Ach, I really must be going; it's after eight o'clock, and Mrs Muller is waiting supper for me.'

Kramer watched him hurry off, then turned just as Zondi emerged from the interrogation room. 'Well, Mickey?'

'Still nothing, boss, so I've told Dumela to find them a

146

place to sleep for the night.'

'Fine,' said Kramer.

Zondi locked pace with him as they made their way back up to his office above the courtyard. 'What's next, boss?' he asked.

'I've had a total gutsful today, one way and another, so I suggest we just both bugger off. It's what the Colonel's just done, and he's leading this so-called investigation.'

'But what about the Zuid—?'

'To hell with Zuidmeyer! There's nothing I can do about him until Doc Strydom confirms those bruises were inflicted a long time before death, when the lady supposedly slipped in her shower. By the way, maybe you should know that everyone directly involved in the case has been sworn to such secrecy that their balls will fall off if they divulge one word about it.'

'Hau, so *that* was the soft bouncing sound when you stood up just now. . .'

'Hey, kaffir, just you—'

'Phone!' cut in Zondi.

Kramer reached his desk at the fifth ring and lifted the receiver. 'Doc?' he said.

He was right. It was Strydom on the line, talking in a curious half-whisper, like a man torn between high excitement and extreme caution. It took a few moments for his words to sink in properly, and by then he'd rung off again.

'Boss?' prompted Zondi, as he watched Kramer replace the receiver in its cradle very carefully.

'Those tissue slides of Ma Zuidmeyer's bruises. . .'

'Yes, boss?'

'Doc Strydom says he can't be a hundred per cent sure, but from the look of them under his microscope he's pretty certain the bruising occurred at about the time of death, tying in with Zuidmeyer's version of events. Or, in other words, it now seems it could be the son who's doing the lying.'

'The *son?*' said Zondi, withholding a match flame from the two Lucky Strikes he'd been about to light. 'But why should he want to lie?'

'The mind bloody boggles,' agreed Kramer.

11

'AND what about this chappie?' asked a tall white man in a white coat, pausing the following morning by Ramjut Pillay's cot in the crowded admitting-ward at Garrison Road Mental Hospital. 'Um, Peerswammy Lal, isn't it?'

'That's right, Doctor,' said the Indian male nurse in charge, whose name-tag read *N. J. Chatterjee*. 'He spent all last night under his bed.'

'It was seeming so much safer there,' said Ramjut Pillay, glancing nervously around him at the other patients.

'Of course, of course. People after you, are they?'

'Oh, no! I am really totally unknown and perfectly innocent, Doctor!' Then he dropped his voice to a whisper. 'My fears were entirely connected with the persons who slept with me.'

'Sexual fantasies, you mean?'

'I did not dare to think as far as that, Doctor!'

'H'm, I'm beginning to see what might have brought you in here.' The doctor shuffled some notes. 'Oh dear, we've been making a bit of a nuisance of ourselves up at the railway station.'

'You as well?' said Ramjut Pillay, most surprised.

The doctor smiled kindly. 'No, you misunderstand me,' he explained. 'When I say "we", what I really mean is "you".'

'But if—'

'Don't argue with the doctor,' said Nurse Chatterjee, pressing him back against a nasty hard pillow. 'He is here to make us better.'

Us?

A person could go mad in a place like this, thought Ramjut Pillay.

Kramer woke, rolled over, stared up at the ceiling and saw that it did not belong to Tess Muldoon, neither was it the Widow Fourie's. He was glad of that. Sometimes, on the rare occasions he went out alone and became very drunk, he ended up doing the opposite to what he'd planned while still sober. But here he was, back in the privacy of his own small room, free to do a little quiet thinking with nobody fussing over him or, for that matter, regarding his body with a ballet dancer's detachment.

He put his hands behind his head and went on looking at the ceiling. He wondered idly whether Mickey now had a ceiling in his bedroom, following his recent move from Kwela Village, where the Zondi family had for years lived in two rooms with a stamped-earth floor, to the new Bantu urban development area at Hamilton, eight miles outside the town. Then he recalled the first ceiling he had ever known, damp-stained and sagging, in the dilapidated Free State farmhouse where he'd been born. Born the day before Christmas, because his church-elder father had become so alarmed at the presumption implicit in a child born on 25 December, that he had induced premature labour by having his wife jolted about in a donkey cart the night before and then given some foul brew by a witchdoctor. In a crude sort of way, this ploy had worked, although, as the old man had so often reminded his cronies, the price he'd paid was that it'd made him both a father and a widower in one and the same day. The listening boy, on the other hand, had always thought that it'd also made him a—

Kramer jumped out of bed, breaking his chain of thought, stretched his arms wide and rose on to his toes. 'Ach, that's better...,' he said to himself, and went for a shower, feeling quite different from the way he'd done the day before, when everything had ended up getting on top of him.

The bathroom brought back an immediate picture of Marie Louise Zuidmeyer as he had last seen her, with Strydom's herringbone stitches running right up her middle, after all her guts and stuff had been poked back in again. A massive woman, certainly, but a short one, and in terms of weight, kilogram for kilogram, probably not much heavier than he was.

This tempted him to try some experiments in the bath. First, he tested the slipperiness of the bath while dry, and found his feet stuck to it. He tested it again, after sprinkling it with some water from his landlady's hair-rinsing device. This

149

hardly made much difference. He dropped in a bar of soap and stood on it. If he placed himself correctly, his foot shot from under him immediately, but time and again, when he simply stepped on it, willy-nilly, all that happened was that the soap went flying, squeezed out from beneath his instep. And so, he finally concluded, slipping on the soap in a shower was not so much an accident as a *freak* accident – something which might happen, strictly by chance, perhaps only once in a hundred years.

Unlucky Marie Louise Zuidmeyer, then, who had got no further than her fifty-fourth birthday before these long odds had caught up with her. Or, unluckier still, the others who had suffered a similar fate, for rumour had it that they'd all been quite young men.

Crouching by the bath, Kramer wondered how else – short of being grabbed and made to fall – Mrs Zuidmeyer could have lost her footing. Then he had an idea. What if the soap had been left lying around on the floor of the shower after the last person had used it? This could easily have created a not-too-noticeable *area* of slipperiness and, if her foot had landed anywhere on it, over she would have gone. Pleased with this theory, he gave it a practical trial by smearing shampoo over the bottom of the bath and then stepping on it without looking. He almost had a bad fall.

'Bull's eye,' he murmured to himself, and reached for the hot tap to run his bath. 'It also explains why I saw no soap there. If the shower had been running for hours on top of that, then what was left would've completely melted and gone down the plughole.'

But his hand came back and he scratched himself with it under one ear instead. Mrs Zuidmeyer – and this wasn't disputed – had been a woman who'd liked a long bath, just as he did. It stood to reason, then, that she'd not step in under a shower until the water was running hot; in fact, he had known very few people prepared to step into showers while the first cold drips were still contained in the nozzle.

So what effect, then, would perhaps a minute of running water have on the slippery surface left by a bar of melting soap? He again made use of his landlady's hair-rinsing device, and discovered that shampoo on the bottom of the bath was dissolved and rendered harmless in seconds.

'Not so clever,' he muttered, and this time turned on the hot tap.

The plumbing gave a clunk, and after the tap had been running for a moment or two there was another clunk and it spat out about a half a glassful of rusty-coloured water before returning to normal. By the time his bath was poured, and Kramer lay stretched out in it, most of the flakes of rust had sunk to the bottom out of sight, but one managed to become washed up on to his chest where he mistook it at first for a small scab he hadn't known about. He gave it a dab with his finger, studied it, and flicked it at the wall.

Then another idea struck him, so forcibly that when he sat up he created a small tidal wave and sank the soap-dish. 'Where's that bloody nozzle?' he said, feeling the floor at the side of the bath for the rinsing device. 'What if we put a whole load of shampoo in there, so it's still coming out when the water's hot?' He unscrewed the nozzle, squeezed the remainder of his shampoo into it, and emptied the bath so that he could complete the experiment. It was only a partial success. The shampoo continued to be released through the nozzle for a good minute or more, but the mixture it made with the water then covered the bottom of the bath with a pretty carpet of bubbles that didn't prove very slippery at all. Moreover, unless one were very shortsighted, bubbles such as these would be spotted instantly, exciting caution and bewilderment.

'Will you be in there much longer, Mr Kramer?' his landlord called out anxiously, with a rap on the bathroom door. 'The wife is on tenterhooks. We think we may have found the answer.'

'Two minutes at the most,' Kramer reassured him, grabbing up a towel.

After all, for years and years now, they had been the ones using this bathroom as a laboratory, which really gave them first rights to it. They'd even had extra shelves fitted to hold the vast selection of aperients, laxatives and purgatives with which they experimented endlessly in various permutations to little or no effect, spending hours on their test-bench in the corner. 'I've been thinking,' Kramer had once remarked to the Widow Fourie, 'if they could only get together with a group of like-minded people in California or somewhere like that, they could set up the Bowel Movement."

Back in his room he finished drying himself and then took a clean shirt, socks and underwear from one of three cardboard boxes beneath his divan. Another of the boxes held his tax forms, car insurance policy and other personal documents, while the third was used for odd items of shopping, like spare jars of instant coffee. He had left his suit neatly arranged on the one chair he allowed in the otherwise furnitureless room, and his shoes, which had been cleaned by the house boy, he fetched from outside his door. In no time, he was dressed, had dragged a comb through his hair, and was on his way, shaving himself with a battery-powered razor.

Perhaps his experiment with the shampoo in the nozzle hadn't worked out too well, but nonetheless he felt pretty sure he'd come close to an answer there. Close enough, anyway, to make his first stop the home of Willem Martinus Zuidmeyer.

Modern pipe-cleaners, like certain CID lieutenants he could name, simply did not have the *spine* to them they'd had in his younger days, reflected Colonel Muller, as he struggled to clear an obstruction in his new briar.

'But, Colonel, I could hardly go on searching personally all night,' Jones was whining. 'I'd got the warrant issued, I'd put out the alert, plus a detailed description. What more should I have done? It's not my fault – or even Gagonk's – that nobody has yet reported a sighting.'

'You should have stayed out all night, like you say – Tromp would've done.'

'Huh! Do you know where he was last night? Round at the Albert bar—'

'Jones, that is none of your concern. I thought I'd made it very clear to you that I needed something new to give the press today, and that *I needed it very badly,* for reasons that

152

don't concern you, either. Now, if you'd arrested this postman, and he'd been able—'

'Why not let slip to the papers about the sword, Colonel?'

The pipe-cleaner jammed fast and buckled. 'God in Heaven, my patience is almost at an end, Jones. . .'

'The idea of a sword would make a real sensation, though, sir!'

'Exactly, you damned fool! It would also leave us looking bloody stupid. Or have you forgotten that all we have of this sword is the very tip? What if the thing turns out to be just a long dagger? What if—?'

'I can't really see that we'd do ourselves any harm by just—'

'You can't? Headlines *this* high, saying: "South African Police fail to find murder weapon"? Or "South African Police *think* sword killed writer"? Is that the kind of publicity we in the SAP want? As the Brigadier says, here is a God-sent opportunity – and you know he's a very religious man, so he really means that – to show the world we are not the incompetent fools, who only know how to kill kaffirs, that we're usually portrayed as overseas. On the contrary, this is our chance to conduct a very professional and impressive investigation in full view of the media, come up with the right culprit, give him a fair trial, and then break the bastard's neck on the gallows. Understand, now?'

Jones reddened, creating an unpleasant effect akin to watching a corpse regain its colour during embalming. 'Er, ja, Colonel, I'm sorry. It's just I . . .'

'Of course, if you'd like to come up with the murder weapon instead today,' added Colonel Muller jocularly, having suddenly managed to dislodge the obstruction in his pipe's mouthpiece, 'I'd be prepared to forget my displeasure.'

'Sir? But I thought Jaap's blokes had searched Woodhollow and the surrounding area from top to bottom?'

Colonel Muller sighed and threw the used pipe-cleaner into his waste-bin. 'A jest, Jones, just a jest. . . Call me a sentimental old fool, but I'd hoped for a smile then. Has any of the rest of this little discussion of ours actually got through? You know what to do now?'

153

'I'll not stop till I've caught this coolie, sir!'

'Thank you, Jones,' said Colonel Muller.

Zuidmeyer was sitting on his garage floor, staring dully at a pile of *Popular Mechanics*. It took him two or three seconds to register that Kramer had just wished him a good morning, and about as long again for him to turn and glance up. His face was haggard, his small bristly moustache now almost facetious, and his eyes hadn't lost their haunted look – if anything, they'd been visited by fresh spectres.

'My son's gone,' he said.

'How do you mean, sir?'

'Gone. I went out to buy some cigarettes last night, and when I came back the boy had gone.'

'Did he take any stuff with him? Clothing, money – that type of thing?'

'I'm not sure.'

'You've looked in his room?'

'Glanced in through the door, but. . .

'Then, you don't mind if I go in the house, sir?'

Zuidmeyer waved listlessly towards it. 'Help yourself, young man. The boy's room is the small one at the rear. Do you think they'll be bringing the dog back?'

'Dog, sir?'

'The one that ran away yesterday. It was only a pup.'

Kramer shrugged.

'That's why I'm waiting outside here, keeping an eye for them.'

You could be a very clever man, Willem Martinus Zuidmeyer, thought Kramer, as he took the path to the front door of the house, or a sicker soul than anybody has realised. Did he never use the dog's name, either, just as he never used his son's name? Had he always kept the world at arm's length from him?

There was mess in the house. That was the trouble with treating something as an accidental death: none of the usual precautions were taken to ensure the scene was secure against pollution. One or other of the Zuidmeyer males, perhaps both of them, had littered the living-areas with beer-cans and cigarette-ends, none of which rested in a companionable pair anywhere. The bathroom, however, which had a separate lavatory adjoining it, looked as though nobody had been into it since the body's removal, and the bristles of the tooth-brushes over the washbasin felt bone dry.

But, first, Kramer went to inspect the small bedroom at the back. It was tidy enough to be a cabin on a spaceship. Apart from a few selected items on the desk beneath the window – a globe of the world, a gadget from which five metal balls dangled on thin wires, a quartz alarm clock – everything else seemed to have been tucked away, out of sight, in sleek storage units arranged against its walls. Even the bed, which was more of a bunk really, formed part of one of these units, and had a panel of buttons beside it that apparently worked everything from the lights to a hidden music-centre some-where. Drawer after drawer slipped soundlessly out to reveal its tidy contents; none of those containing clothing showed any sign of having been rummaged through in a hurry, neither was it obvious that much, if anything, could be missing. Reaching up to the last of the cupboard space, and sliding back the matt-textured pale-blue doors, Kramer found, as he'd half-expected, row upon row of science fiction novels, mostly in paperback. Interesting, the contrast be-tween the father and his son, who appeared to have opted out by escaping to other worlds altogether.

Then Kramer saw the message, scrawled with a blue felt-marker on the full-length mirror fixed to the back of the bedroom door.

TAKE A GOOD LOOK AT
YOURSELF, PA
(if the cops
want me I'm at
Marlene's)

With that little mystery solved, Kramer made sure that Zuidmeyer hadn't come back into the house, and then returned to the bathroom.

Woodhollow was deserted except for two Bantu constables,

posted to guard the property, when Zondi drove up to the front steps and got out. It was a dull, overcast morning, the sky heavy with rain clouds, and the flowers in the carefully tended garden had lost their vivid brightness.

'Come on,' he said to Naomi Stride's three servants, 'you get out of the car, too; there's nothing to be afraid of.'

'Hau, but the spirits are bad in this place!' wailed Betty Duboza, the maid, cowering in her corner of the Ford.

She had been working herself up to this, all the way from the vehicle-yard, and her husband, Ben Duboza, the cook, had been almost as tiresome. For a couple in their fifties, who affected sophisticated white manners and even spoke English with an almost white accent, it was surprising they felt no shame in behaving like a pair of raw peasants straight from the bush.

'I said "come on",' repeated Zondi. 'Your duty to your employer is not yet over. If you can help us find out who killed her, then—'

'I will come,' said Harry Kani, the stocky gardener, opening the front passenger-door. 'I am a Presbyterian, which protects me from ignorant superstitions.'

'And I, an Anglican!' retorted Ben Duboza.

'Good,' said Zondi, 'so you're coming also?'

The cook almost opened his door, then shook his head.

'Harry, what do you know of inside the house?' Zondi asked the gardener.

'I know only the kitchen, Detective – it is not my place to go in any other room. I know the kitchen, because it is from there I fetch my food.'

'But have you never peeped into other rooms from the outside? Eavesdropped on what is being said?'

'Who, me, Detective? Harry Kani is a most trustworthy and—'

'Listen, I was once a garden boy, and a house boy, too,' said Zondi, 'so don't pretend more than I can believe – is that understood?'

The gardener grinned and popped his knuckles.

After careful examination, it seemed beyond a doubt that the shower nozzle in the Zuidmeyer bathroom had not been tampered with. If any attempt had been made to unscrew it from the pipe delivering the mixture of hot and cold water, then this would have cracked the three or four coats of white enamel paint covering the join. But quite plainly this paint was intact – and had been for some very considerable time.

So how else could someone have filled the inside of the nozzle with, say, a viscous, slippery substance?

He could have injected it, using a hypodermic syringe, thought Kramer. But, again upon examination, this theory collapsed: all the holes in the nozzle were far too small to admit even the finest needle.

That 'getting warm' feeling stayed, though. Something *had* to have been introduced to the shower to make Mrs Zuidmeyer take such a tumble – unless, of course, freak accidents happened a lot more often than the laws of chance allowed for.

Getting down on his hands and knees, Kramer peered at the shallow porcelain base to the shower, and felt its surface with his fingertips. It was no more slippery than the bottom of the bath had been, back at the house where he rented a room. Then he felt along the edge of the porcelain base. Behind the plastic curtain on the far side, over to the right where one end of it hung anchored from a cleat in the rail above, his fingertips skidded slightly. He withdrew his hand and rubbed thumb against forefinger, sensing between them a very slippery substance indeed. It appeared colourless, but had a faint scent of pine.

Next, he took off his shoes and then stepped into the empty bath, hoping to be able to see behind this piece of curtain without having to touch it. But it was too close to the yellow-tiled outer wall, and he had to lift it slightly away. There, on the outer surface of the shower curtain, was a shiny streak that smelled and looked exactly the same. It occurred about a metre from the floor. There was a second streak of the stuff at about his chest level, but nothing higher than that.

'Oh ja, very clever . . .,' he muttered. 'Just how did it get there? In that narrow gap against the wall and window?'

He went up on tiptoe and took a look at the sill of the

157

window's fanlight, which was slightly ajar to keep the bathroom aired. There, on the sill, was another small drop of the stuff.

Had someone stood outside and squirted it through the gap? No, that would have meant it making a mark all the way down the outside of the shower curtain. On top of which, this method would hardly have ensured that sufficient amounts of the fluid reached the floor of the shower unit; for that, one would have to have something to duct it there directly.

In the next instant, Kramer saw exactly what must have happened. Someone had run a small-diameter plastic tube through the gap under the window, down the wall behind the shower curtain, and then into the porcelain base. He had waited until Mrs Zuidmeyer had stepped under the shower, and then he'd injected his slippery fluid through the tube. Once this fluid had done its work, he'd then withdrawn the tube, and on the way out it'd dripped twice on the shower curtain and once on the window-sill.

Rubbish! he thought. Mere fantasy.

But the idea stuck. It fitted all the observable facts. It made sense. It just had to be right.

Refinements then began occurring to him, such as the notion that a clear plastic tube had been used, making it even less likely to have been noticed. Now, where had he seen plastic tubing like that? Didn't garages sometimes use it for fuel-lines? Near the carburettor, so one could see whether petrol was being delivered?

His immediate reaction was to want to go straight round and take a look at what Zuidmeyer had in the way of spares in his workshop. He paused, however, and made himself assess the situation more carefully, before deciding to do two other things instead. First, using the corner of a piece of toilet paper, he soaked up a minute sample of the shiny substance from the shower curtain, and stowed it away for forensic examination. Second, he stole out of the back of the house, using the kitchen door, and inspected the area immediately beneath the bathroom window.

It was a flowerbed, about almost a metre wide, planted

with daisies. Being as wide as that meant that, if his theory were correct, then the person with the plastic tube would almost certainly have had to step on to the flowerbed at some stage in the process. But the surface of the flowerbed, made up largely of small dry clods of earth, appeared undisturbed.

Kramer crouched down and began lifting the top layer of clods away. He did not discover a layer beneath them that had been trodden on and then covered again, but he did find a curious damp patch on one of the clods he set aside. A patch that smelled faintly of pine.

Why, of course, he thought, the tube must have been placed in position from *inside* the bathroom, leaving one end dangling within easy reach of the edge of the lawn outside; hence no footprints on the flowerbed.

Then he twisted round and checked to see how exposed a position this was. The property backed on to a large timber-yard, which had a corrugated-iron fence higher than a man. To the left, the kitchen extension blocked the view of those neighbours. To the right, no neighbours could see through, either, because of a trelliswork screen densely covered in a granadilla vine. Or, in short, someone squatting there would be invisible from all directions, including the bathroom, which was fitted with a rather high, frosted-glass window.

To Gagonk Mbopa's extreme annoyance, the second chapter of *The Last Magnolia* contained no further mention of the two adulterers who'd so enlivened Chapter One, but was taken up instead by an endless description of a half-witted Zulu whose ludicrous ambition it was to become a Member of Parliament. Not only did this idiot keep brooding over his job as a garden boy, his Bachelor of Arts degree, and the dead flowers he had to sweep up from under a magnolia tree, but he also seemed to have absolutely no sex life at all, apart from a strange admiration for female prime ministers.

So he decided against starting Chapter Three, flung *The Last Magnolia* into this desk drawer, and took himself out into the courtyard. The prisoner on loan from the jail was busy digging a hole for the new rose-bush, which lay wrapped in a huge sheet of brown paper beside it. Mbopa was just about to go over and check on his progress when the telephone rang, making him hurry back into the Bantu detective sergeants' office.

'Any sightings yet?' asked Jones.

'No, Lieutenant, everything's dead quiet. Just one call from the Municipal Police, asking if we'd made the arrest last night in case they wasted their time today keeping a watch for—'

'All right, all right, I've got the picture! I'm still here at the bus station, double-checking, but I'll be back to pick you up in about twenty minutes for another look around Gladstoneville. By then the duty officer will have got someone organised to take over the phone again from you—OK?'

'OK, Lieutenant.'

Tims Shabalala shambled in, flicking with his short rhino-hide whip at the almost bare buttocks of two terrified urchins who were handcuffed together and carrying several bundles.

'Look,' said Mbopa in Afrikaans, so he wouldn't be understood by them, 'I don't want a lot of screaming and wailing going on in here today, Shabalala – not while I have important things to hear on the telephone.'

'So you hope, Gagonk! Let me tell you now, that coolie is far, far away, and the Colonel will be transferring you and the jackal to fight SWAPO in Namibia tomorrow!'

'Huh! That will be Zondi and Spokes! Just you wait, me and Jones—'

Shabalala laughed rudely, and said in Zulu to his prisoners: 'Come on, you whore's whelps! Empty out those bundles so I can see properly what you've got.' Then switching back to Afrikaans, he added: 'Relax, Great Elephant, these two have already confessed as I caught them red-handed. And, if I wanted to know more, just one crust of bread would make them say anything; they are so hungry their breath gives a terrible stink. Can you smell it?'

The phone rang and Mbopa snatched it up.

'Gagonk,' said Colonel Muller, 'why are there no roses on that new rose-bush you bought me?'

160

'Colonel?'

'I've just taken a look from the balcony, and no roses can I see.'

'But that is right, Colonel. The boss by the garden shop tells me that you must plant it first and wait. They are never sold with flowers already growing, the boss says.'

'Rubbish, man! That was the whole idea of a new rose-bush, so I could have something nice to start my day with. Where did you buy the thing?'

Mbopa found the receipt, which he was keeping to use when making that sly bastard Zondi pay his half-share, and read out the firm's name, address and telephone number.

'Someone is about to get a call from me,' said Colonel Muller in a voice that made Mbopa want to duck. 'God in Heaven, anyone would think I hadn't enough on my plate today!' And he slammed his receiver down.

'Hay-bah-bor...' said Mbopa, very relieved that was over.

'Ramjut Pillay?' said Shabalala.

'No, it wasn't about that; it was the Colonel. He—'

'Isn't Ramjut Pillay the name of your coolie postman?' interrupted Shabalala, hefting a tattered paperback in one hand.

'Why? What's this about?'

'It's the name written inside this book,' said Shabalala, 'above an address in Gladstoneville.'

The two urchins shrank back as Mbopa lunged across the room and made a grab. 'Where did you get this from?' he shouted.

'It was in this big bag with a plastic raincoat,' said Shabalala, grinning.

'That we not steal!' piped up one of the urchins, who looked about nine and the older of the pair. 'True's God that we find just lying – no person was near it.'

Shabalala brought his whip down across the shoulders of the other urchin, who shrieked, burst into tears, and sobbed: 'True's God, true's God! We never steal the big bag! It was left just lying!'

'Lend me the whip,' demanded Mbopa. 'Come on, quick,

Shabalala!'

'There is no need; I believe them – the other one has wet himself now. Why not ask where the bag was found, Murder Squad detective, or must a humble Housebreaking sergeant do all your work for you?'

Mbopa scowled but managed to restrain himself and put the question.

'L-l-last night . . .' said one urchin.

'After buses st-stop,' his companion blurted out.

'I asked *where*, not when, you street rats! Answer, or I'll—'

'By station!'

'Park by station!'

'Railway Street?'

They nodded.

12

'So THERE YOU ARE, you bastard,' grunted Kramer, finally running Piet Baksteen to ground in the State mortuary. 'This is the third place I've had to look.'

'Third time lucky!' said Baksteen, who stood alone in Van Rensburg's small office with the smell of brandy on his breath.

Kramer grinned. Trust Baksteen to have discovered the secret of the locked desk drawer, the key to which Van Rensburg wore around his neck on a greasy length of string. Trust Van Rensburg, come to that, not to have realised that the lock on that drawer was easier to pick than a camel's nose.

'So what's brought you down here, Baksteen, besides the free booze?'

'The Mad Doctor – another of his strange enthusiasms.'

'Strydom? Ach, not more of those snails again?'

'To be fair, properly prepared, the extract can help distinguish between white blood and black blood, but he—'

'Should leave that kind of thing to the experts?'

Being something of an expert himself in the field of biochemical analysis, Baksteen shrugged kindly, as people so often did when Christiaan Strydom, MD, was the topic of conversation. 'Actually, this time the idea's his own and it might even prove a help to us in the lab. Without getting too technical, and trying not to bore you, the hypothesis is—'

'Hold it, Piet, you're over my head already,' said Kramer, producing the cigarette-packet in which he'd placed his forensic samples from 146 Acacia Drive. 'And, anyway, I'd be more interested in what you can find out for me about this stuff.'

'Er, can we...?' Baksteen gave his little black beard a tug, as he glanced uneasily out of the windows surrounding Van Rensburg's office. 'I'd rather move to somewhere else in case—'

'Oh, so Van is around? I thought he must be away on a removal.'

'No, he's out at the back, accusing Nxumalo of keeping meat in the fridge,' said Baksteen, making for the post-mortem room.

Kramer followed his lanky figure through, and then produced the piece of toilet paper on which gleamed, despite the paper's absorbent qualities, some of the substance he'd found on the shower curtain.

'What's that? Jesus, it can't be semen!'

'Well, that's a relief,' said Kramer. 'But don't you buggers in the lab ever think of anything except—?'

Baksteen had taken the sample from him and was sniffing it. 'No good. Too great a mixture of other smells in here,' he said. 'I think we'd best go outside ourselves.'

They were just in time to see Van Rensburg turn his back on a very solemn-looking Bantu constable who broke into a broad grin a second later.

'That bloody Nxumalo,' complained the mortuary sergeant, coming stumping up, 'that's the second time in two weeks I've found goat hairs on a fridge tray.'

'Sure it *is* goat hairs?' asked Baksteen.

'As sure as a man can be, Mr Baksteen, but naturally he denies it.'

163

'Then, let me have some, and I'll get it analysed.'

'You will? You'll do that for me?'

'Anything to help a colleague, Sergeant.'

Van Rensburg beamed, and then said, very pointedly, with a sideways look at Kramer: 'You, Mr Baksteen, sir, are what I call a real white man, a *proper gentleman.*'

'Think nothing of it, hey? Now, let's take another sniff at this and see if the smell can give us our first clue.'

'Can I join in, too, Mr Baksteen?' smarmed Van Rensburg. 'I've always been really good at smells.'

'Ja, I'd noticed,' said Kramer.

'I've got it in one, Mr Baksteen! That's DH–136, sir.'

'DH–136, Van? All I can pick up is a pine scent.'

'Ja, but a DH–136 pine scent,' insisted Van Rensburg. 'Sort of like a detergent only it's also a disinfectant, cleans like magic. You must have noticed it in the p.m. room.'

Baksteen looked at Kramer and then back at Van Rensburg. 'Well, thanks for the suggestion, not that there aren't dozens of detergents on the market, all smelling of pine. On top of which, it may not even be a—'

'It's not just the pine, Mr Baksteen – ach, I can't explain. I tell you what, though, let me show you. . .' And off he went into the mortuary, returning only moments later, huffing and puffing, with a very large white plastic container. 'OK, now take a sniff of this stuff as well, and you'll see it's identical.'

'I'm off,' said Kramer, who simply hadn't the patience. 'I'll be phoning the lab at four for a result, hey?'

'But, Tromp, with all the possibilities there are, that's asking for a—'

'Then stop arsing about with Balls-ache the Bloodhound and get on with it, man.'

Somewhere, Zondi felt sure, he had a scrap of paper that the Lieutenant had given him, bearing a telephone number at which Theo Kennedy could be contacted. He wished he'd taken the trouble to glance at it, imprinting it on his memory, because he wanted Naomi Stride's servants off his hands and quickly. This whole stupid exercise of bringing them out to Woodhollow had proved, as he'd half-expected, a complete waste of time, and there were other things he could be doing. Like, for instance, finding out exactly what all the fuss was about Ramjut Pillay, the Indian postman, of which he'd heard rumours while picking up his police car this morning. He was certain his judgement of the man could not have been so wide of the mark that he'd overlooked a devious criminal brain beneath that childishly innocent exterior.

'Ah!' said Zondi, and took off his hat.

The scrap of paper was tucked behind the leather band inside it, and within seconds he had dialled the number and could hear the ringing tone.

'Hello, Vicki Stilgoe, here.'

'Good morning, madam, it is Detective Sergeant Zondi speaking, Murder and Robbery Squad. I have a message I must give to Boss Kennedy.'

'Oh, yes?'

'Madam can kindly pass on the message?'

'Madam can do better than that. . .' There was the clunk of the receiver being dropped on to a hard surface, and then, faintly: 'Theo, my sweet? It's the police; some boy with something to say to you. Come on, Mandy, off Uncle Theo's lap!'

'Hello, can I help you?'

Zondi again identified himself, and then explained that the dead woman's servants had been brought back to Woodhollow.

'The problem is, sir, now we have finished with them, they ask what they must do. Is the boss's wish that they stay working for him, or are their jobs at Woodhollow finished? They are very worried, sir, and—'

'Oh God, poor old Betty and Ben! And I suppose Harry the gardener is there, too?'

'Yes, sir.'

'Look, I'd best come over right away and see what I can do to put their minds at rest. I'd not given any of this a moment's thought, to be honest! See you in two ticks, Sergeant.'

An unusual man, thought Zondi, as he replaced the receiver in Naomi Stride's studio, who talked to you just as

165

though you were another human being. Perhaps the Lieutenant's own judgement hadn't been at fault, either, when he'd dismissed the idea of his being a suspect.

'Detective?' said Harry Kani, appearing at the window.

'You have found something?'

'I have *thought* something, Detective. Will you allow me to show you?'

'Right,' said Jones, drawing up beside the Railway Street public park and clipping the kerb, 'which bench did they say they'd found Pillay's bag under?'

'This one by the drinking-tap, Lieutenant,' replied Mbopa, pointing to it proudly. 'Marked "Non-whites Only".'

'I can read, hey? And I don't know why you keep on sounding so bloody pleased with yourself; it's not as if you did anything special by asking Shabalala if you could look through the stuff those piccanins brought in with them. I had already organised a check on both lost and stolen property – so this bag would have turned up, whatever happened.'

Mbopa frowned, quite sure there was a flaw in that argument somewhere. 'Ermph,' he muttered.

'So the bag', said Jones, 'must have been deposited here some time between Pillay leaving home in Gladstoneville and eleven o'clock, when the buses stop running. The first question we ask ourselves is, why?'

'Because he dropped it, Lieutenant?' suggested Mbopa.

'Quiet while I'm thinking. . .'

Mbopa noticed a stealthy movement, over by the old Victorian bandstand in the middle of the small, triangular park with its threadbare lawn. Little by little, like a blood-red sun rising above the stage of the bandstand, the face of a huge white drunk appeared, and peered at the police car warily.

'I can't see him just dropping the bag and not noticing,' murmured Jones. 'Therefore it stands to reason he must've dumped it, wanting to get rid of two things that would help identify him: the book and the raincoat.'

The drunk was scratching the side of his nose with a hand bandaged in a filthy handkerchief.

'Don't just sit there!' snapped Jones, jabbing Mbopa in the

ribs with his elbow. 'Take some interest, for Christ's sake! Tell me, for example, how anyone could be stupid enough to dump incriminating property in full view of everybody.'

'Maybe, sir,' said Mbopa, nodding towards a litter-bin just behind the bench, 'Pillay hid his bag in there, hoping the street cleaners would throw it away, but a drunk went looking into it, didn't like the contents, and just left it lying under where he'd been sitting.'

'Possibly,' said Jones. 'Next question, why did he choose this park to dump his stuff in?'

'Maybe, sir,' said Mbopa, 'he did not want to be found with incriminating matter on a train. At the last minute, his idea was to leave it behind in Trekkersburg.'

'A train? But the Railway Police have already checked their Occurrence Book for yesterday, and they swear that nobody answering Pillay's description—'

'With respect, Lieutenant, the Occurrence Book tells you only of arrests and other police matters. Why, if he had the money to travel, would they ever notice one coolie among so many?'

'But the ticket-seller for non-whites doesn't remember his description, either, and I'm talking about the bloke who was on duty two-to-ten yesterday.'

'Well, then...' Mbopa shrugged. 'It is all a big mystery, Lieutenant.'

Jones opened his car door. 'I'm going to go and see that Occurrence Book for myself. You stroll around the park, talk to people, try to find out whether anyone here saw Pillay yesterday.'

Mbopa followed him out reluctantly. Strolling around parks, talking to people, had never been something he was terribly good at; most people took one look at his approaching figure and left before he could get a word out. In a less namby-pamby world, a couple of rounds from his Walther PPK would easily overcome this problem of course, but such were the crosses a real man learned to bear.

'Hey, you!' boomed Mbopa, pointing a finger at an old Coloured lurching towards a bench beside the grandstand. 'I want to chat – come here.'

167

The white drunk dived out of sight, which was interesting, and the old Coloured, having made a faltering turn to see who had called out to him, took off as sprightly as a springbok, leaping three black drunks in a row.

'Bastard,' grunted Mbopa.

Up came the white drunk's head again, to show only the bloodshot eyes. There is something worrying that idiot, thought Mbopa, and wished he could go round, grab him by the scruff of the neck, and find out what it was.

'Lieutenant, sir,' he said when Jones returned, grimfaced from the station, 'maybe you should interview the white man hiding over there. He is acting in a manner both strange and suspicious.'

'Immaterial!'

'Sir?'

'Haven't you worked out yet why there is no trace of him at the station?' snapped Jones, heading for the car.

'Pillay had changed his name, boss?'

'Huh! Do you think that'd be enough to fool me? No, it was because, thick head, *Pillay was never at the station yesterday*. Leaving his bag here was simply a trick to make us think he'd gone somewhere by train, while all the time he's probably still in Trekkersburg, laughing at us behind our backs!'

It hadn't been a bad thought on the part of Harry Kani, the late Naomi Stride's gardener, conceded Zondi. So far, all the emphasis had seemed to be on the murderer having used Jan Smuts Close to reach the property, whereas, as Kani pointed out, the killer could have used the servants' path up through the wooded slope from a main road on the far side.

However, when all was said and done, now that Zondi had explored the path to the fence at the foot of the slope and had found nothing, the net gain was just one more hypothesis. To be sure, motorists could be asked in the press whether they'd seen a car left parked there on the night in question but, in terms of immediate significance, the score for the morning was still zero.

Slowly, Zondi made his way back up the path to the back

lawn of Woodhollow, pausing only once to double-check on a mark that may have been made by a large footprint. Then he reached the top and was pleased to see Theo Kennedy at the side of the pool with Kani and the two Dubozas, both of whom were looking very much more cheerful.

'Sergeant Zondi?' asked Kennedy, extending a hand as he walked up.

Zondi shook the hand in white fashion, and said: 'Thank you, sir, for coming over. Would it be convenient for me to leave them with you and—?'

'Hau, hau, hau!'

'What is it, Harry?' asked Kennedy.

'All these bits of rubbish people have thrown in!' protested Kani. 'Who could have done this thing?'

No doubt, thought Zondi, the cigarette-packets, sweet-wrappers and peanut-bags had been tossed into the pool by uniformed onlookers before the body's removal on Tuesday.

'It's all right, Kani, I can have them—'

'But the madam is very strict about such matters for fear they will cause a blockage in the filter! See down there?' And he pointed to a small grating in a corner of the deep end of the swimming-pool, a couple of metres below where they were standing. 'There is rubbish all over. Also, what is that object?'

'Object?' echoed Zondi, crouching in an attempt to take a better look.

'It glitters orange,' said Kani, 'like a jewel.'

'Yes, I can see it now, too,' agreed Kennedy, squatting by Zondi's side.

'Stuck between the second and third bars of the grating. Very peculiar, isn't it? Why hasn't it been spotted before?'

'Could it be, sir,' suggested Zondi, 'because this is the first dull day since the investigation began, and there is not a bright dazzle coming off the water?'

'You're right. Shouldn't we try to find out what it is?'

'Hau, I cannot swim, little master!' said Kani. 'Never have I been in this water.'

Kennedy looked at Zondi, who shrugged and admitted: 'My swimming has been only in a shallow river as a child, sir.

169

I know how to stay on top, but not how to dive beneath!'

'But there's no other way we're going to get at it, is there?' said Kennedy, standing up. 'I tell you what, I've an old costume in the house somewhere: so, if the police won't have any objection, I'll go in and put it on.'

It took Zondi a second or two to realise he was actually being deferred to, then he nodded gratefully and Kennedy ran off.

'Who are these?' whispered Betty Dobuza, inclining her head slightly to the left.

Zondi glanced that way, and saw a beautiful white child, with small dents in her cheeks, coming across the lawn towards them followed by a shy-looking woman in very plain clothes and a headscarf. 'Some new friends of your little master's,' he deduced. 'Neighbours from where he lives. But tell me, Betty Duboza, is that frown on your face the same frown that your madam would always give if Boss Kennedy brought strangers to her house?'

And he knew he was right, because Ben Duboza grinned from ear to ear.

Faced with an indefinite delay on the Zuidmeyer front, while Baksteen analysed the samples taken from the shower curtain, Kramer decided to stop driving about aimlessly and pay a call instead on the offices of Afro Arts. He was curious to know exactly what had led to Theo Kennedy's broken romance of a month ago, and secretaries, like servants, were often as good as a fifth column when it came to the activities of their lords and masters.

Afro Arts was the middle shop in a row of small businesses in an arcade off Trekkersburg's main street. On one side was a stamp dealer's, and on the other Camera Mart displayed shelf after shelf of secondhand photographic equipment. Afro Arts's own window was black, save for an oval gap in the middle through which could be seen a clay head, lit by a small spotlight. He pushed open the door, which announced *Retail and Wholesale* in gold lettering, and stepped into a pleasing gloom. Here and there, more small spotlights picked out select examples of pottery, clay heads, reed basketry, woodcarvings and Zulu beadwork, leaving the rest of the showroom a dim jumble of countless other goods, like some sort of treasure cave.

'If you're another reporter. . .'

As his eyes adjusted to the low light, Kramer saw a young brunette standing behind a cash register at the rear of the shop, her arms folded across two enormous breasts. It was a shame the rest of her was equally enormous.

'Reporters are what I have for breakfast, lady. Tromp Kramer, Trekkersburg CID.'

'Thank goodness for that!' She smiled, showing perfect teeth, and switched politely to fluent Afrikaans. 'Ja, Theo was telling me about you – he said you'd been very kind to him, poor soul. But he's not coming in this morning after all, you know.'

'He's not?'

'He rang me not long ago to say he's having to go over to his mother's house to see about the servants. Quite frankly, I'm amazed at how well he's managing – he's *such* a sensitive man – but I suppose he could still be in shock. My grandma was like that, went right through Gramp's funeral, never used her lace hanky once, and then, three weeks later, in the middle of *South Africa Today* on the television, she bursts into tears and howls and howls!'

'Hell, hey?' said Kramer, taking out his Lucky Strikes. 'You don't mind if I—?'

'No, please do! I can't agree with all the fuss there is these days about smoking, you know; I personally find it so *manly*. But where was I?'

'Telling me about your grandma, Miss – er?'

'Winny, Winny Barnes – but weren't you quick to notice I wasn't wearing a ring! I suppose that's what being a detective is, training yourself to—'

'Ach, I'm sure I'm not the first bloke to check to see if the lady's still available, hey? But you were saying about your grandma?'

'Look, I'd better get you an ashtray – oh, and while I'm about it, how about a coffee?'

'Winny, I'm dying for one, but only if it's not too much—'

'Don't be silly!' she said with a girlish laugh, and disappeared sideways through a bead curtain into the back, keeping her eyes on him.

Kramer watched her go, shook his head and murmured: 'Tromp, there are times when you should feel bloody ashamed of yourself, old son.'

But he didn't allow this to influence him unduly when she returned with the coffee, the ashtray and an eau-de-cologne respray job, saying: 'I should've asked whether you liked milk. Theo does, and so I just automatically. . .'

'With milk is exactly right, Winny. No, no sugar, ta.'

'You're sweet enough as it is?'

'That's what my old ma always tells me – but, then, she's prejudiced.'

'Oh, I don't know. . .'

Kramer smiled at her and she giggled, crossing her legs with a loud rasping of nylon tights. 'What about Theo,' he asked, 'is he a sugar man?'

'Two lumps; one in tea.'

'Got it all pat, haven't you? How long is it you've worked for him?'

'Would you believe it, it's only been about a month, although I've known Theo for longer than that, of course, because he used to come into my dad's shop – he's Camera Mart – for a chat when trade was quiet, and that's how we two met, you know. Liz was still his assistant then; they sort of set Afro Arts up together, and I wasn't the only one who thought it would go on to them getting married and everything, although she was a bit highly strung, being so artistic, and sometimes there were terrible rows me and my dad could hear right through the wall. But they weren't *serious* rows, if you know what I mean, not those ones before about six weeks ago. It was things like Theo painting his Land-Rover to look like a zebra and Liz having a tantrum, saying it clashed with the "image" she'd tried to create for him in the way the shop was arranged, the lights and that. In fact, as he only painted the Land-Rover in August, we thought it was the same row they were having on the morning she first went storming out, right past our window.

172

Theo came round to see my dad, very upset, and they talked for ages, after which my dad caught Liz next time she went by and had her in. But she'd got into such a state by then, what with these phone calls still going on, that she wouldn't listen or give Theo a proper chance. She said she just didn't *trust* him any more, and that was that. I suppose there were two more big rows, she announced that she was going to the Cape to do design there and, next thing, Theo came round and asked me if I'd like to help him. He knew my dad didn't really have much for me to do, and I'm hopeless with anything mechanical like cameras, and so, well, here I am. Mind you, I'm also his sort of secretary, so what with keeping the accounts, seeing to the Customs forms and—'

'My God, no wonder he speaks of you so highly!' said Kramer, putting down his coffee-cup. 'But what sort of phone calls were these?'

'She never says who it is, but I always know straight away when the—'

'You mean you've had them, too?'

Winny Barnes nodded, redoubling her chins. 'There's just this very sexy woman's voice that says "Is Theo there. . .?" '

'And?'

'Well, there isn't an "and", really. Theo talked to her once, that was in the beginning, but since then he slams the phone down or tells whoever else answers it to do the same. That first time, he says, she went on and on saying how much she loved him, although he'd never heard her voice in his life before. He's got a private theory it's somebody's secretary being put up to it by her boss, probably an old schoolfriend of his or a business rival – but Liz has to start imagining things. She asked my dad how she could be sure Theo wasn't chatting to the woman while she wasn't in the shop, and every time he went away on a trip there was Liz, telephoning the hotel and embarrassing him by asking the management if he'd booked a double room. It finally got to the stage that she was questioning the reason for every trip he made, and then she just walked out on him, poor pet.'

'About a month ago?'

'That's right. I could never understand Liz myself, being so quick to think the worst. Granted, nobody could call her pretty, and she *was* very flat-chested, with a funny nose, but that didn't matter to Theo, you could see he was devoted – you know, like John Lennon and Yoko? No? Well, never mind, all I'm saying is that she was very silly in my opinion, and I told her so. "Don't look a gift horse, Liz Geldenhuys," I said, and then she started crying and saying she'd always known she could never keep him for long, being so plain and coming from such a different background – her dad's just a bulldozer driver, and *terribly* crude. Oh, yes, I learned that to my cost when he tried coming in here afterwards to give poor Theo a good thrashing, you know! And she went on about how Theo's mother had treated them, the one and only time she was invited to Woodhollow, and had argued about what they were doing here in the shop and, goodness me, she did go on and on! In fact, I started to think she *wanted* to cause a break-up, just because she couldn't bear the strain of waiting for it to happen anyway. Do you know what I mean?'

'Ja, I think you've probably got it in a nutshell,' agreed Kramer, stubbing out his Lucky. 'By the way, Winny, when was the last time this mystery lady tried ringing Theo?'

'Oh, somewhere towards the end of last week – perhaps Thursday.'

'And there've been no more calls since?'

'I should hope not! I'm sure that whoever it is realises how cruel that'd be after what's happened!'

'A joke's a joke, you mean? What do you remember about the calls you yourself have answered? Any noises in the background? People typing? Traffic?'

Winny Barnes sucked her thumb and thought. 'Once or twice,' she said, 'I *think* I heard music.'

'What music?'

'The tune? Oh, it was too quick for that.'

'No, was it pop or what?'

'Classical.'

'Opera? Four violins and a drum?'

'A big orchestra, like ballet or on the radio on Sundays'

'So your ears aren't just a pretty shape,' said Kramer, rising and backing off with a wink. 'Bye for now, Winny. . .'

'Tromp! – er, do you want me to contact you if she rings again?'

'You might as well, hey?'

'Oh, and sorry if I talked too much. I'm always doing that and spoiling things.'

'I loved it, honest!'

'You did?' she said wonderingly, and looked as though, God forgive him, her happiness was complete.

Little Amanda shrieked with delight as Theo Kennedy surfaced once again, coming up with a huge splash from the bottom of the swimming-pool and gasping for air.

'Isn't Uncle T'eo *funny*, Mummy?' she said, jumping up and down. 'Just like Danny and Delilah! Go on, Uncle T'eo, do that again!'

'It looks – as though – I'll have to,' said Kennedy, treading water. 'Damn thing won't – budge.'

'Danny 'n' Delilah! Danny 'n' Delilah!'

'You know who they are, don't you, Sergeant Zondi?' said Amanda's mother, turning to him. 'The star dolphins down at Durban aquarium. Ooops, darling! You nearly fell in then. Take nice Sergeant Zondi's hand as well, then you'll be much safer when we're both holding on to you.'

With his children almost grown-up now, it'd been a long time since Zondi had last had such a small hand in his own, and it felt good there. He returned Mrs Stilgoe's smile and, to his astonishment, saw something in her eyes that gave him a tingle of excitement.

'Harry,' said Kennedy in Zulu, still treading water, 'now I've got my breath back, what are the chances of my pulling that grating away? Is it detachable? What precisely is the design of the thing?'

'It is a deep hole, about a leg's length, with an outlet in one side of it that goes to the filter and the pump, little master. The grating fits on top of it in such a way that, if you pull it first to the left, then you can easily lift it to get underneath.'

'Then I'll give that a try, because grabbing at that jewel thing isn't getting us anywhere.'

'It still looks like a jewel, sir?' asked Zondi in English.

'Very much so.'

'Couldn't it be something of your mother's?' suggested Mrs Stilgoe.

'Oh, no, she was never into jewels, gems, or anything like that – would have thought it *very* immoral.'

'But don't people sometimes buy diamonds and things when they're going overseas? You know, to get round the currency restrictions by—'

'Even worse!' said Kennedy with a laugh and then a sad smile. 'You very obviously never knew her, Vicki! Mum would have a fit at the very thought of any form of smuggling. Actually, the thing looks almost too big to be real, even allowing for how the water magnifies, and it could just be glass, a huge bead with facets cut on it or something. Anyway, here goes again!'

As Kennedy dived, Amanda laughed and jumped up and down, bringing Zondi's attention back to her mother. But Mrs Stilgoe had her eyes on the swimmer, and so he looked instead at the child, wondering whether his head wasn't being turned slightly by being in the company of whites so extraordinarily relaxed and friendly in their behaviour. In fact, on reflection, never once had he – not even as a domestic servant – been trusted to hold the hand of a small white female before, although it'd been quite different when it had to come to the brothers.

'Mummy, sure this boy a good boy?' said Amanda doubtfully. 'He's doing a stare at me.'

'Sergeant Zondi's *not* a boy, Amanda! Wherever did you—? Good heavens, Excalibur!'

And Zondi looked up just in time to see an arm coming up out of the water with a sword in its hand.

13

KRAMER sat alone in his car beside the public telephone box for almost ten minutes before finally getting out to dial the number Control had supplied him with. He wished there'd been a telephone directory in the box so that he could have looked up the number for himself. It made him uncomfortable to think those six digits would now have been written down somewhere, a permanent record of one of the nastiest suspicions he'd ever had.

So nasty, in fact, that common decency alone should have instantly banished it from his mind.

He dialled.

After a couple of rings, the other receiver was lifted. 'Hello . . .?'

'Hello to you.'

'Tromp?'

'The very same.'

'What happened to last night?'

'Up to my ears.'

'Pardon? If you'll hold on a tick, I'll get the kids to turn that down. We're right in the middle of—'

'I only wanted to say I could be around a bit later, OK?'

'Can't wait, *mon cheri*. . .'

He hung up, aroused. He couldn't help it. Face to face, all else had been upstaged by those bewitching green eyes and her firm smoothness, but on the telephone, disembodied ballet teacher Tess Muldoon had proved to have one of the sexiest voices he'd ever heard.

'Control to Lieutenant Kramer. . .'

And in the background, music, orchestral.

'Control to Lieut' Kramer. . .'

'Ach, bugger off!' he protested, having returned to his car for a long, uninterrupted think. 'Tell the Colonel to—'

'Control to Kramer, urgent message ex Bantu DS Zondi.'

He reached for his hand mike and pressed the 'send' button: 'Ja, Kramer here . . . Let's hear it. Over.'

'Message reads, "Murder weapon found, Woodhollow".'

Gagonk Mbopa just had time to close his eyes and make a grab for the dashboard. Less than a second later, the car left the road, mounted the pavement and collided with a fire hydrant, slewing round again into the path of an oncoming vehicle. There was a loud blast from a horn, a shriek of brakes, and another collision, battering the car back against the hydrant. A huge jet of water shot into the air.

'My God,' said Jones, his hands on the steering-wheel, his eyes staring ahead of him, 'whoever would believe it?'

Mbopa, kneeling wedged between the front seats and the dashboard, had a panicky moment when he thought he'd not be able to breathe.

'Those two bastards've gone and done it again to us!' said Jones. 'Tricked the Colonel into sending us on a wild goose chase after some crazy coolie, while they go behind our backs and...'

'You maniac!' Mbopa heard someone shouting. 'You total bloody idiot! Have you seen what you've done to my breakdown truck?'

'It's too much,' said Jones. 'Much too much. You agree, Gagonk?'

'Umph.'

'Speak up, man.'

'Can the – ooof, Lieutenant, please help me to. . .?'

'Maniac!' bellowed a burly, bare-chested motor mechanic as he reached the driver's window. 'What the hell made you do a thing like that? Just driving off the road suddenly without any rhyme or—' Then he noticed Mbopa on the floor, with his head in Jones's lap, and his eyes bulged. 'Jesus H. Christ O'Reilly,' he gasped.

'Unbelievable,' murmured Jones. 'Gagonk, you and me have got to find a new way of going about things, hey?'

At which point, the burly mechanic's eyes almost started from his head, and the municipal traffic officer, who arrived at the scene on his motorcycle a few moments later, could hardly credit his own ears at first.

There were already a dozen vehicles parked outside

Woodhollow when Kramer arrived, having thought he'd just set up a land-speed record crossing town from the telephone box. This annoyed him, making him wonder what game Zondi was playing at, until he realised that Control would have felt duty bound to inform Colonel Muller of the message's contents before relaying it on to him.

'Where's everyone?' he asked the Bantu constable standing guard at the front door of the house.

'Round by the swimming-pool, boss,' said Zondi, emerging at that moment. 'I've been listening for the car.'

'So it paid off after all, hey, Mickey?' said Kramer, as they took the garden path. 'Or are you personally responsible for putting your hands on—?'

'No, no, boss. It was a mixture of the garden boy and Boss Kennedy.' And he related the sequence of events leading up to the discovery of the sword in the pool's filter trap. 'The big help', he said, 'was probably not having the sun dance on the water.'

'Bet it's dancing now,' grunted Kramer, glancing up at a sky that was rapidly becoming a brilliant blue again. 'Who's here? The Colonel?'

Zondi nodded. 'Many, many people. It is like a big picnic, boss.'

'H'm, more like a bloody circus,' said Kramer, as the back garden came in view.

Captain Tiens 'Tickey' Marais of Fingerprints was there, with his red nose, white gloves and baggy yellow trousers, crawling along the springboard, but his was not the only act. Jaap du Preez, long hairy arms flailing, was going ape in front of a huddled group of his uniformed officers, and behind him two members of the police diving team, glistening like sealions in their black wetsuits, were heading a beach ball back and forth in the shallow end. Over on the right, little Amanda Stilgoe was turning cartwheels.

'Hello, Tromp!' said Colonel Muller with a ringmaster's gusto. 'It's all go here, hey? I'm just waiting to make my big announcement!'

'Colonel?'

'To the press and television about the sword! I've invited

179

them all up.'

Kramer raised an eyebrow, knowing Colonel Muller's little weaknesses. 'Not the news that we've only just found the murder weapon, sir? That could make you—'

'No, no, what I'm doing is *releasing* the news.'

'Ah,' said Kramer. 'Then I assume there's no doubt—'

'Tiens has already checked, and so has Piet Baksteen: the broken-off tip we found in the deceased lady fits the rest of the sword exactly.' Colonel Muller dropped his voice and added, with a wink: 'Naturally, you realise why I'm getting the press in like this? And am even prepared to allow them to take pictures in the sun-lounge and her study? Because, my friend, it'll cause such a fuss and a fly-around that—'

'The Zuidmeyer case will be quite safe from their unwelcome attentions, hey, Colonel?' said Kramer, not bothering to hide a cynicism that always surfaced in him when the talk was of killers.

'Exactly, Tromp. I'm glad we're of the same mind on this,' replied Colonel Muller blithely. 'Now I think you'd best have a word with Piet, who's in the house somewhere, looking at the sword. Personally, I think our main hope lies in getting pictures of it into the papers and on to the television news. Swords aren't so common in this country, which means, with any luck, maybe this particular sword will be easily remembered by someone.'

As Kramer started towards Piet Baksteen, he thought for a moment of first going over to Theo Kennedy and asking him how he was feeling today, and whether he had ever had any contact in the past with his mother's friend, Theresa Mary Muldoon. But Kennedy seemed wrapped up in Amanda's antics, and so he decided to leave the man looking happy for a while.

Piet Baksteen was in Naomi Stride's study, holding a sword upright above his head and sighting along the blade, as though preparing himself to go outside and swallow it.

'Well, Piet, what's there to add to your previous assessment?' asked Kramer, flopping into the comfortable swivel chair at the desk. 'Or do you still think it's a crudely made imitation?'

'Here, handle it for yourself, Tromp,' he said.

The sword had a narrow, four-sided blade about a metre long, tapering down to where it'd lost its point. The hilt was bound with thick string that had then been sprayed with gold paint, and to protect the user's hand there was a piece of wood, also sprayed gold and with a hole through it, fixed at right angles where the blade itself began. This cross-piece and the top of the hilt had been decorated with big glass beads, glued down and given settings of more gold string.

'What is it, just a play-play sword?' asked Kramer.

'Close!' said Baksteen, raising a thumb to him. 'But why not simply a *play* sword?'

'Sorry?'

'I mean "play", not as in kiddies' fun and games, but as in theatre. Here, give me it back and I'll show you a few things. . . See these marks on the blade, and these dents in the wood? This thing has been used against another sword, which proves it wasn't made just for decoration, to hang on the wall or whatever. See this blade? It was never meant to have a hilt like that, more the Three Musketeers' sort with a metal bowl to guard the bloke's fingers. And if you look carefully, *here*, you'll see it could've had a guard on it like that before being converted. In short, Tromp, I think what we have here is an actor's sword which gets changed about from one play to another, to save all the sweat of trying to make a new blade. The genuine article would cost a hell of a lot, let me tell you.'

'Uh-huh, and that theory agrees with your original finding – you know, that the steel wasn't tempered properly. . .' Kramer took the sword again and stood up to try its balance. 'Hey, a snag.'

'What's that?'

'Actors would never fight each other with the point we found sticking in Ma Stride; they'd have a bobble on the end, or a cork or something.'

Baksteen sighed and shook his head. 'If people took the trouble to *read* the reports I put in, instead of constantly relying on Tickey's hearsay, then you'd already know that I found fresh file marks on the point, and that my conclusion was that the sword had been recently sharpened.'

'Touché,' said Kramer, swishing off the head of a dead flower in a vase on the desk. 'Now truly amaze me, Professor, and tell me exactly, to within one kilometre, where this sword originated.'

'I – er, could have a bloody good guess.'

'Oh ja?'

'In fact, it's so good I'm afraid of getting it right. I distrust anything that's too simple.'

'Let that be my worry. Come on, man.'

But Baksteen held back, nibbling on his lower lip. 'I'll make it your guess, then,' he said. 'What's about this size, black and blue, and has recently been stuck up all over Trekkersburg?'

'A midget bank clerk who gets tripped over a lot?'

'No, I'm being serious. Two more clues: it's oblong and made of paper.'

'Stuck up all over – ah, like a poster?'

'A poster with lettering and something drawn on it. . .'

Kramer closed his eyes, cursing Zondi for never being about when he needed him, and then suddenly had a glimpse of a poster he'd seen near the carpark on Ackerman Street. 'There's a skull being waved around and two buggers swordfighting.' he said. 'Across the top – ach, one word.'

'*Hamlet*,' said Baksteen, with a shrug, 'for what it's worth. The University's latest Shakespeare production. You could always start by seeing whether any of their old props are missing, I suppose.'

'You're right,' said Kramer.

With lunch in the admitting-ward over, and most of it on the floor, walls and in the other patients' hair, Ramjut Pillay was becoming even more determined to escape from Garrison Road Mental Hospital before his rather remarkable mind suffered any permanent impairment. Perhaps this showed a little, because Nurse Chatterjee kept a very close eye on him, as he moved from barred window to barred window, assessing the height of the surrounding walls.

'What interests you so much out here, Peerswammy?'

182

asked Nurse Chatterjee, finally coming to stand beside him. 'There is very little to see except the sky.'

'I have a great fondness for the sky, sir.'

'Of course, I was forgetting. You are a parachutist – not so?'

Ramjut Pillay curled his toes, deeply regretting such foolishness on his part. 'I am certainly a fellow requiring much outdoor exercising. Would it be permissible for me to take a short stroll?'

'No, it wouldn't – not today. Not until it has been decided which ward you are to be sent to. Is there something else you would like to do? Read an uplifting magazine? I have a *Reader's Digest* put away you are most welcome to.'

So Ramjut Pillay retired to his cot and made a start on an article entitled 'I Am John's Gall Bladder'. But even though he was most curious to learn how such an organ could be persuaded to talk – by jingo, these American chappies were endlessly ingenious – he got no further than the first page before becoming lost in his thoughts again.

What he had to do, he told himself, was to become classified as a low-risk patient as soon as possible, which would presumably mean being moved from behind these barred windows and big barred door to a ward where the security was at a sensible minimum.

'Yes, yes,' murmured Ramjut Pillay, nodding. 'We must have patience in the serenely passive manner of the Mahatma. . .'

'What was that?' asked Nurse Chatterjee, looking up from the duty desk.

'Oh, nothing whatsoever, sir! I was very merely talking to myself.'

'Do you often do that, Peerswammy?'

'This article on the gall bladder is a huge enlightenment, Nurse Chatterjee. Have you perhaps read it?'

'Do you ever hear voices? You know, in your head?'

'Sometimes another side to me will—'

'Will what?'

'Er, why do you ask, Nurse Chatterjee?'

Nurse Chatterjeee made a careful note on a card. 'Just get

183

on with your reading, Peerswammy Lal,' he said kindly. 'Nothing for you to worry about. . .'

'I've just been making a few phone calls,' said Kramer, as he came out of the house and joined Zondi at the side of the swimming-pool. 'Got myself an appointment with some English Department bugger at three.'

'What's this all about, boss?'

'I'll explain to you in a minute. First, take this and hold it for me.' He handed Zondi a long brown-paper parcel. 'It's the murder weapon, hey? I think it'd be more tactful if I haven't got it with me while I'm having a few words with young Kennedy.'

'But he's gone, Lieutenant.'

'Why's that?'

'He didn't want to be here when the reporters come.'

'Ach, of course! I should've thought of that sooner. In fact, it's surprising he stayed as long as—'

'That was because of the child, Amanda, boss, who wanted to watch the divers. She makes Boss Kennedy laugh, and he spoils her very much.'

'Not a bad kid, really.' Kramer looked over at the tree beneath which they'd been sitting. 'What did you think of the mother?'

'She acted very friendly towards me, Lieutenant. I. . .' Zondi looked at him for an instant and then away again.

Kramer shot him a curious glance. 'Are you blushing under all that brown?' he asked. 'If so, this'll be the first time I've ever seen it.'

'It's nothing, Lieutenant. I was treated very well. Have you heard that Gagonk and Jones have been involved in a road accident?'

'What, again?' said Kramer, and laughed. 'Fatal?'

'I'm sorry but it's bad news: both are alive and—'

'Zondi, just a minute, man!' said Colonel Muller, coming up whisking a long bamboo cane he'd found somewhere. 'Where do you think you're going with my prize exhibit? The photographers and television people will be here any minute.'

184

With an impatient sigh, Kramer turned away. 'I'd best go and change that appointment to half-past three,' he said.

Jones winced as he tried to unlock the driver's door of his replacement car. 'Bloody hell,' he grumbled. 'Something's happened to my wrist; it's gone all stiff and sore. *Now* what do I do? Get myself another boy from Housebreaking or somewhere?'

With a wince of his own, Mbopa weighed up the pros and cons of the situation. If Jones took on Tims Shabalala as his driver, then he, Joseph, would have to go into Housebreaking and Theft to keep up its numbers. On the other hand, if there was one thing he hated doing, it was driving badly, as he'd be obliged to do in view of his reputation with his 'little pink chauffeur.' Either way, it seemed, his pride was going to suffer greatly.

'No ideas?' said Jones.

But his pride, thought Mbopa, would possibly suffer the most if he left the Murder and Robbery Squad. Just say this Pillay proved the key to the murder of Naomi Stride – and his strong hunch that this was so had been growing apace all day – then there'd be no fine photographs of him in the newspapers for Zsazsa Lady Gatumi to cut out. All he had to do was picture her, sitting forlornly beside an empty scrapbook, scissors poised, for his mind to be made up.

'Lieutenant,' he said, so respectfully that he very nearly was sick, 'I have heard it said that not long ago you came from the police college, where your teaching was much admired.'

'Naturally,' said Jones. 'But what's that got to do with—?'

'Forgive me, sir, interrupting, but if your skills as a teacher are so great, and Mbopa promises to pay every attention, could not even I learn from you *very* quickly?'

'Let you try driving again, you mean?'

'Please, Lieutenant.'

Jones looked him over and pondered. 'You've got a point there,' he finally conceded. 'It could be better not to change you. You don't smell the way Shabalala does, for example. By the way, you mustn't let what I'm saying now go to your head, hey? You've just been exceptionally lucky in your glands. And it's also true, I suppose, that I won't have to go explaining everything about Pillay all over again to some other thick head, when further time-wasting is not in my interest. But I'll require a promise. . .'

'Anything, sir.'

'That when you're at the wheel you'll do, without question or hesitation, anything I say.'

Mbopa mumbled.

'Louder man! Let's hear it!'

'I promise, Lieutenant,' said Mbopa, and was thrown the car-keys. 'First stop the main post office?'

Jones waited until he was in the rear seat before asking: 'Did I say we were going to the main post office?'

Mbopa shook his head. 'It is that I have been thinking, Lieutenant. Do you remember when we were there yesterday? There was this other churra postman who came into that boss's office and told us that Pillay was on a bicycle in the town.'

'Ja, ja, man, I can remember all that! What's it got to do with anything?'

'We wasted much time looking for him in the town, sir. And what was happening while we were wasting that time?'

'I'm the one who asks the questions,' said Jones cunningly.

'Then this is my answer, Lieutenant. While we were there, Pillay was given the chance to return to his home, get his money, and escape over the hill. In very short words, sir, that other churra postman must be Pillay's accomplice and the one who knows his secrets, maybe even where he is hiding today.'

There was silence from Jones while he absorbed all that. 'H'm, fairly good,' he finally conceded. 'You have got that one right, but do you know this other churra's name?'

'I can recognise him, Lieutenant.'

'Then what are you dilly-dallying around for, Gagonk? Christ, man, put in that key, turn it, and select first gear – I always remember it as the one nearest the ashtray.'

Kramer waited out of sight inside the house until the

photographers and television crews had finshed with the sword and Zondi was able to return it to him. Carefully, he replaced its brown wrapping, while explaining Piet Baksteen's theory that the weapon may have come from the University. Then he handed Zondi a note.

'See those names, Mickey?'

' "Miss Theresa Muldoon, also known as Tess," Zondi read out. "Miss Liz Geldenhuys, Kennedy's former shop assistant. . ." '

'What I want you to do now is to take another crack at Betty the maid. Put those names to her, ask for anything she can remember. What I'm particularly interested in is whether Ma Stride and Muldoon ever discussed Liz Geldenhuys in Betty's hearing, and what they might have said. Also, Liz Geldenhuys made one visit to this house, which didn't go down too well. Find out more about that, too, if you can – OK?'

'I can try, boss, but. . .' Zondi shrugged.

'Ja, I'm sorry, it's a bit of a balls-ache, but you could find she remembers things easier when you hit her with specifics. Meet you back at the office about five?'

Some men in white came into the ward and took away everyone except for Ramjut Pillay. Much relieved by this, he left his cot and rushed to the lavatory in the far corner, absolutely bursting after almost twenty terrifying hours during which he'd dared not turn his back. Then he returned to carry on with a most Gandhi-esque article in the *Reader's Digest*, 'Living with Your Conscience', that'd had him in its thrall for quite some time now.

The tall white doctor dropped by, followed by a group of young persons wearing stethoscopes in conspicuous places, and spoke to Nurse Chatterjee in a low murmur. Twice he used the word 'delusion', and once he mentioned 'parachutist', which made the young persons chuckle. One of them remarked: 'Whoever heard of a non-white making a jump? He *must* be schizo.' What that meant, Ramjut Pillay had no idea, but he was far more concerned by the effect the *Reader's Digest* article was now having on him.

'Do not feel slighted, Peerswammy,' said Nurse Chatterjee, coming over when the doctor and his young friends had departed. 'You are still with me because your case cannot be decided by snap decision on the doctor's part. He says it has many unusual qualities to it.'

'But how much longer before I–?'

'Two days, three?'

'And then I will be cured? Allowed to go?'

'It will first be necessary to keep you under further observation, before – er, we decide that,' said Nurse Chatterjee. 'Reconcile yourself to at least a month within our portals, Peerswammy.'

'A month!'

'Keep going with your reading,' said Nurse Chatterjee cheerfully, returning to his duty desk. 'It will greatly help to pass the time away!'

It will not, thought Ramjut Pillay. It will simply make matters very, very much worse. Just the first two pages of 'Living with Your Conscience' had been enough for him to tremble, on reflection, at the thought of all the wicked acts he had so recently committed. Not that they'd seemed bad at the time, of course, but now he'd partially filled in the questionnaire contained within the article they had assumed their properly monstrous proportions.

Step One, the article advised, *identify the most serious wrong you have done, and then take steps to make amends, if possible. You will probably find it's something that relates to another person.*

To what other person? To Peerswammy Lal himself? No, decided Ramjut Pillay, he had fully deserved to have mercilessly ruthless truths said about him. To the little man in spectacles who had been chased by Tomato Face? No, not him, either, for he should have known better than to stare so rudely. To Mistering Jarman, for having absconded with the mail? No, the mail wasn't really *his*, so that hardly counted. But who else was there?

Suddenly, his conscience pricked him so sharply he almost cried out. And there before him, in his mind's eye, he saw the naked and defenceless body of the novelist lady, Naomi Stride, of whom he had taken a most despicable advantage by sneaking into her sun-lounge without his Post Office boots on.

'Fiendish, fiendish cad,' Ramjut Pillay castigated himself under his breath. 'How can I ever be making rectification? Dead and gone, dead and gone...'

By seeing that her death is avenged, you fool, said another side to Ramjut Pillay, which had been very quiet for the last hour, but now spoke up as coldly logically as ever, if somewhat reluctantly.

'And how am I doing that, my fine fellow?' he scoffed.

'The letter, you fool – the letter! You know that holds many clues the CID need urgently to help them go in the right direction and not take wrong turnings! See that you get it to them.'

'Why, of course!'

Then Ramjut Pillay realised he was thinking out aloud, and glanced at Nurse Chatterjee. But luckily the good fellow was too busy fiddling with a small tape recorder to have apparently noticed anything.

Betty Duboza was a different woman in her own home, even though it was part and parcel of Woodhollow, hidden away on one side behind a screen of hibiscus. Grave and gracious, pouring out the tea with the aid of a silver strainer, she served both Zondi and her husband Ben without so much as the clatter of a cup in its saucer. And her other hand, when she held out some small biscuits on a plate, didn't shake at all, either.

'Yes, I remember the night the little master brought Miss Geldenhuys to dinner,' she said. 'The madam was unhappy.'

'The madam called her "Miss Geldenhuys", never anything else,' added Ben Duboza, with a wink for Zondi's benefit.

His wife ignored him. 'We thought her manners at the table were' – Betty Duboza shuddered – 'were manners we were not used to at Woodhollow. She did not *once* touch her finger-bowl, and during the meat course she held her knife like a *pencil*, my dear! So terribly embarrassing.'

'You found it embarrassing, too?' Zondi asked Ben Duboza.

'Hau, I never saw this little missus, Sergeant. Remember, I

189

am working as chef boy in the kitchen.'

'No, it was just me and madam,' continued Betty Duboza, settling back in a velvet-covered chair that went with her extraordinarily well-furnished room. 'We could not believe our ears, either, at some of the things she said. It was never "Excuse me", but "Hey?", and she kept on coming out with "Ach" at the start of almost every sentence. We could see that Theo was trying not to be embarrassed as well, being so infatuated with this strange creature, but as the evening progressed even his smile was wearing thin. What puzzled us most, of course, was what he could *see* in her, for her figure was dreadful and her features were worse than plain. In the end, it just had to be her talent as a window-dresser he was exploiting, while clearly, in her own way, she was exploiting him. We noticed that, halfway through dessert, she began watching Theo and had learned to use her fork as well as her spoon by the time dinner ended. It simply wasn't *on*, we decided, and the sooner it ended, the better. Oh, yes, even for the girl, for he would eventually see her with the same clear vision, once his infatuation had passed, and she would find herself rejected. Would you care for another drop in that?'

Zondi, bemused, was a second or two late with his response. 'No, no, thank you, Mrs Duboza,' he said. 'And Miss Muldoon? You said you know her as well.'

'Sweet little Tess – a bit batty at times, but so refreshing,' Betty Duboza confirmed with a quick half-nod. 'Another drop for you, Ben?'

Not once, during the long interrogation last night, had the woman given that quick half-nod, realised Zondi. A very distinctive nod, expressing the personality of someone terribly sure of herself, caught up in her thoughts, not unaware of how brusque it might seem to others. A nod which must once have belonged, not to Betty Duboza, but to someone else.

'Now, where was I?' she asked, setting down her teapot again.

'Wife, speak Zulu,' muttered Ben Duboza, who had started to look very ill at ease. 'There is no need all of a sudden for English, and hasn't Sergeant Zondi always done us the courtesy of addressing us in our own tongue?'

'Tess', his wife continued in English, 'was appalled when she heard how Theo was selling his soul in all directions. We had her round here the very next day, and·the madam spoke to her for hours about the problem. But, of course, without being seen to be interfering, there wasn't much anybody could do. Tess said she thought it'd sort itself out soon enough, and thankfully it did. The girl proved to be an utter hysteric, started accusing poor Theo of all sorts of shady things, and... Well, my dear, they parted and it was over, thank God. The last time Tess stayed here for the night, we could even have a little laugh about it.'

'*You* did not have a "little laugh about it",' said Ben Duboza, putting his tea aside on the floor, which earned him an immediate scowl. 'All you did was take the two madams out their coffee after dinner to beside the swimming-pool.'

'I laughed when I came back to the kitchen – not so?'

'I don't remember,' he grunted.

'Well, I did.' She gave that quick half-nod again, and crossed her thick ankles in a way which only a woman with trim ankles would think of doing. 'I do hope I have been of some use to you, my dear. There's nothing else I can think òf, not at this moment.'

'Many thanks,' said Zondi, rising and placing his teacup on her tray.

The cook politely walked him as far as the hibiscus, where Ben Duboza shook his head again and murmured in Zulu: 'Bad, bad spirits. . .'

'Cheer up, my friend!' Zondi replied, also in Zulu. 'At least Boss Kennedy has promised you that you still have your job, and soon he will be here at Woodhollow to change the way things feel.'

'Huh! All that didn't seem so bad while she was still alive, but now! You do realise who you've just been speaking with, Sergeant?'

'Of course,' said Zondi. 'The dead.'

14

THE UNIVERSITY BUILDINGS were a mess and a muddle,
scattered all over a slope above Trekkersburg in among far
too many trees. No wonder the local paper continued to
report disappointing results for first-year students, thought
Kramer; it probably took the poor little buggers their first six
months to find their classrooms.

So he didn't even attempt to search for the English
Department, but went directly to the old main building, with
its clock tower and dome, and sat outside it until he
recognised a face from the mug shots of minor dissidents kept
by Security. All he had to do then was slightly raise one
finger, and after a glance at the aerial at the back of the car the
student almost dropped his books and hurried over.

'Full Marx,' said Kramer, enjoying his private pun. 'Where
do I find a bloke who calls himself Doc Wilson?'

'Deputy Head of English?'

'The same. You can take us to him?'

'But you must be. . .'

'Ja, police – so don't try to run away, hey?'

Looking like someone who wishes he could turn his collar
up so friends won't recognise him, but having been foolish
enough to come out in just a T-shirt and jeans that morning,
the student slunk along as fast as he could, which suited
Kramer perfectly. He had by now begun to develop Piet
Baksteen's distrust of a simple solution, and wanted to
eliminate the University from his enquiries as soon as
possible.

The student led the way into a modern building that was
more glass than concrete, and then into a passage with a long
grey carpet and numbered doors on the right. He pointed to
the third door down and stopped.

'He should be in there,' he said, very pale.

'Fine,' said Kramer. 'Oh, and if you hear any screams, it'll
only be this thing.'

One glance at the brown-paper parcel being wielded in
Kramer's left hand was enough. Off went the student, even

paler, and after a quick rap-rap on the door marked *Dr W B Wilson* Kramer walked in with a smile. The gullibility of students, and of dissidents in particular, never failed to delight him.

The room, in one sense, was empty. In another, it was doubtful whether anyone could have packed into it more shelves of books, more piles of papers, or more cigar-ends into its ashtrays, which were perched everywhere. For decoration, it had an oil painting of a nude woman coloured purple – her head was so badly drawn it didn't help to distinguish her race, either, which made it difficult to decide whether Wilson's admiration for her was entirely legitimate – and a human skull, minus its lower jawbone, on a corner of the cluttered desk. Beyond this desk, which had a chair that looked more like a wooden throne, the wall was almost all a sliding window.

Weaving his way through an untidy arrangement of low chairs, Kramer went to the window and looked out. A pasty-faced man of about forty, with long greying hair swept back over his ears, old-fashioned granny glasses, and a cigar jutting from a thin, curvy mouth, was basking in a deck chair with a book balanced upright on his fancy waistcoat.

'Doctor Wilson, sir? Lieutenant Kramer, the CID officer who phoned you earlier on.'

'Wot? Ah! Whoops!' said the Deputy Head of English, struggling to get up.

'Stay where you are, if you like, sir, and I'll come out.'

' "Not so, my lord; I am too much in the sun..." '

'Whatever suits you best, sir,' said Kramer, puzzled to know why Wilson was looking at him as if he expected him to clap or something.

'Act I, scene i,' said Wilson. 'I tend to become besotted.'

'Ja, it's often best to wear a hat,' said Kramer, backing into the office. 'Mind you, today started out overcast.'

'Um, take a pew,' said Wilson.

Kramer couldn't see one. So while Wilson settled down on his throne he took the skull off the corner of the desk and sat there, as was his habit in Colonel Muller's office.

' "Alas, poor Yorick," ' said Wilson, pointing to the skull.

'Must've been quite an exam,' agreed Kramer, who could also make up bullshit when the occasion demanded. 'And the Yorick family don't mind you keeping it?'

Wilson threw back his head and made a sound like a donkey being castrated. 'Excellent!' he said. 'Superb! Must remember that!'

Kramer put the skull aside and drew the sword from its brown-paper wrapping. 'What I'd really like you to try to remember, sir,' he said, 'is whether you have ever seen this weapon before? Would you like to hold it?' And he handed it over, hilt first.

' "I know a hawk from a handsaw . . ." '

'You do, sir?' said Kramer.

But there was no way he could make himself sound impressed. Wilson would be bragging next that he knew his arse from his elbow. Just like a big kid, he was, bouncing about on that throne, saying weird things with that show-off's look in his self-absorbed little eyes, expecting grown-ups to tell him how clever he was.

'Good God,' said Wilson quietly. 'Where did you get this?'

'Why, sir?'

'It's Laertes'.'

'He's what? A student here?'

Wilson looked up. 'It's a sword we used in our recent production of *Hamlet*,' he said. 'These are the glass beads my wife found for it in her mother's trinket-box. I'd no idea it'd gone missing, none at all. This could be rather serious.'

'Oh, it is, sir,' said Kramer, pleased the man had at last decided to act his age.

'You didn't say on the telephone where you'd found it.'

In the circumstances, what with it being the English Department, Kramer decided to allow himself a little poetic licence. 'Ach, we found it sticking in the side of Naomi Stride, sir.'

'Naomi Stride!' Wilson almost dropped the thing, before going several shades lighter and gulping. Then he held the sword away from him, gazed at it, and said very softly: ' "I will speak daggers to her, but use none. . ." '

'Then you didn't like the lady?' asked Kramer.

'Actually, that was more *Hamlet*, I'm afraid. You're familiar with the play. Know what *Hamlet* is about?'

'At a guess, it must be about a village, sir. Aren't hamlets—?'

'A *village*, did you say? How original! Life seen as a macrocosm?'

Kramer just looked at him, quite sure they were both speaking English, and in a place that was actually *designed* for English, and yet once again he had the bewildering feeling that neither of them was really communicating. Something had, however, struck home when he'd suggested that Wilson had disliked Naomi Stride, so he decided to try a variation on that theme. And if he stuck to inviting 'yes' or 'no' answers not much could go wrong.

'You knew Naomi Stride, sir?'

'Yes and no.'

'Sir,' said Kramer with a sigh, taking the sword back, 'please explain.'

'Yes, I did know Naomi Stride the writer, just as I know Jane Austen, from having read and studied her books. But no, I didn't know – what was her married name?'

'Kennedy.'

'Mrs Kennedy, the person, as it were, I never knew, apart from seeing her across the room at a few functions, and having appeared on the same platform as her on one occasion.'

'And why was this, sir? Wasn't she a world-famous writer, living, as it were, right on your doorstep? Wouldn't it be in your interests to know her and, instead of maybe just theorising, get to hear first-hand how she sucked her books out of her thumb?'

Wilson smiled slightly, then hunted for his matches to relight his cigar. 'Setting aside for the moment the academic point you have raised, which clearly invites one to define what one means by literary criticism, and could well—'

'Sir, could we set that part of it aside for good?' asked Kramer.

'If you like,' said Wilson, dispersing the smokescreen around him with a flap of his hand. 'Your question was, why didn't I want to know the woman. The answer is, Lieutenant, *she* didn't want to know *me*. I'm afraid that some of my criticism, directed at her more recent work in particular, did not go down frightfully well.'

'You pissed her off, you mean? Why, what was it about her recent writing you didn't like?'

' "The lady doth protest too much, methinks. . ." '

'Ja, and the Security Branch would agree with you, but—'

'No, no, it's this streak of *feminism* that's come creeping into things, accentuating an already rather humourless—'

'Sir,' said Kramer, 'this sword. That's what I really came about. Any idea why it isn't still where you expected it to be?'

Wilson stood up. 'Let's go over and start some enquiries,' he said.

At last, thought Kramer, someone who speaks my language.

Zondi returned to CID headquarters, feeling very much at a loose end. He had definitely collected some useful information during his brief visit to the Dubozas, but he hadn't any idea what to do with it, other than to store it in his memory until the Lieutenant showed up.

So he wandered into the Bantu detective sergeants' office to ask Tims Shabalala for further gratifying details of Gagonk and Jones's accident. Tims wasn't there, but Wilfred Mkosi was, strumming on his guitar.

'And there was Good Dog Gagonk on his knees, his faithful snout in his master's lap,' sang Mkosi. 'Neither one, alas, was dead, but when the traffic cop came along his face went red! Oh, what were they doing? What were they doing?'

Zondi clamped a hand over the guitar strings. 'Exactly, what *were* they doing?' he asked. 'What is this nonsense I've heard about them thinking the man Ramjut Pillay is a major suspect?'

Mkosi put his guitar down and began to roll a cigarette. 'I have not seen Gagonk today, Mickey, so I cannot give you an up-to-date. I just know they have been rushing around, looking for him everywhere.'

'But why?'

'Yesterday, the postman ran away from home, after spending all night engaged in mysterious activities in his bedroom. He took all his money and vanished.'

'What else?'

'Gagonk says much evidence was found in the bedroom, pointing to the man as being of a highly criminal nature. He had, he says, many, many disguises.'

'*Disguises*? They didn't have any idea where he had vanished to?'

'Not last night, but they did put out a description to all SAP stations, the Railway Police, the municipal police and all the rest. Do you want to see it?'

'Too right. I can't imagine how that poor fool couldn't have been caught by now.'

'Then, I think you'll find a carbon of the Telex in Gagonk's wire basket on his desk,' said Mkosi, licking his cigarette-paper.

Zondi found the carbon copy lying right on top. He read no more than the first two lines before beginning to chuckle.

'What's so funny, Mickey?' asked Mkosi, folding his long thin legs under him. 'I didn't notice any Gagonkish spelling mistakes. . .'

Catching up the carbon copy, Zondi turned to him and said: '*Where* did they get this amazing description? Where? Pillay's forty, if a day, and no mention of his needing to wear glasses, or what kind they are. But that's nothing when you come to his height and weight! One-seventy-six centimetres and eighty-one kilos! This makes him tall and sound a real muscle man, whereas he'd be lucky if he weighs half so much, and his height is only—'

'The figures are wrong?' gasped Mkosi, beginning to share the joke.

'Wrong?' said Zondi, suddenly aware that he was jeopardising a golden opportunity to settle a few more old scores. 'Oh, no, my friend, pretend I never said that.'

'You never said that,' said Wilfred Mkosi happily, picking up his guitar again. 'And anyway, if you did, what a pity I was singing my new song too loudly to hear it. . .'

． ． ．

Kramer had to bend almost double to fit under the stage in the main hall of the University. Wilson shuffled ahead of him, pushing aside the wicker baskets of costumes and tea-boxes of props that kept getting in his way, and eventually reached an old plastic rubbish-bin in which an assortment of stage weapons was standing, point down.

'As you see, Lieutenant, they're the very devil to get at.'

'Ja, but what I also see is that this place under the stage isn't locked, it hasn't even got a bolt on it, there's a notice on the door saying "Drama Club Store", and the hall was wide open, too.'

'Yes, but one simply doesn't think of anybody wanting to—'

'Have you no Bantus working on the premises? What if one of them gets upset with his boss and comes here to get himself a—'

'Our Africans just aren't like that!' said Wilson, shocked.

'Oh, so they've all got degrees, too?'

'I don't think this argument is entirely apposite, quite frankly.'

'You're right,' agreed Kramer, picking over the other swords in the bin. 'We've already established that anyone could come in here, with an excellent chance of not being noticed, and help themselves to whatever they liked.'

'Er, the main building *is* locked after dark.'

'Always?'

'Well, not when there's a function on, either here in the main hall or perhaps in one of the side rooms.'

'And how often is that?'

'During term-time?'

'It's been term-time ever since the play was on, hasn't it?'

'Every other night at least, I suppose,' said Wilson lamely.

Kramer took out a sword with a cup over the hilt to protect the hand. 'Why didn't Lay-whatsit use this one?'

'Laertes? Funnily enough, he rehearsed with that one, but our costume designer wanted something more in keeping with the flamboyance—'

'So who adapted the murder weapon?'

'Er, I did – from another foil that was a bit battered. I think that, as the producer, one should remain infinitely flexible, catering to the—'

'So that's why you know the thing backwards and it's still going round in your head?'

' "These are but wild and whirring words. . ." I become, as I admitted earlier, besotted, obsessed – on top of which, *Hamlet* is one of our examination pieces this year, and Shakespeare *is* my special study.'

'How do you test somebody on watching a play?'

'Oh, they don't have to watch it so much as read and reread it.'

'But aren't books the things you read? I thought the whole idea of a play was to sit there and see—'

'The *ideas* can be – well, just take the raw plot of the thing. A son who discovers his father was murdered so that his mother can marry his—'

'It's a murder story?'

Wilson gave a little laugh. 'Well, in a way – a bit of a ghost story, too, if we're resorting to such terms, plus a sad love story in which Hamlet's girlfriend is driven mad and he loses her.'

' "God in Heaven," ' said Kramer.

The men in white brought in a cross-eyed old Hindu who had burned his feet in an attempt to simulate the fire-walking ceremony, held every Good Friday at the temple down Harber Road, by standing on his daughter-in-law's electric stove with one foot in the curry and another in the rice. He screamed and shouted a great deal, not because he was in pain – he denied having felt a thing – but because he resented having been interrupted in the middle of a spiritual exercise.

But Ramjut Pillay was barely aware of his presence. He was wrestling with his conscience, and it had him pinned to the mat, demanding that he find a way to get the anonymous letter on cheap blue paper with ruled lines into the hands of the CID without further delay. An impossible task, of course, for a poor fellow locked behind bars and with high walls surrounding him.

For an instant, he toyed with the idea of going to Nurse Chatterjee and telling him that, quite frankly, he was as sane as the next man, and had only *pretended* to be a parachutist to get himself out of a bit of a fix. But the problem was that Nurse Chatterjee would doubtless want to know more about this bit of a fix before he'd let him go, and that could lead to even sorrier complications.

If only, Ramjut Pillay reflected bitterly, he had taken up that course he'd seen offered in mental telepathy, then he could send his thoughts out through those bars to that nice understanding fellow, Sergeant Zondi, telling him where the letter could be found. He was sure that Sergeant Zondi would be so delighted to be put on the right track in finding the murderer that he would arrange for his release from Garrison Road Mental Hospital and no questions asked. But, having stupidly neglected to take the course, just as he'd neglected to take one in self-hypnosis before having a tooth out, he had only himself to blame again for his unnecessary suffering.

Ramjut Pillay sat up in his cot with a jerk, filled with the joy of a marvellous inspiration that only his rather remarkable mind would be capable of. It must have been thinking of correspondence courses that had done the trick, for he had suddenly realised *there was a way* of sending his thoughts out between those bars without his needing to accompany them. He would post Sergeant Zondi a map, giving the location of the clueful letter in the hole beneath the tree, and enclose a short note explaining its significance! A short *anonymous* note, perhaps? Yes, yes, even better! Later, when the murderer was caught, and the police were pleased with him, he might then reveal the note-writer's identity, but in the meantime he would remain safely where he was, with a beautifully clear conscience worthy – dare he think it? – of the Mahatma.

Jumping out of his cot, Ramjut Pillay felt for a pen. But he had no pen, and what he'd also overlooked was that he had no paper, envelope or stamp. Then, just go and see if Nurse Chatterjee has what you want in the drawer of the duty desk, whispered another side to him. Go quickly, while he is distracted by that noisy old fool in the corner.

Ramjut Pillay nipped over to the desk, then hesitated.

What good would this act of theft be to his conscience? Look, grumbled another side to him, I have just about had enough of your cowardly scruples.

'Peerswammy?'

'Nurse Chatterjee! I did not see—'

'Is there something I can do for you? Something you'd like?'

'I – er, was partially wondering, um, if it would be all right for me to, providing it causes no inconvenience. . . I would like to write a letter.'

'Why, of course, a letter,' said Nurse Chatterjee, with a kind smile, just as though he'd been half-expecting such a request. 'I have only the humble-type stationery available in the hospital shop, but you are most welcome to it. An envelope, too?'

'Many, many thanks,' said Ramjut Pillay.

Then gaped when Nurse Chatterjee handed him a pad of cheap blue writing-paper with ruled lines.

' "Though this be madness, yet there is method in it. . ." '

'You've taken the words right out of my mouth,' said Kramer, as he and Wilson walked back across the campus to the English Department. 'Mind you, we can't go assuming there is a connection between the murder and this Hamlet bloke.'

'I thought you said Naomi Stride's husband was dead and that the girl—'

'Ja, but there's no proof she was messing around with any uncle that would make her son get all upset about it.'

'What do you know of the circumstances of her husband's death?'

'A heart surgeon who had a heart attack.'

'Poetic irony!'

Kramer frowned, not being aware of having said anything that rhymed, but he was getting more used to Wilson's ways by now, and let it pass. 'No, the mad part is really the bloke using a sword that could be traced so easily.'

'What if the culprit *is* mad and indifferent to the consequences?'

201

'H'm, you've got a point there, but only maybe. Who had this sword in the play?'

'Murray James was Laertes – a nicer, more harmless boy you couldn't wish to come across.'

'Would he have known Naomi Stride?'

'I very much doubt it! And, anyway, he's been in hospital since the last performance. Broke his leg, silly bugger, during the party afterwards.'

They went into the English Department building and back into Wilson's ivory tower. A dark-haired man, with fierce brown eyes and a big beard, was standing at the window, smoking a pipe.

'Ah, Aaron,' said Wilson, stopping short. 'Come about those essays?'

'You're bloody right I have. I'm not going to be accused of marking too high when what's happened is that I've managed actually to *teach* the bastards something. Which is more than can be—'

'But, er, could this wait until a little later? I've someone with me.'

'So I see. Who is he?'

'Say about half-past four?'

'A fencing instructor?' said the man, smiling unpleasantly as he pushed past Kramer and the sword. 'Or your new bodyguard, Wilson? Very wise, because when I come back you're going to bloody need one.'

'Now, Aaron, there's no call for—'

'By the way, I've just read your paper on J M Coetzee. It's crap.'

The door slammed.

Wilson took a seat on his throne and got his bounce back. ' "So full of artless jealousy is guilt"! That was Aaron Sariff – didn't introduce you as the man's enough of a screaming paranoid as it is, without telling him you were a policeman. You've heard of the Jew being persecuted down the ages?'

'Uh-huh.'

'Well, that's the Jew they mean – you've just met him!'

And Wilson did another of his castrated-donkey impressions, making it sound as though the delicate operation had been performed by banging together two house bricks, while Kramer lit a Lucky Strike.

If he hadn't become burdened by a strong hunch this man could be useful to him, he'd have been off like a shot long ago.

Knowing nowhere else that he might pick up the missing postman's trail, Zondi had headed for Gladstoneville. It had been just his luck to come across a serious accident at the point where the dirt road began, which had meant having to stop and give assistance until the ambulances came.

But now at last, his suit stained with blood and his tie left behind on someone as a tourniquet, he was on his way again. He'd never thought he would hold a young Indian beauty in his arms, which had somehow made it worse when she'd died there.

Ramjut Pillay's house had no number, and he had twice to ask directions, before finding it at the foot of a low hill topped by wattle-trees. A fierce-faced old crone, with a bright dab of scarlet between her eyebrows, sat in a cane chair on the sloping veranda. She glared at him as he climbed out of the car, and took up a fly-whisk.

'Police, mama.'

'No menfolk are here, no men,' she quavered. 'You would not hurt an old woman.'

'Where are your menfolk, mama?'

'My son is run away and my poor aged husband goes looking for him.'

'Where does he look?'

She made a gesture with her fly-whisk that seemed to take in the best part of the Southern Hemisphere.

'Much too tiring, mama,' said Zondi. 'I will just take a look in the house, so I can say to my boss that I have been here, and then I will leave you in peace again.'

'Peace? What peace can there ever be', she wailed, deftly killing a fly, 'for the mother of Ramjut Pillay?'

The telephone rang, and Kramer was surprised when Dr Wilson held it out to him, saying: 'Someone for you,

Lieutenant – Baksteen, is it?'

'Kramer here.'

'Tromp, it's Piet, ringing you from the lab. I thought this was where I might find you, and the switchboard lady—'

'Piet, your guess was right. This is where the sword came from. Only next time wait until I get a chance to get in touch myself. I'm in the middle of—'

'I was right? Good God, now I won't be able to sleep tonight! But the sword wasn't why I've rung. I thought you were in a hurry for a result on those pine-scented samples you gave me at the mortuary this morning, and it's after four.'

Kramer needed a moment to switch thought-tracks. 'Oh ja, the Zuid – the stuff you were happy to say wasn't semen?'

'Believe it or not, Tromp, Van Rensburg was spot on – it *is* DH-136, the detergent he claimed it was. I had to start somewhere, and it matches up exactly. What's more, I've been in touch with the distributors, and they assure me there's not another detergent on the market with exactly the same components, as the stuff's patented.'

'Well, I'm buggered! These distributors, what are they called?'

'Buchan & Layne Wholesale. Very helpful, very nice people. While I was on to them, I thought I might as well ask for distribution details. They say DH-136 isn't available through ordinary retail outlets, and they're the only suppliers in Natal.'

'Is it poisonous, that it's not on sale to the general public?'

'Ach, no, nothing sinister like that, Tromp. There'd simply be no demand. DH-136 is biological in its action and designed for a specific, usually industrial, purpose, namely disinfecting and cleaning areas where there's lot of blood lying around. Blood's funny stuff, you know; it isn't all that easy to—'

'*Industrial* purposes, you say? Like what?'

'The obvious ones,' said Baksteen, sounding a little surprised by the question. 'You know, such as cleaning up butcher's shops, slaughter-houses, chicken—'

'The municipal abattoir?'

'Same difference! Hey, don't tell me this connects up with

something you know already? And there I was, thinking I'd really surprise you!'

Zondi sat cross-legged on the horsehair mattress in Ramjut Pillay's lean-to and examined a pen he had found tucked behind a wooden rafter, together with a bottle of lemon juice. His first assumption had been that the juice was taken as some sort of medicine, and the pen had been used to stir it with. But why dip the nib end into the lemon juice, when the other end would work just as well? It was obvious the nib would have to be washed before taking any ink now.

Or had Pillay in fact been writing with lemon juice? No, that was absurd, for the liquid would surely leave no mark.

Putting the bottle and pen aside, Zondi looked round at the mess left on the floor by Mbopa and Jones, and then at the array of uniforms in the corner. Disguises! Most wouldn't have fitted Pillay in a hundred years, except perhaps the Scout uniform. It had made him a little sad to note that each of the others matched one of the terrible courses the poor fool kept taking, not having noticed that the signature of Dr Gideon de Bruin, principal of the Easiway College, was seldom written in the same hand twice.

Then Zondi caught sight of a stamp album, pushed between two Superman comics, and took it down. He flicked to the page headed *Great Britain* and saw a very new-looking stamp stuck there. He jumped to his feet. But when he used Pillay's magnifying glass to check the postmark he found that the stamp had been cancelled in London more than six months ago. A sheet of paper started to slip out of the album as he was replacng it, but it was blank and of no possible interest.

'Just a minute,' Zondi muttered to himself, and gave the blank sheet of paper a sniff. 'Cra-zeee brother! Lemons!'

Then he tried the magnifying glass on it, and found tiny scratchmarks such as a pen nib would make, although he could not pick out any actual writing. Perhaps Baksteen would be able to shed some light on the matter, he thought, and pocketed the paper while intensifying his search, irritated less by the stink of horsehair than by the flies which kept settling on his bloodstained clothing.

'A penny for them,' said Wilson, lighting a fresh cigar.

'What?' Kramer, who had been lost in thought, wondering what to make of the DH-136 discovery, looked away from the courtyard. 'Ach, sorry, hey?'

'That was one of your forensic experts on the phone, I take it? Fascinating business that, the way they come up with secrets from beyond the grave, as it were. "The sheeted dead did squeak and gibber!" – and all that. Has he managed to produce many clues for you so far?'

'A few, not that they all make sense yet.'

'Such as?'

'Stuff that was sprinkled around the body, making the murder seem even more weird and ritualistic than just the sword had done.'

'I'm intrigued.'

Kramer looked at him, noted that he was acting his age again, and decided no harm could be done by taking the man further into his confidence, as this might be useful later on if the *Hamlet* connection were ever established. 'Between you and me, sir, Naomi Stride was left surrounded by pansies and a herb called – ach, it's some woman's name.'

'Rosemary?'

'Very quick!'

'I admit I was probably ahead of you, Lieutenant, once I'd heard the word "pansies".' And back came the show-off's gleam to his eye. 'You'll allow me one final quotation?'

'Ja, go ahead. . .'

' "Rosemary, that's for remembrance" and "Pansies, that's for thoughts" – *Hamlet*, Act IV, scene v, and spoken, I might add, by Ophelia.'

'Who?'

'By the girlfriend.'

Zondi ran into his new house, undressing as he went. He rolled up his bloodstained suit, threw it into a corner of his bedroom, and dragged the shirt off his back.

'Wife!' he called out, opening their wardrobe. 'Where is my other suit? My old one with the silver thread?'

But Miriam appeared to be out, despite the fact that the front door had been unlocked. Ever since moving to Hamilton, she'd gone in for socialising on a scale hitherto unknown, and time and again was to be found gossiping over at some neighbour's house. Her excuse was, of course, that now the twins had grown up, and the other children were older, too, there was not the same need for her to be always at everyone's beck and call, bent over the ironing-board in the kitchen.

'Where is it? Where is it?' muttered Zondi, scattering their scant selection of garments along the brass rail and making the wire hangers squeal. 'If she has sold it, there is going to be much, much trouble...'

But the Lieutenant's radio message had been to get down to CID headquarters as soon as possible, so that would have to wait. He grabbed his only other pair of trousers and his brown sports jacket, took a clean white shirt from the pile of three, and did most of his changing behind the front door, being very impatient to get on the road again.

From the sound of it, they'd at last had some sort of big breakthrough.

On his own way back to CID headquarters, Kramer stopped off at Buchan & Layne, the wholesalers. Like Piet Baksteen had said, the staff were very helpful and pleasant. Yes, they supplied DH-136 to the municipal abattoir in Lawrence Street and, yes, they knew this for a fact. They showed him invoices.

He drove on, intending to see the Colonel before catching up with Zondi, then had another thought. He couldn't be too careful before forming a conclusion. He detoured left and parked his car outside the State mortuary.

Pulling back the fly-screen, and then banging open the door, he shouted out: 'Van!' A loud exclamation came from the refrigerator room, and when he looked in there, Van Rensburg was leaning against the wall, a hand clasped over his heart.

'Please, Lieutenant, never do that again, sir!' he pleaded, very shaken. 'My nerves will not stand it.'

'Your nerves? Hell, you've never mentioned having any nerves before, man.'

'Well, I've got them now, sir, and I don't mind telling you they're shot. Do you know what's happening inside my fridge? What I've got in there?'

Kramer glanced into the dark, foetid chamber, and shook his head. 'No, I don't – and I'm not that interested right this minute. I want to know what else you can tell me about DH-136.'

'Ah, yes,' said Van Rensburg, brightening. 'You know I was right first time?' He emerged from the refrigerator room and said to Nxumalo: 'Try banging a stick against the trays, and see if that frightens it off, hey?'

Nxumalo obeyed with a grin.

'All I really want to know about DH-136', said Kramer, moving to the post-mortem room to get away from the noise, 'is whether it's slippery underfoot.'

'Slippery? Hooo!'

'Very?'

'So slippy, Lieutenant,' said Van Rensburg, miming what looked like a hippo's pirouette on ice, 'that the firm warns you about it every time they deliver! Oh ja, you have to be very, very careful with the stuff, as I am forever telling Nxumalo.'

'I see, so—'

'Not that you can stop less sensible people than myself from doing stupid things with it,' went on Van Rensburg, really warming to his subject. 'Last April Fool's Day, for instance, some young idiot at the abattoir poured DH-136 on the ramp where they herd cattle up from the lorries to the guy who shoots them in the head. Total shambles, all the poor bloody cows sliding down again on their arses, kicking shit out of the lorry boys, and quite a few head even made a bolt for it. The rep who told me said Lawrence Street looked like a bloody rodeo!'

'Who was it that pulled this stunt with the DH-136?'

'Ach, one of the young clerks in the office.'

'Is he still there?'

'Hell, no! He was sacked so fast he was on his way home before the first of those cows bit the dust!'

'Ta,' said Kramer, and started to leave. 'By the way, did Piet Baksteen give you a result on those goat hairs? Had Nxumalo been lying to you?'

Van Rensburg's face fell instantly; the deeply worried look came back to his eyes. 'Er, apparently not, Lieutenant. Nxumalo certainly couldn't be responsible for what Mr Baksteen found, not in a million years.'

'Then, what were they?'

With a glance over his shoulder, Van Rensburg whispered: 'Giraffe hairs, Lieutenant. . .'

'Giraffe?' Kramer began to grin. 'How in God's name could *giraffe* hairs get in your fridge?'

'Shhh, not so loud, sir! That's the very question I myself put to Mr Baksteen, and do you know what his answer was? Why my nerves are in this state? "Van," he said, "the only scientific explanation I can offer for this phenomenon is that you've got yourself a poltergeist down there." '

Nurse Chatterjee paused beside Ramjut Pillay's cot, causing him hurriedly to hide a sheet of cheap blue ruled paper beneath his pillow. 'What is this, Peerswammy?' he said, picking up the pad. 'Not a blessed word written yet?'

' "One should always compose oneself," ' said Ramjut Pillay, remembering an uppermost thought he'd pondered one morning, ' "before one composes a letter" – a piece of advice I am finding highly helpful.'

'You will not leave it too long, will you? My shift is only twelve hours, so I am away again at seven, when Nurse Mooljum will be in charge.'

'No, no, my composition is almost entire already! I am

209

most grateful for the facilities.'

'My pleasure, Peerswammy! Oh dear, a new patient. . .'

He bustled off, and Ramjut Pillay retrieved the hidden sheet of paper, turned it round the right way up, and fell to work again. How he chuckled – very softly, of course – as he saw the fruit of his latest and greatest inspiration blossoming before him. It was a work of sheer genius.

Gone were his plans to send Sergeant Zondi a map. Gone were his ideas of making direct contact with him, which would have involved admitting at some stage that he had absconded with a little of the mail that fateful day.

No, what he was doing now would have only one effect: it would give the CID another chance to open the post arriving at Woodhollow and to find the very same anonymous threatening letter among it, written on the identical paper and word-perfect.

Or almost word-perfect.

Gracious me, thought Ramjut Pillay, I must have read the thing umpteen times that tormented night, and yet I cannot remember the name that began *Riche* properly. It came in front of *Act II, scene ii* and *"The pen is mightier than the sword"*. What about *Richelieu*? No, that still didn't look right. But at least *JUW* was spelled as it had been.

'And finally', said Kramer, shifting the position of his feet on his desk, 'I wrote down for this Doc Wilson the line in double quotes typed on the end of Naomi Stride's last page. You know the "two, comma, two" that had us so fooled?'

Zondi nodded, doodling "*II, ii!*" on a report form.

'Ach, he didn't bat an eyelid, man! Came straight out with the answer! It stands for "Act II, scene ii", when you're talking about a play.'

'Hau! And did this Doc Wilson give you the reason why the killer chose to make this reference, boss? Did it explain the motive?'

Kramer took out his notebook and opened it at a page marked with his last supermarket receipt. 'Wilson said the whole scene was summed up in the final words spoken by Hamlet. "The play's the thing wherein I'll catch the conscience of the king." '

'Boss?'

'Apparently Hamlet suspects the king was the bloke who murdered his own pa, so he puts on a play about a murder to make him blush and fart and give himself away. "Hey, hang on there," I said to this Wilson, "remember it's a lady, not a king, that's been murdered in real life. How does that fit in?" "Ach, no problem," he says, "the lady – that's Hamlet's ma – was also guilty." Then we really started arguing, because I couldn't see how this was even close to being a motive in the Stride case. In the end, he said he would think about it some more, and in the meantime he's given us a copy we can look at, but I still stick to the mad-popsie theory.'

'You mean Miss Liz Geldenhuys? But, boss, if—'

'Now, listen to me, Mickey. At last we know one thing for definite about this murderer: it's somebody who knows the play *Hamlet* – agreed?'

'Agreed, boss.'

'We also have reason to believe this person is of the female sex, because it was a woman's words that the killer used the pansies and the rosemary to symbolise. A young woman upset by "thoughts" and "remembrances" who has lost the love of her life, OK? Someone so bitter that even using a sword would seem—'

'But, boss, what would turn her bitterness against—?'

'Just wait till I'm finished, hey? We have evidence to suggest that Liz Geldenhuys was such a woman. She was badly treated by the deceased, who did not think her fit for her son, and who may even have plotted with Tess Muldoon of the sexy voice to drive her away from young Kennedy. Just say that, after leaving Afro Arts, Liz Geldenhuys somehow found out about this – wouldn't that give her more than enough motive for revenge? Just say, also, that first she wrote a whole lot of letters to Ma Stride on the sort of cheap blue paper her kind would buy, but Ma Stride just ignored them, never answered? That could have been the fatal snub, Mickey – and, one other thing, remember that Liz Geldenhuys had been to the house that night with Theo, and that would have given her a chance to see its layout and know her

211

way around.'

'This young woman who goes mad is also in Act II, scene ii, Lieutenant?'

'Of course, man – but check it yourself if you like.' Kramer tossed across a dog-eared stage copy of the play. 'The name's O-something. Ophelia?'

Zondi opened it. 'Is this play a big poem?' he asked. 'All these short lines. . .'

'Ach, no, it's more likely the crude printing in those days. You'll notice they can't bloody spell, either.'

'Hau, "Kwa Hamlet by William Gagonk"!'

Colonel Muller walked in. 'What you two find to laugh at just amazes me,' he said, and Zondi sprang to his feet. 'Tromp, what's this you've been telling Piet Baksteen about the sword being the University's'?'

'Colonel, I was just on my way to see you, sir,' said Kramer, getting up, too. 'I first wanted to get Zondi here out on his bicycle, making some urgent follow-ups. How are Jones and Mbopa doing? Have they caught up yet with Ramjet Pillbox?'

The Colonel's brow darkened. 'Don't talk to me about—' Then, glancing at Zondi, he said: 'Fine, finish off giving your orders, by all means, but I want you in my office in exactly two minutes.'

'My orders are, boss?' asked Zondi, as soon as he had gone.

'Mickey, you've got the broad picture now?'

'I think so, Lieutenant. First on our list is to find Miss Liz Geldenhuys, and then we must see if she—'

'Except none of that is your concern right now.'

'Boss?'

'I'm switching you to the Zuidmeyer job.'

'Hau!'

'Unofficially, of course, old son. In this case, what we know for definite now is how the lady was made to slip and kill herself. Who dreamed up the idea is a different matter, but at least I think we can safely say it was one of two known suspects, the father or the son. At the moment, the son is most under suspicion, because of Doc Strydom's opinion concerning the bruise marks, but we must keep an open mind

212

and—'

'Prove it was the father, because that is what we believe, boss?'

Kramer cuffed his hat off, but caught it before it reached the floor. 'Hey, kaffir, just you watch it, man!' he said with a wink. 'Now, here's a couple of things I want you to check out for us. Ready?'

It wasn't until Ramjut Pillay had folded his masterful copy of the anonymous threatening letter sent to Naomi Stride, and had sealed it in its envelope, that he realised something that made him feel quite ill.

There was Nurse Chatterjee, absorbed in a first edition of the evening paper, across the front of which the headlines read NAOMI STRIDE SLAIN BY SWORD, and here he was, Ramjut Pillay, about to address a letter to her! A letter, moreover, which he had to hand to Nurse Chatterjee if he wanted it posted.

We have made terrible slip-up, thought Ramjut Pillay. Speak for yourself, said another side to him, Naomi Stride wasn't her only name, little do many people know.

'Euphrates!' exclaimed Ramjut Pillay.

'Bless you,' murmured Nurse Chatterjee, engrossed in the murder case.

Mrs Kennedy, Ramjut Pillay printed on the cheap blue envelope, wishing its flap had had a nicer-tasting gum. Then he hesitated and glanced back at Nurse Chatterjee's paper.

Woodhollow In Pictures – See Inside said another heading in red letters.

Now what do we do, wondered Ramjut Pillay, when Woodhollow must now be one of the most famous addresses in the land? Instantly recognisable by an astute chappie such as Nurse Chatterjee?

So another side to him simply took over, and wrote *30 Jan Smuts Close, Morningside, Trekkersburg* – the correct address, little did many people know.

'Done,' said Ramjut Pillay.

He experienced only one more bad moment after that, which was when, having arrived at Nurse Chatterjee's desk, he noticed the dateline on the newspaper. This acted as a reminder that the anonymous threatening letter would now be arriving at Woodhollow *days* rather than merely hours after the deceased's decease. Another side to him, however, reasoned that as the first letter had been late the second letter ought to be late as well.

'You have completed your epistle?' said Nurse Chatterjee in a friendly way, but without bothering to look up from his paper. 'Just slip it into my drawer, Peerswammy, there's a good fellow. Now, why would anyone wish to kill this poor lady with an old sword of all unsterile things?'

'Ho-hum,' said Ramjut Pillay, for whom the newspaper's dramatic revelation that day had come, false modesty aside, as really no surprise at all.

Far, far away, Mbopa could hear the sound of people speaking long words, and then, through a swirling white mist, he thought he saw the hand of Zsazsa Lady Gatumi reaching out to him. She laid this hand very briefly on his forehead, and not where she generally placed it, which surprised him. He grabbed for her buttocks, but was pushed back.

'Signs of life anyway, Nurse,' some white man remarked.

'Built like a bloody tank,' said another. 'Took half the steering-column with him on his way through the windscreen, apparently. That's how they found him, sitting in the road, going *barp-barp* and wiggling the wheel this way and that.'

'Isn't quite the story I heard,' said the first voice, growing steadily fainter. 'The ambulance crew said he was sitting on his boss's *head* doing the *barp-barps*, using the poor bugger's nose as his hooter, and saying, "Which way *now*, you damn fool jackal?"'

The Colonel stared disconsolately at the badly chewed mouthpiece of his new briar. 'You'd never believe I bought this just last Tuesday,' he said. 'The strain has been terrible, and now . . . and now . . . Well, you heard it for yourself, Tromp, two CID vehicles written off in one day, and Jones having to be given blood by the gallon.'

'Hell, think of the nice rest it'll be for him, Colonel, not having to go out in his big cloak tonight on the off-chance some popsie's left her window open.'

'Tromp?' said Colonel Muller, mystified. 'What sort of allegations are these?'

'Ask Mrs Muller, sir – we had a talk about it at the last police ball. But, before all this, you were saying. . .?'

'I was saying – h'm. Oh ja, Jones asked for a pen and paper while he was still in the ambulance, and he wrote what looks like a name on it. Here, see for yourself. Could be worth a follow-up; he obviously thought it important.'

Perswami Lall, the note said.

Kramer thought a moment, then decided the quickest way of getting rid of this particular irritation would be to pocket it. 'Fine, sir,' he said, 'and how do you rate what Zondi and me have come up with today?'

'It's, er – well, not easy to *co-ordinate*, Tromp.'

'You'd like more information first, sir?'

'Please.'

'Then I'll be going, hey? I—'

'By the way, what did you think of this picture?' asked Colonel Muller, pointing to something under the heading *Police Divers Who Made Sword Find*. 'I look quite nice in it, don't I?'

'You're doing a great job on the publicity, sir.'

'Talking of which, anything new on the Zuidmeyer front?'

'No, Colonel, nothing worth repeating,' said Kramer, who had already made up his mind to save everything until after the arrest, when it'd be too late for anyone to interfere with him. 'In fact, I think they're both still in a state of shock and inclined to talk nonsense, so I was leaving further interviews to tomorrow. It'll only take one of them to change his story, and it could end up as just an accident after all.'

Colonel Muller looked pleased, then said with a wag of his pipe: 'But what about Doc Strydom's evidence about the bruises?'

'He was never a hundred per cent certain, Colonel.'

'Ja, that's true. I hear he's sent some slides down to Durban for a second opinion. OK, fine, and so it's this Liz Geldenhuys you're after right now?'

'As soon as I find out where to contact her, Colonel.'

'Well, man, here's the phone – ring up your plump lady friend at Afro Arts; there's just a chance she's still on the premises, even if it's after five.'

So Kramer dialled and waited.

'Afro Arts, but I'm afraid we're closed for business now. Could you call again in the morning?'

'Er, It's the CID here. Winny Barnes, is she still around?'

'I like that!' she said, switching to Afrikaans.

'Ach, so it's you, hey? Tell me, Winny, any idea where I can contact Liz Geldenhuys?'

'Yes, I've got an address somewhere, mixed up in her tax whatsits I've still to send in. Just a mo. . . It's 24 Sweethaven Avenue, which is near the aluminium factory and the drive-in. Anything else I can do for you, Tromp?'

'Ach, not right away. But thanks, and see you, hey?'

The Colonel watched him replace the receiver. 'What's the problem, Tromp? Why the funny look? You've got the address, what more do you need?'

'No "funny look", Colonel; and, as you say, I'm ready to go, so I'll go. Thanks for your help, sir.'

That was twice I've lied to the old bugger tonight, thought Kramer, as he went down the stairs. Once about the Zuidmeyers, and again when what must have been a funny look had crossed his face. Disembodied, he'd just discovered, overweight Winny Barnes had a very sexy voice on the telephone when she spoke in English.

Zondi turned left into Lawrence Street and cruised slowly past the municipal abattoir. The place had been rebuilt two or three years back, but looked no more inviting than its red-brick predecessor. The slaughter-house itself had no proper windows, just narrow fanlights very high up, and the only access appeared to be the huge doorway, now closed, at the top of the offloading ramp. Three enormous cattle-lorries were parked in the yard, which had a new chain-link fence around it, but the carpark was empty outside the adjacent small block of offices. Then another doorway to the slaughter-house came in view, round the far side. A sort of crane projected from above it, equipped with block and tackle, and below this was a loading-bay. Zondi left the street and drove along the dirt track towards it. What interested him were the half-dozen huge waste-disposal bins, hazy with flies even at this hour of the day, and surrounded by other garbage packed into big black plastic bags.

The stench was terrible. He stopped breathing through his nose and got out. Behind the row of garbage-bags he found four used DH-136 containers, tied loosely together with a length of string through their handles. He unscrewed each of the four containers and poured their contents into an old baked-bean can. The liquid was slow and viscous, but before too long he had about a cupful; more than enough, he calculated, to make the floor of a small shower lethal.

'So what does this prove, Lieutenant?' he murmured to himself.

Simply that a person did not have to work at the abattoir in order to get hold of some of its DH-136, not while the rubbish dump remained accessible to anyone who chose to venture in off a street that was generally deserted after five o'clock.

The light was fading fast and the man with his head under the bonnet of his battered Buick was using a cigarette-lighter to see by.

'Trying to find a petrol leak?' asked Kramer. 'They tell that method never fails.'

The man looked around with a scowl, then opened his watery eyes wide.

'My God, if it isn't the great train robber himself,' said Kramer giving his trousers a hitch. 'How goes it, Bippy? Still sleeping snug as a bug, hey?'

This brought the scowl back. Some years ago, Bippy Unwin had boarded the overnight mail train to Johannesburg, forced the guard at gunpoint to heave a pile of sealed canvas bags out of the guard's van, while the train was slowly climbing the escarpment above Trekkersburg, and had then jumped out after them into the night. Which was when things had started to go wrong for Bippy Unwin. He broke his nose on a tree trunk and twisted his ankle on landing. He had hobbled back down the line, snuffling so loudly that he'd been followed by two herd boys in search of a sick calf, and then had made a discovery that demonstrated how travel really did broaden the mind. Never having taken a night train anywhere before, Bippy Unwin had been unaware that the South African Railways always used lead seals on its big canvas bags of bedding rolls to prove nobody else had slept in them.

'Are doo here just to tordure a man?' he asked, his nose never having fully recovered.

'Ach, no, Bip – far from it, hey? I was trying to raise somebody across the way at number 24. Doesn't look like anyone's at home and I see all the windows are shut.'

'Dey're away.'

'Oh ja?'

'Dast Sadderday. Geldenduys took dem all to his brudder's farm. His daughter's dot been doo good.'

'You mean Liz? She also went with them?'

Bippy Unwin nodded.

'How far away is his brother's farm?'

'Dunno, but it's dear Dundee.'

'Oh, so they're still in Natal? You don't know the farm's name, do you?'

'Dope.'

'You're right,' said Kramer, 'and you always have been.'

The second of Zondi's two enquiries for the Lieutenant was proving something of a tall order. 'Find out for me, Mickey,' he had said, 'where this girlfriend of young Jannie Zuidmeyer lives. Her name's Marlene.'

Not much to go on, and made even more difficult by the fact that Zondi hadn't the slightest idea of what either of them looked like.

He dared one trip down Acacia Drive, knowing how conspicuous a black at the wheel of a car would be in such a neighbourhood, but saw nobody in the vicinity of the Zuidmeyer bungalow, let alone Jannie and Marlene sitting in front of it having sundowners, as he'd fantasised for a moment.

His eye did catch one thing, however, that he found encouraging. Parked beyond the shiny red Datsun in the driveway at 146 Acacia Drive was a motor scooter which looked like it belonged to a young man, to go by the unnecessary number of rearview mirrors sticking out from its handlebars. This indicated that Jannie Zuidmeyer had to be either at home or visiting someone within very easy walking distance. Young white males, in his experience, never went anywhere on foot that would take more than five minutes, although, show them a rugby field and they'd run up and down it for hours.

Narrowing down Jannie Zuidmeyer's whereabouts could be done by telephone, of course, and if Zondi limited himself to a couple words, spoken with a guttural Afrikaner accent, then he reckoned he could get away with it. More than a few words, however, and Major Zuidmeyer, who'd been no fool whatever his other reputation, would be on to him in a twinkling.

So Zondi drove a little way out of the neighbourhood, found a telephone box near a small row of shops, and tried dialling the Zuidmeyer number. The phone rang and rang. His gaze wandered over a wall plastered with old posters and stopped at a faded blue one with black lettering. HAMLET, it said, and beneath that gave other details, including the name of the actor in the leading role, *Aaron Sariff*. The play had been over for three weeks, Zondi noted.

'Hello?' said a drunken voice.

'Jannie?'

'He's at Marlene's.'

'Where?'

'Marlene's! Marlen Thomas's! That must be you again, Adrian. Didn't I tell you to say "Where, please, *Major*"? Next time, don't forget your manners, or I won't answer, you hear?'

And down went the phone, leaving Zondi with more than he'd hoped for, and an insight into the pathetic state of the man's mind.

Twice, while working his way through 'Improve Your Wordpower' in Nurse Chatterjee's copy of *Reader's Digest*, Ramjut Pillay had been sorely tempted to sneak a look at the correct answers. But he had resisted this urge steadfastly, knowing that it would jeopardise that most precious state of mind any man could aspire to – a perfectly clear conscience. His conscience had been clear for almost two hours now, and already he could sense something of the rather remarkable aura others would soon detect in him, making them want to come and sit at his feet.

Nurse Chatterjee looked over his shoulder. 'My goodness, you are courageous to tackle such imponderables,' he said admiringly. 'My personal knowledge of English would never be up to it. Have you received some special training?'

'A great deal,' admitted Ramjut Pillay. 'Ask me anything from Algebra, Part One, to Zoology, Part Two.'

'English Literature included?'

'I have perused the works of Dr Watson, concerning the great Sir Sherlock Holmes, much of Mr Michael Spillane, and, of course, there is my daily dipping into Oxford's Collected Aphorisms and Sayings in search of an uppermost—'

'Aha,' said Nurse Chatterjee and went off.

How rude, thought Ramjut Pillay, then realised that a new patient may have arrived, and looked up, anxious it wouldn't be anyone too noisy or frightening. To his mild surprise, the tall doctor in the long white coat, whose name he'd gathered was Schrink, had returned to the ward and was sitting at the desk, reading something with lively interest.

'Remarkable, quite remarkable,' Ramjut Pillay could just hear him murmuring to Nurse Chatterjee. 'That confirms my interpretation entirely. At first glance, of course, it purports to be the work of an almost complete illiterate. All these block capitals in the wrong places, the spelling, the grammar – or lack of it. But, as I said the moment I set eyes on it, sound habits die hard, they may even pass unnoticed! Or was it conceit, do you think, that compelled him to give the precise source of the quotation, "The pen is mightier than the sword"? Most people would probably wrongly attribute it to the Bible or the Bard, and yet, unconsciously one assumes, he simply cannot allow himself to be counted among them. He makes a slight concession to his feigned illiteracy, I suppose, by placing the source before the quotation, rather than after it, but the unthinking arrogance endemic among lesser university intellectuals and their ilk is still there. The whole episode being triggered by this "slain by sword" newspaper on your desk, wouldn't you say?'

'My very self-same conclusion, Doctor,' said Nurse Chatterjee.

'We can thank God for that, Nurse. Had I merely been handed this note, without any notion of where it had come from, then I would have immediately informed the police. It is simply charged with paranoid delusions and, as for the fantasy represented by the sword in the quotation, I would be very much afraid there would be some attempt to fulfil it. What truly alarms me, I must admit, is that I doubt very much that I'd have pointed the police in the right direction. Most certainly not towards a – ah, a member of your race, shall we say?'

'Then what would your advice have been, Doctor?' asked Nurse Chatterjee. 'I am meaning, who would you have suggested to the police to check over?'

'An intellectual, more than probably associated with a place of learning, someone who already displays paranoid tendencies – they could not be entirely supressed, running at this level – and a person, dare I say it, of Semitic origin? The spelling of "Jew" must surely be familiar to even the least educated among us, but to deny this knowledge so vigorously, while having no trouble with a complex word like "Richelieu", *is to deny too much*, in my estimation. Or have I lost you there?'

'No, no, not in the least, Doctor! You are saying that by pretending to know nothing the man would hope nobody will suspect *him* of being the very thing he knows nothing about.'

'Precisely. You've a good mind, Nurse; see that you never miss a chance to use it. But back, I'm afraid, to the more mundane matter in hand. I see from these notes you've practically confirmed paranoid schizophrenic, what with these voices, et cetera. Anything else to add?'

Ramjut Pillay just went on staring at them, hearing every word being said, but finding himself so devastated he could neither move, utter nor blink.

'Good God, Nurse Chatterjee, look! Now we appear to have become catatonic!'

16

IT WAS seven o'clock exactly when Kramer arrived at Azalea Mansions, parked beside the zebra-striped Land-Rover belonging to Theo Kennedy, and went to knock at his front door. He noted the time while waiting for an answer, and wondered how Zondi was progressing. So far, his own efforts to achieve anything had been abortive. He had tried every house in Sweethaven Avenue, asking if anyone knew exactly where the Geldenhuys family at Number 24 had got themselves to, and had ended up none the wiser.

He was about to turn away from yet another door, and to try the Stilgoes' instead, when Theo Kennedy opened up, looking delighted to see him.

'Sorry about the delay,' he said, 'but I went to the bedroom window to see who it was first. Come right in, and I'm sure Vicki'll be just as—'

'Ach, I've got just a quick question I could ask you out here.'

'Wouldn't hear of it, Tromp,' said Kennedy, glancing back over his shoulder and lowering his voice before adding: 'Got a lot to thank you for, you know. Without Vicki – and Amanda – I don't think I could've handled the last few days.'

'That's what neighbours are for, hey? They'd probably have offered—'

'Listen, I'm still grateful, OK? Vicki's been marvellous, even encouraging me to have a good cry when I've needed it, and that's helped as well.'

Kramer hoped for his sake it'd been more than a weep in the arms of a willing woman. Death, he had always found, was best encountered by its opposite, by the act which began life. To be sure, it included its own little death, but not until there had been a joyous affirmation of what being alive could mean – and even what a soul was, although he generally left that side of things to the Widow Fourie, while he lit a Lucky.

'No, we haven't – not yet,' said Kennedy with a smile, having picked up something in his expression. 'Vicki's keeping me at arm's length; she says I'm still too vulnerable. There'll be time enough.'

'Oh ja? So it's like that, is it?'

'It's – well, I'm not even bothering to think about it. I'm just glad it's happening and, if we're wrong, that'll be an end to it, before anyone gets hurt.'

Amanda won't see it that way, thought Kramer, as he followed Kennedy through into the living-room. That's the little lady you should be watching out for.

'Hello, again,' said Vicki Stilgoe, 'although we really only just saw each other by the pool this afternoon. Were you very busy?'

'Like a buffalo with its bum on fire,' said Kramer, noticing with some relief that she appeared to have eyes only for Kennedy. 'I did come out later to say "How goes it", but by then you'd pushed off before the circus properly started.'

She laughed. 'Theo, isn't that how I described it? That incredible colonel making those divers rehearse and rehearse, so you wouldn't need to get mixed up in it!'

'*And* so there wouldn't be too much egg on our face,' Kramer pointed out to her. 'Uniform were meant to have searched every inch of the place. Still, as Zondi -'

'What a nice, gentle man he is. Amanda adored him.'

'Oh ja, he's saved my life a few times.'

'How many?' asked Kennedy, tapping an invitation on the

Scotch-bottle he was holding.

'I'll take a dozen – or do you mean how many times Zondi's pulled the trigger?'

Kennedy laughed, and poured a large tot. 'You're being evasive.'

'Not really. Nine times.'

'Good God, he's killed nine people?' said Vicki Stilgoe.

'Nine occasions, I should have said, because sometimes the bastards were in batches. Ach, if you want a head-count, around fifteen.'

'*Fifteen?*'

'You realise what that means, don't you, Tromp?' said Kennedy, handing him the Scotch. 'There's an old saying to the effect that, if you save a man from death, you're responsible for him for the rest of his life. Something tells me I'd hate to be responsible for what you get yourself—'

'Actually, Mickey and me are quits, hey? There's about fifteen on my side, too.'

'That's *thirty*,' said Vicki Stilgoe, staring at him. 'Thirty people – almost a busful! – between you.'

'Not counting the ones who didn't surprise us, of course, Mrs Stilgoe.'

'Not more! Well, you've certainly surprised *me*, Tromp – and, please, it's just "Vicki".' She got up and reached the drinks cabinet before Kennedy could intercept and take over. 'Don't be silly, Theo; I hate feeling one of those helpless women!'

'*I* wouldn't mind feeling a—'

'Now, then! I think I may have to call a policeman!'

But Kramer only half-heard that. He, too, had been surprised by his disclosures, and was wondering what on earth had prompted him to make them. Not even with Zondi had he ever started totting up before, and he had only just stopped himself from going on to give the number they'd sent to the gallows. Then he noticed that, when Vicki Stilgoe sat down again, she did so a good metre further away than before, and that's when he smiled. His instincts had, presumably, been making sure he'd not attract another of her tingling looks, not now or at any time in the future when it might ruin a good thing for a good bloke like Theo Kennedy.

'Is this just a social call?' she asked, a little stiffly but trying to sound friendly.

Kramer took a sip of his drink. 'First of all,' he said, 'let me tell you what I found out up at the University this afternoon.'

'Lieutenant Kramer's not back yet?' asked Colonel Muller, entering the office a moment after Zondi slipped the copy of *Hamlet* under a docket. 'Come, I want to show you something.'

Zondi followed him down into the courtyard.

'There,' said the Colonel, pointing. 'What's that on the new rose-bush?'

'One yellow rose, Colonel?'

'Right, a rose! Which Gagonk Mbopa had the cheek to tell me you couldn't get already growing when you bought a rose-bush. I had to go to a lot of trouble today to get it exchanged, and I want you to tell him that when you visit him in hospital.'

'In hospital, Colonel?'

'He's been in a traffic accident, but it's mainly just bruises and concussion. Lieutenant Jones is the one in a bad way – multiple lacerations.'

'Hau, shame!'

'A terrible shame,' agreed Colonel Muller. 'Where am I supposed to get two new vehicles from? They don't grow on trees, hey? And certainly not on rose-bushes!'

Zondi laughed at his joke and, taking advantage of the change in mood, risked putting a question that was bothering him. 'Colonel, sir,' he said, 'on a point of informtion, can you tell me what sort of a name "Rosencrantz" is?'

'Rosencrantz? Rosencrantz? Where have you come across that?'

'Just in a book I was reading, sir.'

'Ach, if it's "Rosen" with a "crantz" added on for swank, then I'd say it was definitely Jewish.'

Kennedy shook his head hard, as if to clear it. 'Rosemary and

225

pansies, Laertes' sword – I can't keep up! And what precisely is the relevance of "Act II, scene ii"?'

'I've got Doc Wilson working on that, seeing as he's the *Hamlet* expert.'

'Now I'm lost, too,' said Vicki Stilgoe. 'Why *Hamlet* in particular?'

'I see what you mean,' agreed Kennedy. 'That could have been an allusion to any play with a second act and a second scene.'

'Ja, but as everything else is *Hamlet* it stands to reason,' said Kramer.

'Not necessarily, surely,' said Vicki Stilgoe. 'Whoever this is seems to be someone with a – well, literary bent, I suppose you'd call it – and that could mean the link is with some other. . . Are you sure you've got nothing else to help you pin it down?'

Kramer shrugged. 'Nothing we've come across so far, hey? There's a chance we'd know more if Theo's ma had kept some letters she had recently, but she went and burned them.'

'Oh, what sort of letters?'

'All we know is they were written on cheap blue writing-paper with lines, Vicki. Tess Muldoon saw her reading one of them two Saturdays ago, and looking a bit upset. The pity of it is, Theo's ma didn't tell her what was in it.'

'Huh, that doesn't surprise me,' said Kennedy.

Kramer turned to him. 'Why's that? I thought Tess and your ma were in cahoots?' And then, mindful of his conspiracy theory, regarding the ousting of Liz Geldenhuys by a woman with a sexy voice, he added less than truthfully: 'I got the impression from Tess that they shared secrets, and would be willing to sort of do anything to help each other out.'

Kennedy threw back his head and laughed. 'Secrets perhaps, but the rest isn't Tess!'

'Sorry?'

'Tess Muldoon, let me assure you, Tromp, is the sort of person who never gets involved with *anyone else's* problems. She's like a sleek, green-eyed cat: beautiful to look at, lovely

226

to stroke, I'd imagine, but totally "bugger you" in her attitude when it comes to humans demanding anything more of her. My mother often said she'd have liked to unburden herself on occasion to Tess, "but it would've been like asking one's Siamese if one could borrow a Kleenex".'

Vickie Stilgoe giggled, and Kramer, who needed time to think, said: 'I didn't know your ma made jokes, hey? They say her books were always so serious.'

Kennedy nodded. 'We had rows about that, too – it spoiled some of her best writing. She'd put everything into, say, a scene in a Bantu males' hostel, and then forget it was only because they found things to laugh at that they didn't go stark raving crackers. I used to become very restless, reading them, and not know quite why, until I spotted what the mistake was. Mum's answer to that was "Don't you realise, Theo, I *weep* when I write those bits." She bottled up a lot.'

'Although, where Liz Geldenhuys was concerned, your ma didn't exactly bottle up what she thought of her table manners and how she kept saying "Ach" in front of her sentences.'

'Mum didn't say a word about that to her!' Kennedy went pale. 'How the Jesus—? Oh, I see, Tess again! Well, that's that bitch written off!'

'Not Tess, another source,' said Kramer. 'But, while we're on the subject, do you think your break-up could've had anything to do with—?'

'Look, Tromp, I know I might be a bit touchy about my mum at the moment, but I still think I've every right to resent what you seem to be implying. She could have a very wicked tongue in private, just as she could in her books, but she wasn't the sort of person to go hurting someone like Liz. And, besides, my mother's never tried to interfere directly in my life, however much she may have—'

'Ja, I'm sorry, Theo, but I have a job to do, hey? And you can't deny, man, that *somebody* has interfered in your life until very recently. I'm talking about the "sexy voice" phone calls.'

'God, you leave no stone unturned! What has all this to do with anything?'

'These calls, Theo, can you tell me if—?'

'Look, I've not heard that bitch's voice since the day before Liz walked out, and so what relevance—?'

'Winny Barnes says the last one was only last week.'

'Yes, and I was away. I've been away every time she's phoned since Winny came to work for me. I still can't see what the hell you're driving at, Tromp!'

But Kramer suddenly saw something then. He saw Winny Barnes lift the receiver in her father's boring photographic shop and begin a series of telephone calls. He saw Winny taking over as assistant to Theo Kennedy, a man she plainly idolised, and he even saw her pause outside a jeweller's window, her eye caught by a tray of wedding rings.

'If I might interrupt,' said Vicki Stilgoe, 'time to pop next door.'

To give him his due, Nurse Chatterjee had stayed on after his shift ended in an effort to placate Ramjut Pillay, and because his relief, Nurse Mooljum, could hardly be expected to pick up the pieces single-handed. But Ramjut Pillay was in no frame of mind to give anybody his due, not even the Devil himself.

Ever since regaining his voice and the ability to move, he had been loudly denouncing Garrison Road Mental Hospital as an institution filled with traitors and unspeakable cads, while prancing about, exposing himself, on the top of the ward cupboard. Nothing would make him listen to reason. Nothing would make him come down again, and the rest of the patients were becoming over-excited.

'Look here, Peerswammy, kindly replace your pyjama trousers and—'

'Ho, ho, so the great Dr Schrink is back!'

'Kindly stop referring to me—'

'Showing us where we are Jewish!' demanded Ramjut Pillay.

'Peerswammy, you're missing the point. In saying—'

'We are *not* missing our point. Just you looking, Dr Schrink, and you will see it is entirely uncircumscribed!'

Nurse Chatterjee came a step closer. 'But nobody said you

228

were Jewish, Peerswammy Lal, old fellow. What you over—'

'Nobody said', Ramjut Pillay echoed bitterly, 'that this was a place where an honest face was not to be trusted! Once a letter is sealed, it becomes—'

'But you shouldn't have sealed it, Peerswammy, that is altogether against hospital regulations. We have to read all correspondence before it is leaving here, to make sure nothing that is offensive—'

'By jingo, you just think yourself lucky I am trying to emasculate the Mahatma! If that were not so, already your traitorous dog's body would – betrayed again! O woe is Ramjut Pillay!'

Men in white had leaped up from nowhere, catching him completely off guard, so intent had he been on replying to treacherous Nurse Chatterjee.

'Ramjut Pillay?' he heard Dr Schrink repeat after him. 'What is going on? Pillay, Pillay, Pillay . . . rings a bell somewhere. Some sort of police notice we had circulated to us?'

'I have seen none, Doctor,' said Nurse Chatterjee. 'Have you, Mooljum?'

'Typical of the organisation in this place,' grumbled Dr Schrink. 'I'm still waiting for those figures on drug dosages to surface again. Oh, well, what I propose is, unless something else happens, that we have another word with him in the morning, once the sedative has properly calmed him down, and then possibly get in touch with them. I'm curious to know who this Mrs Kennedy could be.'

No, no, *no*! pleaded Ramjut Pillay.

But he could only do so by blinking, because he was again unable either to move or to utter, having been gagged and then strapped most cruelly into a straitjacket.

There was a whole shelf of books by Naomi Stride above Theo Kennedy's stereo equipment, noted Kramer. The next shelf up was almost empty, apart from a road atlas, a dictionary and a few African ornaments.

'Vicki'll be back in a minute,' said Kennedy, returning to

229

the living-room. 'That was Amanda. Bruce is looking after her, but she won't go to sleep until she's been kissed goodnight.'

'And you're now included in the bedtime parade, hey?'

Kennedy nodded. 'Mind you, as I think I mentioned to you before, Mandy and me have been friends for some time now. You got any kids?'

'Mine isn't the job for them.'

'You don't think it'd be right?'

'Have you ever been to a police funeral? They fire guns at the end.'

'The salute?'

'Uh-huh. You should see those bloody kids jump.'

Kennedy stared at him, then turned away slowly and went over to the bottle of Scotch. He poured himself another tot, put a dash more in Vicki Stilgoe's tumbler, and came back to sit opposite Kramer. He offered him the peanuts.

'No, like I said, Theo, I'm doing fine, thanks.'

'I've been thinking,' said Kennedy. 'Putting two and two together. I can't believe what I've come up with, but I'm going to have to ask you if I'm right. Are you forming some sort of theory that Liz Geldenhuys is mixed up in my – in what's happened? Because, if you are, that's crazy!'

'You can't see there's a possible motive?'

'In that she blamed my mum for our splitting up? Or even, if my worst two-and-two is right, for being behind those calls to the shop?'

'Look, Theo, I've satisfied myself your mum had nothing to do with them, but from Liz's point of view she could've easily—'

'Stop! Please, just stop right there. You don't know Liz, you've never even set eyes on her, or you'd realise how totally ridiculous the whole idea is.'

'Then maybe I'd better see her for myself, hey?'

'On what pretext?'

'Oh, any information concerning your ma that she can think of which could be relevant to our investigation. I'll tell her we're going round everyone who knew her, which is true.'

Kennedy took a sip of his Scotch. 'Fine,' he said. 'Well, I suggest you do that as soon as possible. You know where she lives?'

'Ja, Sweethaven Avenue, only she's away up near Dundee at the moment,'

'Oh, yes, at Mooikop, her uncle's place. She took me riding there a few times.'

'Well, then,' said Kramer, 'perhaps I'd better—'

'At last,' said Vicki Stilgoe, with a mother's sigh, as she rejoined them. 'Some nights I could strangle Miss Moppet, but she's asleep now. Sorry, am I intruding—?'

'Don't be silly,' said Kennedy, getting up to bring her drink over. 'I've just been persuading Tromp to get a bee out of his bonnet.'

'What I can't understand—' she began.

'No, let's hear,' said Kramer. 'It's often a help to have someone right on the outside give their opinion, and female intuition's not always too far wrong.'

Vicke Stilgoe smiled at him, although her eyes still said he scared her, and sat down on the sofa. 'What I find baffling is why so much time is being spent on Theo's mother's personal or, if you like, family side of life. Surely, this could all have happened because she was, first and foremost, a famous writer.'

'So far, Vicki, we've no evidence to confirm that.'

'You haven't?'

'Listen, anybody could have gone up to the University and taken that sword from under the stage. Second—'

'Oh, come on,' she said. 'What about the bookish symbolism of the rosemary and the pansies? That reference to Act II, scene ii? Doesn't that all point to the motive, or whatever you call it, being somehow connected with writing?'

But Kramer, who'd had some fine honey from bees in his bonnet in the past, merely thanked them both for their hospitality and went on his way again, armed with Liz Geldenhuys's present address.

Zondi picked up the phone. 'Lieutenant Kramer's office. Yes,

231

Dr Wilson, will you hold on a minute, please – the Lieutenant has just walked in.' Then he cupped his hand over the mouthpiece and said: 'Any luck, boss?'

Kramer nodded. 'And you?'

'Both times. The father could have taken all the DH-136 he wanted from the rubbish at the abattoir, and Marlene Thomas's address and telephone number are here on your desk.'

'But where is my tea?'

Zondi grinned and handed the receiver to him.

'You've got something for me, sir?'

'Ah, Lieutenant! "A hit, a very palpable hit"!'

'Oh ja?'

'But before I go into Act II, scene ii,' said Wilson with a chortle, 'I have some intelligence for you.'

'You don't think my IQ's high enough as it is, Doc?'

Shrill donkey sounds. 'Superb! Must remember that! But what I intended to convey is that one of my staff has told me that Naomi Stride was among the audience on the first night. Another of my staff, who must also remain nameless, has also informed me that Aaron Sariff – you met briefly, remember? – had sent a play he'd written to Stride for her opinion, and had not been terribly pleased with her response. Yet another colleague—'

'Hell, you've been busy, hey?'

' "Not single spies, but in battalions", what?'

'Ja, what did this other bloke say?'

'Apparently, Aaron Sariff found out from a student who you were, and made a devil of a fuss about it, saying there were secret police everywhere, turning the University upside down and threatening the freedom of democracy. He also wanted to know, from me, whether you'd had a search warrant to look under the stage. Enormous fun all round.'

'Not that I can see why you're telling me all this, sir.'

'You can't? Thought it might amuse you – and Stride being here on the first night does establish a closer link with the play, doesn't it?'

'Yes and no,' Kramer enjoyed saying. 'From what I've read about her, Naomi Stride encouraged all the arts in the district, which would include seeing plays put on, not so? Can you get back to Act II, scene ii?'

'Ah, of course.' There was a shuffling of papers. 'I've spent hours on it, mulling over the possible significance of the scenes within the scene. Tends to give your "mad girl" a bit of a knock, of course. Ophelia's perfectly sane at this stage – it's Hamlet who's acting up a bit, pretending idiocy. Oh, and while we're touching on the significance of the pansies and the rosemary, I think I ought to point out that there is always the danger of being too literal in one's interpretations. Just because Ophelia spoke those words about "thoughts" and "remembrances", it wouldn't preclude a man from using them for his own ends. "Show me the steep and thorny way to heaven" – there, you could use that yourself, couldn't you, but, again, those are Ophelia's words, you see! And so—'

'And so?' prompted Kramer, doodling a jumping bean on his memo pad.

'Themes, themes, themes, none of which quite matched up – no wicked uncle et cetera, nothing to get one's teeth into. What I ended up doing was going through it line by line, disregarding the context, seeking only something that had the sense of immediate and undeniable relevance. I was appalled.'

'Appalled, sir?'

'Devastated to think that I could have failed to see the one and only truly apposite line right at the start. The line that has *got* to be the one – it shrieks at you.'

'Ja, go on, sir – I'm ready to write it down.'

'Here goes, then, Lieutenant: "many wearing rapiers are afraid of goose-quills".'

'And?'

'What "and" could there possibly be? *There it is* . . . Rapiers, rapiers, Lieutenant! Naomi Stride was killed by a rapier! The precise word, you see, not merely the rather vague word "sword", which embraces sabres, two-handed—'

'I see that, sir, but what has goose-feathers got to do with anybody?'

'Goose-*quills*, Lieutenant. Never heard of quill pens? Dear me, you must've. Even today, still a potent symbol of the writer, and so what this line means is—'

'The pen is a bigger bastard than the sword, sir?' said Kramer, wincing as another donkey joined the papal choir.

'At last, Lieutenant, you've pipped me to it! "Beneath the rule of men entirely great, the pen is mightier than the sword", Edward Bulwer-Lytton – I've just looked it up. And – would you believe it? – by some extraordinary coincidence those lines appear in Act II, scene ii, of his *Richelieu*!'

There was one of those pauses where Kramer felt he was expected to clap, but he spent it instead putting a large cigar into the mouth of the jumping bean on his memo pad.

'You do see the difference between those two quotations, don't you?' said Wilson, and there was the flare of a match. ' "Many wearing rapiers" invites an immediate association with the actors, and the "goose-quills" with—'

'The plays critic from the *Trekkersburg Gazette*?' said Kramer. 'You see, Doc, much as I appreciate your efforts, it still doesn't point to a motive, does it?'

'But aren't you being a bit hasty when you say that?'

'Ja, maybe,' Kramer grunted. 'I tell you what, I'll sleep on it – OK?'

'Sleep on what, boss?' asked Zondi, handing him his tea as he put the receiver down.

'Bloody Act II, scene ii.'

'Hau, a very cunning scene, Lieutenant! This Boss Hamlet—'

'Not you as well, hey! Give us—'

'But I found a line in it, boss, that could have been spoken by Mrs Stride in reference to Liz Geldenhuys.'

Kramer had a little tea first. 'Oh ja, and what was that?'

' "Lord Hamlet is a prince, out of your star", boss – which the father of the young madam Ophelia tells her, so she will not think of marrying with him. You know something also, boss? The last book Mrs Stride was writing had such a story also. There is this university teacher with a daughter—'

'Mickey, enough!' protested Kramer. 'My bloody head's going round, and I can't take another bloody clue, fancy theory, or anything else, understand? If it's not straightforward, *I don't want to know*.'

Zondi nodded and went back to his table, where he marked his place in *Hamlet* before dropping it into his jacket pocket. He started sharpening pencils.

'H'm, this should be straightforward enough,' murmured Kramer, reaching out for the slip of paper bearing Marlene Thomas's address. 'And your tea's bloody terrible, so we might as well get going, hey?'

By the light of his torch, bright with fresh batteries, Zondi continued to pick his way through this very strange and tantalising story, many parts of which he just had to skip. Other parts were no harder than the bible the nuns had given him when he'd left the mission school, which was how he knew words such as 'harlot' and 'delve', having once looked them up in a dictionary long, long ago. There was also something vaguely Zulu about the elaborate greetings people kept giving each other, and he enjoyed trying to fill in the missing verbs, as in: 'I must to England.'

Go to England? Sail? Travel?

He looked up. But it was not the Lieutenant who had come out on to the front veranda of the small bungalow. It was probably Mr Thomas, father of the girl Marlene. The man lit a cigarette, looked at his watch, and began to pace back and forward, stopping occasionally to listen outside a softly lit window.

After another ten minutes of *Hamlet*, Zondi found his concentration wandering. It was really too difficult. So he began to skip whole sections, stopping only when the words were short. He gave a grunt. Often these lines carried a very strong, satisfying meaning: 'I must be cruel to be kind. . .' How well he understood that, and then, with a start, he seemed to remember one of the old nuns having actually used those very words to him, the time he had been caned for not doing his homework. It made a bridge through the years he was afraid to step on.

There was a clatter from the veranda. The man had gone indoors again. A minute later, the Lieutenant emerged, walking slowly and sadly.

Zondi put *Hamlet* back in his pocket and started the car. He

235

had acquired a taste for searching for those simple lines and, if the night wasn't going to go on too long, he would search for some more.

Kramer sighed and took out his Luckies, lit two and put one in Zondi's mouth for him, as he was driving. 'Ja, Mickey,' he said, 'it must be a terrible thing to know that you have been the cause of the death of your own mother.'

'Boss?' Zondi glanced at him. 'Was Jannie there? Did he—?'

'I spoke just to his girlfriend, Marlene,' said Kramer, picturing her again as she sat hunched on a worn living-room sofa, her eyes swollen with crying. Not a pretty girl, but cuddlesome and plainly intelligent. 'Jannie has been talking to her almost non-stop. About how much he hates his father, how terribly his mother had suffered each time he had one of his "mishaps" then took it out on her, because he didn't like the reprimands he got from his seniors. But what Marlene can't understand is why, when Jannie has told her a hundred times his father made his ma slip, he first came to her and said: "Oh Jesus, Marlene – it was an accident, a terrible, terrible accident." And three times since then, when he's been very upset and crying to himself, the word "accident" has slipped out. Marlene didn't spell it out for me, but I saw what was eating her up. Listen, Jannie runs in and says: "Oh Jesus, Marlene – there's been an accident, a terrible, terrible accident." Fine, nothing to do with him. But if he says "it was a terrible accident"—'

'I've got it, Lieutenant. Hau, you mean he killed his mother by accident?'

'You wouldn't know this, Mickey, because I never told you all the details but, thinking back, I've known all along that Zuidmeyer was the first to use the bathroom every morning. Then, for once, he doesn't use it, he goes off to sulk in the garage, and it's his wife who steps into that shower. A shower which, as I see it, Jannie has made lethal before going off with the dog. He comes back expecting his pa to be dead, but who's lying there in the bathroom?'

'The Lieutenant is sure that—'

'So far, the facts fit, and once I've had a little chat with him I think you will find they fit even better.'

Zondi dropped speed. 'Sorry, I was not thinking, boss – did you want to go and talk with Jannie now, back there in Acacia Drive?'

'Actually, he was there at Marlene's, out cold in their spare room. I – ach, tomorrow, Mickey, tomorrow. He's old enough to do the rope dance, so one more night with young Marlene. . .'

As if endorsing this view, Zondi put his foot down.

'One good thing, though, Mickey!'

'What's that, Lieutenant?'

'The look on Zuidmeyer's face when I tell him.'

17

THAT NIGHT, Zondi dreamed very little. His sleep was so deep that when he awoke the next day his first thought was to wonder where he was. For years, there had been splintery rafters and corrugated asbestos roofing above him, walls of unplastered red brick on four sides, and a damp, stamped earth floor to make his bare feet sting on a winter's morning. But now, as he lay there, alone in the big bed that he and his wife Miriam had once shared with two of their children, it was like being in a neat whitewashed box with a flat lid, and when he rolled over he could see its warm green carpet. The Widow Fourie had sent him that, the same week as he'd shifted the family from Kwela Village to Hamilton. She had apologised, saying it was a little old and worn in places, but Miriam, who'd never owned any sort of carpet before, had been moved to tears.

'Wife!' Zondi called out, sitting up in bed. 'Wife, how is the time?'

Miriam put her head round the bedroom door. 'It is still early,' she said. 'I am ironing your suit, so you stay there a few minutes until it is finished. What was your big hurry yesterday, that you threw it into the corner all crumpled up? And whose was the blood?'

'Oh, just a road accident – and then I had to go quickly on a job for the Lieutenant.'

Miriam disappeared again, and soon he heard her humming away to herself and the thump of her iron. He looked back at the carpet, smiling as he recalled how, in the old days at Kwela Village, she had scored lines across the stamped earth to simulate the planking of a wooden floor. A very houseproud woman, was Miriam Zondi, and it was the greatest pleasure of his life to know that now she had a house to be proud of.

Admittedly, the place had only three rooms in place of two, a cement floor, and there was still no bathroom or separate kitchen, but at least the outside lavatory had a proper door on it, instead of the wooden flaps provided at Kwela Village, and everything looked new, having recently been slotted together. Who knows? In a few years, they might even have electricity, and then some of the Widow Fourie's other presents – the secondhand steam iron, for example – could come into use, too. He began to daydream. To imagine things that he might buy in the meantime. A small black-and-white television set, perhaps, like the people next door already owned, running it off a twelve-volt car battery. No, a paraffin refrigerator would please Miriam more. It was going to be a hot day again.

'Hau!' he heard her exclaim in great surprise.

'What is it, wife?'

'Come! Come and see this! Will you be angry with me?'

Zondi sprang out of bed and went through into the parlour. His suit, sponged and pressed, hung neatly over the back of a chair. On her ironing-board, Miriam had a sheet of blank paper.

'I found it in your jacket pocket,' she said. 'I thought it was for a letter you wanted to write, so I decided to put the iron on it to take out the creases. Then, straight away, there was this writing! Like a magic trick! Like witchcraft.' And she shuddered.

'Let me see,' said Zondi, reaching her side and looking down.

Sure enough, what had previously looked like a blank sheet of paper was now covered in pale-brown script under the heading: *Highly Secretive Thoughts With Reference Most Untimely Decease Of Late Naomi Stride (Professional Name)*

'Do you know what it means?' asked Miriam, putting her iron back on the stove to heat up again.

The Widow Fourie brought Kramer breakfast in bath, as she called it. The doughnuts went in the soap-rack, and the ginger beer in the tooth-mug. Then she stood in front of the mirror and dragged a brush through her head of thick blonde hair, tugging hard to get all the knots out. He liked to watch her doing this, as it made her heavy breasts bob gently, almost in slow motion.

'It's just as well it's another hot day already,' she murmured, her hair-clasp held between her teeth. 'If it wasn't, you'd have this mirror all steamed up. I don't know how you can stand water that a cook could boil eggs in.'

'So you've guessed my little secret, hey?' he said, reaching for the tooth-mug. 'But, let me tell you, it's a lot cheaper and less embarrassing than a vasectomy.'

The Widow Fourie smiled and glanced back at him. 'That last sleep did you good,' she said. 'Was it a nightmare that woke you up?'

'It was you shaking me, my girl, so don't start trying to establish alibis.'

'You were already almost on your feet, Trompie. I've never seen you so upset. What was the dream about?'

'Ach, some court or other.'

'I tried to guess, but all you kept saying was "It was the father, the father, not the son!" And you were crying for your ma.'

'Ach, rubbish,' said Kramer, and submerged himself.

The Widow Fourie stepped away from the splash this made, and put her clasp back in her hair. The soap in the water began to sting Kramer's eyes, so he sat up again, wiped his hand on a towel, and took a doughnut.

'Ma!' came a voice from the passage.

'Oh, for a life without kids . . .,' the Widow Fourie grumbled good-humouredly. 'What is it, Piet?'

'Ma, Uncle Trompie's office is on the phone!'

'I'll go,' she said, unbolting the door. 'See you don't get jam on the sponge again, hey? You made little Suikie think she was starting her first period.'

Kramer lay back and watched for his toes. They surfaced and stared back at him, the nails as blank-faced as an identity parade. The one he'd stubbed didn't stand a chance of course, having turned a nasty black. He remembered the nail missing from Naomi Stride's left foot, and his fists clenched. Like Tess Muldoon had said, for all her faults, a good woman. Tess Muldoon with the biggest spice-rack he'd ever seen. Rosemary.

'Ach, that was just Mickey,' said the Widow Fourie, coming back into the bathroom with a mouthful of toast. 'He must have done one of his impersonations for Piet. How long has he been playing tricks on the telephone? It's new, isn't it?'

'But he never usually rings me here. What's the message?'

'He says he'll be over in fifteen minutes to pick you up, Tromp. He's got some paper that he says makes all the difference to the Stride affair.'

'Oh ja? Then you'd better bolt the door again.'

'For why?'

'You said my last sleep did me good, hey? Fifteen minutes is just time for another.'

Nurse Chatterjee removed the gag and began unstrapping Ramjut Pillay. 'Good morning, Peerswammy,' he said, 'and what a bright beautiful morning it is! Can I take it that all is now forgiven and forgotten?'

'Forgotten?' said Ramjut Pillay hopefully, still groggy with the effect of an injection in his bottom.

'Quite so,' said Nurse Chatterjee. 'Even your curious reference to one Ramjut Pillay.'

'Oh, good, good. He's a most terrible fellow, that.'

'So you know him?'

Something warned Ramjut Pillay that somehow he was discussing matters he had resolved to ignore, but his feeling of euphoria, induced no doubt by a very clear conscience, made him say: 'Oh, only very slightly in passing.'

'A big fellow, strongly built, tall, aged thirty-one?'

'True, very true.'

'And a postman?'

'He—' Ramjut Pillay stopped.

'Why won't you confirm or deny? What are you hiding?'

'It is indeed a bright and beautiful morning, Nurse Chatterjee. It reminds me of a morning when my uppermost—'

'Then perhaps the police had better see you after all,' said Nurse Chatterjee. 'I have already told the doctor there would be no need, but maybe you have inside information and can assist them in their endeavours.'

Information did not come more insider, reflected another, truly transcendental side to Ramjut Pillay.

Zondi stopped the car a kilometre back down the road from the home of the Widow Fourie and handed Kramer the sheet of paper that Miriam had ironed for him. 'This I found in the Indian postman's room out at Gladstoneville, boss.'

'Let's have a read, then.'

'Lieutenant, maybe I should explain—'

'It's bloody funny ink, hey? What is it? Blood, watered-down?'

'Lemon juice, but none of that matters, boss – just look at what he says.'

So Kramer ran an eye over it:

Highly Secretive Thoughts With Reference Most Untimely Decease Of Late Naomi Stride (Professional Name)

———

1) Murderous blow struck from left side
2) Murderer ignorant fellow

3) No warning received of calamity to come
4) Deceased of Jewish persuadings
5)

Kramer frowned. 'What can you see that I can't see, Mickey? This looks to me to be complete rubbish. Or, at least, it's only what he saw with his own eyes, read about, or sucked out of his thumb.'

'The Lieutenant is quite correct, it is rubbish,' said Zondi. 'But when I read it I was reminded there was something we have not looked at too closely that could greatly simplify the case.' And he pointed to the heading on the sheet of paper.

'I still don't get it. . .'

'The words "most untimely", boss.'

'And so?'

'The phrase in English, boss, means "before her time".'

'Ja, I know that – and it's true. She was still quite a young woman.'

'That is what I thought when first I read it, Lieutenant,' Zondi went on. 'Then while I was looking at it again, in case I had missed something, I was helped by those words to remember that, in another sense, Mrs Stride had died *after her time.*'

'Kaffir, you're going to have to explain it better, hey?'

'I mean she died after her time here in South Africa, after when she should have left to go to England.'

Kramer took out his Lucky Strikes. 'Christ, I'm beginning to see what you're getting at. The question you're really asking is, who knew she was still around?'

Zondi nodded and accepted a light.

'As a matter of fact, Mickey, I put that to Theo Kennedy on the first day, but ever since then, with so many theories and clues to follow up, I'd completely forgotten this angle.'

'Maybe somebody hoped we would, boss. Maybe that is why there are so many clues.'

'Ach, no,' said Kramer, shaking his head. 'There's not been that many really, and why it got forgotten mainly was because....' He thumped a fist on the dashboard. 'Jesus Christ, it's been our whole approach! Right from the bloody

242

start, we've been doing nothing but look for the motive. Why, we kept saying, why kill this nice lady? That's where it began, with Jones's bullshit theory about her being killed for her money. We find the sword and the *Hamlet* link-up, and we're still saying, why? I get the idea about Liz Geldenhuys, and this time I think I know why, but not even then do I ask myself the truly practical question, *how*? I must be going out of my—'

'You asked yourself "how" with Mrs Zuidmeyer, boss,' Zondi pointed out, starting the car.

Kramer gave a bitter laugh. 'Whoever starts by asking why in a domestic murder? We could all give a million boring reasons. But when it's a world-famous person we're out of our depth, hey? Jesus, with Naomi Stride, the answer can't be boring, we tell ourselves, so the "why" gets all-important – or something.'

'Or something,' Zondi agreed with a nod. 'Where to now, boss?'

'Right back to bloody Square One, old son.'

Colonel Muller, as co-ordinator in the case, had the call rerouted to him. 'Yes, Doctor, we're still interested in the whereabouts of Ramjut Pillay, very interested.'

'Well, I hope I'm not wasting your time, but I've a patient in my admitting-ward who claims to have some knowledge of him.'

'He's an Indian, too?'

'That's right. Aged roughly forty, claims to be a para-chutist.'

'Never!' Colonel Muller laughed and had to catch his pipe. 'Did he admit himself down the chimney?'

'I was attempting to give you the details of his case, Colonel,' the doctor said coldly. 'Mental illness is hardly a suitable topic for jocose and—'

'Ach, I'm sorry, hey? But if he's in that sort of a state I doubt if he'll be any good to us. Has he given you any information about Pillay?'

'No more, at this stage, than would indicate he knows him.'

'H'm. I tell you what I'll do, if you give me your number and the name, I'll put that in the file in the meantime.'

'45300. And it's: P-E-E-R-S-W-A-M-M-Y L-A-L.'

'Got it. Many thanks for your help, hey? 'Bye...'

Funny, thought Colonel Muller, that name was not altogether unfamiliar.

Zondi took the car in behind the zebra-striped Land-Rover, and stopped. The parking-bay beside it was this morning occupied by a grey Ford pick-up. Theo Kennedy was round the front of it, with Amanda seated on his shoulders, talking to a big, loose-limbed man above the sound of a portable radio-cassette player belting out vintage Simon and Garfunkel.

'Must be Bruce, Amanda's uncle,' said Kramer, noting the man had the same colour hair and the same chin.

'But younger, boss?'

'By a couple of years, maybe,' agreed Kramer, opening his door. 'With luck, this won't take anything like that.'

'Tromp!' said Kennedy, and Amanda added her greeting, too. 'How did it go with Liz? I was just about to phone you. Oh, I'm sorry: Vicki's brother, Bruce Newbury – Tromp Kramer.'

'Glad to meet you – but I'd better not shake,' said Bruce Newbury, showing a right hand mucky with grease. 'I've just been under to check the gearbox seals.'

'They're buggered?'

'Totally. So much for my day off. I was going to go fishing.'

'Borrow the Land-Rover, like I've said,' offered Kennedy.

'No, you might be needing it, and, anyway, I've got to have my transport working; it really bothers me otherwise.'

'Can Bruce take Amanda?' asked Kramer. 'It's just that—'

'Bruce's busy; she can go and talk to Zondi,' said Kennedy, putting her down. 'All right, Amanda? There's a good girl!' And she ran off.

Kramer followed Kennedy into his flat and into the kitchen.

'Coffee, Tromp?'

'Nothing right now, but you go ahead. I didn't make that follow-up on Liz Geldenhuys.'

'You didn't?' said Kennedy, taking down four mugs. 'Was that because Vicki and me steered you in a more promising direction, the literary link-ups and that?'

'No, it was because I realised what a bloody fool I am, man. Whoever did that to your ma had to be someone who knew she'd be still at home on the night of Monday – stroke – Tuesday.'

'Naturally.'

'And I've never asked you for a list of who they might be.'

'Phew! But. . .'

'But what, Theo?'

'Where does one begin? The travel agency knew she'd changed plans, the security people, probably the milkman, and that's long before you come to her friends. No, wait a moment. . .'

'Ja?' said Kramer, plugging in the electric kettle for him.

'While she was here last Saturday, I remember laughing – because she wasn't often sly about things – when she said she'd not let on to more than a handful of friends that she'd postponed her London trip. If they wanted to phone her, they had to use a code and give three rings first. Oh, yes, and *that* was why she'd let Betty and Ben leave as planned, so they wouldn't be at the house to answer the door. She said it was a heaven-sent opportunity to work undisturbed, more especially as she'd just broken her "jinx" on the book and wanted to make the most of it. Do you know, I'd almost blanked all that? It was just you asking—'

'It's part of shock, man. Don't you feel still in a bit of a dream world?'

Kennedy nodded and went on spooning instant coffee into four mugs. 'Nothing is very real. But what's your excuse?'

'Sorry?'

'You still haven't switched the kettle on.'

They laughed, and Kramer flicked the toggle down. 'You've just made me realise something else,' he grunted. 'I've been obsessed a lot with the idea your ma had threats made to her in those blue letters I mentioned. Fine, I could be right, threats had been made, but what I missed is that the blue-letter business must've *already been sorted out* for her to be unafraid to stay alone in the house, no servants and no friends coming round, for even those few days.'

'In other words, the blue letters were a red herring of your own making?'

'Uh-huh, and a lot of time has been wasted.'

Kennedy took the milk from the refrigerator, and stood for a moment, looking out through the window at Vicki Stilgoe and her brother, chatting together as a start was made on repairing the gearbox. But he probably wasn't seeing them at all; his eyes had a far-away glaze to them. 'Unless', he said softly, 'Mum was wrong in thinking the blue-letters thing had been resolved. You know what I mean – some dangerous crank who'd been locked away, but escapes again.'

'H'm, very unlikely,' said Kramer, finding himself sneaking a look, out of sheer habit, at a rent bill that'd just been opened. Embarrassed, lest Kennedy had noticed this, he added: 'Hey, we've strayed from the point a bit! We were talking about who'd have known your ma was at home. Can you give me a list of names?'

'I can try.' Kennedy took down a kitchen jotting-pad and accepted Kramer's ballpen. He was about to start to write, when he stopped and scratched behind an ear. 'There's something wrong with the logic of this,' he said.

'Wrong, how?'

'Very wrong. Give me a minute, and I'll see if I can pin it down.'

Amanda played with the radio mike, and squeaked with delight each time Control came through with a message. 'Boy,' she said in the intervals of silence, 'boy, make it talk – or I'll tell the missus.'

'We may not talk on there, Amanda; it is for Lieutenant Kramer only.'

'The man who sits here?'

'Yes, that is the Lieutenant.'

'Mummy doesn't like him.'

'Why is that?'

'Mummy says he's horrible and shoots people.'

'He shoots only very very bad people.'

'Uncle Bruce is bad, but only sometimes. Make it talk!'

'Soon it will talk again.'

'Can Uncle T'eo talk to it?'

'No, Boss Kennedy is not a policeman.'

'He's a nice man and Mummy says he's a nice man, too.'

'What does Uncle Bruce say?'

'T'eo is a big softy-pofty!'

'Control to Lieutenant Kramer. . .'

Zondi took the radio mike. 'Bantu DS Zondi, receiving for Lieutenant Kramer, over.'

'Give it to me! Give it, boy!'

'Control. Message reads: "Suspect Peerswammy Lal to be found Garrison Road Hospital, interview immediately, Colonel Muller." Over.'

'Gimme! Gimme! Gimme! *Uncle Bruce!*'

'Message received, Control. Over and out.'

'You, what do you think you're doing, hey?' said the uncle, appearing at Zondi's open door. Then his eyes switched to the child and he smiled. 'Amanda, I'm talking to you. You're being a nuisance, I can see that, so you'd better go inside to Mummy.'

'This boy pushed me! Hit him, Uncle Bruce! Hit him!'

'Amanda, you're going to get a smack in a minute!'

'It's OK, boss. The little girl is—'

'She's been acting up all morning, let me tell you. Sorry about this.'

Zondi watched Amanda dragged away, kicking and screaming as only a truly spoiled child can do, beside herself with fury. Then he realised he still felt chilled by the look in the eyes of Bruce Stilgoe when first he'd reached the car.

Vicki Stilgoe came into Kennedy's kitchen. 'Theo,' she scolded, 'you shouldn't have inflicted Amanda on poor Sergeant Zondi – you will apologise to him for me, won't you, Tromp? She's been an absolute little bitch this morning, right from the moment she got up.'

'Been sweet as pie with me,' said Kennedy. 'Here, this is

yours, Vicki.'

'Lovely. Thanks,' she said as she was handed the mug. 'This one's Bruce's? I'll take it out to him.'

Kennedy watched her go with a hint of concern on his face. 'I think she's been having another row with Bruce,' he confided quietly. 'They're not terribly alike, and she can't wait for him to move to his own place. He's been here about six weeks while he finds his feet. Came down from Zimbabwe when—'

'But you were saying?' Kramer prompted him, who could never stomach too much domesticity.

'Yes, had it on the tip of my tongue, hadn't I?' said Kennedy, lifting his own coffee. 'I know, it's simply this. If my mother wanted only a few people to be in the know about her postponing her trip, then it stands to reason she'd have told them who the others were, and have asked them not to tell anybody else.'

'Ja, agreed.'

'So you've got this small group of people – three or four, at most – and one of them decides to commit a murder, using knowledge that only they share. But, if he did that, the others wouldn't take long to work out it *had* to be one of them, and by a relatively simple process of elimination they – or the police – would know who the culprit was.'

'Bloody hell, you're right,' said Kramer, wishing he'd had this talk with Kennedy earlier. 'And so it can't have been one of the people she told, or they'd have seen the risk involved. But who *wouldn't* see the risk?'

Kennedy shrugged. 'Logically, it could only have been someone who didn't realise there was a risk in the first place. Somebody, for instance, who didn't know she was keeping quiet about still being here.'

'Now we're getting somewhere!' said Kramer, lighting a Lucky Strike. 'An outsider who caught sight of her after when she was meant to have left?'

'He'd have to have been quick. She said she'd not been out of the house except to see me on Saturday morning, and she drove straight here and straight back. I know that because she rang me with something she'd forgotten to add to my list of things to see to.'

'Fine, but somehow he caught sight of her, knew she was still around, and that she'd be working late, the house still unlocked—'

'Now, that *is* a point,' interrupted Kennedy. 'She only "burned the midnight" when she was really up against it, a deadline, something like that. And yet she hadn't been working for weeks on end, because of the writing block, so how would an outsider work than one out?'

'I suppose going to England this week was a deadline, hey?'

'But how would an outsider know that, either? Christ, *I* didn't realise, until she came round and told me, that she was intending to work on the book all the hours God sent, right up to the very last minute.'

'Then, did you tell someone?' asked Kramer, before he could think of a less blunt way of putting it.

Kennedy flinched. 'No, I'm certain I didn't. I never talk about my mother or her work to anyone, in the ordinary course of events. In fact, the only time I've discussed the matter at all – until now – was with her, out there by my land-rover last Saturday morning.'

'Who was with you?'

'Nobody. Bruce had been working alongside me, but he'd gone inside for a Band-Aid before Mum arrived. Then Vicki nipped out to call Amanda and switch Bruce's radio off, and then we were completely on our own. That's when this discussion about burning the midnight oil took place – I remember feeling relieved we were on our own, because the rows me and my mother always ended up having were, well, a bit strong-worded at times. I sparked it off by saying she was overdoing things, and would be a gibbering wreck by the time she reached London. I wish now I'd had a chance to introduce Vicki to Mum, but I'd barely said more than "hello" to her at that stage and... Oh, well.'

'Ja, that's life for you, hey?'

'Or death,' said Kennedy quietly.

'Theo, you mustn't dwell too much,' warned Kramer. 'To go on with what we were saying, if there was nobody out there on the carpark, except your ma and you, what about above you?'

'Sorry, I don't quite follow. . .'

'There's a balcony running along just above this window, isn't there? So the people upstairs can get to their flats?'

'Oh, I get you. Someone could've eavesdropped from there, you mean?'

'Correct. Can you remember seeing anyone?'

'No, I don't think so. They could've been ducked down behind the balcony wall, I suppose, but that sounds a bit melodramatic.'

'Even so, who lives above you?'

'I've no idea. People come and go a lot from these flats; they're often just a stepping-stone in their lives. We've had construction workers, bohemian intellectuals of different sorts, varsity students, young marrieds, divorcees – God, do you realise what I've just said?'

Kramer nodded. 'Do you know the names of any of the students?'

'No, but Vicki might, or we could try—'

'Theo, you leave this just to me, OK?' said Kramer, starting to leave. 'And don't say anything to the others at this stage. I don't want things going wrong because a suspect feels he is being stared at or anything like that – are you with me?'

'All the way, Tromp. I'd much prefer it if the others didn't get involved.'

They walked outside, and Zondi came up.

'Ja, Mickey, what is it?'

'Radio message from the Colonel, sir. He wants us to go and fetch a suspect, Peerswammy Lal, from Garrison Road Mental Hospital, reference Ramjut Pillay. The matter is now very urgent – a letter on blue paper.'

'A letter on blue paper?' Kennedy said, his voice catching, as Vicki Stilgoe moved protectively towards him.

'Ach, take no notice,' said Kramer. 'That'll have bugger-all to do with this case, let me promise you.'

'But surely. . .' began Vicki Stilgoe.

'You don't know the officer behind it, Vicki, or you'd agree with me, hey? See you all later maybe.'

'But, boss,' whispered Zondi, as they neared the car, 'that lady is right. A blue letter and the postman who—'

'Sod Ramjet Pillbox, Mickey, I've just come up with a bloody good lead of my own that—'

'Lieutenant, you have made this kind of mistake before, and we have been in much, much—'

'What do you want to do? Change places with Gagonk?'

'Ermph,' said Zondi, and tossed him the car-keys.

18

COLONEL MULLER'S new briar was in danger of having its mouthpiece bitten off. 'What the hell do you mean?' he stormed at Control, managing to snatch his pipe from his teeth just in time. 'Lieutenant Kramer hasn't acknowledged yet? That's *three times* my order has gone out!'

'Ja, Colonel, I know,' said the radio operator, standing to attention beside his desk. 'Twice his Bantu's taken the message, but since then nothing.'

'How often have you tried?'

'Every two minutes, Colonel.'

'I don't believe you, Hedge!'

'But it's true, Colonel – just look in my log.'

'Then, why aren't they answering?'

'Maybe they're not in the vehicle, Colonel.'

'But there have been two messages already!'

Hedge shrugged. 'They could've been in a crash, sir. CID's always—'

The briar dug deep into his belly. 'You, Hedge,' hissed the Colonel, 'are a funny man, a proper comedian. Consider yourself forthwith on transfer to Namibia.'

'Jesus, Colonel, I was only—'

'They tell me things are very serious there, so what they need is a joker, Hedge! Ja, and try telling your jokes to SWAPO; see if they laugh more than me, hey?'

Then, turning about, Colonel Muller stamped out of the room, grabbed Tims Shabalala by the arm, and commanded him to go straight down to Garrison Road Mental Hospital and bring back Peerswammy Lal for immediate interrogation.

'Hau, most gladly, Colonel, sir,' said Shabalala, slipping his thick wrist through the thong of the rhino-hide whip he always carried.

Azalea Mansions, as Kramer had noted when glancing at Theo Kennedy's rent bill, was owned by A K Coates & Son, which had its offices in a new building opposite Trekkersburg General Hospital. As though to rival its neighbour in providing an air of brisk, clinical efficiency, Coates & Son had opted for white walls, green rubber tiles, metal furniture, a rude receptionist and a pile of the oldest magazines on offer outside an outpatients' waiting-room.

'No, Mr Coates, senior, cannot see anyone without an appointment,' said the receptionist, browsing through a bridal catalogue.

'He's disabled, hey? Carries a white stick?'

'That's nice,' the receptionist murmured to herself, pausing at a colour plate of a honeymoon négligé.

'But where's the bag he's going to need to put over your head, lady?'

She looked up then, for the first time. '*What* was that you said?'

'Mr Coates.'

'All right, you've asked for it. . .' She leaned towards her intercom and pressed down a switch. 'Mr Coates, there is a very abusive man out here. I think I need some assistance.'

'You see,' Kramer said to her, as the door marked *A K Coates, Snr* was yanked open and a big man came hurrying out, 'it never fails.'

Zondi had decided to keep well away from the car, and certainly out of earshot of its radio. He crossed the street and paused to look over the bank of flowers arranged outside the entrance to the hospital. The flower-seller ignored him;

252

Trekkersburg General took no Bantu patients, making it immediately obvious he wasn't a customer.

Curious to see inside the building, Zondi went back to the car very briefly to pick up one of the large manila envelopes that lay scattered on its rear shelf, and then walked past the flower-seller and into the air-conditioned reception-area. A black hospital guard in a khaki uniform immediately barred his way.

'Messages at the side door, brother,' he said.

Zondi turned the envelope round and pointed to its printed markings. 'SAP,' he said. 'Important documents that I must deliver personally.'

'To what person?'

'Lieutenant Jones.'

'You have proof of identity?'

Zondi flipped open his jacket to allow the guard a glimpse of his Walther PPK in its shoulder holster and the knife in his waistband.

'Hau, brother, I do not know what to do. Will you come with me?'

They went over and stood to one side at a large counter where five white women snapped at people who asked them questions. From time to time, looking awkward and anxious, black deliverymen would hurriedly approach the counter from the street, place cellophane-wrapped bunches of flowers at the far end of the counter, and hasten away again. Eventually one of the white women came over to the guard.

'What do you want?'

'This is a policeman, madam. He has here important papers for his boss. He says he must give these to him by his own hand.'

'Rubbish. We can't have him wandering everywhere with ladies just in dressing-gowns. Tell him to put his boss's name on it, and we'll see he gets them – nothing ever gets lost here. Well, go on.'

So the guard said in Zulu: 'My apologies, brother, for the rudeness of this ignorant person. Can you do as she said?'

Zondi addressed the empty envelope and had it snatched from him. But, just as he was leaving, he had an idea and said to the guard: 'Brother, there is one other item to go to Lieutenant Jones. If I bring it here in ten minutes, will you place it on the counter for me?'

Mr Coates, senior, was a man who liked to talk rugby, and as the sport was considered so important by the police that rugby training was carried out during duty hours, he not unnaturally expected Kramer liked to talk rugby, too.

'Now, let me guess what position you played,' he said, knitting together two huge hairy hands and placing them behind his shiny bald head. 'Wing?'

'Wing,' said Kramer to save argument, having an antipathy to all games that weren't played for real. 'But you say your brother-in-law took on the Lions for Rhodesia?'

'That's right – and scored the first and last tries of the game, I'll have you know! Now, there was a hard man for you – truly hard. His natives on the farm were terrified of him, worked like niggers even when he wasn't around. One day, you see, his induna gave him some cheek, so he picked the old bugger up, held him in the air, and he dropped him, right on this harrow. Luckily for the coon the tractor wasn't pulling it at the time, or he really would have had some wounds to lick. Well, from then on, so they tell me, that induna was almost as hard as he was, really drove the boys under him, and Denis never had any trouble bringing in the biggest tobacco crop in the whole district. Of course, this was some years back, before Rhodesia became Zimbabwe and the whole place went to—'

'That list of tenants, Mr Coates,' said the receptionist, coming in and glaring at Kramer as she handed it over. 'Mr Jeffery says it's fully up to date, and when you've finished with it could he have it returned to him, please?'

Coates gave her a leer, which restored the smugness to her face, and a moment later the door was closed behind her. Then he slid a computer print-out across the desk.

'Help yourself to anything you want on it,' he said. 'And don't take any bloody notice of Jeffery; he's a proper old woman, never passed a ball in his life. If you'd like that to keep, you keep it; I can always get another one done.'

Kramer, partly distracted by the thought that he was grateful never to have passed a ball, either, as it sounded agonising, glanced across the column headings. Flat number; name; marital status; occupation; income; deposit; rent; number of other occupants; period of lease; service charge; arrears; garage number, if applicable. He could not have wished for more.

'There are a few students, like I said, aren't there?' asked Coates, getting out from behind his desk to practise a golf swing. 'Mind you, I've got a strict policy as far as letting to kids at the varsity goes. The only ones I'll take are sportsmen – you know, forestry, agriculture, chemistry. . . I certainly don't want a lot of arty-farty ones with the long hair and girlie complexions smoking Christ-knows-what on my premises and having their multi-racial orgies. If they say Fine Arts or English, they are *out*. Even History can give you trouble.'

'Ja, there are a few students, very few,' murmured Kramer, disappointment setting in, 'and they're all women.'

'Every one of them plays a sport, though!'

'Couch rugby?'

Coates barked a laugh. 'That, too, I wouldn't be surprised! Now, you know, that reminds me of the time after I'd played against East Griqualand—'

'Just a sec, sir,' said Kramer, noticing something. 'One of your tenants doesn't seem to pay any rent, hasn't any occupation, no income, didn't put down a deposit – in fact, the name's the only part that's filled in.'

'Ah, yes, I know which one you mean,' said Coates, suddenly looking ill at ease, almost embarrassed. 'But her, I can vouch for personally. It's, er, what you might call a bit of a private matter.'

Kramer raised an eyebrow, while he also tried to picture this great heap of slackening muscle lowering itself on to the petite form of Vicki Stilgoe, lying back with her eyes closed and thinking of the rent bill. But somehow, adept as he was at turning his gut with insights of this kind, the trick wouldn't work this time.

'Nothing like that!' exclaimed Coates, returning hastily to

the dignity conferred on him by his big leather swivel-chair. 'Denis's daughter.'

'The bloke who played for Rhodesia?'

'Denis Newbury, that's right – wife's sister's late hubby. And she's gone, too, of course, the wife's sister. Bastards butchered the lot of them. Vicki and little Amanda were the only two to come out of it. That induna I told you about? Somehow he got them up into the rainwater-tank on the roof before the terrs had fought their way past Denis and young Gary – Vicki's husband, the farm manager. That's where the police found them the next day, still in bloody water up to Vicki's neck, the dead induna floating round – Denis'd spied him up there, and blasted him between the eyes, naturally thinking he was up to something – and, well, that was it. A terrible sight, it must've been, and all the bloody tobacco-sheds up in smoke, which is typical terr thinking.'

'But what about Bruce, if you say only two—'

'He was in the Selous Scouts, fighting the terrorists in the north. But how would you know his name?'

'Ach, I know him and Vicki, Mr Coates. They're next-door neighbours to—'

'Of course! That poor young sod Kennedy – a bit soft to look at, but a good business head. How's he coping with it?'

'Not bad, considering. H'm, so Vicki is your—'

'I know what you're thinking,' said Coates defiantly, looking down to make an unnecessary adjustment to his gold tie-pin. 'You're wondering why Madge and me don't have her still living with us and the girls at Riverbend? I suppose she's already had her moan to you about being "kicked out" and all the other things she's said to people we know, including quite a few at the country club, where Madge plays bridge and had almost to stop going.'

Kramer shrugged. 'Ach, she has implied something of the sort about relatives not giving a damn,' he improvised, 'and I'll admit I got the impression they were a bunch of real shits, hey? But, not knowing the ins and outs, I hadn't really—'

'Shits? *Us?*' exploded Coates, going the colour of the jersey he must have worn in the match against East Griqualand. 'That really is the bloody limit! If it wasn't for the kiddie, I'd have that bitch out of that flat tomorrow and on her arse in the middle of the road! "Ins and outs", you say – you can't imagine what we had to put up with, during that first year she stayed with us. Oh, yes, a whole year, and do you know how many servants we lost? Five! Madge was nearly at her wit's end finding new ones and trying to train them, only for that spoiled little bitch to upset them so much they just took their clobber and went. Now, I had great admiration for Denis as a rugby player, nobody can take that from him, but when it came to that daughter of his he must have been so soft with her it couldn't be true. Madge said maybe it was because the terrs had killed all her family and her husband that she treated natives that way, but what about the way she treated Sheryl and Jacky? She thought our daughters were her servants, too! She was forever telling them to fetch things for her, to do this, do that, see to Amanda because she wanted to read. Read, that's all she did, lie by our pool and eat bloody chocolates and make remarks because if Sheryl eats two chocolates she puts on four pounds. Never a nice remark for them when they'd got dressed up for a dance, and if we had any young men to the house she would monopolise them the whole time. I can remember Jacky crying and coming to me and saying: "Daddy, it's not fair; Vicki's got her arm around Tony, and it's *us* who're engaged!" My daughters are just a little younger than her, you see.'

Kramer nodded, and imagined them as both having the figures of prop forwards. 'I'm surprised, though, Mr Coates, you didn't think of trying to marry her off to someone, hey? That would have got her off your hands and—'

'Jesus Christ, don't you think we tried that? I mean, it was two years since Gary'd passed on—'

'Oh, she didn't come straight down here from Zimbabwe, then?'

'No, she stayed with friends after it happened – Gary had no family – and waited for Bruce to get compensation from the Government for the farm. Denis had left it it in his will that the farm was to go to both his kids together, you see, which would have left each of them bloody well off. I can't explain to you the whys, hows and wherefores, but those bastards never paid one cent, not one bloody cent to them. Mugabe's lot had taken over, of course, and the place had been allocated as a co-operative or some rubbish for natives to turn to wreck and ruin. Well, I suppose Vicki's friends got the hell out, the same as us, and so she asked if she could come down to us, as we were her only relatives. Bruce hung on, trying to get justice done. But, as you know, the Scouts got themselves quite a reputation for what they did to any terr they found, so he never stood a hope. He just had to give up in the end, and I've fixed him a job at a shoe factory here in town. It's a scandal what's happening in Zimbabwe over compensation: some get it, some can whistle in the wind. But I was telling you. . .?'

'About marrying her off.'

'Not a chance, not with her attitudes. Nobody was good enough for her. I don't know how often Madge tried to point out, really nicely, that a woman with a child already isn't going to find herself another husband so easily, and she would have to lower her sights a little. Once, just once, we thought we'd pulled it off. A divorcee, well off, educated, loved books and plays same as she did, a bloke missing his own kiddies, who tried really hard to get Amanda to like him. But, no, that little madam would turn down her lip whenever he came near, and that was it! With Vicki, it was Amanda who did the choosing! Madge had a talk to her about this as well, and warned her the child was getting too spoiled for its own good. You know what she said to my wife? "Don't worry about us, Auntie Madge. When Amanda and me see the right father for her, we'll see that we get him for ourselves." "Then he better be rich!" Madge told her, and she said: "Oh, I'll see that he is." Because that was something else. Vicki had told me she'd be getting compensation from the farm, and so I lent her money for clothes, over and above the pocket money I was already giving her for free. It was never, never enough. This made it my turn to talk to her, and what she said took my breath right away – shit, it really did. She said: "Uncle Arthur, I was born to money, I grew up with money, and I will marry lots of money – then I'll pay back the measly amounts you're making such a fuss about."

Marry? By this stage, she hadn't got a chance in hell! Her reputation as a spoiled, snobby little bitch was too well known, and all the blokes were giving her a wide berth, I can tell you. Despite, I should add, she was so over-sexed – at least, on the outside – with the way she walked, acted bold as brass, that even my brother, who's a Born Again Christian, came round three nights running when she first arrived.'

'How did she leave?' asked Kramer, folding up the print-out and stowing it inside his jacket. 'You just said you told her you'd had a gutsful?'

Coates glanced at his intercom and then back at Kramer. 'Have I your word this won't go any further – you won't take action or anything?'

'Hell, that wouldn't be playing the game, would it, Mr Coates?'

The black sergeant slapped his left hand with the handle of his rhino-hide whip, showing every sign of impatience with how the interview was proceeding.

'Will you stop making that noise, hey?' complained the man with a pipe just like Sir Sherlock Holmes. 'You're interfering with my co-ordination.'

'Sorry, Colonel, sir, but if you want this man to—'

'Hasn't he talked enough? My head is spinning! Now, like I say, give me a chance to look through all these notes I've made.'

Ramjut Pillay was very grateful to him for intervening, as he had found the sight and sound of that whip a grave distraction for a fellow bent on making a full and complete confession. This was something he had dreaded doing, but now that it was over it was as though a great weight had been lifted from his poor shoulders.

'You know something, Shabalala?'

'What is that, Colonel, sir?'

'I don't know if we should believe one word of what this loony's been telling us. You know when I rang the Post Office just now? They say this man must be an impostor. A Mr Jarman there agrees that they have a postman called Peerswammy Lal, but he also says that this postman is out on his rounds at this very minute.'

'Hau, Colonel!'

'Moreover—'

'But, with humble respect, sir, that is elementarily explained – I am Ramjut Pillay, never Peerswammy Lal!'

'Look, how many times must we go through the same thing? You can't be Ramjut Pillay, either, because you don't fit his bloody description!'

'Then the description is wrong, most gracious sir. There is a simple way of supplying proof.'

'What's that?'

'You are merely presenting before me Detective Sergeant Zondi. He has great admiration for me and my many degrees of learning, which he will vouchsafe for upon his arrival.'

'Oh ja, and you think that getting Zondi on the bloody radio is simple?' growled the man whose name, Ramjut Pillay had gathered, was Colonel Moola.

Still a little stunned, Kramer related to Zondi everything he had been told by Arthur Coates, the uncle of Vicki Stilgoe and Bruce Newbury, Theo Kennedy's new-found friends from next door.

'And that's something else, Mickey,' he said. 'After Coates found she had been using his daughter's credit cards, and got rid of her by putting her up in Azalea Mansions, she came back to him with a complaint. She said that being in an upstairs flat wasn't safe for Amanda, and she wanted to change places with a tenant on the ground floor. She actually told him which flat – it was the one she's in now – and made him move the people out and into her old one.'

'Hau, boss!' said Zondi, just allowing the car to take whatever road it pleased. 'She has a big, big cheek, that young madam! Why did this Boss Coates just do what she told him to? It is like she had some kind of blackmail to use.'

Kramer nodded, lighting them each a Lucky. 'My thought exactly, then I remembered him saying she was "over-sexed, at least on the outside" and I had him then. It was obvious he'd made some pass at her, and had got her knee in his whatsit. Not that he'd admit it, but, Christ, I thought I'd have to give him mouth-to-mouth.'

'Not nice, Lieutenant,' agreed Zondi, mirroring his expression of revulsion, and accepting the Lucky between his lips. 'And so?'

'Well, doesn't it all add up, hey? Vicki gets kicked out, moves to Azalea Mansions, and Amanda finds herself this nice man downstairs, who's often out mending his bloody "zebby car". Vicki hears whose son he is, and a plan starts to form. She gets herself moved down beside him, but keeps a low profile. She knows what her aunt says is true, she's maybe not much of a catch with a kid, and perhaps she's seen Liz Geldenhuys with Theo. Right, so the first thing she does is get rid of Liz. She pays a call to the shop, sizes her up—'

'But how does she know she's at the shop, boss?'

'Ach, because she must have eavesdropped on them, or maybe Amanda met Liz and she told her. That part wouldn't be difficult. She tries the game with the telephone, using her real "over-sexed" way of speaking, and soon Liz isn't coming round to the flat any more, so she knows this side of her plan has worked. Now she mustn't allow Theo time to find another woman in his life, and so she has to work fast. My guess is that she sends for Bruce to do the dirty work – Jesus, you must've heard what a homicidal bunch of psychos those Selous Scouts were – and boom-boom, he sticks the sword in Ma Stride, she kicks the bucket, and Vicki has the son at his most vulnerable.'

Kramer smashed his fist into the dashboard, making Zondi glance across sharply.

'Hau, what is the—?'

'Who was it that threw the poor bastard into that bitch's arms, hey? Who made it all so easy for her she must've been pissing herself with laughter behind his back?' Kramer hit the dashboard again, even harder. 'You don't know how I—'

'But if this theory is all true, boss, she would have got Boss Theo without your help, just with the child going out to him, and her asking him round for a coffee maybe, like a neighbour at that time would.'

'What do you mean by "this theory"? Can't you see how everything fits, right down to her copying Liz Geldenhuys's shy manner, guessing that quiet, shy ladies were Kennedy's type? Later, of course, once she had the wedding ring on her finger, that could all change, but—'

'And it also fits', agreed Zondi, 'that if she liked plays and books she would know how to use the *Hamlet* trick to make it look like some person at the University was behind the killing. But, boss, what I do not understand is why the brother would be willing to help her in—'

'Ach, Mickey, I'm surprised at you!' said Kramer, sucking his knuckles. 'He had bugger-all money but, if he did what his sister asked, soon she'd be married to a millionaire, man! Kennedy could be made to set him up, perhaps give him a partnership in Afro Arts if he was going to keep it – all sorts.'

Zondi took a dual carriageway leading out of town. 'And so,' he said with a long sigh, 'although it pains us very much, we must admit that Lieutenant Jones was right at the very beginning. Mrs Stride was killed for her money.'

'Bastard! But it was also for her son – he was just as much a legacy, hey? Shocked out of his head, in a bad dream, clutching on to a kid with big dimples, clutching her bitch mother, too, thinking God was trying to say sorry for what—'

'Boss, boss, boss,' Zondi remonstrated quietly, 'you are hitting yourself with a stick that has not yet grown from the seed.'

'What else do we have to work out? It's all as—'

'We still do not know the big "how" concerning Boss Kennedy and his mother being overheard.'

'Bruce was up on the balcony.'

'No, boss, you said he was inside, getting a bandage.'

'Vicki eavesdropped when she came out to—'

'No, boss, they spoke of working late *after* that.'

'Then, I don't know how, old son. But I do know who and bloody why, and I'm going to nail those two bastards, somehow or other – *and* quick.'

'Quick will be—'

'Bloody Jones,' grunted Kramer, flicking his cigarette out of the car window, half-smoked. 'What makes it worse is that, if I'd used my head, I would have caught on to all this a lot sooner. Christ, it was staring me in the face – literally!'

'Boss?'

'A look in her eyes, Mickey. Twice I got it, and it sent a bloody tingle right down to my – Jesus, a hell of a look, I can tell you. My mistake was getting it mixed up with flirting, with that special sort of laughing look that makes you feel the hunter and that the woman is your prey. Have you any idea of what I mean?'

Zondi, who seemed to be concentrating unnecessarily hard on an open stretch of road, nodded very slightly.

'But, of course, the look meant I was the hunter that my *real* prey was playing games with, running circles around, only I didn't realise it! Why the laugh?'

'Oh, nothing, Lieutenant,' said Zondi. 'Boss, to change the subject a little, how are you going to catch these two quick? It is still all theory that has to be tested before an arrest can be made.'

'Then we'll just have to think of a quick test, hey?'

'Maybe I have done so, boss. . .'

'Then, why the hell are we—?'

Zondi grinned. 'It's all right, we are already travelling in the right direction. Have you not noticed which road this is?'

Tims Shabalala brought the car to a halt at the entrance to Trekkersburg General Hospital and Colonel Muller got out, carrying with him the sheaf of very confusing notes he had made during his interview with the mental patient known for administrative purposes as Peerswammy Lal.

His temper was hardly improved by having to wait at the reception counter for someone to notice him, and he spoke very sharply to the woman who eventually came up and said, 'What?'

But things improved a great deal almost immediately after that, when a very pretty young nurse arrived in no time at all to show him up to Lieutenant Jones's ward on the sixth floor.

'Tell me, how is the Lieutenant this morning, miss?' Colonel Muller asked in the lift. 'Has he got enough blood now?'

'Still a little pale, and not very cheerful, I'm afraid,

Colonel.'

'But Jones is usually like that, hey? Maybe the doctors ought to know.'

'I'll see that I tell them. By the way, I hope you don't mind me saying this, but Sister insists you're not with him for too long. You seem to have an awful lot of things with you to show him.'

'Ach, no, he doesn't have to go through all of it. I just want to try to find out exactly what he was hoping to get from a certain Peerswammy Lal. There could be a mix-up of suspects' identities, you see, and perhaps I'm really supposed to be talking to a postman.'

The nurse looked up at the floor-indicator lights. 'Almost there,' she said. 'When you come out of the lift, you'll find Lieutenant Jones in a side ward on the right, two doors down.'

'Ta, and thanks very much, hey?' said Colonel Muller, raising his hat gallantly to her as he backed out of the lift into a food-trolley.

'Oops, that was nearly your pipe broken!' she said, picking it up for him. 'You won't smoke in here, will you? Sister's terribly strict about that.'

'No, I promise not to light it,' said Colonel Muller. 'Many thanks again. . .'

Then he went to the second door down, and peered in. Something like an Egyptian mummy turned to look at him from the bed. It made Colonel Muller think of a very bad film he had once seen, filled with screaming women and police inspectors he would not have given two cents for to have on his staff.

'Morning, Jacob. All right if I come in?'

Jones nodded.

'Well, it's good to see you awake anyway,' said the Colonel, moving a chair over to his bedside. 'And they tell me Mbopa was discharged from Peacevale Hospital late last night, which you will be glad to hear. What I have to query you on won't take long. My, these are nice arum lilies, hey? Who sent them to you?'

'My ma, Colonel.'

264

'Are the chocolates from her, too?'

'My landlady, Colonel, but they say I can't have any yet. Would you like one?'

Colonel Muller glanced at them, conscious of Mrs Muller's view of grown men who spoiled their figures with too much sugar, and shook his head. Then he noticed another present, just behind the chocolate box.

'Now, that's very pretty! Who sent you the yellow rose?'

'Just arrived, before I woke up.'

'But who's it from?'

'Can't reach, Colonel.'

'Ach, then I'll read the card for you – just a sec.'

There was a clatter, which left Colonel Muller's new pipe snapped in two where the black plastic mouthpiece met the briar of the stem.

'Colonel, sir! What's the matter? What does it say?'

The get-well card had only two words written inside it: *Love, Gagonk*.

19

SIMON AND GARFUNKEL were once again building a Bridge over Troubled Waters when Zondi nosed the car up behind the zebra-striped Land-Rover at Azalea Mansions. All that could be seen of Bruce Newbury was a pair of feet sticking out from under the grey Ford pick-up. Nobody else was about.

'Bang goes half our script,' murmured Kramer. 'But tell me, Mickey, where did you get this crazy idea from?'

'Act II, scene ii, boss.'

'Ja, I bloody thought as much. You ready?'

'Almost, Lieutenant.' So saying, Zondi took a pin from his lapel, drew its point hard across the back of his left hand, and then slapped the scratch it had made. 'One more minute, and it will look very very serious. . .'

'Uh-huh, that's a neat trick.'

'Long, long ago, I worked three months at the city hall. There was a big wrestling match every Friday night. The wrestlers would put a pin in their towel and cut their foreheads before the last round. The other man knew this, and would hit them there. Then the blood would come and the crowd would go mad.'

'It looks good already, Mickey – shall we go?'

They got out of the car and Kramer went over to the grey pick-up. 'Bruce, we're back, hey? Zondi's cut his hand – Vicki got any Band-Aids?'

'Just hang on a minute. . .' Bruce Newbury wriggled out from beneath the pick-up and squinted against the light at Zondi's dripping fingers. 'Er, ja, just go and ask her. She's inside with Amanda, making lunch.'

'Go on, Mickey, knock at the door, man.'

Zondi left them and went over to do as ordered.

'How'd he manage that?' asked Bruce Newbury, getting to his feet and wiping grease off his hands on to his overalls. 'Been in a fight?'

'No, just putting something in the boot of my car. It's a surprise – can you help me with it?'

'If my hands are clean enough. Who's it for?'

'Ach, for Theo, so I'd like to move it while he's not out here. He's in his flat?'

'Ja, finally got round to phoning undertakers.'

'Abbott does a really good job – I'll tell him. It would be terrible if he got one that tried to put make-up all over his ma's face. Did you ever see her? Like last Saturday, when she was here?'

'No, never set eyes on her. I'd cut my hand myself, actually, and was inside, in the bathroom, putting stuff on it.'

'Or in the papers?'

'Only one picture, when she was very young, and they all seem to use it.'

'Ja, well, anyway, she never used even lipstick herself, so it would make her seem terrible. Can you help us now?'

'Lead the way, man, lead the way.'

So Kramer led the way, and saw Zondi going into the

Stilgoe flat just as he reached the rear of their police vehicle. He unlocked the boot, took a deep breath silently, and let the boot lid fly up.

'Jesus Christ!' exclaimed Bruce Newbury, staring huge-eyed at what the boot contained. 'How——?'

It was the head of Naomi Stride, curls and all, sculpted by Kwakona Mtunsi and then given a quick coat of whitewash to change the colour of the clay to something approximating plaster of Paris.

'Why the gaping jaw, Bruce?' asked Kramer. 'It wasn't meant to be *that* kind of surprise, you know – just nice for Theo to put in his sitting-room.'

'Well, you hardly expect——'

'But you knew who it was, didn't you? Even though she's aged a lot since that old picture in the papers.'

'Now what are you trying to——?'

'Shhh, quiet a moment,' said Kramer.

The only sound was that of Simon and Garfunkel.

Glancing away at the radio-cassette player, Kramer added: 'And I now know how you eavesdropped. That thing doesn't just play tapes, does it? You can pretend to switch it off and instead press down the button for "record".'

Then Bruce Newbury sprang a surprise of his own. 'Act naturally,' he said, smiling over the barrel of a .357 magnum, wrapped in an oily rag. 'Walk into our flat. Don't try anything.'

'Hell, I thought I *was* acting naturally,' said Kramer, cursing himself inwardly for scoring points about the tape at just the wrong moment. 'In fact, I was acting my arse off.'

Zondi was rinsing his hand under the cold tap in the Stilgoe woman's bathroom while she fluffed out some cotton wool and found a bottle of antiseptic.

'Tell me,' she said, 'what were you and Amanda talking about in the car earlier on?'

'She wanted to use the radio, madam, but I had to explain it wasn't for games.'

'Oh, she gave me the impression you'd had quite a little chat. There'd been questions.'

Zondi smiled. 'What child does not ask questions, madam?'

'That isn't what I mean.'

'No, madam?'

'You're used to children, are you, Sergeant Zondi? You've got kids of your own?'

'I have twins and—'

'You're good with them? With kids?'

'Vicki,' said Bruce Newbury, from out in the passage. 'Could you ask Sergeant Zondi to step out here a moment? Tromp wants him.'

Zondi immediately turned off the tap and made for the door.

'I'm sorry, old son,' said Kramer, as he saw Zondi's eyes widen. 'I think I pushed making the king feel a prick about his conscience a little too hard.'

'Shut up!' barked Bruce Newbury. 'You, boy, stand in front of your boss, and, Kramer, you stand right up close to him. Good. Either of you make a move, and I'll only have to fire once – this magnum will go through both of you. Now back slowly down the passage.'

Kramer and Zondi obeyed. Vicki Stilgoe appeared at the bathroom door with a look of astonishment.

'Stay in there, Vicki, till I'm past you!' said her brother. 'I don't want you getting in the way of this.'

'But, Bruce, what the hell has happened?'

'Let's get them into the lounge first. Go and close the front door, so Kennedy will think they're interviewing us, and won't want to get involved.'

Kramer saw her go down the passage and push the door closed. She did not notice that the latch on the Yale lock was up, which meant Kennedy would not need a key to get in.

'Just keep on backing, very slowly,' said the brother. 'Where's Amanda, Vic?'

'Playing in her room.'

'Lock it.'

Following them, Vicki Stilgoe turned the key in the last door in the passage. Kramer, with Zondi bumping against

268

him, moved backwards into the living-room and on to a green rug. His mind was curiously intent on inconsequential detail. He noticed a carved African figure, just like the one in Afro Arts's window, and a large colour photograph of Amanda in a gilt-edged frame. He stepped off the rug and back on to the parquet flooring, then felt the window-sill in the small of his back and heard the clatter of the closed venetian blinds. The room was pleasantly cool and dim.

'Stop exactly where you are,' orderd Bruce Newbury. 'Vicki, shut the door.' He shook the oily cloth off the magnum.

'But Bruce,' began Vicki Stilgoe, closing the door.

'They'd come for us.'

'How do you know that? Surely we—'

'The tape-recorder, the lot. He tricked – he had a head in the car.'

'A *head*? Whose head?'

'That terr-loving bitch's.'

'Jesus, I just don't believe this!'

'No, a model, some sort of bust. But it looked so real I—'

'You fool!'

'Why call Stride that?' asked Kramer. 'A "terr-loving—" '

'Read the fuckin' book!' snarled Bruce Newbury.

'What book?'

'Hers, *Winter Sun*, you ignorant Boer bastard.'

'He can't; it's banned here,' said Vicki Stilgoe with a short laugh.

'Should be banned every-fuckin'-where. Now, you, kaffir, take your gun out by the grip, using thumb and one finger only.'

'Hau, I have no gun, boss! I am only a Bantu and we—'

'Don't try to bullshit my brother, nigger! We know you've got a gun; the stupid bastard behind you blabbed that last night!'

'Oh, so that's why you're all nerves today, and put a magnum in your tool kit?' said Kramer. 'You're right; I should've—'

'Then, shut it now, kaffir-lover! And you, boy, you'd better do what I say bloody quickly!'

Zondi slipped his hand inside his jacket, withdrew his Walther PPK and held it out, dangling in front of him.

'Now chuck it on the floor at my feet.'

Zondi obeyed, and Bruce Newbury kicked it under the sofa without taking his eyes off them for an instant.

'Hell, I thought I'd forgotten something when I was dressing this morning,' said Kramer, with a tut-tut. 'Would you believe I—?'

'Cut the jokes, you big ape. You do the same, but step sideways half a pace so I can watch.'

Kramer took out his Walther PPK, and tossed it at the man's feet. It was also kicked under the sofa.

'Now what happens, Bruce?' asked his sister.

'We'll have to go, that's all. The kaffir we can dispense with, and his boss can drive us in his own car. It'll be good cover.'

'That's too risky. Kill them both and—'

'No, it's our best chance. If Kennedy sees us leaving, we can say we're—'

'But, Bruce, this bastard's not to be trusted! Not even with a magnum in his back.'

'I know what I'm doing, Vicki, so shut up, OK?'

The man was lying, thought Kramer. His best chance of escape *was* to kill both police officers, in the quick, silent way in which he'd been trained.

'Boy,' said Bruce Newbury, 'put your hands in your pants pockets, right in deep.'

While Zondi did so, Vicki Stilgoe said: 'Shit, I've just realised something! We should have guessed, Bruce.'

'What?'

'Things were going wrong. Kramer was in the kitchen nearly half an hour this morning with Theo, but Theo wouldn't say afterwards what it'd been about. That was the first time he hadn't told me everything.'

'So?' Bruce Newbury shrugged. 'Too late now. Here, come round this side of me and take my gun, so it never stops pointing at kaffir-lover there. Boy, you better not try anything, either. Start moving to the right.'

Vicki Stilgoe took over the magnum, and her brother moved a pace from her side, his eyes now fixed on Zondi.

'Those things have a hell of a kick,' remarked Kramer, nodding at the gun.

'Why do you think it's aimed at—?'

'Ach, penis envy, lady,' said Kramer.

But his eyes were on Bruce Newbury, as the man moved slowly towards Zondi. 'Boy,' said Newbury, 'I want you to take a rest, sit down on that couch. Sit well back and make yourself comfortable.'

Or, in other words, thought Kramer, get off your feet so you won't stand a snowball's hope in hell of dodging what comes next. A momentary distraction was essential now, whatever the cost.

Kramer took a step forward, saying, 'Now, listen—'

'*Stop*,' hissed Vicki Stilgoe, and her brother turned, poised.

'The word is "freeze", hey? I only wanted to—'

'*Not one more move* or you get it. Hurry, Bruce!'

Her brother sprang at Zondi. The slashing chop to the throat should have been fatal, but Zondi's razor-edged knife met the force of the blow and took two of the man's fingers off. He screamed and spun round, whipping blood across his sister's face, and her first shot, fired almost blind as Zondi dived for the floor, went into Newbury's shoulder, blasting bone over Amanda's picture. Kramer dived, too, grabbing the rug and giving it a violent heave. She lost her footing and fell over backwards, her second shot going into the ceiling, just as her reeling brother crashed down across her legs. Kramer stamped his foot on her right wrist, and Zondi scrambled across the floor, his suit a terrible mess, to disarm her.

'What in God's name—?' gasped Theo Kennedy as he charged into the room and stopped with a jerk, his voice almost inaudible to half-deafened ears against the background of a child screaming. 'Vicki? This is unbelievable!'

'Ach,' said Kramer, opting for the gentlest way he could think of putting the poor sod in the picture, 'we were just demonstrating to your ex-girlfriend here that Zondi and me

271

don't always shoot people.'

The news of the arrests in the Stride case reached Colonel Muller while he was taking a break from interrogating the alleged Peerswammy Lal to go through his morning's mail. One item had left him very badly shaken.

It was an old newspaper cutting that came in a brown envelope, and it had no covering letter. It dealt with the alleged suicide in Johannesburg of an Indian political detainee, Ahmed Timol, aged thirty.

Colonel Muller read again what the CID chief had told *Rapport*:

'Timol was sitting quietly on a chair. Security police were with him. At one stage two of them walked out of the room. Then Timol suddenly jumped up and headed for the door. One security policeman jumped up and ran to the door and stopped him. But the Indian then stormed towards the window and jumped through it. No one frightened or touched him. The post-mortem will show this.'

And then Colonel Muller skipped to the comments made by the deputy chief of the security police, who had explained there were no bars on the tenth-floor window as nobody could break in.

'We, who know the Communists, know that when they plan to use violence they make their people swear an oath to commit suicide rather than mention the names of their comrades. They are taught to jump out before they are interrogated.'

To which the deputy security chief had added:

'We threaten no one and assault no one, and therefore we assume no one would want to escape from the tenth floor. It was an ordinary enquiry. Bars are not needed. Only senior officers handle these situations. They are not children and they remain within their rights and prescribed duties.'

Strydom, reading over Colonel Muller's shoulder, remarked: 'Well, I'm not so sure I understand why you're in such a state, Hans. What I'd come in to tell you is really far more—'

'But, Doc, can't you see the connection with Zuidmeyer?'

'Zuidmeyer never had anything to do with the Timol affair. If you look at the date on that, you'll realise that he was—'

'Ach, don't start being pedantic, man! Isn't the tenth floor enough of a common denominator?'

'Ja, but—'

'But nothing, man! How is it that, out of the blue, I get sent this thing? What does it mean? Does it mean someone has got wise to the Zuidmeyer case?'

Strydom looked at his watch. 'It could do, I suppose,' he said, 'although I've certainly said nothing about it to anyone, and I can't imagine who else could have done.'

'What about Van Rensburg?'

'Huh, he's got his mind on other matters! I've just had to talk him out of getting in an exorcist – or, rather, some witchdoctor Nxumalo recommended. Did you hear about Piet Baksteen's not-so-funny joke he played on him?'

'God in Heaven, jokes at a time like this? I must get hold of Tromp and tell him to—'

'That's what I came about, Colonel. Tell Tromp that I've had that second opinion on Mrs Zuidmeyer's bruises, and it seems I was right: those marks she had must have been made by Zuidmeyer trying to revive her.'

'So the son was lying?' said Colonel Muller, reaching out for his phone as it began ringing. 'Ja, Colonel Muller here. Tromp? And what have you been doing all morning, may I ask? I've got – *What was that?*'

And, for the time being, he forgot all about the mystery of the old newspaper cutting. Never, what with *Time* and *Newsweek* and *Der Spiegel*, not to mention all the television crews, had he ever had a morning quite like it. On top of which, in a bid to regain her freedom, and carry on caring for Amanda, Vicki Stilgoe declared she was prepared to turn State's Evidence against her brother, Bruce Newbury, and tell the police anything they wanted to know.

Very slowly, so gradually it was impossible to see as it happened, the sun moved a barred pattern across the floor of the room in which Ramjut Pillay had sat waiting since long before lunchtime to be dragged away in chains, thrown in a deep, dark dungeon, there to be left to do true penance for his many sins.

'Don't you like carrot soup?' asked the black sergeant, who sat watching over him and tuning a guitar. 'It must be almost cold now.'

'Bring only bread and water to Ramjut Pillay, kind jailer,' he said with a quavering voice, savouring his guilt to the utmost as the Mahatma must have rejoiced in his own state of holy enlightenment.

Guilt, Ramjut Pillay had discovered, was an attitude of mind he could be really jolly good at, and the more he allowed himself to feel guilty, the greater became his awareness of his true self. Already, another side to him had become faint and feeble in its attempts to be heard above the beating of his breast.

'Then, I will have it,' said the black sergeant, reaching for the tin mug.

I am guilty, thought Ramjut Pillay, of making this poor man a more wretched prisoner behind these bars than I am, for if it were not for me, then he could leave the room and have the carrot soup heated up for him.

'Yergh,' said the black sergeant, spitting the carrot soup back into the mug. 'There is a fly in it! Why didn't you tell me, you cunning bastard?'

'I am guilty of not knowing!' cried out Ramjut Pillay, tearing a rent in a little more of his clothing. 'I am guilty, too, of the death of that unfortunate insect, which could not have been drowning if I had drunk my carrot soup! Strike me, beating me about the head, grind my bones beneath your lovely feet!'

But the black sergeant laughed and said: 'Everyone feels guilty in a police station, which is good, but you mustn't worry about a fly – maybe it had a heart attack.'

Disconcerted, Ramjut looked at him.

'No, what you should worry about', the black sergeant continued, 'is when Lieutenant Kramer sends for you. But try to be quiet now, for there was a big arrest this morning, and I must compose my song about it.' And he picked up his guitar.

But before he could pluck the first note the door crashed open and there stood a smiling Sergeant Zondi with bloodstains on his shirt.

I'm off, said another side to Ramjut Pillay.

Toying with the old newspaper cutting on his desk, and noting it had traces of Cow Gum on the back, Kramer shook the receiver and held it to his ear again. 'That's better; this phone takes a bit of a hammering. Now, what was that you were saying, Major Zuidmeyer?'

'I was confirming that Ahmed Timol was never in my charge – it was after my time anyway. Why do you ask?'

'Ach, the Colonel and I were just talking about what a tough deal you had, and now the tragedy of your wife on top of it, and the name was mentioned, that's all.'

There was silence.

'Major, are you still there?'

'Last night—'

'Ja?'

'Well, I'll admit I'd had a few. Started looking through our old snapshot albums, remembering the good days with Marie, when we were both young and stationed out in the bushveld. The simple life, a few faction fights, cattle theft; now and again, a stabbing, some arson – haystacks and the like. Then my scrapbooks, because I got quite a few nice little write-ups from the courts when I first joined the CID. Marie was the one who had time to keep it up, and I noticed there were a few I'd personally not have included. Two were about this same Ahmed Timol, and there was a gap on that page where another cutting had been pulled out. Whether or not it pertained to Timol, I can't say, but it struck me as strange the name should come up again in conversation like this.'

'I didn't realise you'd done rural work,' said Kramer,

beckoning to Zondi, who had just appeared in the doorway with a cowering little Indian. Then he covered the receiver's mouthpiece with a hand, and added: 'I won't be long, Mickey. Put the kettle on for tea.'

'Oh, I was on a horse for four years,' said Zuidmeyer. 'The best kind of policing there is for a youngster.'

'Which reminds me, is Jannie home yet, sir?'

'He came back last night at about eleven. We didn't talk, but I respect that. He needs time to adjust.'

'And today?'

'Funnily enough, he's just phoned me. He wants me to go down to some lawyers' office at four – Grant & Boyd-Smith, do you know where that is?'

'Grant & Boyd-Smith? No, Major.'

'Oh, well, I can find out from the phone-book. He says his ma left her will with them, although it's news to me she had one. With me working all hours, they became very close over the years, of course, and so—'

'Major, I'm sorry to interrupt, hey? But the Colonel's just come in and wants me to interview this prisoner in the Stride case.'

'Ja, I heard about the arrests on the radio, a newsflash. That was excellent work, young man. But I won't keep you, so I'll say 'bye for now.'

' 'Bye, Major.'

'Boss?' asked Zondi, as soon as the receiver was replaced. 'Was the cutting from the son?'

Kramer nodded. 'I'm pretty sure it must've been, Mickey. He was probably too young when all that was going on to know his pa had already left Security by the time of the Timol business. But, as for what he thinks he'll gain from giving the Colonel a seizure this morning, don't ask me.' Then, turning to the prisoner, he said: 'Well, Ramjet, what are we going to do with you, hey?'

The little Indian raised his handcuffed wrists in front of his smudgy round glasses, bent his bandy legs at the knee, and would have fallen prostrate before Kramer, had not Zondi pulled him upright again.

'Behave,' said Zondi. 'This is not the temple.'

'O Mighty and Vengeful Lieutenant, do anything with me that you will! Great are my sinnings against postages and against persons, and I am never denying that I am most guilty!'

'Too right you are, if only a quarter of what you say here is true,' said Kramer, tapping Colonel Muller's notes. 'But all that really interests me, Ramjet, is whether this blue letter is hidden in a hole under a tree near your house.'

'True, true, in a plastic bag as exhibit numbering five!'

'Oh ja, so the white ants won't have got it? That was smart of you.'

'It was?' said Ramjut Pillay.

'While you were fetching him up, Mickey,' Kramer said to Zondi, 'I had the Colonel on the line. Vicki Stilgoe's explaining the lot now – including this blue letter. She says she could never understand why we hadn't acted on it, because it clearly made it seem as though a Jewish bloke at the varsity could have been Ma Stride's killer.'

'But he wasn't, boss, so how did she——?'

'Ach, man, she wasn't stupid. She planned it so we'd find out the bloke was innocent and then we'd go on to try to find out who'd tried to frame him.'

'On and on and on, boss?'

'That's right, until we got sick of it and gave up, but always keeping us thinking it had to be someone intellectual Naomi Stride'd put in one of her books.'

'Hau, a good plan, boss!'

'Which would have worked perfectly, maybe, if our four-eyed friend here hadn't buggered off with it. Oh, and by the way, you know the other blue letters before it? Which she used to build up the idea of a series, if it went the way she planned?'

'The ones which upset Mrs Stride so she wouldn't show them to her friends? Were they threats?'

Kramer couldn't help a smile. 'No, just criticisms of her writing, really putting the knife in where it hurt. So it wouldn't have mattered if she *had* shown them to her friends – only, as Stilgoe expected, she——' The telephone rang. 'Ja,

Kramer here. OK, Colonel, I'll be along in two minutes.'

'*Two minutes* will be deciding the fate of Ramjut Pillay?' the little Indian said, going again at the knees.

'One minute,' said Kramer. 'Take his cuffs off, Mickey.'

'But O Mighty—'

'Listen, Pillay, it could be we owe you a favour, hey? But, more important than that, do you realise how much bloody paperwork it's going to take to bring a case against you for withholding this evidence? Statements from the Railway Police, the loony-bin, doctors, nurses, your work colleagues, God knows who else? Which is to say nothing of all the charges the Post Office will want us to add on? So what I suggest is this. That we get that stuff back from under the tree, and we'll change your story to read that you gave it to Sergeant Zondi on Tuesday when he first interviewed you in Jan Smuts Close. Have you got that?'

'Only, if you were possessing these documents, sir, then—'

'What difference does that make? We weren't fooled by the blue letter, that's all, which is why we didn't follow up on it. Do you understand now? Can you get that guilty look off your face?'

'There it goes, by jingo!' whooped Ramjut Pillay.

Vicki Stilgoe was watching Colonel Muller's every move. It was the least of the things which made him uncomfortable about having her in his office. Never, in all his days, had he encountered a woman so cold, so controlled, so totally without any discernible conscience.

He reached for his telephone and dialled Kramer's number. He lit another of the cigarettes he kept in a drawer for emergencies, and pulled a face at the thin, acrid taste the thing had when compared to his pipe tobacco. He felt very angry with whoever had bought a yellow rose and a greeting card that morning. He wished he knew his identity, because it would definitely cost the swine the price of a new briar. If not a meerschaum.

'Tromp, Tromp, Tromp, answer, dammit!' he said under his breath, for it had been five minutes since he'd last rung the

278

man's office, and he could not imagine where Kramer could have got to in that time.

'And am I expected to go on just sitting here?' asked Vicki Stilgoe.

'That's right, you go on just sitting there,' said Colonel Muller, dialling the duty officer's number. 'But don't worry, there are no more questions I want to ask you.'

'None at all?'

He glanced at his query sheet.

'Was it your brother who got Mr Kennedy to waste his time waiting in a Durban hotel on the night of the murder?'

'Yes, we wanted to provide him with a cast-iron alibi so that the police would leave him – *and* me – alone.'

'Why did you pick last Monday night to kill the deceased?'

'It had to be after a weekend, so it would look as though the threatening letter had been posted to arrive on the Monday.'

'But why not the Monday before?'

'Amanda had her birthday.'

'Or the Monday before that?'

'We weren't ready. Bruce was still scouting the lie of the land.'

'You realise now you left it too late in a sense?'

'It was a mistake we couldn't have known about.'

'It was why you got caught.'

'No, that was due to a different mistake.'

'What mistake?'

She looked away and gave no answer.

Once again Colonel Muller dialled Kramer's number, but again had no reply. He decided to give him one minute before there would really be trouble.

'Mrs Stilgoe, what was your—?'

'Fatal error?'

'If you like.'

'Not realising. . .'

'What?'

'That everywhere that Mary went her little lamb was sure to go.'

'You're talking in riddles, woman!'

279

'Nursery rhymes, Colonel. Out of the mouth of babes.'

'Now, I warned you!' said Colonel Muller, and turned to the two policewomen sitting quietly in the corner. 'Keep a strict eye on her. I'm going down to the Lieutenant's office again. I can't imagine what questions he could still find, but he must get the chance if he wants to.'

'Colonel Muller,' said Vicki Stilgoe, showing her first sign of emotion by tightening the grip of her clasped hands, 'May I ask *you* a question?'

'Make it a quick one, Stilgoe. You heard I'm about to—'

'It was him, wasn't it?' she said with sudden vehemence, almost spitting the words out. 'That little black bastard, Zondi.'

'Who did what?'

'Noticed.'

'Riddles again.'

'Amanda keeping on saying "boy", which wasn't very *liberal* at all, was it? Rather spoiled the image I was busily trying to—'

'Ach, I don't think the average Bantu even notices when—'

'So the first chance he got of getting my daughter alone he started asking her questions about Bruce, about what Bruce thought of Theo – oh, yes, I managed to get that much out of her. But what else did he ask?'

Colonel Muller shrugged. 'I have heard nothing of this conversation.'

'Don't lie to me! That's what—'

'See she doesn't leave that chair, all right, girls?'

Colonel Muller closed his door behind him, glanced down at his rose-bush for consolation, and went along the balcony. Kramer's office was empty. A pair of handcuffs lay on the desk. The electric kettle was boiling itself dry.

Then, taking up Kramer's memo pad, he stared in bewilderment at what had been scrawled there: *G & B–S/Rooms 1019/1023*

Zondi had his foot down.

'Go,' urged Kramer, 'go, man!'

They jumped the red, missed a bus by the thickness of a

bus ticket, and straddled the central white line, horn blaring.

'Boss, why are we doing this?' asked Zondi, going through another red light. 'What was that phone call you suddenly made to Grant & Boyd-Smith? I was telling Ramjut where to wait and I couldn't quite hear—'

'A pair of good Afrikaner names.'

Zondi chuckled. 'Grant & Boyd-Smith? They are so English that—'

'Exactly, Mickey. Then what was a dyed-in-the-wool Afrikaner woman like Marie Zuidmeyer doing taking her business to them, when the town's full of solicitors' firms like Brandsma and Du Plessis, Van der Merwe and Kros? I rang them to ask where they were situated.'

'And?'

'I've already told you the address, Chadlington House. Right opposite the *Trekkersburg Gazette*, where half the world's bloody press is busy using its Telex facilities.'

'Boss, that still is not an answer.'

'It bloody is, old son. Can you guess what floor Grant & Boyd-Smith has its offices on?'

'What floor?' repeated Zondi, going through another red and leaving two cars to untangle themselves. 'Hau, not the—?'

'You've got it,' said Kramer. 'And it's just gone four o'clock, the time Jannie told Zuidmeyer to be there.'

Thirty seconds later, Zondi screamed to a stop across the street from the *Trekkersburg Gazette*, and they jumped out. The lobby of Chadlington House was empty and the lift stood open.

'Christ, we're in luck!' said Kramer, as they dashed for the lift before the doors could close. 'Hit ten and hope.'

The lift doors took a lifetime to close, but the lift itself was swift. It rose with gathering speed, so that when it stopped at the tenth floor Kramer felt his stomach surge up and come down again. Considering what else his stomach was doing, that was the least of its tricks. With a rubbery sigh, the lift doors parted.

'Rooms 1019 to—'

'To the right, Lieutenant!' said Zondi, getting a head start.

Kramer caught up with him and they pounded down the wide corridor towards a suite of offices with a glass front and the name of the firm, *Grant & Boyd-Smith,* in a discreet shade of gold. There was a grey-haired woman seated behind the reception counter, powdering her nose. She must have been slightly deaf, because when they burst in through the door, she jumped so much that she powdered the left lens of her bifocals.

'Goodness, what on earth—?'

'The Zuidmeyers!' said Kramer. 'Quickly, where are they?'

She looked too startled to comprehend.

'The father and son? Four o'clock appointment?'

'Oh, oh, yes, to see Mr Boyd-Smith. He's running a little late as usual, I'm afraid, so they're in the waiting-room. But can I ask you—?'

There was a hoarse shout and then the sound of breaking glass.

Kramer shouldered the waiting-room door almost off its hinges. The first thing he saw was a gaping hole in the window, and through it the neon-rimmed letters that spelled out *Trekkersburg Gazette* along its rooftop. Then as Zondi stepped to his side he became aware of a movement to his left and behind him. Zuidmeyer was crawling backwards on his hands and knees, his eyes staring at the window and his mouth agape.

'Jannie!' he said, noticing Kramer. 'Jannie, my boy Jannie!' And he raised a shaking finger to the window.

Faint shrieks and the sound of braking came from down in the street.

'Check, Mickey,' said Kramer.

Zondi crossed to the window, leaned out, turned a little grey and brought his head back in with a shake.

'Jannie, Jannie, Jannie!' sobbed Zuidmeyer, getting himself into the corner and curling into a ball. 'Not one word!'

'What in—?'

Kramer turned. A smooth-looking man, grey above the ears, impeccably dressed and manicured, was approaching the doorway. 'Mr Boyd-Smith? Don't come in here, it's a police matter. But I'd like to ask you one question.' And he held out his warrant card.

'Y-yes, what is it?'

'Do you hold the will of a Mrs Marie Louise Zuidmeyer?'

'We don't handle wills; we're strictly—'

'Thank you, sir, I will be out to explain in a minute,' said Kramer, and shut the door in his face. 'It was a complete set-up, Mickey.'

Zondi nodded and looked out of the window again. 'Already there are cameras, boss,' he said. 'And a man with a movie one, across there in that window.'

'Jannnnniiie...' howled Zuidmeyer. 'Why? Why? Why?'

'Major, it's Tromp Kramer. Can you tell me what happened here?'

Zuidmeyer knelt and looked up, his eyes no longer haunted but lit by a terrible light. 'Nothing, Nothing! I came in. I. . .'

'Go on, sir.'

'I said to the boy: "Well, I'm here. What's all this about?" He looked at me. He said nothing. He—'

'Don't stop, Major!'

'The boy looked at me. He said *not one word*. I said: "Jannie, I'm asking you a question!" Then he smiled. Just smiled! Then he turned and he took three big steps and he—' Zuidmeyer pitched forward on to his face and beat the floor with his fists. 'Why? Why, why, why? For the love of God, *why*?'

'It's a pity you were alone in the room with him, and we have only your word for all this.'

'What?' said Zuidmeyer, staggering to his feet. 'What're you—?'

'As your wife's inquest will show,' said Kramer, with a glance at Zondi, 'your boy had something he wouldn't want to confess to you, Major Zuidmeyer.'

ABOUT THE AUTHOR

James McClure was born in Johannesburg, South Africa, and grew up in the capital of Natal, Pietermaritzburg. While working for three major newspapers there, he became a specialist in crime and court stories. After emigrating to Great Britain, he worked at the *Scottish Daily Mail;* in 1965, he became deputy editor of the Oxford Times Group of weekly papers, a post he held until 1974, when he resigned to devote more time to writing. McClure is most familiar to American readers for his novels, of which he has written seven. He has twice won the Crime Writers Association's Dagger Award. He is also the author of *Spike Island,* a highly praised portrait of a Liverpool police precinct.

***Other mysteries you'll enjoy from
the Pantheon International Crime series:***

Peter Dickinson

"Sets new standards in the mystery field that will be hard to live up to."
—Ruth Rendell

Hindsight	72603	$3.95
The Last Houseparty	71601	$3.95
King and Joker	71600	$2.95
The Lively Dead	73317	$2.95
The Old English Peep Show	72602	$3.95
The Poison Oracle	71023	$3.95
Sleep and His Brother	74452	$3.95
Walking Dead	74173	$3.95

Reginald Hill

A Killing Kindness   71060 $2.95

"A cause for rejoicing....Sparkles with a distinct mixture of the bawdy and the compassionate."   —Robin W. Winks, *New Republic*

Who Guards the Prince?   71337 $2.95

Hans Hellmut Kirst

The Night of the Generals   72752 $2.95

"One of the finest detective novels from any source in many years."
—*New York Times Book Review*

Hans Koning

Dewitt's War   72278 $2.95

"I recognize in this book all the subtlety of my fellow writer Koning."
—Georges Simenon

Peter Lovesey

The False Inspector Dew   71338 $2.95

"Irresistible...delightfully off-beat...wickedly clever."

—Washington Post Book World

Keystone   72604 $2.95

James McClure

"A distinguished crime novelist who has created in his Africaner Tromp Kramer and Bantu Sergeant Zondi two detectives who are as far from stereo-types as any in the genre."   —P.D. James, *New York Times Book Review*

The Artful Egg	72126	$3.95
The Blood of an Englishman	71019	$2.95
The Caterpillar Cop	71058	$2.95
The Gooseberry Fool	71059	$2.95
Snake	72304	$2.95
The Sunday Hangman	72992	$2.95
The Steam Pig	71021	$2.95

William McIlvanney

Laidlaw   73338 $2.95

"I have seldom been so taken by a character as I was by the angry and compassionate Glasgow detective, Laidlaw. McIlvanney is to be congratu-lated."   —Ross MacDonald

The Papers of Tony Veitch   73486 $2.95

Martin Page

The Man Who Stole the Mona Lisa   74098 $3.50

"Full of life and good humor....His novel is a delight."   *—New Yorker*

Julian Rathbone

"Right up there with Le Carré and company."   *—Publishers Weekly*

A Spy of the Old School   72276 $2.95

Vassilis Vassilikos

Z   72990 $3.95

"A fascinating novel."   *—Atlantic*

Per Wahlöö

Murder on the Thirty-First Floor   70840 $2.95

"Something quite special and fascinating."   *—New York Times Book Review*

Elliot West

The Night Is a Time for Listening   74099 $3.95

"The major spy novel of the year."   *—New York Times*

Look for the Pantheon International Crime series at your local bookstore or use the coupon below to order. Prices shown are publisher's suggested retail price. Any reseller is free to charge whatever price he wishes for books listed. Prices are subject to change without notice.

Quantity	Catalog #	Price

$1.00 basic charge for postage and handling $1.00

25¢ charge per additional book

Please include applicable sales tax

Total

Send orders to: Random House, Inc., 400 Hahn Road, Westminster, Md. 21157.

Please send me the books I have listed above. I am enclosing $_____ which includes a postage and handling charge of $1.00 for the first book and 25¢ for each additional book, plus applicable sales tax. Please send check or money order in U.S. dollars only. No cash or C.O.D.'s accepted. Orders delivered in U.S. only. Please allow 4 weeks for delivery. This offer expires 7/30/87.

Name _____

Address _____

City _____ State _____ Zip _____